NO ESCAPE

By Joseph Hayes

THE DESPERATE HOURS
BON VOYAGE (with Marrijane Hayes)
THE YOUNG DOCTORS
THE HOURS AFTER MIDNIGHT
DON'T GO AWAY MAD
THE MIDNIGHT SUN
CALCULATED RISK
THE THIRD DAY
THE DEEP END
LIKE ANY OTHER FUGITIVE
MISSING . . . AND PRESUMED DEAD
THE LONG DARK NIGHT
ISLAND ON FIRE
WINNER'S CIRCLE
NO ESCAPE

NO ESCAPE

A NOVEL BY
JOSEPH HAYES

DELACORTE PRESS/NEW YORK

Published by
Delacorte Press
1 Dag Hammarskjold Plaza
New York, N.Y. 10017

Manufactured in the United States of America

First printing

Designed by Rhea Braunstein

ıLIBRARY OF CONGRESS CATALOGING IN PUBLICATION DATA

Hayes, Joseph Arnold, 1918–
No escape.

I. Title.
PS3515.A942N6   813'.54   81-12470
ISBN: 0-440-06438-4   AACR2

To Marrijane
as always,
with love

And with thanks, too,
to James Oliver Brown
and Arthur M. Bell

IT was simply a matter of coming home, leaving the car in the driveway as usual, opening the front door of her own house, and then, of a sudden, knowing that from this moment on her life would never be the same.

At first she saw only that the small Duncan Phyfe table in the front hall had been upended. Violently. One delicately carved satinwood leg lay apart from it on the carpeted floor. The mirror was still hanging on the wall but the heavy antique frame was askew and the glass had been smashed. She caught a brief glimpse of herself reflected in the sharp stellated glitter: the image distorted, grotesque, as if it, too, had been shattered. She could not recognize the face that stared back at her.

I love you, Brenda. Always remember that. Nothing else matters.

She moved, with slow reluctance, into the living room. And stopped. And stared. The cobbler's bench was on its side. Ashtrays, magazines, the ivory chess set, all were scattered over the carpet.

The sofa stood on its end against the wall.

The mantel had been cleared and its pale stone length looked naked. Above it the wall was bare: the oil portrait of herself, which Donald had insisted she have painted, was lying in the litter on the floor, faceup. The canvas had been smashed through—by his huge fist or by a furious kick? The picture stared up at her, a mockery of her own face.

I believe you, Donald. I do believe you love me. But it's a kind of love I don't understand, or want.

Stunned, staring at the havoc, beginning to quiver inside, she stood motionless in the grip of incredulity. She should not have told him. Not this morning. But it was Saturday and Toby had gone ice-skating at the home of friends in Brookfield and they had been alone in the house together. He had been himself, then: composed and quiet, even cheerful, and not drinking. So she had decided to get it over with. It had to be done. The sooner she told him, once and for all, the better for all three of them.

Divorce? What the hell are you talking about, Brenda?

Outside the living-room windows the forsythia was promising to bud yellow soon in spite of the patches of dirty snow that remained on the sweeping lawn. And Donald was standing—tall, wide-shouldered, his blond hair setting off the handsomeness of his clean-shaven boyish face, his blue eyes clouding with disbelief and growing shock—but not anger. Please, God, don't let him lose his temper—make him talk with me again, the way we used to.

You've threatened this before, Brenda, but always after we had a row or when I was drinking too much.

This time it's different. I've thought it through. I'm not even saying it's your fault. Maybe it's mine. I often think it must be.

Are you saying you don't love me anymore?

No. I don't know about that. I'm saying I can't take any more.

You'll always love me. The way I'll always love you. We both know that.

No, don't touch me, please.

And he had not tried to touch her again at that point. But he knew his power. He always knew. *Did* she still love him?

She walked over the rubble now, stepping over the shards of broken glass and trying not to notice the primitive African wood carvings and the small Eskimo animal sculptures in black stone strewn over the Oriental rug. Her legs threatening to cave in and her mind sick with horror, she went to open the double doors leading into the dining room—and halted.

More devastation. The Chippendale breakfront flat on its face.

Broken jagged fragments of Wedgwood and bone china scattered everywhere. Was all the lovely Waterford crystal gone, too? Yes. Everything. The dining table itself was on its side. She did not go in, or to the breakfast room or kitchen beyond. Was this happening really? *Had* it happened?

What lawyer, who?

Does it matter now? I've talked with him, that's all.

I don't believe it, Brenda. Who?

Not that it matters: I've talked with Preston Brice.

Preston Brice? You would choose a good-looking one, wouldn't you?

Now don't start that. Please. Preston and Lucy Brice are one of the few truly devoted couples we know. I've known both of them since grade school.

How well? How well have you known the bastard?

She couldn't remember what she had answered. It didn't matter now. She had to move. At once. She had to do something. But what? She drifted helplessly to the door of Donald's study.

He had smashed every bottle of liquor in the house. The room reeked of alcohol and the sharp jagged edges of the breakage glinted in the pale late-winter light that fell across the small room. His desk was intact but the file drawers had been emptied, their contents helter-skelter everywhere—blueprints, contracts, letters, folders—on the floor, across his desk, everywhere, everywhere. Still, even with the wildness and violence of the drunken act flickering in her mind, she did not feel the rage that she knew had to come. Could it be because the framed photograph of herself still stood unharmed and upright on his desk?

Brenda, I swear to you: I'll never touch another drink.

It's not that, Donald. Not that alone. I wish it were.

She had not tried to explain that it was something *more* than his drinking—something deeper and more fundamental. She hadn't told him because she hadn't known exactly what it was. And still did not.

She retraced her flagging steps to the hall now, trudging through the debris. She realized, going up the wide carpeted stairway, that the quivering sensation in her stomach had become a trembling through her whole body. Even though her step was firm, she wondered whether she was going to be sick.

Who is he, Brenda?

There's no one, Donald. I know it's hopeless to try to convince you of that but I don't love anyone else. I don't want to love anyone else.

What's his name?

Let go of my arm, Donald. I've already told you. There's no one.

Lies. More lies. I've known for a long time this was coming.

So have I, I think.

No one else is going to have you—ever.

Damn it, you're hurting my arm!

I'm sorry. I wouldn't hurt you, Brenda. I'm sorry.

You're always sorry—afterwards.

You belong to me.

I don't belong to anybody. I belong to myself. Whoever the hell I am.

There's never been anyone else for me, Brenda. There never will be! In the whole ten years we've been married. No one.

I believe that, Donald.

I love you. Only you. Nothing else matters.

Wrong, wrong! Much else matters. Toby, for instance. Toby matters. His room matters. And look at it.

A shambles. More havoc. Oh, Donald, couldn't you at least have spared Toby? If he sees this—the electronic toys crushed, the small television screen kicked in, his carved wooden animals and birds strewn everywhere—if he sees this, he'll start to stutter again. He'll throw up. Toby even hates violence on television. His tender eyes will take on that stunned expression. They'll fill with the tears that you, Donald, have always considered unmanly. Oh, Donald, he's only eight years old. He'll be sick when he sees this. Sick.

No.

Toby will not see it.

She moved along the upper hall, still too stupefied, still too appalled, to force order into her thoughts. She was shaking all over now.

Toby needs a father. Have you thought of that, Brenda?

Now we're beginning to talk. Let's be reasonable, darling—I mean Donald.

You said darling—

Old habits, Donald.

You still love me!

I don't know. That's the truth.

You know I'll never let you take Toby away from me.

I don't want to do that. But things have been happening to him. To all three of us.

Toby needs a father. We need each other, all three of us.

Do we, Donald?

No. She was staring into the bedroom. Her bedroom. Hers and Donald's. She had gone slack all over. Her blood was running thin and her eyes were stinging and hot, although her body felt cold. She leaned against the doorframe.

The bureau drawers had been flung across the room one by one, their contents tumbled everywhere. Her dressing table was on its side, the mirror miraculously intact, but the bottles and combs and brushes in a jumble on the floor. The closets were empty, the doors open—ransacked. Her clothes, and his, were on the floor in heaps. Her English Davenport desk lay on its side. The chaos was total except for the Queen Anne bed. Her bed. Hers and Donald's. It stood naked, stripped of all its coverings, its mattress exposed, barren and impersonal.

And no longer hers.

She felt as if she had been raped. Disgust flooded her like poison. The entire house, which had once been hers, had been ravaged, pillaged. Plundered in a drunken orgy of rage and hate.

Yes, hate, Donald, not love—hate!

And she had been raped by a stranger.

The anger came then. Finally, while she stared at the bed, it came scalding and blinding.

Let's talk later, darling. No one else is here. And I haven't been drinking. Let's go upstairs. Now.

Please, Donald, it's too late for that.

I'll show you how much I love you.

I'm due at the library. I promised to help on the used-book sale this morning.

Little Friend of the Library, Brenda Forrest. You're my friend, too.

I'm sorry, Donald. That's all over.

That'll never be over.

I mean it. Don't try to force me. I'm going.

I've never had to force you. Not you, Brenda—
I'll be back around noon—
You're not going!
Don't hit me, Donald. You're never going to hit me again.
Brenda, come back here. You'll never get away from me! I'm
warning you. You'd better come back now or you'll be sorry, you'll
be goddamned sorry, Brenda!
Was she sorry?
No.
She was not sorry now because she knew what she had to do. It
had been decided for her. She realized that she was no longer
shaking—not a quiver. Empty, drained, she felt a vast quiet settle
through her whole body.
She started down the stairs, then stopped herself halfway to the
bottom. She would need clothes. She and Toby would need
clothes. What else? Money. It was Saturday; the banks were
closed. Her father might have some cash. How much did she
have? There was always a little in the safe in the study.
She was choking with rage now, sick with it. But the trembling
had gone and her mind was focusing and functioning.
Whatever she had to do, she'd do it. And fast. Before Donald
returned and staggered into the house, possibly more dangerous,
more out of control—
Abruptly fighting down panic, she turned around and, moving
fast, climbed the stairs again. Her legs were steady, her mind
clear, icy clear.
I love you, Brenda. I'll always love you.
Comfort me with apples—where had she read that? The Bible?
Comfort me with apples for I am sick of love.

———□———

"I'm sorry, Mr. Forrest. The bar doesn't open till one on Sat-
urdays, you know."
"Bars open all over town, Clarence." Why hadn't he stopped on
his way? Why had he come here anyway?
"Sorry, sir. Club rules. It's less than half an hour now, sir."
Clarence was walking away. Still grinning. Superior bastard.
Why was everyone against him? Who the hell was Clarence, a
barman, to make fun of him?
He could go out and get into the Mercedes and drive back into

town. He'd have a drink inside his gut in ten minutes. Or he could go to the office. FORREST AND SON, BUILDERS AND PLANNERS. Always a bottle of Jack Daniel's in his desk drawer.

Then he remembered: he must have some in his locker. He headed for the stairs.

God, what a dreary empty dull place the Lake Club was on a Saturday morning.

Going down the carpeted stairs to the gym, he went weak and cold, picturing the devastation, remembering how savage and murderous he had felt. He had always known something like this would happen—that he'd do something like this. Or worse. Remorse churned in his guts. As he turned into the locker room, he felt that familiar sick hatred: You slimy bastard, you don't know what you're doing. Or what you'll do next. What the hell is happening to you anyway?

Brenda. A wave of tenderness engulfed him. Maybe she hadn't come back from the library yet. Maybe he had time to go back to clean it up before she had to look at it.

Brenda, I'm sorry. Brenda, I didn't mean it—

There was only an inch of whiskey in the bottle. He swilled it down and felt the burning, the good fiery sensation that he knew would be followed by a sweet surge of peace—

The locker room was empty but the stench of sweat and soap and tennis shoes and disinfectant calmed him. He'd always felt at home around gymnasiums. And then he remembered why he'd come: to sweat the booze out of his blood. So, without changing clothes but taking off his heavy tweed jacket and shirt, he worked out on the parallel bars until his shoulders and arms knotted and throbbed with pain. And begged for more. He continued when his muscles threatened to collapse, and when his body was dripping and his mind blanking, every nerve and tendon twisting and taut, he still forced himself to go on.

You deserve it, you bastard. Worse. You deserve much worse.

Finally he gave up and staggered toward the sauna area. Hating himself. Our home, our beautiful *home*—you crazy bastard, what did you think you were doing?

He stripped down then and took a cold shower, the frigid blast cruel and stabbing—a paroxysm of agony.

Forgive me, Brenda.

She always has. She always does. She always will.

But could he ever forgive himself?

After dressing and then passing the lounge and bar, without being tempted to enter—I'll never drink again, Brenda, ever!—he emerged from the clubhouse into the gray, chill, dreary day. He felt purged.

Driving the lakeshore road toward town, he did not try to rid his mind of the pictures of Brenda—her fragile face tinged with sun on the deck of the sloop, the waters of Long Island Sound glittering; her soft full legs and softer breasts; her black hair flowing in the wind—

He had to see her now. Brenda alone, before Toby came home from skating in Brookfield.

In the center of the town, which looked bleak and gray, he turned at the stoplight at Main and West Street and then again onto Deerhill Avenue, a wide residential street of handsome old houses under high bare-limbed oaks and maples. He passed the sprawling stone-fenced estate that had once belonged to his mother's family, the huge house now owned by New Yorkers, strangers. Memory brought inevitable sadness. And a deep familiar bitterness. And anger. *Don't look at me that way, Donald. You're only a child. What do you know about a woman's needs?* But he had known, even then. *You may tell your father whatever you think you know. Or imagine you know. Your mother's not as old as you think. And she's still beautiful, too—to some people.* The vain selfish deceitful bitch—were all women like her?

No. Brenda was not like her. As beautiful, *more* beautiful—but not like *her*!

I didn't mean what I said, Brenda. I don't know why I say things like that. I know you've never let another man touch you. I know, I *know*!

He made two more curving turns and then he saw the house. The lovely simplicity of its classic colonial lines, its blinding whiteness against the dark sky. His house. His and Brenda's.

We'll start over, Brenda. We'll buy whatever you want. We'll do it together. We'll shop every antique store in New England. We can afford it. We'll start over and, you'll see, our whole life will be different. *I'll* be different, darling. You'll see, you'll see—

But when he stopped the car in the driveway and as he stepped out, he saw the front door. It stood wide open.

And he knew there was no one inside.

———□———

Driving, she could not rid her mind of the picture of the house. Or of the rage. She remembered that last moment of blank irrational fury when, with the suitcases stowed in the rear of the Lancia, she had been tempted to go back into the house and set a match to it. Finish the job, to hell with it, all of it!

But instead she had only left the door open and had driven to Brookfield and picked up a surprised but unprotesting Toby, who stared at the luggage with questions in his blue eyes, but unspoken. She had explained that they were going on a short vacation. Since he didn't ask where—are all eight-year-olds so tight-lipped and self-contained?—she had felt obliged to say more. So she made the decision that, until then, she had been dreading and postponing. They were going to Florida, she told him. For a short time anyway—to get away from the winter, as Dr. Kellerman had suggested the last time Toby had pneumonia, remember? A sober nod of blond head in reply. Was it a lie? Would it be necessary to go on lying to him? Or should she blurt the truth and devil take the hindmost? Did the child suspect she was lying? Or did he know? Why start off this way? The bitterness and sick disgust had turned into a chill, enveloping sadness as she drove.

The Lancia Zagato ate up the miles. Oh, it was a lovely car— large for a sports car, teal blue, fast, sleek, smooth. Thank you, Donald. Always generous and never more so than when tormented by remorse, guilt. He had surprised her with the gift while her left jaw was still aching from the flat-handed blow he had struck the night before, three or four weeks ago now, after returning from the Lake Club: *I saw the way you were dancing. I saw the way you were looking at him!* She had not even known which *him* Donald was referring to. The past. Gone. Forget it, put it behind you, Brenda. Forget.

Florida. Sunshine and palm trees and a blue sky. She had been there only once, as a child. Donald always preferred the islands for their winter vacations. Or Bermuda. He'd charter a boat and sail it himself. But Florida—she knew no one in Florida.

Except Charlene Conrad. Charlene Scherwin now. Or was it Conrad again now? *I'm celebrating my freedom in Sarasota.* A scribble on last year's Christmas card—a picture of a white egret on a sandy beach incongruously framed in a conventional Christmas wreath. *Take a breather from winter, come down to this land of milk and honey and we'll relive our college days. The mat's always out.*

She pictured Charlene in her mind. Tall, athletically handsome rather than beautiful, with brown short hair and quick gray eyes and a manner always threatening to explode with one enthusiasm or another. What—other than divorce—had happened to Charlene in ten years? She'd probably be a total stranger now. And how could she impose her own difficulties, her confusions and pain, on someone she probably wouldn't even recognize?

Miles later Toby said, "I saw a bluebird at the pond. Pete said they're mean. Is that true?"

"It must have been a jay," she told him, relieved to be talking—and on a trivial subject like Toby's odd but endearing fascination with wild birds. "Jays are around this time of year; bluebirds are small and sweet and they go south for the winter."

"Like the wild geese."

"Only not in those formations we watched in the fall. Bluebirds are supposed to symbolize happiness, did you know that?" Hesitating, she glanced at him.

"I know what *symbolize* means," he said somewhat loftily so that she almost smiled.

"Someday you'll have to read Thoreau. The bluebird carries the sky on his back."

"You read a lot, don't you?"

"I used to read a lot." Maybe now she would be able to read more. Or less. Much less, since she'd have to find a job. There'd been only $310 in the safe in the study. She'd had only sixty-three in her purse. And her father had insisted that she take all the cash he and her mother had in the house—another ninety. He had not asked her why she needed it and, very carefully, she had not told him what she was doing, or why. Without saying so, she had let them both think she was only going on a shopping spree.

The bluebird of happiness.

She realized for the first time that she had not cried.

The snow continued, off and on, in flurries. Then it began to fall heavily, floating and white, causing her to slow down.

"I won't need my ice skates in Florida, will I?" Toby asked.

"You can learn to water-ski," she said.

But her mind was drifting like the quiet snow.

Skating on the pond in Hawleyville. The night sky close and full of cold stars and the skaters sailing in couples in the light of the bonfires on the shore. A radio playing—the Gershwin-Berlin-Porter tunes that, in a day of rock music, they had discovered, as if it were a miracle, that they both preferred and loved. Donald holding her. His arm strong but gentle around her, his back lean and muscled under her arm, hands clasped, his thick blond hair glowing in the wind, his fine young face tranquil with happiness as they glided together, their breaths separate on the winter air, then mingling as their mouths met while they sailed, together, together—

Enough! Enough of this. The aching emptiness in her body moved up into her mind. It was over. The bluebird had flown. The bluebird's promise had been a trick. Instead of happiness, desolation. So be it. Accept it, Brenda. You have no choice. Not now.

With dusk the driving became more hazardous and with darkness, the snow still falling, going farther seemed foolish, even reckless.

"Are you hungry?"

"Not much."

And it was true. In the dining room at the Holiday Inn Toby made a valiant but vain effort to eat his Salisbury steak. To please her, she knew. But she did not urge or entreat, only thankful that, whatever he might be feeling or thinking, he had not begun to stutter. It had been his recent tendency to stutter that had helped her reach her decision. Her own meal grew cold on her plate and she drank five cups of black coffee. On the way back to the room, after she'd purchased a package of cigarettes from a coin machine, Toby asked his first question: "Is Daddy going to be with us in Florida?"

"Daddy's pretty busy, you know." Could she go on evading?

"He has to get the new shopping center built in time to open in May." *Should* she go on evading? "He's behind schedule, you know."

"Does Daddy work too hard?"

"Sometimes."

She didn't add: when he's not drinking. It was not yet time. But did she have the right to spare him? Was she sparing him or only trying to stave off the inevitable?

Or had Toby already guessed more than she was giving him credit for? Face it, Brenda: What you fear, what you dread, is that expression of hurt and childish misery that can leap into that face. Even before he could speak at all, Toby had been so sensitive, so vulnerable, that a quick angry word, even a dark glance, would cause that small face to tremble, to twist, threatening to disintegrate. So that she had found herself almost incapable of reprimanding him, however gently; she still had to force herself to reproach or correct him for fear of seeing that stunned and regretful expression take over his blue eyes; and by now she knew the awful chaotic compassion that invariably assaulted her while she watched, often forcing her to turn away.

Ensconced in the room, Toby sat on the end of one of the two wide beds, watching television. She sat in the only chair, smoking a cigarette and wondering, with a flutter of apprehension, where Donald was. Had he returned to the house, discovered them gone—then what? It was her first cigarette in three years and it tasted bitter and dry. Why had she bought them? Why didn't she stub it out? Toby changed channels again, cutting off the images of violence on the screen.

Where was Donald, damn it? Had she covered her tracks? What tracks? She hadn't known where, exactly, she was going—how could *he* know?

Charlene Conrad. Charlene Scherwin, *née* Conrad. She looked up the area code, dialed 9, and then information in Saraşota. Yes, there was a Charlene Conrad (not Scherwin) at 1168 Westway Drive. Charging the call to the room, she dialed through and Charlene answered.

No mistaking that voice: "Brenda? Brenda Whittier?"

"Forrest, you idiot!" Brenda, at once infected, as always, by her old friend's lusty, still youthful ebullience, almost shouted: "*Née* Whittier, *née.*"

Charlene chuckled. "You sound like a horse that has to sneeze," she said.

And, astonished, Brenda laughed and then found herself stretched out on the bed, holding the phone and listening, trying to interject protests as Charlene demanded where she was ("We're somewhere near Richmond"), and then quickly estimated miles and driving time ("I'll expect you Monday evening!") and then rushed on to explain that here she was alone in a big Oriental house with the beach within spitting distance out the front doors and that it was still midseason without a decent motel room available even if she'd *allow* her to go to one. "It's wild, pet. The house belongs to this playwright and his family and it's been vandalized twice while they weren't here so I'm house-sitting while he, poor fellow, is doing a production on Broadway. You said 'we'—does that mean I'll finally get to meet that handsome wretch I only shook hands with at your wedding?"

"Donald's not along. Toby's with me. He's eight now."

A long pause. Should she say more? Charlene would have to know. But not like this, not on the telephone. . . .

"Well, if it's serenity you're looking for, pet, this is the place." Charlene already knew. That weird intuition of hers. "The house is Japanese and those people believe in tranquility when they're not chopping off heads. Give Toby a kiss for me and ring me after you pass the airport and the Ringling Museum on the Tamiami Trail. And Brenda—"

"Yes?"

"You'll survive. We all survive."

"Thanks, Charl."

That deep-throated laugh again. "For what? Listen, pet, with your looks you have nothing to fret about. You hang on to that, hear? You're *you.* *You're somebody.* That's the first trick—hang on to that idea. You're somebody on your own!"

It was then that she cried for the first time. She went into the bathroom and drew a tub and with the water tumbling to drown out her sobs, she sat on the edge of the tub and wept.

After her bath she stood naked in front of the mirror and studied her face. Framed in long black hair, it looked small and delicate, still girlish. And her deep brown eyes, almond-shaped and deep-set, stared back at her. Did the pain show? The loss? The terror? *You'll survive.* Yes. But how? *You're you.* But who was she?

Would Donald, discovering what she had done, allow her to find out?

Wearing the pajamas and robe she'd reclaimed from the rubble on the bedroom floor, she returned to the room where Toby was now lying on his bed, reading one of the books she'd retrieved from the chaos of his room.

"I don't see why," Toby said, "I don't see why I couldn't have packed my own things. You didn't even bring the Peterson's bird book."

"Sorry, darling," she said. "I'll get you another one at a book-store in Sarasota."

"Does Daddy know Charlene?"

"Not really. They only met once." At the wedding. On the lawn of your grandparents' home. A day of sun and champagne and laughter and wide-brimmed summer hats. But she must not think of that now. "You want to study the maps with me?"

"Sure."

Any more questions? No. Not now. Not yet. If only she had the courage to sit him down and tell him the whole truth, clear and straight! But what would it do to him? She couldn't face that now. She didn't have the strength. The *guts*, she told herself harshly.

After she had kissed Toby good night and he had hugged her in a ritualistic sort of way, she lay in semidarkness—are any motel rooms ever really dark?—and realized that she was not going to sleep. She couldn't lie here *thinking*. She couldn't turn on a light to try to read. Read what? She didn't even have a magazine or newspaper. Trapped.

How long would the cash last? She'd left with about $460, total. She'd had to pay cash for the gas on the New Jersey Turnpike because she carried only one oil company credit card, and there'd been sandwiches and Cokes along the way instead of lunch. How long could the balance last? She had the Gulf Oil credit card for gas and, she'd noted at the desk, Holiday Inn also honored that card. Although Donald had the others, she herself had none of them. Oh, she had department-store credit in Danbury and Westport and at Saks and Bloomingdale's in New York—but only because Donald had signed the necessary papers. She'd never, until now, been concerned with whether the whole system was fair or unfair. But she felt a pang of outrage now. And what about the joint checking account? Could Donald close it out to shut off funds? Certainly. All he had to do, Monday morning, was to withdraw whatever the balance might be. Would he?

Yes.

Or would he talk to the bank—he knew everyone and everyone loved and admired him and he *was* the son of one of the men who'd done the most to turn Danbury into the thriving industrial center it had become after the demise of the hatting industry— would he talk to the president of the bank and arrange to find out where, in what town, she cashed her first check to get cash?

He'd do it if he thought of it. She couldn't risk cashing a check.

It *is* unfair. Foul! She was a prisoner still. *His* prisoner.

"Mama—"

So he was still awake. "Yes, son?"

"You can cry again if you want to."

He knew. He couldn't have heard her in the bathroom but he knew.

She threw back the covers and stepped to his bed. She lay down beside him and felt his small arms go around her, felt his soft breath on her cheek. She reached to touch his cheek; it was dry. Thank God.

She held him till he slept in her arms and then, an eternity later, she drifted off into a shallow, fitful sleep.

But she did not cry again.

———□———

"Odd Don Forrest being at the club alone. Is Brenda sick?"

"Apparently she's walked out."

"Oh, Preston, no. They always seemed so happy together. Well, it does prove that you never know what goes on between other people, doesn't it?"

Or *inside* them, Preston Brice thought as he drove the yellow Cordoba along the deserted road that hugged the edge of the lake.

It was late and the pavement was covered with a white treacherous film of snow although no more was falling. But the heater was purring and the car had begun to feel warm.

"I'll speed up," he said, "if you'll make it worth my while when we get home."

Lucy laughed drowsily and said, "Not tonight, hon. The older the twins get, the more hectic Saturdays seem to become." She yawned audibly. "Donald wasn't polluted, was he?"

"I have a hunch he's been drinking all day. But you can never really tell about Donald." He had never been able to decide whether Donald Forrest's reserve and composure reflected a calm inner strength or whether it was a facade, possibly erected unconsciously, that concealed some churning turbulence inside. "I thought he was going to slug me a while ago."

"But why? If telling me isn't a sacred legal no-no."

"He wanted to know where Brenda went."

"Did you tell him?"

"If I knew, I couldn't tell him. But I don't. When she talked to me on Monday, she didn't mention leaving. But after the way Donald acted tonight, I sort of hope she's gone to Nevada or someplace. Frankly, I'm curious as hell but I'd just as soon not handle a divorce case involving friends."

"Especially after what Brenda told you . . ."

He grunted a laugh. "Don't probe, angel. Go to sleep and leave a guy his professional ethics."

"I'll find out."

He laughed again. "How? By making it worth my while?"

"You've got yourself a deal! Stop lollygagging. I'm wide awake now."

So he eased the big car forward, excited at once, and pleased. Brenda had been carefully evasive in her single explanatory consultation but what little she had hinted at had been partially confirmed tonight. And Donald's insistent questions had suggested even more.

Don, be reasonable. I can't tell you something I don't know.

You have to say that, pal. I understand. What're you afraid of—that if I find her, we'll patch it up and you'll be out your fee? Hell, you won't be paid at all if you take the case. She doesn't have any money of her own, you know—

Damn it, I don't practice law at the Lake Club. I came here to have dinner and a few drinks. Buy you one?

I know how she'll pay you. You've always had a yen for her, haven't you?

Christ, Don, you have to be smashed to say a thing like that. Now I'm going back to my table. I'll talk with you Monday in my office if you want to. Maybe she'll just walk in before then.

But Preston doubted that. He remembered her smooth delicate face and deep dark eyes: vulnerable, hurt, but fixedly, quietly determined. Small wonder that Donald was jealous of her—a rather ordinary sort of hoyden in high school, Brenda Whittier, now Mrs. Forrest, had developed into an arresting and lovely, not quite beautiful, woman.

"Let him go around," Lucy said.

Preston had not realized that there was a car behind him. Close behind. Much too close, with only the two cars on the road and snow on the ground.

"Let the idiot pass, hon. We're not in *that* big a hurry."

So he allowed the Cordoba to slow down.

But the car behind did not swerve left to pass. It slowed too.

In the rearview mirror he could see only a shadowy bulk behind the glare of light, but it hugged the solid yellow no-passing stripe. Then, around a curve, the solid yellow gave way to a broken white line, but still the car behind did not pass.

It was then that the suspicion took root. That drunken fool hadn't followed them from the club, had he? If so, why? Probably to carry on the scene when they arrived home. Well, let's get it over with. He increased his pressure on the accelerator.

Ahead the narrow road ran in a twisting pattern of curves, with the lake stretching flatly off to the right, dark and wide, only a few lights dimly visible on the far shore. The water, beyond a low protective barrier of rustic timbers, glittered in the headlight beams. And on the left, across the road, stood bluffs of dark brown stone.

He couldn't stop here. He pressed the pedal closer to the floor.

"Lock the doors," Lucy said. "I don't like this."

"Can you make out what kind of a car it is?"

The tires were beginning to protest in screeches and the rear end fishtailed on a sharp curve.

"It looks like a Mercedes," Lucy said, her head turned. "What does he want?"

"It's only Donald Forrest," he reassured her. "He wants something I don't have, but—"

The Mercedes changed course and swung left, charging until it was alongside. Preston didn't take his eyes from the road. The road was now blocked. If another car or truck came from the opposite direction around a curve, a head-on collision could not be avoided.

The Mercedes did not pass. It stayed alongside. And when Preston eased the gas feed even lower, the Mercedes also increased speed.

"What's he trying to do?" Lucy cried. "He'll kill us all!"

Kill. With a sickening anger Preston realized that that was what the man—he had to be mad!—was trying to do.

Because now the gray side of the Mercedes was edging closer to the cream-colored fender of the Cordoba.

Automatically Preston gave ground without swerving. And at the same time he eased up on the gas—if the two vehicles scraped together at this speed, it would be disaster.

"Is your seat belt fastened?"

Gripping the wheel, his whole body rigid and his breath tight, he decided to edge his car to the left, but not sharply, with caution.

It did not work. Donald—a stiff fixed profile behind the wheel of the Mercedes—did not give ground.

And there were only a few feet of gravel shoulder between the edge of pavement and the heavy loglike fence on his right.

Donald was trying to force them into the lake!

Inexorably the heavy curved body of the Mercedes came closer. Had he lost his mind entirely? Or had fury taken over completely? Madness! Recklessly then, sharply, Donald swung the wheel and the Mercedes made a sudden sharp turn. Against the side of the Cordoba.

There was a tremendous grating sound, a terrible jolting. Cursing, Preston had to fight to hold the wheel. He heard Lucy scream as her side of the car scraped along the timbers. He felt his seat belt biting diagonally into the flesh of his chest. His arm seemed to be ripped from his shoulder. And, for only a few yards, the car, still charging forward, was trapped between the Mercedes on one side and the heavy barricade on the other.

Then the wood on the right gave way and he realized that the pressure and the horrendous sound on the left had stopped but that the water of the lake was alongside and that, unless he could somehow stop the forward movement of the car, it would be engulfed. As he drove the brake pedal to the floor and struggled to swing the wheel to the left, he saw the taillights of the Mercedes moving off fast, disappearing around a dark, craggy outthrust of stone.

—— □ ——

At breakfast Toby, his eyes on his pancakes, said, "Let's go back."

Carefully, drinking more black coffee, she said: "We've come this far, darling."

"We could be home by dinner time, couldn't we?"

"Don't you want to go to Florida?" Silly question. Absurd. She had not slept well, or long. Her nerves were taut, jumping. "Your aunt Charlene has a place on the beach."

"I don't have an Aunt Charlene."

"Well, you do now. Don't you want to swim in the Gulf of Mexico?"

His blue eyes met hers, stabbing. "I want to go home."

"Well, we're not going home!" We have no home. You should see what your *daddy* has done to your home! "Is that all you're going to eat?"

His eyes wavered. At once she was sorry. She braced herself to see the pain and hurt twist his face.

But instead she saw his eyes harden, and it was with something like relief that she heard him say, "The pancakes stink."

In the parking area, the car packed, she turned to realize that he had dropped something heavy, with a clank and metallic clatter, into the trash container. He climbed into the car, his frail shoulders set defiantly.

"What the hell did you throw away?" she demanded.

"My ice skates."

She drove. Fast. The ground was covered with a white film of snow but the pavement was wet. The traffic was light on the interstate. Sunday morning. How had she come to be here—Virginia, of all places!—on a Sunday morning?

How had she come here? It was the question that she would have to face, the question to which she was not sure there was even an answer. It had happened slowly but with a terrible inexorability over the years. At first his love, his intense concentration on her to the exclusion of all others, especially the women who had flirted with him in both obvious and subtle ways—yes, for most of the ten years of their marriage she had relaxed with satisfaction, even joy, in the certainty and security of his devotion. They had made love with delight and abandon, sometimes light-heartedly, playfully, sometimes with a furious, consuming passion. They had enjoyed themselves, and each other, and Toby. And she had not recognized the flickering storm signals. She'd been too happily and securely blind. But then . . . coming to see his helplessness in the grip of suspicions and dark fears that, she realized in time, he hated as much as she did, she also came to see that some poison, perhaps deeply old and only freshly released in his blood, had somehow intensified in its deadly virulence until his mind had become its victim, overwhelmed, paralyzed, twisting in pain and lashing out with cruelty.

Even now, trying to see the thing as a whole, she could not pinpoint a particular scene between them, or a particular place, or even the year when their lives had begun the subtle change that had brought her here with such terrible inevitability—here, hundreds of miles from the only town that had ever been home to her.

And why? Would the whole pattern remain a mystery that she would never understand? Was the drinking a result or a cause? Or both? Certainly as the boozing took over, it had come to *seem* the cause. And she had blamed it and Donald as if by some mighty exertion of human will he could cure the whole complex malignancy. And often—God, how often—she had blamed herself, wondering helplessly what *she* might have done. Hopeless, hopeless . . .

Quiveringly aware of the straight-backed figure in the bucket seat beside her, she thrust the past aside. There were more immediate, more practical considerations. Could she, for instance, still type? She'd paid part of her tuition in college through typing jobs. And Donald's electric portable was in the trunk—how had she had the good sense to retrieve it from the trash on the floor of the study? She didn't even know whether it would function. Or whether she could still operate it.

Country on both sides now. Fields. Pines. Reddish earth. The sky threatened rain. And to hell with it.

Where was he now? And what was he doing? She could see him entering the house, staring at the desolation, discovering the emptiness—what would he do? He would either explode into more violence or, more likely, be overcome by remorse. The sad familiar pattern. He would be amazed and sickened by what he had done. Lost. Lonely in the big house . . .

You're crazy, girl. To think this way now—to *care*.

She remembered the time she had suggested, not angrily, that Donald should see a psychiatrist. He had erupted in fury. *A shrink? What the hell do I need with a shrink!* And then—her mind flinched away from the scene—then he had thrown her to the bed and had ripped off her clothes, his eyes cold, cold. . . .

She blanked her mind, forcibly, anger running mercifully through her blood. Hate? No, not hate. She could never hate him. Even if she should. She could not hate Donald.

Because you still love him?

She did not know. Not yet.

After miles of silence Toby spoke: "Daddy's not c-c-coming, is he?"

Eyes fixed on the road, the hated stutter echoing in her mind, she heard herself speaking in a low, level tone: "No, he's not coming, Toby." But he will—he will if he ever learns where I am. "He's not coming, darling, because I've left him. We're separated and I'm going to get a divorce. Do you understand what that means?"

"Y-y-es."

"I'm sorry, dear. I'm so terribly, terribly sorry." She didn't say, It has to be. She didn't say, It's a matter of survival. She didn't say, It's for your sake, too.

Another few miles. Not many. The car was like a small boat on a vast rolling sea. She struggled with despair. And guilt. And another kind of anger—why the hell should *she* feel guilty?

At last Toby said, very softly: "Don't w-w-worry, Mama. We'll have a g-g-good time anyway."

She could not speak. Toby reached and turned on the radio. Voices singing hymns. She had forgotten it was Sunday. She wished she still knew how to pray. She wished she could thank God—anybody—for Toby.

Broken half-remembered lines of poetry came to her: *For us, like any other fugitive . . . like all the flowers . . . and all the beasts that cannot remember . . . . it is today in which we live.*

Today. Now.

"I'm h-h-hungry."

She turned off the interstate into a sleepy small town. Bought sandwiches and Cokes at a diner, then drove the side streets till she found a small shaded park. With a playground: swings and a slide. They ate. They played. Astonishing how a child's mind can shut out the past, the future. She pushed his swing, her body responding gratefully to the physical exertion. Toby laughed. And then, while he climbed the steps of the slide over and over, she sat and vigorously pumped the chains of the swing until she was swooping so high that she was looking at the quiet streets and modest houses through the leaves and boughs of the immense trees.

Then it started to rain and they ran, whooping together to the car, and then they were back on the superhighway again. Fugitives, but alive.

No more was said of Donald. Or where they were going. Or why.

The afternoon passed slowly, pleasantly. It was as if, her decision accepted by Toby, she could now drive through the steady rain without despair or anger or even fear.

For those few long hours at least.

The country became more hilly, lovely in a wet, raw sort of way, with fields—was that cotton growing?—and barns and farmhouses blurred but visible through the gray downpour.

And then, at dusk, the rain stopped.

"Mama, are you t-tired?"

"No. Are you?"

"N-n-not really."

So they drove until after eight, then located another Holiday

Inn—thank God for the Gulf card, because the cash was going fast—and, passing the lighted pool on the way back to the room after a huge dinner which they both devoured ravenously, Toby asked: "Is it too c-cold to go swimming?"

Swimming. A horrible scene flashed in her mind: Donald on the deck of the sloop he kept in Westport, Donald throwing Toby's screaming, protesting body into the Sound. Her panic. Donald's slightly drunken laughter: *It's the only way he'll learn, Brenda.*

The panic turning to terror as she dove into the depthless water. And Donald's amused but derisive smile when she and Toby clambered aboard. Toby had refused to cry, but the bafflement in his face had torn her apart. And he had stuttered then for several weeks and had never again gone sailing.

"Why don't we wait to swim till we get to Florida?" The evening air was surprisingly warm. They were in Georgia and it had not rained here. "I'll teach you how, Toby. I really will."

Would he ever learn? She'd tried over and over since that summer afternoon and had failed as often as she tried. Whether he would admit it or not, the child was terrified of deep water. Would he always be?

So much to do. So many wounds to try to heal. But she did not feel so rebellious tonight. Or overwhelmed. She slept in her own bed and Toby slept in the other one, his quiet breathing, not quite a snore, lulling her tired mind until she, too, drifted gratefully into a soft and dreamless sleep.

———□———

"Donald," Emily Whittier said very softly, her tone husky with compassion, "dear boy, we've told you each time you called: we have no more idea where she is than you do."

"I'm sorry to get you out of bed." His tone was contrite, boyishly abashed—and Emily was convinced that his remorse was genuine. "I guess I didn't realize it was so late."

"We're worried, too," Randy said from the deep chair where he always sat, usually reading. "But she's a big girl now. Her mother and I have decided she might just need time to sort things out." He studied Donald. "I'd offer you a drink but I'm not sure you should have any more, are you?"

And Donald smiled, as if he were amused, agreeing. "I haven't had much else to do for two days." But then, as if he didn't want to give himself excuses: "Oh, hell, Randy, we both know I drink too much, right? I've been trying to taper off." A flash of smile, his bloodshot blue eyes warmly bright of a sudden. "It hasn't got me yet."

Emily, drawing her robe around her fleshy body, said, "It's not like Brenda not to phone. But she's probably as distraught as you are." And it was typical of the girl to try to spare her father any anxiety. Emily wished now that she had warned Donald, one of those times on the phone, that Randy's doctor had suggested that he take a leave of absence from the college for a semester or two and had warned him against any intense, emotional stress. "I'll brew some fresh coffee, Donald. If you'll drink it." Then, in the dining-room arch: "It won't do you any good to ask for any, Randy. You know what the doctor said." It was the best she could do in the circumstances—was Donald in any condition to take a hint? Oh, how she wished Donald hadn't wakened them.

From the kitchen she could hear their voices through the small pleasant house.

"I'm on the ropes, sir. I admit it. I don't blame Brenda. All this is probably ninety percent my fault. I can be a bastard. Maybe being alone like this is good for me really. Forces me to *think*. About all the ways I've let her down. One thing I want *you* to know, though: I do love her. I love her more now than I did when we were first married. Do you believe that, sir?"

"There are so many different ways of loving."

And, hearing Randy's soft, evasive tone, she knew: Randy had wanted Brenda to be loved in the gentle, steady way that he had always loved both of his women—his daughter and his wife. A shudder of gratitude and selfish satisfaction went through her.

"She could have a car accident. She never did get the hang of that car."

"I wouldn't worry on that score, Donald. Brenda's always been a careful driver."

"I had one myself. Last night. Not much but it's getting messy. Other guy's threatening all sorts of charges soon's court opens in the morning. Christ, my whole life's a mess all of a sudden!"

She returned to the book-lined living room that looked like an extension of Randy's small library. Donald, tall and leonine, was pacing in long, slow strides. The poor boy—he usually looked and acted so self-contained, so inwardly confident and strong. At least in her presence. Too much so, Randy had once or twice suggested, but she had ignored his passing remarks—after all, Randy had always wished their Brenda had married . . . well, otherwise. Although Randy wasn't one to verbalize disappointments that could not be remedied. But, having worked so hard to achieve his various degrees, he had always had an amused contempt for what he called spoiled little rich boys in his classes. She sat on the worn, comfortable sofa.

"It's so lonely," Donald said, staring out the window at the modest, quiet street. "I never knew anyone could be so lonely."

Randy glanced at her, his gray eyes reflecting her own compassion. "I imagine," he said mildly, "that she's lonely, too."

"That worries me, too," Donald said, and crossed the room to resume his seat in the wing chair by the small fieldstone fireplace. "Even with Toby—oh, she's lonely all right. But then, she never loved me as much as I loved her."

"Not," Randy said, "in the same way, perhaps."

Emily saw Donald's lean, athletic body stiffen. "What do you mean by that?"

Randy tilted his small gray head and shrugged, almost imperceptibly. "We all love in different ways, don't we?"

"Do we?" The blue eyes were sharp now and Donald ran his hand, once, through his blond hair. "Maybe you'd better explain that, Professor."

Emily said, "Donald, don't you think that, since tomorrow's a workday—"

But Randy slid his gaze to meet hers and she subsided. Her blood had begun to pump and her stomach was fluttering.

"There's no need really to explain it," Randy said. "There are all sorts and degrees of love. And definitions within each of us. Any mature mind accepts that. If the world were simple, it'd be a pretty damned dull place, wouldn't it?"

The room was very still then until Donald spoke. "You're saying I don't love her." He stood up. "Isn't that what you're trying to say?"

"I'm saying you may love Brenda more than she loves you—"

"That's pretty damn obvious."

"And you may love her in a different way. Possibly in a way that . . . that doesn't satisfy her."

"I knew I shouldn't have come here." He began to stride up and down again. "I knew all I'd get was more blame and your highfalutin ideas and more lies!"

"We haven't lied to you, Donald," Randy said. "We don't know where she is and I suspect she prefers it that way."

"Yes," Emily added, "if she wanted us to know she would have told us when she borrowed the money."

Donald came abruptly to a halt in the center of the room and looked, eyes kindled darkly, from one to the other. "Money? You didn't tell me she borrowed any money."

"Ninety dollars," Emily said, startled at the change in him. "It was all we had in the house."

"Then you *did* lie to me!"

Randy stood up, shaking his head. "We thought she was a little short on the weekend and wanted to do some shopping. As the kids say—no big deal."

"Why didn't you tell me?" Donald demanded. It was almost a shout. "She took every cent there was in the house, too."

"Well," Emily heard herself ask, "it's her money, too, isn't it?"

"She always had all the money she ever needed!" Donald's face was clotted red and he was bellowing now, fists clenched. "More than most women! More than she ever had before! More than *you* could ever afford to give her!"

Shocked, Emily took several steps backward. This was incredible. She didn't even recognize the man standing here in her own living room.

"Donald," Randy said, "look here—we know you're over-wrought. We understand that—"

"You're glad." A whisper now, almost inaudible. "You're both glad she left me." It was an accusation but his eyes looked hurt and stunned. "You've never liked me, have you? You're like everybody else—you pretend you like me but you really hate me."

"That's simply not true," Randy said. "Emily and I both—"

But Donald's face contorted again and he made a slashing open-palmed gesture, shutting off Randy's protest. "No one ever loved me in all my whole goddamned life."

Emily's impulse then was to reach out a hand, to step toward him, even to take him into her arms. No one should have to live believing that . . .

But then Donald spoke again, in a bleak whisper: "Except Brenda. She was the only one. And that was a lie, too."

Again Emily and Randy exchanged helpless glances tinged by bewilderment and compassion.

"Donald," Randy said, "you're going to have to get control of yourself. Give Brenda a chance, why don't you? You must have seen this coming—"

"Go on, Professor." Donald had turned his head and now his heavy gaze, almost mocking, was on Randy—as if he were waiting, or urging. "You know Brenda better than anyone, don't you? You're the only one who ever really understood her, right?"

Frowning now, Randy straightened. He looked very small, very frail, as he faced the younger, taller man. "No one ever really understands anyone else completely—it's childish to expect that. But I'm not blind, Donald—"

"Go on, go on—

"Brenda hasn't been herself for some time. Or happy."

"She's talked to you, told you about me. Behind my back."

"Not once. I do know Brenda, yes. Too well even to expect that." And then something else came into his face, his voice, and his eyes hardened for the first time. "But I know a bruise when I see one. And sometimes I even know a lie when I hear one. And there have been times lately when I've been tempted to demand to know. Hoping that if I did, I wouldn't give in to my own savagery the way you do."

When he stopped speaking, there was a long silence. Emily felt a pang of pride, a thrust of intense love. She had not seen. Or even suspected. But Randy had known—and had protected her by not saying. Yet he, not she, was the one who was ill.

Finally Donald said—and this time the mockery was clear and ugly: "So you think you know Brenda, do you?"

"Reasonably well, yes. As I said, no one ever knows another person completely."

"Shit," Donald said.

It was, Emily realized, the first time she'd ever heard that particular word in this house. "Donald, you're not yourself—"

But it was Randy who interrupted: "Maybe he is, Emily. Maybe he's being himself for the first time. Go on, Donald."

"You don't know the first goddamn thing about your lovely innocent daughter, Pop." And when Emily heard herself gasp, Donald ignored her and took a long unsteady step toward Randy. "Listen, Pop—do you know your daughter's been sleeping around all over town? Think about *that*. She's been laid by half the men in the Lake Club. *Know* her? She's got you conned just the way she's had me. You don't know what that little bitch has put me through!" His tone was low and harsh and furious. "Now, get this, get this, Pop—she's hired a lawyer to get a divorce and she's paying him off by letting him screw her in his office!"

He whirled about and strode toward the front door, shoulders canted at an arrogant, satisfied angle. She caught sight of Randy's face—tight and hard and pale with shock—and something inside her erupted. As Donald reached the door and opened it, she moved, heavily but swiftly. She grabbed his shoulder, swung his body around, and brought her palm across his face. The sound exploded and she wondered, as Donald's face twisted into a grin, whether she would strike again.

But then the door closed and she was standing there staring at it. Incredulity and hate, nausea and disgust and anger—a black river of poison gushed and surged through her.

Slowly she managed to turn.

Then she saw him.

He was sitting in the chair. Slumped. His eyes were open and they had a strange expression of astonishment in them. They looked at her and his lips tried to smile reassuringly. But all he could do was shake his head.

———□———

They awakened very early, almost simultaneously, and refreshed.

"Hi."

"Hi, yourself."

"Are w-w-we in Florida?" The stutter was still with him but not worse. "Will we b-be there today?"

"By nighttime if we move."

"Let's move!"

Within an hour the sun appeared, not hot but warming. She

pulled into a rest area and they folded down the canvas behind the rear seat but could not remove the sun roof because there was no place to store it until the car was unpacked.

How many more miles? Was it the powerful little car itself that fought to shoot forward or was it her own eagerness? She had to struggle to control it—no money to waste on fines for speeding and the roads bristled with patrol cars.

It's Monday. He should be at work. If he's still in Connecticut. And if he isn't? Maybe he's so confident you'll come back that he's gone to Vermont to ski. No time now to think of Vermont. All the fine times there, skiing together and laughing and making love. And the bad times which had begun as good times: *Don't you even know when one of those ski bums is giving you the eye? Don't pretend with me, you bitch.*

Oh, God, she couldn't let herself think of that!

He couldn't reach her if she was careful, very careful, step by step. Why this awful sickening panic all of a sudden?

But she'd have to let her parents know where she'd gone. She had to think of them—and Pop's angina. She couldn't let them worry. She'd never confided in either of them. She was too ashamed. Or too proud. And it would have been disloyal to Donald—who had always resented Pop. Mother, yes, but Pop especially. Possibly because he sensed Pop's inner strength in spite of his physical frailty in the last few years. More likely because in his own strange, possessive way he was jealous of her friendship with her father. She'd find a way to talk to him when she was in Sarasota. She suspected that Pop would not really be too surprised. . . .

She could phone Donald's mother. His father, retired, would be at the offices of FORREST AND SON, PLANNERS AND BUILDERS—even though Donald was now in charge. *In name, anyway,* Donald sometimes fumed ironically, as if amused. But resentful. Rosamond, by this time of day, would probably be drunk. (Like mother, like son?) What could Rosamond tell her? No, it was what she could tell Rosamond. Lay down a false trail. *I'm on my way to Arizona. Tell Donald.* Anger erupted again and surged hotly through her. *Tell him I'm on my way to meet my lover: one of my many lovers!* Her mouth was dry and sour. Her mind again brimming with bitterness and a terrible craving for revenge, she warned herself that she could not afford the luxury of punishing him that way.

To hell with it. She was being emotional, irrational. If she stopped to phone, she'd have to use more of the precious cash or charge the call to her home number. And Donald knew people at the telephone company. *If* he learned the call had been charged to his number and placed in Georgia, even before she crossed the state line, he'd *guess* she was on her way to Florida. He might even go through her address book—which in her confusion she had forgotten to search for in the rubble. If he found Charlene's address and put it together with a phone call from Georgia—

What if, what if, what if—a fugitive but still a prisoner. Was her prison sentence only really beginning?

"We're here! Look, Mama, we're here!"

She looked. WELCOME TO FLORIDA.

And her heart lifted again.

Later: "I didn't know Florida had h-h-hills. Like Connecticut!"

And later still: "Oranges. Hanging on the trees! C-c-can I pick one, just one, please?"

They drove through brilliant sunlight that occasionally turned into quick rainfalls. "It's l-l-like the rain's a tunnel and you always know you'll come out at the other end, don't you?"

The monotony of the interstate highway was not monotonous because Toby sat upright beside her, alert for adventure, devouring every sight and sound. "It smells different. The t-trees smell different, and the g-g-grass, too. Even the air!"

Well, the stutter was there but—in time, with luck, with peace—who knows, who can predict? Dr. Kellerman had described the difference between a stutter—the hesitation over and repetition of consonants—and a stammer, that painful and embarrassing struggle of body and mind to produce a word at all. A stutter, he had reassured her, might be associated with a specific and possibly temporary state of emotional insecurity, whereas a stammer could be much more troublesome and more seriously incapacitating. She had read somewhere that Somerset Maugham's stammer had been so severe that sometimes he had had to struggle for as long as five excruciating minutes to utter certain ordinary words and sentences. God spare Toby that, please. Please . . .

By the time they reached the smog and turmoil of traffic in the Tampa–St. Petersburg area, she realized that she had relaxed deep inside. She dared not give herself over to the idea that, because thirteen hundred miles lay between them, she was free. But by refusing to allow her mind to gaze backward or inward, she discovered within herself something she had not known she ever possessed: the ability to live within the minutes as they came and went, as if no others lay behind or ahead. If only life could be lived so, always. . . .

The final miles off the superhighway were, if anything, dreary: farmlands and oaks with hanging moss, and small bleak towns with tin canning factories glittering in the sun and ramshackle roadside stands brilliant with fruit and vegetables, sad-looking weathered farmhouses beyond.

She was not prepared for Sarasota. They passed the Ringling Museum on one side, imposing and lovely, and on the other the airport entrance.

"It's s-so clean, isn't it? Everything l-l-looks *white*, doesn't it, Mama?"

On target again, Toby. And thank you for forcing me to see it.

She phoned Charlene from a booth alongside the busy Tamiami Trail—so-called, she decided, because Route 41 ran from Tampa to Miami on the other coast. The sun was now low in the west, a golden glow lying over the town, and Charlene's voice crackled with joy as she gave directions.

"The sign reads 'Lido Beach.' You turn right—that's west—and head straight into the sun! You'll cross two bridges, that's the Ringling Causeway, everything's Ringling here, including the freaks. If the traffic's not too bad, you'll be here in time to see the sunset. And be prepared, it's nothing less than sensational! Hurry, pet—hurry, hurry."

"You'd better be more specific, Charl."

"Oh, all right, if you have to be so damn prosaic. Now concentrate—"

They had crossed one bridge over the bay, Toby twisting to look back at the white beauty of the town and then ahead into the rich radiance beyond the rooftops and the highrises, when he spoke again, this time in a different tone, hushed and grave and troubled: "C-c-can I ask you a question, Mama?"

Stiffening, she said, "Of course, dear."

"You'll t-tell me the truth, this t-t-time?"

"I'll always tell you the truth, Toby. From now on."

"Would you still b-be in Connecticut with Daddy if I . . . if I had n-n-never been born?"

She thought for a split second that she was going to scream. She pulled the car off the road onto the green shoulder. A horn shrilled from behind. She slammed on the brakes.

"No, no, no, Toby, darling, my baby, it is not your fault, you must not think that, oh, Toby . . ."

And she reached awkwardly across the gearbox; she was clutching to bring him closer when he threw himself over the obstruction and then she had him in her arms, trembling and quivering and holding her as if he were an infant again.

Not your fault, no, and not mine. His. *His*, goddamn him to hell, now and forever, damn him, damn him, damn him!

——— □ ———

Orin Forrest was watching *The Late Show*. Or maybe it was *The Late Late Show*. An old western tonight. Randolph Scott rides again. The good guys against the bad guys. Not too many years ago people said he reminded them of Randolph Scott—same tall muscular body, same square jawline and light-colored hair. Before he lost his hair altogether. And until then strangers had often mistaken him and Donald for brothers. Donald—his thoughts always drifted back to Donald. Stretched out now but not relaxing on the reclining leather-covered contour chair in his paneled den, Orin decided to see this film to the inevitable shootout and then to take two sleeping pills and go up the wide Victorian stairway to his own bedroom, hoping not to waken Rosamond in hers, and go to sleep. He couldn't wait up all night for Donald—he might not come at all.

Yesterday he'd appeared during Orin's favorite Saturday afternoon program, *Wide World of Sports*. What a familiar scene that had been. How many times had they acted it out in one form or another?

The boy suffering the tortures of the damned, his remorse a naked and terrible thing to watch. *I guess I blew it, Dad.* How many times had he heard that, those same words? *She's left me.*

And Orin, his heart writhing with compassion, had asked all the familiar questions, of course, carefully not offering a drink, since Donald had seemed sober. And then Donald had told him of the accident.

And, following the pattern, Orin had promised to have his own attorney look into it.

He heard a sound. Was Rosamond coming down the stairs? Which probably meant that she had run out of booze upstairs. He closed his eyes. He hoped he'd be able to hold off telling her about Brenda—and Donald's marriage—until he was certain Brenda wasn't coming back. Sometimes he felt he'd spent a lifetime protecting Rosamond from unpleasantness and pain—well, if Donald couldn't help being what he was, his old man couldn't help being what *he* was, too. A fool perhaps. To be in love over the years—to *stay* in love—with a vain and utterly selfish woman who herself had begun sadly to realize that she now had no beauty of which to be vain.

But what he had heard, he realized, was the front door opening. Footsteps now across the big center hall. He tensed. Donald came in. He looked like hell but he smiled—that open boyish smile that was always so appealing and that reminded Orin of the good days and the good years when he was young. Surprisingly, Donald seemed to be sober.

"I knew you'd still be up," he said.

"Where the hell have you been?" Even as he spoke, aware of the quick anger mingling hotly with the relief in his mind, Orin recognized that he was falling into the role that he somehow assumed as soon as he saw his son in circumstances like these. "You might at least have telephoned the office if you weren't coming in."

"I knew you'd handle things." Donald sat down on the leather couch. His wide shoulders slouched; he stared at the flickering TV screen as if he wasn't really seeing it. "I've been all over hell and back." He stretched out on his back. "I thought I'd go skiing, but I turned around before I got to Vermont. Any word here?"

"Not about Brenda—no. But plenty of *word*, buddy. Plenty."

"That Preston Brice bastard, right?"

Orin stood up. "That Preston Brice bastard brought formal

charges." He flicked off the TV. "You sat right in this room yesterday and told me it was an ordinary accident. Something about the road being slick and you didn't even know whose car it was. Something about losing your head and driving away."

"Truth, Dad. Honest. I might have known Preston Brice would try to make something out of it. You know lawyers, right?"

"I also know some of the fancy words they use. Like aggravated assault. Like reckless endangerment. Like leaving the scene of an accident involving personal injury."

Donald sat up. "Was anyone hurt?"

"No thanks to you, according to Brice's sworn statement. Their seat belts saved them."

Donald stood up. "They didn't go into the drink. I saw the car stop in my rearview mirror."

"Goddamnit, you better know: Brice is furious! He's bringing charges of attempted homicide. Vehicular homicide, it's called."

"He's crazy."

"*He's* crazy? You didn't mention yesterday that Preston Brice has been engaged to represent your wife in a divorce action!"

"Cool it, Dad. You want to wake Mother, bring her in on this?"

With a fierce assertion of will Orin lowered his voice, conscious of the quivering in his muscles. "Son, we're not talking about driving while intoxicated, or running a car over a fraternity-house lawn after a football game. You're in serious trouble. And speaking of your mother—do you realize what a shock the disgrace will be when this shenanigan hits the newspaper? Her family founded one of the hat companies that put this town on the map."

"Christ, Dad, let's not go over all that again." He stepped to sink into Orin's chair, lowering his lean head into his hands. "So you're against me, too."

"Let's not start *that* whine again. Nobody's against you. Nobody's out to get you. You're your own worst enemy. Always have been."

"All I really care about is Brenda. I kept telling myself while I drove that when I got back, she'd be here. She'd have to be here."

Orin shook his head. "If she's gone to all this trouble, what makes you think that she'd just turn around on her own and come back?"

"She has to."

"*Why* does she have to?"

"She just does. She has to."

"Son, nothing has to happen just because you want it to."

"It's crazy, I admit that. I see her everywhere. Here. On the way north and back. A woman driving. A girl on the street in one of those towns, a dark-haired—" He lifted his face. "She really loved skiing, Dad."

And tennis. And preparing meals. And decorating that big house on her own. Just plain living. Orin knew. He'd even envied his son's good fortune. He had been afraid all along that, somehow, Donald would blow that, too. The poor kid. That was the trouble: You couldn't help loving the boy, feeling sorry for him, and wanting to help—even when you knew he'd brought it all on himself.

"Hell, I didn't even stop for one drink all day. I forced myself. I really love her, Dad. I love her so damned much. I don't even feel alive without her."

I—always I. Should he mention the Forsythe Agency? Not yet.

Instead he sat in the chair behind his desk and said: "Well, you worry about Brenda. I've taken care of Preston Brice." He saw Donald's head lift, his eyes pathetically hopeful. "Don't ask me how. Brice may be sore, even vindictive, but I do business with a good many of his valued clients. It's not good public relations for an attorney personally to get mixed up in legal cases like this."

"You're saying it's all over, right?"

"It'll cost you a new car for Brice. And I don't advise your cutting in on his wife at the Christmas dance."

"Oh, God, Dad—how can I thank you?"

"By never doing anything that foolish again, drunk or sober." How many times had he said that? "And by doing *something* to get control of that temper of yours." He'd been saying that since the boy was five years old. "Next time it might not be so easy. Or I might not be here to bail you out." He took a deep breath. "Or," he added, "it might be something that no one can bail you out of." Like what? His mind veered away.

"I try," Donald said. "Honest. I try like hell." He ran a hand through his disheveled blond hair. "Sometimes, Dad, it's as if I just can't hold myself in. You don't know. It's like there's a kind of volcano gurgling inside—I'm as scared of it as anyone, Dad. Maybe *more* than anyone."

It was the first time, over all the years, that Donald had broken down and talked this way. Orin was moved—and terrified.

"Have you discussed this with Brenda?"

"She thinks I need a shrink." His eyes met his father's: the torment in their depths was agonizing to see. "What I really need is Brenda. If I could even *talk* to her! I tried to get Mac at the phone company to help—you know, tracing calls charged to our house number or any going to her parents' house—but he said it was against policy and even against the law, he thought." He sat back and turned away. "If I only knew where she was. That she was all right. That Toby was okay . . ."

So, unable to bear the misery that he himself had begun to feel, Orin made up his mind. He reached and picked up a business card from his desk. "I talked to a Mr. Michael Collins today." He glanced at the card that read FORSYTHE INVESTIGATIONS—PRIVATE. "Collins says his company can locate anyone. Says they're ninety percent successful in cases like this."

Donald leaped to his feet, reached, and took the card. He did not seem to be breathing.

"The office is on Main Street above Steinberg's Men's Store. It's a nationwide outfit. Mr. Collins said it would be helpful if he had a list of friends and relatives. Does Brenda have an address book, Christmas card list, anything like that?"

"She may have taken it. I'll see." Donald stepped around the desk and Orin stood up. "Thanks, Dad. I don't know how to say it. You won't be sorry."

He reached and clasped his father in a bearlike embrace, one palm slapping Orin's back. Into his father's ear Donald whispered: "I'll make it up to you. And Mother, too. I'll make it up to both of you."

"If you find her, buddy," Orin said, gruffly, "you make sure she knows how much you love her."

"That's a promise, old man. That's a promise!"

And then, after Donald had gone, his father turned off the lamp and did not turn on the television again. He resumed his place in the chair and tilted it as far back as it would go.

Had he done the right thing?

Would he ever know?

He wished he could discuss it with Rosamond. But she'd only have another drink and probably consult her astrology books. What did the stars predict for Donald today, tomorrow? Well, if it gave her comfort . . .

He closed his eyes. He may as well spend the night here—just as well not to infect her with his forebodings. He'd sleep in time.

But his mind wandered on. Had Donald somehow outfoxed him just now? Had he taken advantage, again, not even consciously aware of doing it, of his father's love and compassion?

A dark sense of doom settled over Orin's tired mind. Of helplessness: what more could he do when he had failed so often over the years?

A sense of dread: Will the volcano erupt again?

And against whom?

———□———

The house was low and long, Oriental in general design, but modern, with wide sliding front doors flanked by huge picture windows. Its coral color, framed in black, was sun-faded, so that it had a pinkish seashell hue.

The owner told me it once looked smack across the Gulf, Charlene had said last evening when they'd arrived, *before they built those houses on the beach the other side of the street. But except for one monstrosity, they're beautiful homes and the neighborhood's as quiet as any in town. No condominiums or high rises and very damn little traffic day or night.*

When she saw the interior, the first word that had occurred to Brenda was *serenity.* It was a place of sliding *shoji* panels, alcoves, exquisite Japanese scrolls on grass-cloth walls, a spacious lack of clutter. The living room was very long, its high ceiling draped with brass chains holding huge paper lanterns, its wooden floor laid out in a tatami pattern to simulate an arrangement of grass mats framed in black. Central to the room was a large dropped area lined on two sides by upholstered built-in couches with seats at the level of the surrounding floor. *Voilà,* Charlene had said, *a Japanese conversation pit! You feel you're sitting on the floor but you don't have to fold up your legs like a Buddha.* In the center of the pit was a very low, very large square table on black-lacquered legs, its surface a pattern of inlaid woods of various grains and shades and sizes, all highly polished. A Ming tree, and this alone, graced the tabletop. The rear of the room was glass: a huge panel of plate glass at center, forming one side of the pit, and on either side of this, sliding glass doors leading onto a patio. The cobblestone paving surrounded, on three sides, a sunken, dimly lit Japanese garden. Here there were widely spaced plantings, evergreens nestled horizontally amid huge stones or boulders, a decorative concrete lantern, moss here and there, wood chips and brown pebbles arranged in a pleasing pattern, a miniature waterfall. The sound of water trickling and dropping delicately over stone only added to the almost incredible sense of tranquility.

Even Toby had been impressed. *Neat,* he had said. *It makes you want to-to-to whisper.*

But Charlene, laughing softly, had insisted that they go to the beach to see the sunset before she showed them their rooms. *We'll be in time if we hurry. It goes fast once it gets this low. Believe me, it's worth seeing.*

And so it had been: a slow descent of the huge ball that changed color from orange to red and then, reaching the rim of the Gulf's horizon, seemed to plunge out of view, its movement suddenly visible to the naked eye. Charlene timed it triumphantly from the second it touched the water's distant edge: *A minute and twenty seconds on the nose!* And Toby had said it reminded him of his favorite children's book: the story of *The Red Balloon* over the rooftops of Paris. The afterglow had flooded the world with a golden glow that lasted for hours and filled Brenda with a curious and overwhelming sense of peace. Of hope perhaps.

As they returned through the small hushed woods of Australian pines that served as access from the street to the beach, Toby had said, *I always thought beaches were tan or brown. This one's white!*

She, too, had been astonished. The single time she'd been to Florida, as a child, she and her parents had stayed on the east coast, where the sand was indeed tan or brown. And in the islands, with Donald, there had been beaches of black. But she must not think of that. Or of Donald.

During the night in her room, which was separated from Toby's by a sliding door so wide that it formed half the width of the wall, she had not thought again of Donald. Or of what might lie ahead.

She had given herself over to the serenity of the house and had slept soundly and peacefully in spite of everything.

Now, with the morning sun streaming across the patio where they ate breakfast, Charlene asked, "Do you know how to swim, Toby?"

"Not yet. But Mama's g-g-going to teach me."

"Well then, don't go out above your knees." She stood up, ready to go to work. "There's an undertow from New Pass. And you, Brendie, you make yourself at home. That's an order."

"Aye, aye, skipper," Brenda said, and Charlene was off in her shiny white station wagon.

While they were unpacking the suitcases, Toby asked: "How long are we s-s-staying here, Mama?"

She wished she knew. "Don't you like it here, darling?"

"I l-love it. But n-not forever, right?"

She nodded. Certainly not forever. Whenever Toby said *Right?* that way, her mind flashed to Donald. And then swerved away.

Later, when Toby had gone over to the beach alone—no fear of his going too far out, he'd wade in *ankle-deep* at most!—she set up the typewriter on the built-in dressing table in her bedroom. It functioned as if it had never been crashed to the floor. And to hell with all that. She worked in a slash of sunlight—*she* was functioning, too!—and after an hour or so she began to feel confident, even reasonably proficient. Once you've done it well, it comes back to you. Like swimming.

Swimming.

Toby had not returned so she decided, unalarmed, to go to the beach. Drawing on her one-piece black swimsuit and borrowing a terry beach robe that she found hanging in the bathroom, she recalled what Charlene had said last evening: that she, Brenda, had not changed much over the years. *Same cameo face, same brown eyes flashing at you. Oh, maybe a little different. More wary—is that the word, Brendie?* Yes, that was the word. Charlene herself did not look so much older as more womanly. The tall handsomeness had matured into a sort of voluptuousness that her brief shorts and halter only emphasized. And her brown hair was blond now, long and drawn tight to her head. But her manner was familiar: hearty, outgoing, warm.

Last night, after Toby had asked to be excused to go to the

spacious television room in the rear and later to the bedroom that Charlene had already prepared, Charlene had replenished their drinks, calling Brenda's attention to the massive black-lacquered and intricately carved liquor cabinet that her brother, whose name was Barry, had designed and constructed for the playwright owner. Barry was a widower living very much alone on Anna Maria Island, which, Charlene explained, was the northernmost of the string of narrow barrier islands that included Lido Shores, where they now were, and Longboat Key stretching twelve miles in between to the north. *So I did at least have someplace to go after the so-called trauma of splitting. Which wasn't really that much of a trauma after all. How I survived five years of marriage with that super-bore I'll never understand. He sold insurance but mostly he sold himself. I just stopped buying. When I finally admitted to myself that he was as dull in bed as he was at the dinner table, that was it—sayonara, arrivederci, au revoir, and auf Wiedersehen!*

So here she was now, selling the condominiums that were ruining the peace and beauty of the area. She'd been divorced three years. *Glorious, pet. My own boss and a choice of all the studs, at least until the wrinkles win out over the suntan lotions. Oh, there's a handsome young actor type trying to change my mind, but no thanks, never again.*

They had talked for hours, and Brenda, she later realized, had revealed little, confided less. She couldn't. Not yet. Perhaps never. And she had to admit that at least part of her reticence and reluctance was due more to shame than to loyalty. After the evening with Charlene, though, she did feel less a failure.

Now, going along the curving uncurbed street and then through the deep quiet woods, she began to feel a mounting sense of apprehension. The beach, to her amazement, was all but deserted. Her uneasiness intensified. But almost at once she spotted Toby's blond hair in the brilliant sunlight. He was studying the seagulls as they wheeled overhead and plunged beak-first into the water to snatch a fish. The dark blue water of the Gulf looked vast and the gentle waves lapped in long silver crescents along the white sand. She swam and then later tried to teach him. Again. And failed. Again. Even though he had mastered the strokes, his small body tensed and froze each time she released it and then he began thrashing about in wild panic. Until, after an hour, she had to give up. Damn you, Donald, damn you again.

On the way back to the house, though, Toby said: "I'll do it yet. I'll sh-sh-show him."

It was his only reference to his father all day. But somehow it expressed all the pent-up frustration and anger of an eight-year-old unable, ever, to satisfy the demands of a sometimes contemptuous parent.

We'll *both* show him, she thought, but said nothing.

In the afternoon they explored the town. Even busy and traffic-clogged as it was, it seemed a quiet place. Without urgency. And bright! The sun flooded the white and pastel-colored buildings, and Main Street, when she compared it with the dreary dullness of Danbury's, winter or summer, had a graceful charm. The palm trees and blooming tropical plants everywhere gave the whole place, this first day, an exotic bewitching quality that she found both relaxing and exciting. She could understand why her erst-while landlords, the playwright and his wife, had chosen this place in which to raise their three sons. Would Toby be happy here?

On the bridge over the bay, where sailboat and motor launches and yachts moved on the water in a lazy pattern, Toby cried, "What the hell k-k-kind of bird is that?"

She ignored the *hell*—he could have used worse—and told him it was a pelican perched on the concrete balustrade. " 'A funny bird, the pelican,' " she quoted. " 'Its beak can hold more than its belly can.' "

And Toby laughed, twisting his head and then collapsing in great guffaws, his fists beating his knees in glee. Thank you, Ogden Nash. Or was it Dorothy Parker? It didn't matter. Toby's laughter had made her day.

In the house, later, he discovered a life-size carving of the bird—a stylized, not really abstract, wood sculpture. But by some miracle of art or perception the clumsy ugliness of the creature had been transformed into a thing of beauty. And Brenda remembered: *Any sculpture that's not Oriental is mine. My brother works in wood—anything from abstractions to custom-made furniture. You'll meet him. He's a real loner. And the gentlest of men.*

Charlene returned from work with a gleaming new red bicycle in the back of her white station wagon. "Can you ride it, Toby? Lido Shores is great for bicycles."

But for some reason Toby had never learned to ride. Which he refused to admit. He took the bike, giving Charlene a hug that seemed to please her so much that Brenda's objections withered on her tongue.

Later he returned to the house, knee bleeding slightly and an expression of rueful frustration on his face, which, Brenda realized, was turning pink from the sun. "Please d-d-don't bother, Mama. I know where they keep the rubbing alcohol." Had his stutter slacked off or was she imagining it?

While he was in one of the three bathrooms—Brenda assumed there was another in the upstairs area, which was her landlord's writing studio—the sound of a motorcycle shattered the quiet. The figure that climbed off, removing his helmet, and entered through the sliding panels of the front door, which were kept closed because of the air conditioning, was not really impressive—until Brenda saw his face. In his late twenties, the man whom Charlene kissed lightly before introducing was possibly the most handsome man Brenda had ever seen. At least off the motion-picture screen. Black hair, black eyes, a flashing brilliant smile. His name, Charlene said, was Malcolm Eggers. "Mal, a wandering minstrel. A thing of shreds and patches. Works at the Asolo. That's the local repertory company. He knows our landlord, who made the mistake of introducing us. Now he thinks he's in love with me."

Mal laughed. It was a deep rich laugh but it did not sound phony, or theatrical. "Charlene's already given me *your* biography. Welcome to Florida." His grip was strong. "Maybe you can help me. I can't dope out whether Charl's afraid to admit she loves me or whether she's scared no one could possibly love *her*."

"Both," Charlene cried. "And also, you don't like golf. Let's have a drink!"

Over cocktails on the built-in sofas around the conversation pit, Brenda discovered that she was very pleased. She discovered that she liked Mal—he didn't seem like an actor and didn't even talk like one—and she found herself wondering about Charlene. Not conventionally beautiful, Charlene had developed into a striking woman—but this almost-too-handsome man was younger and, from appearances, could probably have his pick of any of the lonely young things he must work with. Perhaps he saw in Charlene those qualities that had caused Brenda to make that phone call and then to accept Charlene's insistent invitation.

Whenever the conversation veered to the theater or his work, Mal somewhat abashedly smiled and went on to another subject. But she did learn that he had made a screen test and that, at the end of the theater season here, he was going to Hollywood under contract.

When Toby appeared, he accepted the introduction in his usual shy way. His face seemed pinker and his stuttering was, if anything, more pronounced.

So Brenda, who made it a rule never to mention it, was startled when Mal said, "You know something, Toby? I used to stammer. Not stutter, like you, but really stammer."

Toby frowned. And said nothing.

"Mr. Eggers is an actor."

And Toby's head turned to look at Mal again, his blue eyes studying the man, who regarded him as if waiting for a reply.

"Is that your motorcycle out there?" Toby asked.

"You want to take a ride?"

"I c-c-c-can't even ride a bike."

Mal stood up. "Charlene, where's your helmet?"

"I'll get it."

Brenda was about to protest when Mal said, "This is different. I'll do the balancing. All you have to do is hold on."

She waited.

"Sure," Toby said. "Thanks."

Astonished, her heart pounding, she went outside and she and Charlene watched. After the motorcycle and its two riders had gone around the block twice, she relaxed again. Grateful.

"I'm not going to miss the sunset," Charlene said. "Come along?"

"I want to make a long-distance call," Brenda said, and moved toward her blue car.

"Where are you going? There're three phones in the house."

They were facing each other across the front yard, which was not grass but brown pebbles. What should she say? She could not explain. She could not impose her fears on Charlene.

Explain what? That she couldn't risk phoning from the house where she was staying? Why not? If he was using his friends at the telephone company in Danbury to report on calls charged to her home, did it matter whether she called from 1168 Westway or from a pay station less than a mile away? Maybe. Because she could use cash at a booth—there'd be no record of any charge. Was she taking foolish unnecessary precautions? Well, Donald had often accused her of being irrational.

"Mother?"

"Brenda! At last. Are you all right? And Toby?"

"We're fine. How are you?"

"Slightly frantic."

"And Pop?"

Silence.

"Mother—?"

"Randy's not here."

"Where is he?"

"He had a faculty meeting after his last class."

"Mother, I'm sorry I couldn't tell you when I came by on Saturday."

"It's just as well you didn't."

"Why? Donald's come by, hasn't he?"

"Yes." Very slowly: "He's come by. We . . . we told him we didn't know where you were."

"But he didn't believe you."

"Since we didn't know, we couldn't tell him, could we? Brenda, is there anything you need? Ninety dollars won't take you very far."

"Mother, is Donald still in town?"

"I saw him walking on White Street on my way to the hospital. Staggering, you might say."

"Hospital?"

"Oh. Yes. To visit a friend. Mrs. Eugene Brown. Margo. You remember her."

"Vaguely. Mother, I'll phone you regularly. But I'm going to try to get a job so you can't reach me. We're with . . . someone

I used to know. If Donald asks again, tell him we're in Phoenix, Arizona. Tell him I'm living with an old boyfriend."

"Brenda, I know better than that. I also know you shouldn't upset Donald any more than he is."

"You think I've done the wrong thing. I didn't know you were that fond of Donald."

"I'm not. I hate him."

"Hate him? Mother, you don't sound like yourself at all."

"I shouldn't have said that. But it's true, Brenda . . . because of what he's done to you."

"Well, if it'll make you feel any better, he's done less than you think. And less than I thought he had, too."

"I'm relieved. And I know Randy will be. Thanks so much for letting me know, dear."

"I'll do this again. After five. Maybe every day for a while."

"No."

"No? Why not?"

"Yes, do, Brenda, do that. Good-bye!"

"Give Pop my love."

"I shall, dear."

"Mother, are you crying?"

"Of course not. I'm so relieved, that's all. Good-bye now."

But, driving back over the small bridge, Brenda was not reassured. Had Donald staged one of his drunken scenes—or what? She had never heard her mother say she hated anyone before. Ever. And for as long as she could remember, she'd never known Pop to have a faculty meeting on Monday.

Here she was thirteen hundred miles away and fretting about what was going on up there.

The thought of Toby's sunburn, slight enough but painful, brought her back to 1168 Westway. Charlene had put him in a cold tub and Mal had gone. Together she and Charlene prepared him for bed. He was not hungry; the sun had made him drowsy. They placed him on top of the sheet, wearing only his underpants, with a brass dinner gong on the table beside him. On the table also was the carved wooden pelican—which Toby had apparently claimed as his own for the duration. How long would that be?

She kissed him. "We're only a few yards away so ring the gong if it gets worse." But he only nodded, tried to smile, turned on his side, uttered a faint moan, and, before they left the room, was snoring softly, sound asleep.

Over Mexican TV dinners juggled on trays in the living room, Charlene said: "I used to envy you your cameo face and free wild grace, as they say—now I envy you that mysterious little creature in there. One thing I always wanted was a little boy. *Me* of all people!"

Charlene had turned off the air conditioning and had slid open the wide front doors and an incredibly soft cooling breeze was sweeping gently through the house from the Gulf.

"Well," Brenda said, "I'll lay pretty fair odds that your actor friend would be happy to oblige."

Charlene laughed. "Oh, Mal. He's a fool."

"We're all fools."

"His career's just getting off the ground. It's Hollywood and bright lights—make no mistake, he's good—Oscars and everything a boy like that dreams of. What does he need with a beat-up old copout like me?"

"He all but proposed right here in this room a couple of hours ago."

"And now he's up on that stage charming an audience into ecstasy. I'll settle for what I can get. What I have. And take it from me, pet—it is ecstasy in its purest form, while it lasts." Then, as Brenda was remembering how Charlene's frank and fervid accounts of her sex life on campus had always embarrassed her slightly, Charlene said: "Which reminds me—you won't be offended if I disappear at night after Toby's asleep, will you?"

Suddenly appalled, Brenda said: "Charl, I won't chase you out of your own house!"

"Will you relax, for God's sake? It's all arranged. Mal has a room of sorts in an old house in town."

"Of sorts! You'd both be here if it weren't for me, wouldn't you?"

"Now you listen to me, Brenda Whittier. That Donald bastard's done what most of them try to do—he sapped your self-esteem, he's done his damnedest to break you, as if you were some kind of animal who has to be tamed. Tamed *his* way. For *his* ends. They do it in different ways and maybe we do the same to them in a different way, too. But when it goes sour, *kaput*, you need a place to recover, to lick your wounds."

"I won't have it, Charl. No. I'll get a motel room now. To-night!"

"Shut up. There are no motel vacancies this time of year and if you wake that boy, I'll give you a slap across the chops."

And when Brenda, standing now, turned away, Charlene came up behind her to whisper: "I'm sorry, pet. What I mean to say is that you're welcome here as long as you want to stay."

"I know." Was she crying? "I know that." But she had made up her mind regardless. "I'm . . . grateful."

Charlene hugged her once, quickly, and then strolled away. "I don't want your damned gratitude. I want you to get well."

An hour later Charlene, wearing a different pantsuit and carry-ing only a cosmetics kit, stood at the open door. "Lock it, pet. There've been no rapes in the neighborhood but the paper here is full of them. I'll go to work from Mal's in the morning and I have a golf date later. Can you manage?"

"We'll be fine. I'll keep Toby off the beach."

"Before ten and after five—that's the custom here. Only tourists get sunburns. You take care of that kid, hear—if you don't want to answer to me." And when Brenda smiled: "As for yourself. In-dulge. Self-pity's good for the soul. Purging. Ask someone who's been the route."

After she was sure the white station wagon was gone, Brenda closed the sliding panels and went to the telephone on a table in one of the alcoves. She slid the panel shut. She had made up her mind. The sooner the better.

Recklessly—who would think to get a record of calls to Preston Brice's home?—she obtained the number through Connecticut in-formation and dialed through.

"Hello?"

"Lucy?"

"Yes. Who is this?"

"Lucy, it's Brenda. Brenda Forrest."

Silence.

Then: "Yes? What do you want?"

"Is Preston home?"

"He's gone to bed. Can I help you? Have you come back?"

"No. I'm not coming back." That had been decided deep inside and she hadn't realized it. "This is all I want, Lucy. The name of a lawyer in Sarasota, Florida. Someone Preston would recommend."

"Brenda—Preston doesn't want anything more to do with this."

"All I want him to do is to get the name and call me, collect, tomorrow. Area code 813—555-3887. Will you?"

"I'll give him the message."

"Lucy, what is it?"

"What is it? Oh, you wouldn't know, would you? Well, I'll tell you. That husband of yours should be in jail. He tried to kill us Saturday night. He drove us off the road! We're lucky to be alive! Good-bye."

Click. She sat holding a dead telephone.

And now Lucy Brice knew where she was.

———□———

White Street—was he on White Street? Skid Row of Danbury, Connecticut. Donald Forrest, Esquire, and the other drunken bums. What the hell time was it? What did it matter?

Nothing mattered.

Wrong there, buddy—wrong again.

Brenda, where are you?

He was waiting for that little click in his brain. Open Sesame— beyond that was the gray dead world where he wouldn't even try to think.

Brenda, darling, where *are* you?

And Toby. He missed Toby. He hadn't realized how much he missed the little guy till he was cleaning up Toby's room. I'm sorry, buddy. Dad'll make it up to you.

He turned a corner, passed the post office, and crossed Main Street diagonally toward Greene's Hotel. He wasn't staggering. He was almost sure he wasn't staggering. But damned if he could remember where he'd left the Merc. Find it tomorrow. Wednesday. Tomorrow's another day.

Without Brenda.

I cleaned up the whole house, darling. Every room. Did it myself. Even polished the floors. Had the broken furniture, all the trash, hauled away—we'll get new furniture. The best. We'll go on a shopping spree. Have a great time! Remember how we furnished the house, Brenda? All for you, darling, all for you. . . .

It was no longer Greene's Hotel. That was years ago—when he was a kid. It was a motor inn now. But the lounge was inviting. Not as plush as the club's, but dim, with music, and empty except for someone at the other end of the bar.

Brenda, please, where the sweet hell *are* you?

"Hi, Don. The usual?"

"So be it." Whatever your goddamn name is.

"Jack Daniel's. On the double. Righto."

Phoenix. Phoenix, Arizona. Shit! If you were in Phoenix, Brenda, you wouldn't have told your mother. Or if you told her, she wouldn't have phoned to tell me. Conspiracy. All in it together. Lies. You know, Brenda, that when I find out, really know, I'm coming. And you know why. And when you see me, when you realize what I really feel, how I've changed—

"Closing time in ten minutes."

"Another one then. Nightcap, right?"

"You sure?"

"I'm not sure of anything."

Wherever you are, I know what you're doing, you little bitch.

No, darling, I don't mean that, I know you better than that.

"You drinking alone, Don?"

"How'd you know my name?"

The girl laughed. She had a nice laugh. Young. "Don't growl at me, Don." She must have moved down the bar to sit beside him. "Charlie told me. Charlie's the bartender."

You're dancing with somebody, aren't you, Brenda? No, not dancing—kissing. Your body thrust against his, his hands on your back, behind your neck, under your hair—

"You offer to buy me a drink? Well, thanks, Don."

He only nodded.

No, you're not dancing. You're in bed. You're naked. He's staring down at you. That beautiful soft naked, naked body. You're lying there, stark, stripped—

"You walking or driving, Don?"

"I don't know you, do I?"

He's bending over you. I'll kill the sonofabitch if he touches you.

The light girlish laugh again. "What does that matter? We're closing up the place together, aren't we?"

Okay, Brenda. If that's the way you want it, two can play that game. . . .

He looked at the girl. Her face was blurred in the stagnant smoke and pale light. Christ, she was lovely. And a kid. And her tight dress was split deep between her breasts.

"They're turning out the lights. I got a room upstairs. Or the desk will call you a cab."

"Stairs?"

She thought that was funny. "There's an elevator, dummy."

He stood up. He threw a bill to the bar. He felt her hand taking hold of his. Romantic. Romance with a hooker. But damned if she *looked* like a hooker. Hookers don't look like hookers today. . . .

Except for the boy behind the desk, who only squinted at them sullenly over his copy of *Playboy*, the small lobby was deserted. Going up in the tiny box of an elevator, he looked down on her.

"Stop glaring at me, Don. Why do you look that way?"

"What's your name?"

"You look ferocious. Scary. My name's Sandy." She moved closer to him. "I'm just a college girl who has to make a living. Lot more fun than waiting table. And the pay's better."

He wanted to laugh. Couldn't. Where had all the good, fine laughter gone? Brenda and he had had so many laughs. When? How long, long ago now? He felt sick and empty.

"Top floor," the girl said, the tips of her young breasts against him. "All ashore who're going ashore."

He realized that the elevator had stopped moving, stood shuddering, the door sliding open.

He did not step out. Nor did she. He could only stare at her. Lovely, young, lovely—

He caught a whiff of her perfume—sweetly chemical, dried dead flowers, phony. Brenda never used perfume, had her own natural scent, her own bouquet, body and breath. Suddenly he hated the girl. A surge of poison rose in his veins, soured his throat, acid on his tongue.

"How much?" he heard himself snarl.

"Wait till after, Don. I trust you."

But, her face blurring mercifully, he reached, took his wallet from his pocket, and slid out a fifty. Blindly he reached again and shoved the bill into the girl's dress, between her breasts. Her flesh was firm, too firm, hard, and cold.

Her face twisted with chagrin. "I don't do it just for the money," she said, sounding like a disappointed, scolded child. "You don't know what you're missing."

"Like hell. Like hell!" His voice was a hollow roar that filled the compartment and echoed down the narrow ugly corridor. "*Get out!*"

Sandy moved then, fast, cautious, but not quite cowering. Outside the elevator she turned to face him from a safe distance. She looked baffled now, even angry, but frightened. "Whoever Brenda is, I don't know whether I envy her or feel sorry for her."

He punched a button.

"Are you sloshed or stoned or crazy or what?"

The door slid shut. For a split second he felt sorry for her. He wanted to say, *Nothing personal, kid,* but it was too late. He was descending alone.

And trying to breathe.

The aching emptiness inside was like a hunger threatening to erupt into a howl of pain, or into violence.

They're all alike. Inside, women are all alike!

In the small, bleak lobby he asked the surly young man to call him a cab.

Brenda was not like other women.

Or like his mother.

Brenda, no one will ever have you. If anyone else even so much as touches you—

He needed another drink. Only a few more now so that his mind would move closer to that click. The click that would let him enter that dead gray world. . . .

In the taxi he sat slouched deep in the seat. The familiar town passed dimly by outside the window. Cold. A wind now. Dark storefronts. STEINBERG'S: MEN'S QUALITY CLOTHIERS. And above, the dingy office of Forsythe Investigations. *Your father told you correct. We're ninety percent successful in cases like this. They usually go to someone they know. Relative. Old friend. Sometimes it's a man the husband never even heard of. With this address book to work from—hell, Mr. Forrest, it should be only a matter of a few days, maybe even hours.* "Let's move it, driver," he growled.

Wrong, Mr. Collins, wrong. It's not a man the husband never heard of. It's not a man at all. Not Brenda. Hell, she's probably waiting in the house now. *I'm sorry, Donald. I turned around and came back. Toby's sleeping upstairs. You know I could never really leave you, darling.* And, weeping, she would rush into his arms. . . .

When the taxi stopped and he saw the porch light burning, he knew: she was not here.

Standing alone in the hall, he felt the cold emptiness of the house on all sides. No furniture. The walls bare. And the silence.

He went through the motion of phoning the answering service. She had not called either the house or the office.

The sick self-loathing returned. He deserved this.

He had to make it clear to her. He had to make her understand that he had changed.

Then . . . she'd understand, she'd forgive. Brenda still loved him. She'd always loved him. The only one who ever had, the only one. Just as he loved her.

Just as he would always love her. And only her.

And when he found out where she was, when he went to her: *Oh, God, Donald, how I've missed you. I'm glad you've come. Take me home! Take us both home where we belong.*

But as he went up the stairs, aching in every muscle and his mind reeling because he needed another drink, he felt the rage take over. He was, as always, as always, helpless in its fierce hot clutch. Oh, God, this was the feeling he hated most, feared most—this helplessness. As if he had no will of his own—

Sometimes it's a man the husband never even heard of—

If it was a man—

What?

No one else will ever have her. If anyone else even touches her—

What the hell will you do, what *can* you do?

I'll kill the sonofabitch.

You can't kill anyone.

I'd even kill her.

Click. At the top of the stairs, as he moved into the bedroom, the world went dead and gray, then black. And in the instant before he lost consciousness, he had just enough time to be grateful for oblivion as he fell to the bed.

2

"**M**ORNING doves?" Toby asked. "Do you hear them only in the m-m-morning?"

And, pouring Toby more milk, Charlene laughed. "A different kind of mourning. With a *u*. Like . . . sad."

"They didn't sound s-sad to me," Toby said. "Only soft and nice. Like it's a nice way to wake up—the f-f-first thing you hear."

Brenda, seeing Charlene's smile, agreed. It *was* a lovely sound. Peaceful. Soothing. Brenda asked, "How's the sunburn?"

"Oh, *Mama*," he said, shaking his head.

They were having breakfast on the patio that enclosed the sunken garden. The day was dull and unpromising, the sky heavy with rain. Charlene said, "But don't let the mornings fool you. It could be blistering hot by noon. On the other hand, you'd better bring a raincoat, buddy."

Buddy. Donald's word for Toby. And Donald's father's word for his son. Donald. Always back to Donald. But Toby's face revealed nothing. His mood this morning, Brenda decided, was like the Florida weather.

"Which do you want to take in first?" Charlene asked. "I'm going to take the whole day off—no work, no golf! It's Toby's day. Cars of Yesterday, Lionel Train and Seashell Museum, Jungle

Gardens. And if we have time, the Ringling Museum of the Circus. It's a circus town, kid. Don't be surprised to see a midget or two on Main Street."

"Why aren't you coming?" Toby asked, eyes on Brenda, but undemanding.

"I," Brenda said, "I, my dear, am going job hunting."

"Then," Toby said—and it was not a question—"we're not going home." He stood up and went inside, turning in the frame of the open glass doors. "Excuse me?"

Brenda nodded and tried to smile. But failed. It was only natural for Toby to want to go home. Would she have to tell him, sooner or later, what had happened to the place that he called home?

The day was full and busy—and endless. Answering newspaper ads, filling out forms at the employment agencies, interviews. Over a Coke and sandwich at a whitewashed table outside a Dairy Queen at noon, she decided it was not going to be easy. No recent experience? No recommendation or former employers to contact? Heads shook, male and female. Smiles flashed—regretfully, some sympathetic, some amused. But she went on, thinking of the dwindling cash in her purse. And then it rained, a chill wind coming up out of nowhere.

One very tall, very severe middle-aged woman glanced through the window with icy eyes at the Lancia parked along the curb, and said, "There are always plenty of *waitress* jobs this time of year." Well, why not? She could learn. The way she'd already learned that you don't lick self-pity by making up your mind *not* to feel it.

In the office of a printing firm a bald-headed older man with a bulbous face and probing eyes said, "It's late anyway. Let's go around the corner to the Five O'Clock Shadow and explore the situation over a drink." No thanks, Daddy Warbucks.

But by and large people were pleasant and friendly. As were those she encountered on the streets. Some nodded, some spoke, most smiled. And she began to marvel at the contrast between the attitudes here and those in Connecticut. She began, despite the frustration, to like the town more and more. But there was always Toby to think of. Always. What right had she as a mother to uproot a child because of *her* failure as a *wife*?

Then, as suddenly as it had come, the rain was gone. She

crossed the bridges over the bay, the sun burst into brilliance, glistening on the wet pavement and glittering on the expanse of water.

She could sell the car. It was in her name. She'd buy a cheaper secondhand Ford or Chevy. She loved the sleek blue sports car but she needed the money, didn't she? It would buy more time in which to find a job, wouldn't it?

And in one of the advertising offices a woman had said, *I see you majored in art at college. Any professional experience?* None. How many years ago had she given up her sketching? And why? *The woods around here are full of painters but we seem to be always in the market for a really imaginative commercial artist. Sorry.*

Had she left some part of herself back there years ago?

If she stayed and *if* she could find a secretarial job, *if* Donald didn't appear and force her to move on, maybe she could try her hand again. She'd seen something in the paper about a school of art somewhere in town. If, if, if.

She found a parking place on St. Armand's Circle—a small manicured island of grass and paths and palm trees surrounded by elegant shops—and, careful to have enough coins, placed a call to her parents' home again.

And again her mother's warm, cautious voice informed her that her father was not at home.

"Another faculty meeting, Mother?"

"Some delay or other, dear."

"And how's Mrs. Brown?"

"Who?"

"Your friend Margo—is she still in the hospital?"

A long silence. She waited. She had begun to clutch the phone and her hand felt damp.

She heard her mother take a deep breath. "I never could fool you for long, could I, Brenda?"

"Tell me, Mother."

"Your father's doing well, dear. He's out of danger now."

"Danger?"

"He . . . Randy had a slight stroke, dear. But he can talk again. And tomorrow they're going to start therapy."

"He can't *walk*?"

"His left side is affected. Oh, how I hate to tell you. He made me promise not to. We won't know for a while."

Pop. Dear Pop.

"We'll fly back. Tonight."

"No. No, Brenda—that's just what Randy does *not* want. Nor do I."

"You're all alone."

"I have many friends, Brenda. And you know how devoted Randy's students always are."

"Toby and I can stay with you."

"Brenda, I don't want you here. I don't want you in this town."

She did not ask why. A cold hand gripped her heart. And a terrible suspicion stabbed her mind. "When did Pop get sick?"

"Sunday. During the night."

"And when did Donald come by?" Don't answer. I don't want to know. "*When?*" But she knew. "You don't have to tell me, Mother."

"Donald was terribly distraught. He said horrible things. Unspeakable—"

"Mother, I'm going to hang up now. I'll drive. We'll be there Friday evening."

Her mother's voice hardened. "Daughter! You'll do no such thing. He's been calling here and I told him what he caused. I'm afraid I lost control. But you have no idea what a state he's in. He's capable of anything. So you stay where you are. Don't you see, Brenda—I'm afraid for *you*! You stay there, stay away! And Brenda, hear me now: you must not take this on yourself. Oh, I know you. It's not your fault, understand? So you do what I tell you, hear?"

"I hear, Mother. And tell Pop—"

"Pop already knows you love him. And so do I. Good-bye, dear."

Slowly then she placed the phone on its hook. And then drove slowly to the house on Westway, deciding that she would not tell Toby and then realizing that she had not given her mother Charlene's phone number. Perhaps just as well . . .

Everything he touches—he destroys everything and everyone he touches!

He'd always resented her love for her parents. Her own parents—as if that threatened or diminished her love for him. It didn't seem possible. None of what had happened or was happening seemed even *possible*.

Should she go back regardless? What right did Donald have to—

A red Jeep was parked in the crescent-shaped driveway in front of the house. The sliding doors of the house stood open wide and Charlene's white station wagon was nowhere in sight.

Her first thought was that, while Donald might drive one of the company's Jeeps at home, he would not fly down and rent one here. But after the relief came the question: Who was in that house? Then: Had Donald hired someone? To spy, to frighten her, to bring her back by force?

She refused to get out of the car. Don't panic now, you little fool. Hold on.

A figure appeared behind the dark scrim of screen. Slowly it slid open.

The man who stood there was not tall, rather slight. He wore a blue denim work shirt, tan chinos, and dirty tennis shoes. He stepped out. His hair was thick but neatly short, and the deep red color of certain Thoroughbred horses she had seen. His small-boned face was defined rather than obscured by a very short, very neat beard, also dark red.

When she did not move, he said, "Hi, I'm Charlene's brother." Had he sensed her apprehension, her damn-fool anxiety? "You must be Brenda."

She opened the door and stepped out. How much did he know? How much *could* he know since Charlene knew so little herself? "Guilty as charged," she said, extending her hand as she stepped onto the wide unroofed platform that served as an entry porch. His hand was small but the flesh was callus-hard and his grip was quick, startlingly forceful. And she was surprised, too, to realize that he was only a few inches taller than she was. "You're the one who carved the pelican that my son likes so much. Oh, that's not to say I don't." She moved into the big, cool living room. "It's lovely. Your name's Barry and you live someplace called Anna Maria."

He was inside, too. His beard twisted into a smile. "Relax,

Brenda," he said, and she saw his deep brown eyes shimmering with amusement. "I dropped by to bring some oranges. It's a habit." But he made it sound as if he were apologizing. And of a sudden she realized: The man's as embarrassed as I am. And he's shy. He's as shy as Toby often is!

"Charl ought to be along soon," she heard herself say, startled by the fact that she was so conscious, absurdly *conscious*, of his presence. "You want a drink?"

Again that twist of smile. "Not really." Meaning: If I did, I know where the bar is. Or meaning: No thanks, I didn't come to visit. *Or:* Pardon me for intruding? The man puzzled her and she wasn't really sure she liked him. Certainly he was not in the least like his sister. "But if you're going to have one, I'll join you."

Don't do me any favors. "I've been job hunting. I think I need one." But the reason she needed one was that she had a decision to make and she couldn't make it while this stranger was here, damn him.

But she, not he, was the intruder, wasn't she?

"What would you like?" he asked, and as he crossed to the chest that he had designed and constructed, she realized that he walked with a limp. "She usually has everything but gin."

"Scotch, please. Shall I get ice?"

"Ice is for summertime. And tourists. Unless you want it."

"I'll join the natives," she said.

Drawing her legs up under her body, she sank to one of the upholstered couches built around the pit. Relax, Brenda—as the man said. If you decide to go, you can be packed in an hour. And it would be wiser to leave in the morning anyway, if you do decide.

If again.

He sat opposite her across the sunken floor with the huge, low cocktail table between them. He lit a rough-bowled pipe. His brows were red, too, and the thick hair on the backs of his hands looked golden in the sunlight.

"Charlene's going to miss her sunset," Brenda said, wondering *when* she had ever been at such a loss for words.

"Slim chance," Barry said, and Brenda's mind cast about to recall what she knew of this man: he was somewhat older than

Charlene, he must have grown up on the same Wisconsin farm, he was widowed, a loner. *The gentlest of men*, Charlene had said. And obviously he didn't bother with small talk.

"Is that what you do then—carve ugly things like pelicans and make them beautiful?"

He cocked a brow. "That's one of the nicest compliments I've ever had."

"You're welcome." She startled herself by saying it. The whiskey reached the trembling uncertainty deep down. And the lovely serenity of the room began to soothe her, too. And the warmth of the low sun flowing through the open door. Then she realized that she felt no obligation to talk. Even though she was alone here in the house with this stranger. Odd. Very odd.

And he asked no questions. He seemed to accept her presence— to accept her—just as Charlene had done.

"Charlene and I have a friend up on Anna Maria Island," Barry said, blowing fragrant smoke. "She writes children's books. Novels, really. Would you like to meet her?"

"Of course. But I may be leaving tomorrow."

He seemed to ignore that. "She types her own manuscripts. Largely because she hasn't been able to find someone she likes who can also type."

What was he saying? Suggesting? "I'm not a very good typist," she said with caution.

"Maybe not. But she'd like you."

"How do you know?"

"I know Lavinia."

"But you don't know me."

"I know you don't want to leave tomorrow."

"How do you know?"

He shrugged and drained his glass. "You don't, do you?"

"No."

He shrugged again.

She sat up straight. "You know you're talking like an idiot, don't you?"

The shrug again, but the brown eyes gravely on hers. *"You* don't know *me.* Maybe I *am* an idiot." Then the smile, as if to ask forgiveness.

She twisted about and stood up. What was going on? It had

been years, regardless of Donald's cruel suspicions, since she had found herself responding to a man like this. "I think we both are. Idiots, I mean." Suddenly she was angry. At him. At Charlene. At herself. Mostly at herself! "I think I'll go pack."

He stood, too. "Because of me?" His tone was abashed, regretful—boyish now: "Because of me?"

"No. Because of . . . because of my father. He's ill. He needs me."

You stay there, stay away!

A horn sounded and then tires crunching on the stones outside. Abruptly weak with relief, Brenda waited. While Barry took a few limping but somehow graceful steps to slide open the screen door. She saw Charlene hug and kiss her brother—the open affection between them was somehow as amazing as everything that had happened in the last half hour—and then Toby was demanding her attention.

He was carrying a stuffed giraffe and his eyes were brilliant and he moved about while he spoke. "They let me run the Lionel trains myself and there were acrobats on a trapeze at the Hall of Fame, and a magician! And, Mama, listen! There's a house that's like a palace. It was owned by the man who started the Ringling, Barnum and Bailey Circus that we saw in Hartford, remember? And they have birds at the Jungle Garden from all over the world!"

Charlene introduced Toby to her brother. They shook hands gravely, both nodding shyly, unsmiling. And then Charlene flopped onto the couch. "Your son," she said, "got himself involved in a squawking argument with a myna bird. They had to throw us out in order to close up."

"Oh, Mama, you've got to see it! You've got to see the flamingos. I'll take you tomorrow!"

She couldn't say it. But she had to. "Toby—darling, I think we're going home tomorrow." She saw his small flushed face go stiff and quiet. She saw his astonished eyes, and the hurt in them, then the anger.

But she was not prepared for what happened next.

"I'm not going," Toby said. "That's all!" And he hurled the stuffed toy. Wildly. It plopped with a soft thud against the huge plate-glass wall separating the living room from the sunken Japanese garden.

Toby faced her defiantly from across the room.

The tensions of the day exploded in Brenda. "You'll go if I say we're going," she said, and heard the grim harshness in her tone.

And regretted it at once.

Toby whirled about and ran outside.

Charlene turned to follow, then thought better of it, saying, "The sun's too low to hurt him now." Then to Brenda: "If you apologize, it's the end of a beautiful friendship."

"Who's apologizing?" Brenda snapped. Then she glanced at Barry—who, lucky for him, was not smiling.

"Nice to meet you," she heard herself mutter. "Excuse me."

And then she was in the bedroom, furiously opening suitcases on the bed. And beginning to cry. Like the little fool she was, always had been, always would be—

That's when it came to her.

Was it possible?

Yes. Toby was not stuttering.

Toby had not stuttered on a single word since he came into the house.

And her decision was made.

———□———

"Sarasota, Florida, one-one-six-eight Westway, Lido Shores, Sarasota. Do you have that, Mr. Forrest?"

"Florida?"

"Perhaps you should come to my office and I'll have the information typed and ready for you."

"I've got it, goddamnit, but are you sure?"

"Mr. Forrest, if I wasn't sure, I wouldn't be calling you at this time of the night."

"*How* . . . how can you be so positive?"

"The house is owned by a Jason Drake. He's a playwright and he's in New York on business."

"How did you get that address, Collins?"

"Secrets of the trade, son, secrets of the trade."

"Horseshit. You're not Humphrey Bogart. I'm paying for this."

"Cool it, son. Two long-distance phone calls were placed to the home of Professor and Mrs. Whittier, Danbury, from a pay station located on St. Armand's Circle in Sarasota, Florida. The Whittiers *are* her parents, aren't they?"

"You tapped their phone, right?"

"We didn't need to. We have more sophisticated methods."

"Like spies in the phone company, right? *That'll* cost me."

"Look here, Mr. Forrest—are you sure you're in shape to go on with this conversation?"

"Two phone calls. Proves nothing."

"Not in themselves perhaps. Incidentally, we don't know their content. But you gave me your wife's private address book, remember? The only friend she shows in Florida is a Mrs. Charlene Scherwin, with some other obsolete address, but Mrs. Scherwin, now Ms. Conrad, occupies that Lido Shores residence. Less than a mile from St. Armand's Circle."

"What do you want—congratulations? Proves nothing."

"Now listen, Mr. Forrest, I know you're drinking, but now you're questioning my integrity."

"Funny man. Is that all you've got?"

"It's enough. One of our operatives out of our Tampa office confirmed the whole thing. Ms. Conrad drives a white Ford station wagon but only one car is parked at the house now. A Fiat— a Lancia Zagato, to be exact. Blue. You gave me the description and the license number yourself, remember? Now, do you want the telephone number?"

"I won't need it."

"Nevertheless—do you have a pencil?"

"I don't need a pencil, I've got a mind."

"It's 555-3887. Area code 813."

"What the hell do you think I'm going to do—warn the little bitch I'm coming?"

"In case you need any help down there, we have an office in Tampa."

"I won't need any help—unless you're wrong. Then *you'll* need help."

"We are never wrong, Mr. Forrest."

"Even God made a few mistakes."

"If there's anything else we can do—"

"You can fuck off."

"You're welcome, Mr. Forrest."

———□———

Preston Brice had arranged the interview by phone from Connecticut. He had sounded politely distant, as his wife Lucy had sounded on Tuesday night, but he had not referred to Donald except, in answer to her question, to say that as far as he knew, Donald was still in town. But poor Preston had seemed relieved to be recommending his law-school friend, Rex Maynard—it meant *he* was no longer involved.

But the interview in Rex Maynard's small but elegant private office above a bank was not going well. A tall, spare man about forty, with a paunch, freckles, and thinning light brown hair, dressed entirely in shades of tan even to the tint of his shell-rimmed eyeglasses, Rex Maynard was cordial but skeptical. Brenda didn't mind being sized up, but this Rex Maynard was so wary that he gave the impression that he was judging *her*. Or that he was prepared to doubt her.

He had explained the basic difference between the dissolution of a marriage—which was the law in Florida—and a divorce elsewhere. The marriage is merely dissolved. "No one wins, no one loses—hence the term 'no-fault divorce.' " And then he explained that she would have to establish residence in the state for at least six months previous to filing. This was a simple matter of being physically in the state with the intention of remaining here permanently. He could advise her later how to accomplish this to a judge's satisfaction, but meanwhile it would be a good idea to get a Florida driver's license and auto tags and file a Declaration of Domicile at the courthouse.

"Later, you'll need one witness to substantiate residence. *If* that is what you're prepared to do. . . ."

It was not exactly a question but she answered it: "I'm prepared to do anything."

His brows lifted. "You're sure you don't want to live separate and apart for a while?"

"I want a divorce."

"Such a separation could be regarded by the judge as your effort to save the marriage."

"I don't want to save the marriage."

"It might be possible, Mrs. Forrest, to get you financial assistance from your husband in the interim. It's called a separate maintenance action. You did say you've been looking for a job for two days, didn't you?"

"I'll find one. I don't want my husband to know where I am." She felt herself leaning forward in her chair. "Will he have to know? Even *after* six months?"

"Yes and no. There are ways to evade that—which we can discuss if that time ever comes." And when she said nothing, sitting back stiffly, he went on: "The judge must be satisfied that the marriage is *irretrievably broken*. That's the legal phrase. It's always easier all round if both partners agree to this openly and settle their differences prior to the final hearing."

"My husband never would."

Rex Maynard looked thoughtful. "That presents problems."

"If he didn't know—you said there were ways."

Rex Maynard sat forward and placed his elbows on his desk. "Let me ask you this, Mrs. Forrest: Do you think you can hide from your husband for a year?"

"A year?"

"After you've established residence and filed, it will take another four or five months before the hearing. And if Mr. Forrest contests various parts of your case—"

"Such as?"

He tilted his narrow head. "Anything. Residency. Money matters. Custody. But basically the fact that the marriage is irretrievably broken."

"Then what?"

"It would delay the final decision. Especially since there's a minor child. The usual process would be for the judge to enter an order requiring both of you to seek professional counseling. In an attempt—"

"To save the marriage—I know. How long?"

"The period is supposed to be no longer than three months. But facts are facts in the courts today. The judge may not be able to hear your case as soon as the three-month period is over. And if a contest over custody should develop, the case could drag through the courts for a long, long time." He stood up. "I'm honestly sorry, Mrs. Forrest. I can only help you by giving it to you straight."

"That's exactly the way I want it," she said, surprised at the words and her own tone of voice. "You make it sound like forever."

"I have to ask this, Mrs. Forrest. Forgive me." He adjusted the venetian blinds against the sun. "You are not this dismayed because you want to remarry, are you?"

"I don't think I'll ever remarry. But, to answer the question you're really asking—there's no other man in what you call my *case.*" She heard herself take a deep breath. "Although that is what my husband will think. Or does think. What any man would assume, I suppose."

"Mrs. Forrest," Rex Maynard said, quietly, "I'm on your side."

Their eyes met. His were light hazel in color, and flecked. But they still held a certain mistrust. As if what she had already told him about Donald were just possibly the exaggerations or fancies of a wife who, just possibly also, might want her freedom for her own selfish reasons.

"You mentioned custody," she said.

"The law," he said, sitting again, "requires that the parent providing for the best interest of the child gets custody. And although both parents are given equal consideration, the courts here usually award custody to the mother. In the best interests of the child. Most states, but not Louisiana and Florida, will approve joint custody or coparenting. I take it from what you've told me—and your general attitude—this would be out of the question anyway. In your view."

"In my view, *yes.*"

"It's better if the two parents have a definite plan worked out in every detail. But I assume that also is out of the question in your case. Sorry, in the *circumstances.*"

But she did not smile. Could not. "He's no good for Toby," she said. Now there was a mild, contained, *stupid* way of putting it! Toby was not stuttering, was he? "He's not fit," she said. "It would be better for our son if he never saw his father again." True, true—make of it what you will, Mr. Maynard.

"By the way, where's the boy now?"

Sneaky, sneaky. "He's with friends of mine. He's watching a rehearsal at the Asolo Theater. And in very good hands, thank you." Who's on trial here?

"Mrs. Forrest, at the risk of offending you again, I have to ask: Are you a woman of independent means?"

"Stocks, bonds, a family portfolio? My father's a professor. He came from a very poor family of teachers. The answer is no." And then she added: "He's in the hospital now because of my husband."

But, thank God, Rex Maynard decided to ignore that. "Did you and your husband make a prenuptial financial agreement?"

"It never occurred to either one of us." We were too much in love. Oh, were we in love, Mr. Maynard. . . .

"Do you own property jointly?"

"I don't own anything." It's never mattered till now. We never discussed those things. We only enjoyed them. "I don't want his money."

"That may be an emotional indulgence, Mrs. Forrest. Even if *you* don't, what about the boy?"

Unfair. A low blow. "I haven't had time to think about it."

"He is responsible for child support, you know."

"I'll take care of Toby."

"All well and good. For the present. I have a ten-year-old girl myself. Do you know what a college education costs these days?"

"Can't you understand, Mr. Maynard? Haven't you been *listening*? I don't want ever to see Donald again."

"We might be able to arrange alimony. In a lump sum so you wouldn't be dependent on it month by month."

She stood up. Why, why, why couldn't he understand? "This isn't like other divorces. I told you, I told you—"

"Maybe a trust fund for your son, to cover his education—"

"That means dealing with him. Seeing him. Talking. I came to the wrong place. I can't get a divorce in this state. I don't know how Toby'll get his education. I'll find a way!" She was trembling. "I'll take care of Toby. I'll rob a bank. I'll find a way!"

"One last question, Mrs. Forrest. It's important."

She only nodded. But there were no tears.

"Do you fear your husband? Even here? Now? Are you scared of him?"

Yes. She nodded dumbly.

"Tell me this—has your husband ever had psychiatric counseling?"

She shook her head then. Still there were no tears. Every time she'd suggested help, Donald had exploded. With derision. With rage.

"Have *you*, Mrs. Forrest?"

What was he saying?

"Because there's someone here in town I know. A psychotherapist. He's very good, especially in cases such as yours. And he's great with children."

Cases such as yours—now she was no longer a *legal* case, now she was a psychiatric case!

"Sometimes people under stress don't see everything in perspective, they overreact—"

"Especially women."

"I don't mean that at all," Rex Maynard said. "Honest."

"If you're worried about your fee, you'll get it." Irrational again. Don't say any more! "I've heard of clients paying by performing services—"

"There's nothing improper in that. We'll work it out."

An idea flashed into her mind. Out of nowhere. "Ask your friend Preston Brice what Donald accused me of. How Donald imagines I paid Preston! I meant I could *type* to pay you. But I know Donald's mind. Phone Preston Brice, Mr. Maynard—I dare you!"

He came around the desk toward her but she turned. And fled. Again.

Again running. Along a corridor. And then down the elevator in the bank building. And into the parking area behind.

Then she was driving. Blindly. Tears now.

Mrs. Forrest, I'm on your side.

Like hell! She despised Rex Maynard. And she'd come to the wrong place. The wrong state.

She crossed the Ringling Causeway bridges. The bay was glass smooth today, like a lake.

Alive with boats. She saw a small stern-wheeler. A dinner boat, Charlene had said. Well, she'd never have dinner on it now.

But as she rounded St. Armand's Circle and headed north over the small bridge and then down the lanelike road between Australian pines, she realized that although she'd made a fool of herself, she'd also clarified her thoughts.

I don't want to save the marriage. She'd said it, admitted it to herself. *He's not fit! It would be better for our son if he never saw his father again.* True, true, true, at last she'd said it!

Feeling purged and again resolved, she turned into Morningside Drive. Handsome pleasant houses, lawns, and not a soul in sight. And at Westway, where Morningside dead-ended, a bicycle made a sweeping turn and came straight toward her.

Toby.

She eased to a halt. And Toby, straddling the bike, came to a stop alongside. His still-pink face, damp with sweat, appeared in the frame of window.

"Nothing to it," he said.

"How'd you—who—Toby, that's marvelous!"

"Mama, I've been waiting to tell you. I know what I want to be when I grow up."

Peering into his grave eyes, relaxing, she asked: "Do you? What?"

"An actor, or maybe a director."

Not a race-car driver, or fireman—not Toby. "Did Mal teach you how to ride?"

"Nope. Barry. He told me to call him that. He walks like that because he had an accident when he was my age. On a tractor. He's a really neat guy."

"You've had quite a day, haven't you?"

"One of the best." But the blue eyes remained sober, even solemn. "Did you get a job?"

"No."

"Are we going home?"

"No."

"It's okay if you want to. I'm sorry I threw the giraffe at the window."

"We all throw giraffes. I just threw a big one."

"Well, I just wanted to know. So long."

In the rearview mirror, as she turned the corner, she could see the small figure bent over the handlebars and pedaling fast. No stuttering, no hesitation. Then, when she approached the long low house, she realized that she was looking for the red Jeep. But only Charlene's station wagon and Mal's motorcycle stood in the driveway. She felt an odd pang. Disappointment? *I don't think I'll ever remarry.* That, too, was the truth, and in focus.

——□——

"The battered-wife syndrome," Mary Rinaldi said. "The alcoholic husband. We get it all the time."

Rex Maynard shook his head. "More than that in this case. Much more, I think. She told me her husband sent her father to the hospital. I doubted that, too. But he's in Danbury Hospital all right. Stroke. God, did I make a pompous idiot of myself!"

They were seated at a wooden table under huge live-oak trees hung with Spanish moss. Dusk. Most of the other guests were in the high, old-fashioned, northern-style house, but a few were strolling down by the sea wall on the bay.

"Well, Rex, we all do that," Mary Rinaldi said, sipping her vodka tonic. "You at least had the good sense to check her out."

"She dared me to! She even told me what the guy had accused her attorney of—and when I talked to him in Connecticut, damned if she wasn't right. It's uncanny. And Brice says he didn't tell her that, so she just plain knew."

Mary Rinaldi, a tall, brown-haired, chubby-faced young lawyer who was serving her time in the state attorney's office, smiled her cynical, slightly patronizing smile. "And you thought the poor girl might be exaggerating. Or lying."

"I did, so help me. But it gets stickier—are you sure you're interested?"

"Of course I'm interested."

Rex shook his head. "When Brice refused to tell the husband where the wife had gone—because he really didn't know—the husband, get this, ran him off the road with his car! Brice still doesn't know for sure whether it was to scare him or whether the nut was really trying to kill him."

"Maybe the nut himself didn't know."

Rex was peering at her through his brown-tinted glasses. "You sound as if you can dig a character like that."

"You said she told you that he did these wild things because he loves her."

"Love? A man like that, love like that—it's beyond my ken and I admit it."

"There are a lot of women, chappie, a lot of sad, bored women who'd give a lot to be loved that much."

"That way?"

Mary Rinaldi shrugged and smiled her knowing but enigmatic smile.

"That intensely—yes."

"You, for instance?"

"Let's not get personal."

"Sorry."

"Oh, come on, Rex. I've known you and Alison ever since I moved down here. You're one of the few members of the local bar, as they say, who's never made a pass. The answer is yes-me-for-instance, why not?" Her dark eyes met his across the table. "Look, you feel guilty because you doubted her, you didn't offer enough sympathy—"

"She was prickly as hell. I put *her* on the defensive."

"One gets you ten that she's a beauty. Are you sure she hasn't stirred up the male gallantry juices? Maybe even other juices—"

"The gal needs help whether she's a beauty or not! She admitted she's scared. I think she's terrified."

"That he might come here? So that's what this is all about. You want to know whether there's anything my office can do to protect Mrs. X from her husband?"

"Something like that."

"Knight errant on his white charger."

"Maybe."

"Or a dedicated attorney with a conscience. Rex, you know the answer. The legal system, top to bottom, is set up to punish crime, not prevent it."

"I knew you'd say that. What are we supposed to do, then, sit back and wait for this character to—"

"To do what?"

"How the hell should I know?"

"There's Alison waving at us. They're going in to dinner." She stood up and together they strolled, glasses in hand, over the crisp, springy zoysia grass toward the sound of voices and laughter.

"Look, Sir Galahad, maybe you'd better give me the names, her address. Off the record. In case something does happen."

"I'll write it on my card after dinner. What you're saying is that, when it's too late, the law will act."

"Name of the game, chappie."

"Shit."

"My feelings exactly."

But did she know her own feelings? She was faintly jealous of this Mrs. X who had appealed so much to Rex. And she was intensely jealous of Alison, who was waiting in the door of the screened Florida room. But then, while liking her at the same time, she'd been jealous of Alison for years. Was she in love with Rex, after all? While it was true that Rex Maynard was one of the few members of their profession in Sarasota who had not made a pass, he was the only one she wished *would*.

———□———

It happened on the bridge connecting the north end of Longboat Key to Anna Maria Island. She was clutching the wheel to control the car, her palms sweaty, her mind suddenly reeling with dizziness. . . .

"The thing about a director," Toby was saying, "is that he's kind of the boss . . ."

She hated these times, feared them. She'd made it all the way down, all those hundreds of miles, without being attacked this way. Hands shaking, heart pounding, body quivering all over . . .

". . . but I don't know. If you're the director, you don't get to be on the stage when the play's really going on. . . ."

She couldn't breathe. At the end of the bridge she pulled the little car off onto the wide, sandy shoulder and lowered her forehead to the wheel.

"Mama, are you all right? Are you sick?"

"No, Toby, it's nothing. I'll be fine. Give . . . give me a minute."

"What's the matter?"

"It's what they call an . . . anxiety attack." She'd begun to breathe again. It was always the same: they always passed. "Nothing serious."

Nothing serious, Dr. Bell had said. *But people do sometimes*

*mistake them for heart attacks. Cause? You must feel threatened
and insecure about something in your life.*

Nice guess, Dr. Bell. Damned clever of you.

She eased the car onto the road into a line of traffic emerging
from the shaded beach area across the road on the Gulf.

"You okay now, Mama?"

"It's all gone," she said, using one of Toby's phrases. "You hungry?"

"Starved."

They crawled, slow and snakelike in traffic, along the single
road that ran up the narrow island, or key, past restaurants and
small motels and trailer parks.

"Will Charlene be here?"

"Charlene's at dress rehearsal with Mal."

"Lucky. I'm going to rehearsal again tomorrow. And tomorrow
night we're all going to the play, right?"

"Right." Donald's word. "Right, right, *right!*"

She felt his eyes on her in the dusk. But did not try to explain
or excuse.

Following Charlene's directions, they passed another public
beach on the left—the sign read MANATEE PUBLIC BEACH—and,
rounding a curve, she caught a quick glimpse of the sun's afterglow still shimmering on the water.

"Who's Mrs. Davidson?" Toby asked. "Do we know her?"

"Not yet. She's a friend of Charlene's."

"And Barry's?"

"More his friend, I think."

"I hope she's a good cook. People always have hamburgers or
hotdogs for kids. I get my fill of those."

She turned left onto Forty-sixth Street, narrow and with only a
few small, modest cement-block houses, and at the end of three
blocks a barrier with beach and Gulf beyond. A crushed-shell
driveway, almost obscured by Brazilian pepper trees and sea-grape
plants, led off to the right and made a small circle around a banyan tree under which the red Jeep was parked. The house looked
like a gray, weathered beach cottage from the outside but inside
seemed large and comfortable and inviting, with walls of pecky
cypress stained a pale greenish-gray and hanging pots of growing
plants trailing green leaves and colorful blossoms. It was furnished

in a mixture of styles: bamboo and rattan furniture, a heavy sea-man's trunk, an Orozco print on the wall, or possibly an original, maybe a Rivera, and framed impressionist reproductions of various sizes—all of it blended into a warm and charming atmosphere. Rather startling in its unconventionality, at once vivid and yet re-laxing. And Brenda realized, fleetingly, that something inside her-self was responding to it.

Barry, wearing a black open-necked shirt, chinos, and Indian moccasins, introduced them. A large woman of indeterminate old age, Mrs. Davidson had vivid dark eyes and short gray hair that was almost white; she wore an ankle-length skirt and blouse of colorful Mexican design. Although politely cordial, Mrs. David-son seemed at first imposing, even cold. But over wine before din-ner—while Toby spotted a large carving of a gull in flight, which he recognized at once as Barry's, and while he then asked Barry about a large white long-necked bird he'd seen on the beach— Mrs. Davidson sat with Brenda on the wicker sofa and put her at ease. She spoke in a husky, almost guttural voice that seemed nevertheless melodic. "We lived in Chicago all our lives—al-though we'd traveled everywhere—but when Max died, I remem-bered Bradenton Beach." She laughed—a deep, hearty laugh— and said: "And I could afford this sort of place then. Anything on the beach like this would be far beyond my means now. I came also for my health. And look at me. I intend never to die." She stood. "Well, it's potluck tonight. Leftovers. You two men, set up the chairs."

"Can I help?" Brenda asked.

"Of course. Come in to my galley, said the spider to the fly."

And over a long leisurely dinner in an airy screened-in room, where they could see the white-rimmed waves almost at their feet and could hear their soft lapping sound as a steady obbligato, Brenda found herself relaxing again, the strangeness dissolving into a pleasant sensation of well-being. They sat around a large round glass table supported by a huge complex gnarl of gray driftwood. As dusk closed in, their faces were lighted by hanging hurricane lamps encased in split bamboo.

Toby, who in time lost almost all of his usual shyness, pro-nounced the food *terrific*! Adding: "Even if it is spinach." Laugh-ter then, with Toby joining in. Barry, who also seemed less reticent than he had yesterday, teased Mrs. Davidson: "Lavinia always serves gourmet leftovers." They were eating crisp fresh salad with a tart dressing that suggested lemon and herbs and garlic, and a casserole dish that Mrs. Davidson described as "Fish Florentine—snapper, grouper, sea trout, and whatever comes to hand. And fistfuls of nutmeg. Is anyone here old enough to remember a macabre story titled 'A Touch of Nutmeg'?"

"John Collier," Brenda said. "It's in one of the *New Yorker* collections, isn't it, Mrs. Davidson?"

And Mrs. Davidson peered at her with interested, appraising eyes. "Ah, the girl reads. I was sure there were some readers extant in the world. My name, my child, is Lavinia."

During the meal Brenda learned of Barry and Lavinia's relationship in bits and pieces. Both loners—Charlene's word—they shared, she soon gathered, sunsets, evenings of recorded music over wine, philosophy and politics ("bitter civilized arguments," Lavinia called them), and a companionship that Brenda found refreshing and downright enviable.

"We sometimes go fishing, too. But we don't swim together," Lavinia said. "I get up too early. Do you swim, Toby?"

Would he stutter now? Brenda saw his face cloud up. "I can't swim," Toby said. No stutter, thank God, no stutter, please God, never again.

"Swimming," Barry said, his brown eyes on Toby, "swimming is tough, Toby. I grew up on a lake in Wisconsin and I thought I'd never learn. Then one day Charlene accidentally pushed me off the dock. And all I could think of was: Keep your head above water and keep moving. So I let myself go—way deep inside—and by the time Charl got to me, I was actually swimming. Because all of a sudden I *believed* I could do it. I let myself go and after that I never even had to think of *what* to do. I just *did* it."

"Did they make fun of you when you couldn't?" Toby asked gravely.

"Sure."

"Did you ever play football?"

"I never liked it."

"Boxing?"

"I never liked that, either. Do you?"

"I hate it," Toby said.

"Why not?"

"That's right," Toby said. "Why not?"

Barry smiled then—and Brenda avoided his eyes. Something had happened and she didn't know quite what. Only that it had. Then she discovered Lavinia's eyes on her and then she saw Lavinia smile. Their eyes held.

Darkness fell during the meal, and when they stood up from the table, Lavinia stepped to a wall switch. "I take credit for the edibles," she said, "but this is Barry's doing." She flipped the switch and, beyond the screen-wall on the beach itself, a light came on.

Toby gasped, then uttered a low childish sound of delight. They stood staring at a high wooden sculpture embedded at its base in a huge concrete block.

"Sails," Toby said.

But the lighted sculpture was more suggestive than representational: three sails rising at least twenty feet above the base and placed at different angles, yet somehow suggesting wind and motion.

"A birthday gift," Lavinia said. "My seventy-fifth but I won't tell you how long ago he gave it to me. Now—you two stay. Toby, come. I want to introduce you to another friend of mine."

When they'd gone into the house, Barry, without asking, poured more coffee into both their cups, ran a hand over his red beard, and lit his pipe.

"It's beautiful," Brenda said, sitting again.

"It's impossible to steal, but sooner or later some vandal will saw it down just for the hell of it."

"Then what?"

He shrugged. "I'll do another one." His eyes drifted from her and stared out across the dark Gulf. "Charlene says you majored in art—"

"That was a long time ago."

"Were you any good?" It was a gentle challenge.

"I'm afraid I'm not very good at anything," she heard herself say. True, true—she'd failed at everything.

"There are more so-called Sunday painters in Florida than in any other ten states."

"I may try it again. Some Sunday."

Barry's beard twisted into a smile around the stem of his pipe. "Don't buy any paints—I have several kits. Oil or water?"

"I like . . . I *liked* water."

There was a commotion inside—a raw, raucous squawking sound.

"Bobo," Barry explained. "Lavinia's parrot. Fierce and red and loud, but almost completely inarticulate. Does Toby know Portuguese?"

"No. Why?"

"It's my theory that Bobo swears obscenely in Portuguese."

She laughed. Aloud. How long had it been since she'd laughed? Even silently. . . .

Then Toby was back. Ecstatic. "He talks! Mama, his name is Bobo and he can say 'Pretty baby' and 'Go to hell.' "

"He can say more than that in Portuguese," Brenda said, casting Barry a glance.

He stood up. "Toby," he said, "I've got a book on Florida birds at my place. You want to come help me find it?"

"In the Jeep?"

"Sure."

"Mama?"

"Sure," Brenda said, echoing Barry's word, and he winked.

As they left, she realized that until now she had not been aware of Barry's limp all evening.

"Dishes?" Brenda asked.

"Of course," Lavinia said.

And while Brenda cleared the table—what a lovely thing it really was!—Lavinia fed the dishwasher and talked.

Had Charlene told Brenda that Lavinia was a writer? No, but Barry had. Yesterday.

"Novels for children. Does that surprise you? Well, it surprises me. Max and I wanted children very much. And occasionally I still turn out a mystery novel for adults. The old-fashioned puzzle kind. I can't—what's the word?—I can't *swing* with the modern trend. I know nothing about spies and my taste for gore is really revulsion at violence. Consequently you don't know my name. But I have a small but refined following who do not live by the vicarious thrills of television. Does that sound snobbish?"

"In some cases," Brenda said, "snobbishness is only another word for good taste. My father—"

She stopped. Pop. *He's on his way to recovery,* Mother had said when Brenda had phoned earlier in the day. *But, Brenda, you may as well know. I'm afraid his left leg and arm will never be quite the same.* Dear Pop who had never harmed—

Donald again. Damn him, *damn him!*

". . . fifty cents a page."

"I'm sorry, Lavinia." She went into the living room from the porch. "What did you say?"

"Only that you would do better financially with almost any ordinary job—but this *would* give you a chance to be with Toby and there'd be no pressure."

Lavinia entered from the kitchen. And stopped. Then she smiled. "You haven't heard a word, have you?"

"You want me to type for you?"

"Don't look so stunned. I'm not doing you any favors. You could get a dollar a page up North, perhaps more. But that's the going rate in these parts, and all I can really afford."

"It's a conspiracy," Brenda said, delighted, incredulous. "This whole evening's been a plot! You, Barry, Charlene. Spur-of-the-moment dinner. Impromptu. Potluck!"

"I had to find out firsthand whether I'd like you, didn't I?"

"And—?"

"Oh, dear girl, you *have* had a kicking-around, haven't you? Of course I like you. We all like you. You're enough to make an old woman break down and bawl. Here, give me a hug and let's get the tears over with before the men get back."

———□———

Listen, he had told the fresh-punk kid of a pilot when they were taking off from the Danbury Airport in the chartered two-seater, *listen, I've been boozing for six days, I'm hung, and I don't want to talk, so fly the goddamn plane and fuck off, right?*

And over the miles the pilot had sulked—but in silence. While he had longed for a drink, exulting in the fact that he had not brought along a bottle of Jack and, although tempted, had not tried to buy one when they stopped to refuel in Charleston— damned if he'd risk facing her drunk!

After the phone call from Mr. Collins last night, he'd walked the empty hollow house, singing old Gershwin and Porter songs and making plans and drinking until the rest of the world woke up and then it had taken several hours to pack and to sober up at the club and to make arrangements: the car rental in Sarasota; the bareboat charter of a Morgan Out Island Ketch, with power, to be ready and waiting; traveler's checks, letter of credit from the bank, more cash, closing out the joint checking account, which he should have done two days ago—it had been one hell of a day.

But hell was behind now. All the suspicions and torment gone. Clean slate. How could he ever have imagined Brenda unfaithful? He had control of his thoughts now. Control of himself. And soon the bitter, shot-away, sick loneliness of the past six days would be gone, too. His mind was steady—as steady as the confident throbbing engine as it cut through the night. And as buoyant as the plane itself—moving, nose pointed, high above the lights. He knew where he was going, at last—and from now on everything would be different. The elation and certainty had sustained him and now he was here, the plane circling and descending with the lighted pattern of the town and the dark boat-dotted expanse of Gulf stretching away. The joy was stronger than any drink—wilder.

Sarasota, not Phoenix. He'd never believed that lie. But the thought of Brenda's parents brought a painful twinge of remorse. Thinking of what he'd accused her of—had he actually said those things to her own parents? And now her mother blamed him for the professor's stroke. Well, people were always blaming him. Had always done so. Even his own father. Especially his mother. Why was it that everybody always blamed him for everything that went haywire?

The car was a black Cougar. The girl behind the counter gave him the eye. He was used to that. But to hell with her. To hell with everyone but Brenda. He asked directions to Lido Shores while she did the paper work and then, driving south on what the girl had called the Tamiami Trail, he passed a billboard at the entrance to the Sarasota Jungle Gardens and at once he thought of Toby. Why did he always think of Toby *second*—after Brenda? Strange boy. Delicate. Too delicate. Look at him cross-eyed and he'd almost burst into tears. Had to toughen up. That was all that Donald had ever tried to do—toughen him up for his own good.

And Brenda had blamed him for that, too. *You can't make him be like you, Donald. Do you really think you're the perfect image of what a man should be?*

The poison came into his throat as he drove. What if she no longer loved him after all?

He saw a forlorn-looking building on the far side of the wide street, across the palm-lined median of grass: BROADWAY BAR. But he didn't stop. Damned if he would.

Brenda loved him. Had always loved him. As he loved her.

And when she saw him now, when she realized he had come all this way because he couldn't live without her, she'd come into his arms. She'd kiss him. On the lips. Fully. The thought sent a violent tremor of yearning through his body. Through his mind. And the exaltation returned. He pressed the gas pedal down and passed between rows of motels, their NO VACANCY signs lighted, and then, at the stoplight where the street curved ahead, he saw the sign reading LIDO BEACH and turned west without waiting for the red to turn to green.

Son, nothing has to happen just because you want it to. Nothing happens just because you feel it has to. Go away, old man. What do you know? If you're so wise, how come Mother made a fool of you for years? Or did you know? Or at least suspect? Well, your son knew what was going on. Your son knew *early.* He was only a kid when he realized what your dear beautiful Rosamond had to have to satisfy her goddamned vanity.

After crossing two lighted bridges over the bay, he saw a marina on his left, on the other side of the narrow island of grass and palms that separated the traffic—docks and a low handsome building with a sign: SARASOTA YACHT CLUB. It would be here that he had arranged to moor the boat—reciprocal privileges with the Westport club. And it would he here then that they would embark, the three of them, for the cruise back to Connecticut—inland waterway to the East Coast, then slowly, offshore in the Atlantic along the coast, north to Westport, using the sails when the weather was right. He'd have to hire someone to drive Brenda's car back. It'd give them time to be together, the three of them, and to heal the wounds, put the past behind once and for all. If the charter company wouldn't agree, he'd buy a yacht and do it anyway. What the hell is the point of having money if you don't use it to buy happiness? Brenda would love the idea. She loved sailing. And alone in their private cabin, or on deck in the moonlight while Toby slept . . .

He drove around the four or five streets that formed the Lido Shores development, circling every driveway. The area had an atmosphere of quiet understated elegance.

The Lancia was nowhere to be seen.

Westway Drive curved around two sides of Lido Shores. By following it very slowly and driving very close to those rural mailboxes that were on posts directly under the lights, he finally found his way to the 1100 numbers. Then he parked and got out and walked. A few boxes carried nameplates. But none with the name Conrad or Scherwin. None with the name Drake, either.

Sometimes it's a man the husband never even heard of. Cynical, cocksure bastard. If the agency was wrong, he'd tear the office apart! And if it *was* a man—

1168. The number was on a box designed to resemble a Japanese teahouse.

And the house was long and low, with black vertical strips framing a series of coral-colored panels.

And the huge windows on either side of the very wide front door were dark.

Should he knock?

The front yard was not grass but brown stone that crunched under his step. And there was a bicycle.

On the huge platform that served as a simple stoop, he lifted his hand and used the brass oriental knocker.

The sound seemed to reverberate inside. Hollowly.

But there was no other sound. And no lights appeared.

It was then that the rage took over. The scalding anger flooded up in him.

He'd been tricked.

He was choking with fury.

He was pounding on the door with his fists.

They'd tricked him!

Sometimes it's a man—

Then what?

If it's a man—

What?

——□——

"You ought to see his workshop," Toby was saying. "It's a place where they used to make boats. You should see the tools! And it has a smell. A sawdust smell—nice!"

Giving herself over to a warm hopefulness, she drove. The moon was high and full and the road was bathed in a pale blue light so that she could have driven without the headlight beams.

"He gave me a choice of this or a dolphin. Dolphins are those fish that dive in circles." He stroked the polished wooden bird. "I liked this better. It's an egret. That's the kind I saw on the beach and didn't know their name. Was it all right to take a gift?"

"Did you say thanks?"

"Oh, *Mama*."

The whole evening had been a gift. "It was all right to accept it, Toby."

"He gave me the Florida bird book, too. And he promised to teach me how to carve things myself. Mama, why is everybody so *good* to us here?"

"I don't know. Maybe because people, most people, *are* good."

"He's going to take me to a place called Myakka Park. He said if we're lucky we might see an armadillo or even a deer."

"I'm sure you will, Toby. I'm sure you'll see anything you want to see." Maybe even a bluebird, the elusive bluebird . . .

She was thinking of Charlene: *We were never very close when we were growing up on the farm. But I came here when I was at loose ends and somehow Barry and I sort of realized how much we really love each other.*

She was thinking of Lavinia: *Barry was a sad man when I first knew him. Bitter at fate, maybe at God, because he'd lost his wife the way he did. Some crazy unnecessary accident, some drunk driver on a country road at night. Behind that shy mask lives a lonely man.*

She was thinking of what Barry had said, with bashful gravity, when they were shaking hands to say good night: *If you need us, we're here.*

"You don't have it again, do you?" Toby asked.

"Have what, son?"

"Another one of those attacks. What did you call them?"

"Anxiety. No. Why do you ask?"

"You're driving funny."

They were on Longboat Key again, passing a moonlit beach on the right and a trailer park on the left. And moving with incredible slowness. Had her mind wandered that much? She pressed down on the accelerator and shifted gears. The road was all but deserted. The waves broke on long silver crescents and, with the sunroof off, she could hear the sound of the surf.

Lavinia had made a life of her own. On her own. All the many things she did—and *enjoyed* doing! That lovely collection of sea-shells, shelf after shelf of them, and she knew every exotic name of each. And that rowboat on the beach, imagine, chained to one of the concrete pilings under the house. *Featherweight Fiberglas but on those days when the Gulf's smooth as a lake, I row for hours!* And after dinner she'd sat down at an old upright piano and played everything from Mozart to Gilbert and Sullivan and had then placed a sheet of newspaper behind the key hammers to produce a crazy honky-tonk resonance while she pounded out ragtime and boogie-woogie to Toby's astonishment and Brenda's delight. How long since she'd had such an evening, how long . . . ?

After several miles, just as she had begun to think that Toby might have drifted off to sleep, he spoke: "Do you still love Daddy?"

Startled, at once unnerved and alert, she asked with slow caution: "Do you?"

"Yes. Do you?"

"I don't know," she said—uncertain, dumbfounded by her answer. "I think so."

And out of nowhere a sudden wave of tenderness engulfed her. Was it possible? Could she still love him after all that had happened, all he'd done to her, to both of them? Again she wondered how he was. Not whether he would find her or what he would do—but how he himself was feeling. She knew his pain, his seizures of remorse, his self-flagellation—all the misery and guilt. And she knew, too, how much he would miss her. Miss them both. How he would suffer. How he must be suffering. . . .

Even now, at this unlikely moment when she had only begun to glimpse the possibility of her own independence, some perverse part of her nature identified with *his* pain. And she said aloud: "Yes, Toby, I still love your father." She did not add: I will no longer live with him. She did not add: I know it's over but love doesn't die even when the other person does everything possible to kill it. I wish it would die. Until it does, I won't be free, no matter how many miles are between us.

Oh, God, Toby, why did you have to ask? Especially tonight, damn it, why?

But by the time she'd crossed over the short bridge over New Pass onto Lido Shores, Toby had fallen asleep. And it was with a kind of relief that she drove the last few quiet blocks of darkened houses along the long curve of Westway.

There was a black car parked under the high streetlight across the street from the house.

Did Charlene have company? No—Charlene had said she was going to Mal's apartment after dress rehearsal.

She grasped the wheel, going stiff with panic. Should she speed up, drive on?

But it was too late. The figure that stepped out of the car, tall and wide-shouldered, and into the center of the narrow street, blocking it, was the one person she had come all these miles to escape.

———□———

"You've been living like a monk and you know it."

Barry smiled. Dear Lavinia: abrupt, blunt, to the point. She'd been trying to find a way to say something like this ever since Brenda and the boy had left. "Monks get along," he said.

They were walking on the beach, trying to stay on the dry side of the wet surf line. There was a full moon tonight and the white sand, bits of shells crunching under their step, held a soft glow as it stretched away in a curve. It was a good time to stroll. No bathers, no small boats drawn up on the sand, no voices. Far out, across the water, a boat of some sort—possibly a freighter or an oil tanker, only a dot of light moving very slowly. Another world here. The one he had come to cherish: peace, detachment, no complications, no entanglements, emotional or otherwise.

"Monks get along," Lavinia said, "because they sublimate their natural human impulses for some greater spiritual reward."

"Some monks take a vow of silence."

Lavinia laughed. "Touché, dear boy, touché, and not another word."

How much had Lavinia guessed? Probably plenty. That damned intuition of hers.

It was adolescent really. He was a man forty-three years old, not a boy. Was it the delicate cameo face, the lush black hair, the slim body sheathed in white and suggesting soft warmth—damn it, was it her physical beauty that had brought him to this crazy state of quivering excitement? Or . . . was it this and more?

"Did Charlene tell you more than she told me?" he asked in spite of himself—because Charlene had said only that Brenda had always been tight-lipped on private matters. Which he respected, even admired.

"Brenda saw a lawyer this afternoon. But I don't think Charlene knows much more than we can surmise. It's obvious the girl's been through a rough time. She seems to have lost faith in herself. It's a terrible thing for one human being to do to another, isn't it?"

"It is." Already in the few hours since he'd first seen her yesterday, he'd begun, in some deep recess of his being, to hate whoever—and whatever—had put that wounded look, that terrified angry wariness, in those lovely deep-set brown eyes. Is that what had prompted him to say, holding her pliant warm hand for an instant, that if she needed them, they'd be here? What the hell, exactly, had he meant?

He had meant just that.

After having said good night to Lavinia—*Dear boy, why fight your feelings when you should thank the Lord you still have them?*—and now driving to his workshop on the bay side of the north tip of the island, he began to think of Jenny. He had, he thought, schooled himself not to give in to those painful memories. Jenny is dead. That was years ago. Another lifetime. Hadn't he decided, when he sold the farm in Wisconsin—and its house forever empty of Jenny's sunny presence—to put all of that behind? To blot out memory? To indulge himself instead in the work he'd always wanted to do? He'd found a way to survive, after all.

But alone. He had always thought there could never be anyone after Jenny.

Was there someone now?

No.

In the moonlight he parked the Jeep alongside the high dark building and decided not to go into the workshop but to go directly to the boat tied up at the small private dock that was really a part of the old boathouse building. This was where he slept—where he had most of his meals and listened to the hi-fi and read and in general lived when he was not in the workshop or camping or fishing. It was a clumsy old trawler with the rigging removed, originally owned by a professional fisherman in the village of Cortez on the mainland; he'd put in a head and galley and had converted its cabin into a compact living room, teak plywood satin-finished, with a wide sleeping bunk shaped into the bow forming a separate bedroom of sorts. Comfortable enough for two on those occasions when he felt the urgent need for female company—occasions he often regretted, sometimes even *before* the sex, almost invariably after it.

Leaping aboard, he checked the lines automatically and then went down the narrow companionway into his lair.

For some damned reason it had never looked so empty.

———□———

So far, so good—but she had not yet been alone with him. Leaping from the car as it stopped, Toby had rushed pell-mell into his father's arms, crying, *Daddy, Daddy, Daddy, you came! I knew you would. I knew it!* And she had known, too, as she turned her cheek for his kiss and saw the almost bewildered chagrin in his eyes. Less than half an hour ago now, ages really, centuries of polite chitchat and stiff apprehensive chatter.

But now . . .

From his bed Toby asked in a whisper: "Does this mean we're g-g-going home?"

The stutter again. Thank you, Donald. Thank you and damn you!

"Do you *want* to go home?" she heard herself asking. An unfair question, unfair—but she had to know before she faced Donald again in the living room. "Do you, Toby?"

"I d-d-don't know."

There's your answer: simple, truthful, and no help.

"Nor do I," she said—was it only a soothing lie? Reluctance held her rooted in the half-light of the bedroom. And again that dismal wave of helplessness and inevitability broke across her mind, dark and threatening.

She pulled up the sheet and bent to kiss Toby's inscrutable sun-tinted face. "You promised both your father and me that you'd go right to sleep." She heard the sharpness, almost irritability, in her tone when she had intended to convey comfort and understanding.

She turned off the lamp and stepped to the door but paused when Toby spoke: "You promised *me*, too. You b-both promised that if I went to b-b-bed, you wouldn't fight. You gave me your word."

How many times had she made that promise? "I'll try," she said, and moved into the hall, sliding the bedroom door shut behind her. Wondering: How can I give anyone my word about anything? But try she damned well would!

Donald had seemed subdued, contrite, himself uncertain. And during the painful prattle he had not even asked where they'd been all evening although he had made clear that he'd been waiting in the car for over an hour. Nor had he tried to find out by veiled questions directed at Toby—part of his familiar sly pattern of mistrust and suspicion—whether, wherever they'd been, a man had been with them.

Most astonishing of all, he appeared to be sober. Although with Donald it was sometimes difficult to tell. Until the drinking reached a certain invisible point, often you could not even guess how much poison he had put into his veins; then, without warning, the eruption.

The living room was empty.

. Had he decided to leave, to give up? Not Donald. After coming this far. Nevertheless she had to choke down the hope.

The huge sliding front doors were open wide and she could hear, very faintly, the sound of the surf on the beach beyond the houses across the street. The scent of salt was on the light breeze that cooled the room that, by its nature, promised tranquility, serenity.

Then she heard a step on the brown pebbles outside. Crunching. Approaching.

For a wild insane moment she was tempted to draw the doors together, to twist the lock, then to latch the chain between the two panels. *Double protection,* Charlene had said. *At night. We get some weirdos on this beach.*

But a picture flashed into her mind: Donald outside, enraged, hammering furiously with his fists, shouting her name, curses, obscenities—

She thought of the neighbors, Charlene's kindness—

There was a step on the wooden porch and Donald's tall wide-shouldered body loomed in the frame, outlined by the light from the high streetlamp across the street.

No escape. She would have to see it through.

The screen door panel slid open and Donald stepped up and into the room. Running a hand boyishly through his blond hair. Smiling, grinning . . .

Kiss me good night, buddy, he had said. *And get to bed. Your mother and I have a lot of things to discuss.*

He had an unopened bottle of Jack Daniel's in one hand as he strode to the black-lacquered cabinet that served as a bar. "While I was waiting for you to get here, I drove back into town." His broad-shouldered back to her, he twisted off the cap: a harsh ugly sound that she had come to hate. "Joint called the Broadway Bar. On the Tamiami Trail, right?" He was pouring into two glasses. "You know the place?"

And there it was. For the first time. But inevitable. She was tempted to say, *Charlene and I hang out there every night.* But instead she stepped down into the pit and said, "It's called the Tamiami Trail because it's the original route from Tampa to Miami." She sat down. "They're putting in a new interstate, though."

The safety of trivia. But how long could she postpone, evade? His casual quiet was a storm signal in itself.

But when he turned, she saw his face clearly: pale, drawn, his direct blue eyes bleak with torment. Even his step as he approached seemed timid, tentative. And as he extended the glass, she allowed her eyes to meet his gaze, which seemed to beg, to plead.

How's my boy? he had asked Toby. *You still love me?*

You know I do, Daddy.

And now, above her, his eyes were asking her the same question. And she had no answer.

To her own amazement compassion twisted in her as she took the glass. Watch it now, no room for sympathy—he'll use it.

The flesh of his hand touched hers. He drew it back as if he had touched a hot coal. She saw the abrupt brightening of his eyes. No anger—when the rage took over, his eyes went almost black.

But as he turned away and went to sink onto the sofa on the other side of the pit, she could not control the swift turmoil of her own feelings. How desolate he seemed, how vulnerable and filled with pain. Donald, oh, Donald—

But she stifled the quick tender impulse. How many hundreds of times had she been betrayed by her own pity?

Or love. Did she still love him?

He did not speak or lift his glass to his lips. Nor did she. She could feel his eyes on her, devouring her.

Should she drink? No telling, ever, what might change his mood. No telling what casual petty thing might trigger blind, senseless fury. Or worse, his passion. You used to love that, Brenda. You used to take delight in arousing it.

God, what a tyranny!

She took a long defiant swallow, hating the taste, hating the necessity—

"You don't have to drink it," Donald said very quietly, as if he had read her thoughts.

"I love it," she lied, hearing the acrimony in her tone, and hating that, too. "I know you're too polite to drink first. And I know how much you must need it."

Donald reached and placed his glass on the long low table that stretched between them. "That's where you're wrong, baby. I haven't had a drink since last night." She refused to allow her surprise to show. "Since I found out where you were."

Again startled, she said nothing.

"It's what you want, right? What you've always wanted. Well, I've stopped."

It was what she had wanted—but now, did it matter? Did she really care? "I seem to have heard that before, Donald. Several times." A hundred times, a *thousand*!

"I know. Only this time it's different. You really shook me up, darling."

"I've been a little shaken myself."

"I know. I know and I'm sorry."

She nodded. A sense of déjà vu had set in. Again. "You're always sorry."

"You enjoy torturing me, don't you? Well, I've got it coming, right?"

The quivering was still deep inside. And her body was hot, damp with sweat, in spite of the cool, salty breeze. But now there was a strange calm at the core that surprised her and reassured her. "I didn't leave in order to punish you."

"I'm sorry, Brenda. For everything." His tone was firm, his gaze direct and clear and sincere. "Whatever has happened, it was all my fault. And only mine."

She heard the past tense. Now that he's here, does he imagine it's all over? Can he possibly think that?

"You'll see, baby. You'll see."

The future tense now. . . .

"From now on," Donald said, "everything's going to be different, darling. A whole new world!"

And then she knew. He was not asking, he was *assuming*. As he always assumed. . . .

"This time, Brenda, I really mean it."

Déjà vu. Again and again and again and *again*!

Donald stood up. "Listen, Brenda, listen!" He took several steps toward her. His voice took on a fresh youthful exuberance. "I've chartered a boat. I take possession tomorrow morning at nine. A forty-one-foot Morgan, ketch-rigged but with power, too." Tall and again confident, his handsome face bright with that expectant sense of adventure and promise that had always been one of his most endearing qualities, he stepped out of the pit and began to stride around the large room. "We'll take a whole month, two months, take our time. I'll skipper it myself. Just the three of us on board. Toby can have his own cabin! And by the time we're out of these tropical waters, I'll have the kid swimming like a shark!"

Incredulity held her speechless. And amazement. Not at Donald—he always and invariably, childishly, cast the future in the mold of his own desires, needs. No—she was amazed at herself.

Why had she failed to anticipate this, or something like this? She knew Donald—why be shocked or even surprised?

Then, when he had stopped pacing and was looking down at her, the incredulity turned to an anger that she could taste sourly on her tongue. But the solidity at the core held: her decision had been made.

"Well, baby—how about it? This'll be our chance to be together, bind up the wounds, right? Imagine what it'll be like to make love on the deck. Atlantic moon. Sea all around. And it'll be spring by the time we get home. You've always loved spring in Connecticut."

He took a long vigorous step but her voice stopped him. "Home? We have no home!" She heard the strident, bitter rage in her tone and hated it. "You saw to that!"

It was as if she had struck him. His face drained white and his eyes flinched, as if from a cruel and unexpected blow. He looked stunned as he said, slowly: "I said I was sorry, Brenda."

"And that wipes it out, does it? Cleans the slate! That means it didn't even happen!"

"I was drunk," he said reasonably.

"You were drunk and you're sorry, so you didn't really do it." She shook her head and stared through the large plate-glass wall at the beautiful Japanese garden, hating him, hating herself, hating everything. But the calm, firm, hard certainty remained at the core and she felt a new strength.

He was speaking in a rush: "Listen, Brenda, if that's it, the house, listen—we'll start over, refurnish it, together, or if you want, we'll buy a new one. Or build one. Everything *exactly* the way you want it. It'll be something to look forward to as we go north."

He stopped talking and his words hung in an echo through the house. Was Toby listening? Had he heard? How *much* had he heard?

She could not help herself now. "You don't really give a damn for anyone but yourself." She stood up. *"You've* decided. You don't care a damn about me! Or Toby!" It was what she had earlier decided—with doubt. Now she knew—without doubt. "You haven't once asked either of us what *we* want. You don't give a damn for anything or anybody but yourself and you think *we're* part of *you*."

Softly Donald said, "You are. Part of me. Both of you."

"We are *not*. We are separate and distinct human beings!"

Then Donald, frowning, shook his head. "I don't know you when you're like this."

"You don't know me at all, Donald. You never troubled yourself to try."

"I never saw you like this."

"Six days, Donald. Almost a week. Maybe I've changed." Then she added, knowing: "I have changed."

Desperately, then, bewildered, Donald said: "I love you. That's all that counts."

She was shaking her head again. "If you do, Donald, if, even if you do, it's *not* all that counts."

"You're mine. You and Toby both. You're mine."

"Is that what you've come all this way to say? Just that you're sorry and that we *belong* to you?"

"I came to take you home." His tone changed. And his face. "I've been through hell and—" He stepped down into the pit. "You can't hide from me, Brenda. There's no place to hide. No matter where you go, ever, I'll always find you."

"Why, Donald, *why*?"

"Love, baby. Love."

"No," she said. For somehow she had learned, somehow it had been revealed to her here, tonight. If he really loved her, he'd let her go. He'd let her live.

"Maybe," Donald said, "maybe the man had it right, after all."

"What man?"

"Mr. Michael Collins. Said sometimes it's a man the husband never even heard of. . . ."

Careful now, careful—dangerous territory. Thin ice. Acres and acres of cold thin ice.

"Donald, Toby's sleeping." But she did not back away. "You must think of Toby!" she hissed. She wanted to scream, to shriek. But she kept her voice low. "You must think of somebody besides yourself!"

His eyes had darkened. "I am thinking of somebody. What's his name?"

"There's nobody!"

"Where were you tonight?"

Hopelessly, frightened now, trying to judge where she might run if he reached, she said: "We had dinner with a friend of Charlene's."

"What's his name?"

"It is a *she*. A woman writer." Carefully she did not say where. Reluctantly, she did not add: She's given me a job. "She writes books. Not a man—she, she, she!"

"Lies. Is he the reason you came to Florida?"

"I met her only tonight."

"I hate lies," he said. "You know how much I hate lies."

"She gave Toby a book she wrote." But his mind, she knew, had moved beyond reason. Although now, she also knew, it would operate with a cold distorted logic of its own. "It is called *Looking for a Bluebird*."

"What's her name?"

"Lavinia." That was enough—too much. Remember Preston and Lucy Brice: *He drove us off the road. We're lucky to be alive.* "An elderly woman, Donald." She must not mention Charlene's brother. Oh, God, no—

"If she's Charlene's friend, where's Charlene?"

"She couldn't be there." Why was she answering these questions, why? "Her boyfriend's an actor and he had a dress rehearsal tonight."

"Shit."

"Oh, Donald, for God's sake, there's no man, no other man, there never has been." She sat down again. Hopeless, hopeless . . .

His face now the familiar fevered mask of cruelty and distrust that she had come to hate and fear, Donald whirled about and started toward the hallway leading to the bedrooms.

"Leave Toby alone!" she cried, leaping to her feet. "Leave Toby out of this, please, please!"

He halted and turned.

"There's no book, is there? There is no Lavinia."

She stepped up and started toward the hall. "I'll get the damned book."

But as she was passing him, his arm reached out and his fingers dug into her bare arm. "I won't wake Toby on one condition," he growled.

"What?" But again she knew: that husky tone, that look darkening his eyes. . . .

"You know what I want, Brenda. What I always want."

Not shocked, not surprised—appalled, she said: "You're hurting my arm."

Quickly he released her. She moved away cautiously. Charlene was not coming back tonight. What's one more time? But if she gave in now, he would take it to mean what he wanted it to mean. Still, if she did not—

"Strip," he said.

"Not here," she heard herself say, stupidly, vacantly. "Not here, now. What if Charlene comes in—"

"You have a bedroom."

"There's Toby—"

"We're married, aren't we? Toby knows what goes on." But he did not step toward her. His eyes, though, raked her face and body. "Strip naked." His own words were fueling his lust. "You said earlier that Charlene probably won't come home till morning. Strip."

Should she bolt and run? He could outrun her. And there was Toby—

"Donald, it's too *late* for that."

"Shut up. You're my wife. We'll be out of here in the morning before your friend even comes home."

Anger flared. "You haven't heard a damned word I've said."

"You're my wife. Don't ever forget it. You belong to me."

"I don't belong to anyone!"

"Strip. I've been thinking of this for almost a week. Do what I tell you." He took a single step. "Or would you rather I do it for you."

"Listen, Donald. We can't." What do you hope to accomplish by lying, you little fool? "I've got my period."

His eyes went even darker. "More lies. You used that one two weeks ago. You were lying then or you're lying now."

Impossible, impossible! He forced her to lie. He was always *forcing* her to become someone she hated being, someone she was *not*! "You haven't been listening. It's over."

"It'll never be over between us. Get that through your head. *Never.*"

"Donald—do you want me to hate you?"

He shook his head. "You could never hate me, Brenda."

True? Possibly true. But she no longer loved him. *That* she knew now.

"I want to see you, baby. All of you. In the light!"

Before she could reply, he moved. Fast. He stepped and took the neck of the white dress in one hand, ripping it violently, while his other hand snatched and tore the straps off her shoulder until, unmoving, she stood half-naked.

He took a step backward and stared.

She knew that to turn away now, to try to run would only inflame him further.

"If you knew how much I've looked forward to this minute," he said.

What if Toby walked in? What if he was listening—

"Not here," she said, thinking: If I can get him out of the house—

"Where?" Donald asked. "Anywhere you say, baby."

Revolted now, seeing his eyes, *feeling* his eyes on her body, she said: "There's never anyone on the beach this time of night. . . ."

Donald's face changed aspect. He grinned. "I admire you, baby. Always thinking of the kid." He was standing very still. "Take off the rest and we'll go to the beach."

"There are houses on both sides of the street," she said.

The stand of pines giving access to the beach was a city block away.

"Lights have been off all over the island for over an hour."

Could she go out, then break and run, pound on a closed, locked door? Shouting what? Explaining what, *how*?

But Donald took two long strides and brought his body against hers. One arm went around her and drew her close, while the other hand closed over one bare breast. She could feel his penis through her clothes: stiff and pulsing and demanding.

"When I came, you let me kiss you on the cheek like you were saying good night to some stranger after a dinner party. Now kiss me, for God's sake."

His entire body, against hers, was quivering with intensity, and his grip tightened so that she could not move, could not breathe. But it did not excite her.

She was relieved—*glad*. She felt her body stiffen and she went sick and weak. When his lips closed hungrily and hard over her mouth, her lips did not open, could not.

His hand released her breast and crept up to her chin, clutching it roughly.

Her lips remained closed. And rigid. While a new sense of relief flowed through her: freedom. She no longer desired him.

Then he drew his head back, stared down on her face with blind, uncomprehending, hungry urgency. His hand moved slightly to grasp her cheeks between thumb and fingers and, uttering a low growl deep in his throat, he held her face pinched in a viselike grip that shot pain down into her throat and up into her temples.

Her mouth opened.

And hate stabbed her. Rage.

She caught a blurred view of his eyes, cruelly triumphant, and then, while she stood defenseless and furious, she felt his mouth close over hers again. His tongue entered between her open lips, probed, met hers.

The arm around her back tightened. She went faint for a second or two, and then, as if without volition, in a spasm of outrage and rebellion, she bit down, hard.

Her teeth came together over his trapped tongue.

She heard a smothered, strangulated gurgling in his throat. She tasted blood. She felt his body go slack. Then, as he released her, she opened her mouth, gagging, and he stumbled backward.

For a horrible moment she saw his face: contorted, twisting in agony, blood bright in the open cavity of his mouth and gushing between his lips and over his chin. His eyes—dazed with pain, stunned, wide, and incredulous—stared with hate and fury.

Then she heard a mind-splitting roar—a convulsive, savage howl of pain and fury that filled the house.

She moved. In panic. But not quickly enough.

She had reached the sliding screen panel when his hand caught her shoulder, spun her body around. She caught sight of the blue-black eyes, like smoldering coals.

She heard only one word, clogged and thick and liquid, over and over: "Bitch-bitch-bitch!"

And then, a split second before it struck, she saw the huge ball of fist coming up from below.

It exploded on her chin.

Then she sensed that she was falling but she could not be sure.

3

IT was after one o'clock in the morning when the telephone rang in the second-floor hallway of a house on the corner of Cocoanut Avenue and Third Street, in one of the older, less fashionable neighborhoods, only a few blocks from the center of town. The house was big and long ago it had been the residence of one of the first families. Now a sign on the browned-out lawn, under sprawling live-oak trees, read simply ROOMS TO LET.

"Let it ring," Malcolm Eggers said, rolling over; then, sitting up, he said, "Goddamnit!"

Charlene was only half awake, if that, but she saw Mal throwing on a robe over his naked body after he stood up, and again the thought occurred to her: It's not right for a man to be so handsome. Who could be calling at this hour? Everyone who had anything to do with the dress rehearsal had agreed that it had been so horrendous that it would be best not even to discuss it until tomorrow's rehearsal. She could not make out what Mal was saying on the telephone but his voice had dropped to a cautious mumble and he seemed now to be asking questions. Probably some cast member or even the director with some middle-of-the-night afterthoughts. . . .

When the theater season was over, Mal would be going to Hollywood and earlier tonight, depressed, he had suggested again that she come, too. Not on your life, pet. Damned if she, six years older and a happily divorced woman, was going to attach herself to this boy with his career and life opening in front of him.

Stretching luxuriously, content and knowing her own mind, she did not realize he had stopped talking until he was again in the room, closing the door.

"Mal! What's up, pet?"

"Charl," he said, "please don't get excited. I have something to tell you. It was Brenda—"

"Brenda?"

"Something terrible has happened—"

"To Brenda?"

"No. I don't know. Yes. She wanted me to tell you. She needs us. Get dressed."

"What, Mal, *what?*"

"I couldn't get it all straight. Hurry. She's hysterical. Little Toby's been kidnapped."

———□———

Seated stiffly in the alcove off the living room, Brenda continued to stare at the telephone.

Kidnap. Why had she used that word? He had asked so many questions. Trying to calm her. Eager to help. A stranger to her. Charlene's lover. But concerned. . . .

Can a child be kidnapped by his own father?

Can a woman be raped by her own husband?

Yes, yes, yes.

Was she going to have an anxiety attack? Her heart was pounding fast and hard; she could feel sweat all over her body, and a quivering weakness. If she tried to move, she knew the room would reel.

She had to do something. But what?

Her ribs were tight bands of iron, of pain, damming up her breath. Had he broken them when he held her?

Had he broken her ribs to prove how much he loved her?

Her cheeks flared with pain. Her jaws throbbed and her teeth ached and her back was bruised from the harshness of the bare wood floor and the agony in the area of her groin was so terrible that, to walk, she had to stifle the automatic cry that rose, dry and ugly, in her throat.

Love. How had love come to this?

The earthquake inside threatened violence. Her body now was drenched in sweat. And shaking so that she was afraid to try to stand up.

But she could not sit here waiting, doing nothing.

Toby, where are you? Are you cold? Are you so terrified that— Oh, God, Oh, God, Toby, Toby, darling, if he does anything to you, I'll kill him.

Then the hate took over—overwhelmed her completely, body and mind.

Donald had not asked whether she still loved him.

He had not asked: *Do you hate me?*

She would have answered, *No.* An hour ago she would have said no.

But now . . . now she did.

For a moment she felt positive that hatred would devour her completely.

But she couldn't let that happen.

She had to *use* that hate. Find strength in it.

But could she?

She had never, never felt more alone.

And then, out of nowhere, the picture of Barry Conrad's face flashed into her mind: the slightly withdrawn brown eyes, the reddish beard, his gentle, shy voice at dinner . . .

The frenzy and anxiety receded.

She was tempted to telephone him. Who? Barry Conrad. But the man was a complete stranger!

Don't do something stupid now, something impulsive and ridiculous.

Concentrate. If you must act, do something meaningful, constructive, such as, such as . . . ?

Where would Donald take Toby?

No predicting Donald's mind.

Try.

She picked up the phone then—her arm was surprisingly steady—and dialed 0, then 203, the Danbury area code, and then, from memory, the number.

After only two rings, it was Donald's father who answered, as she knew it would be. His voice sounded as if he were wide awake—in the middle of the night.

"Orin," she said, hearing a vibrancy in her tone that had not been there when she spoke with Mal. "Orin, listen. I'm in Florida. Donald found me and he's taken Toby. When you see him—"

"Hey, slow down, girl. He may not come here. Why should he?"

"Because he will. I know the bastard."

"Brenda, that doesn't sound like you. Are you—"

"Bastard, bastard, *bastard*! Your fine son knocked me out, raped me while I was unconscious, and took Toby before I woke up."

"Jesus."

"You may say that again."

"Brenda, are you all right?"

"All right? Oh, I'm just fine. I've never been in better shape in my life."

"I don't believe Donald did that."

"You believe it. You know him. You made him what he is." A long silence. She could hear Orin breathing and then there was another voice on the line: "Brenda, this is Donald's mother."

"Rosamond," Orin said, "please get off the phone up there. I'll handle this."

Rosamond's voice was clouded—with sleep, with drink, both? "Brenda, now you listen to me. It's a bad time of month for anyone born under Capricorn. And with the moon full—"

"Rosamond, goddamnit, get off the phone!"

"One . . . Brenda, I want to ask you *one* question—"

"Rosamond, please—"

"Isn't Toby Donald's son, too? That's all. One question. Good night, little Miss High and Mighty."

Click.

Then Orin's voice: "Sorry, Brenda."

She said nothing. She could not speak. The anger was a cold knot in her stomach now.

"Brenda," Orin said, and his tone sounded tired and very, very old. "Brenda, I hope that when you're my age, no one tries to hold you responsible for something Toby does."

And the anger melted. "If anyone's responsible," she said, "it's me." But did she believe that? No, she no longer believed that.

"Brenda, we all fail. Don't blame yourself." For a second she was reminded of her mother: *I know you, Brenda. Now, you must not take this on yourself.* Orin's voice asked: "Now, dear—what do you want me to do?"

What? Why had she called? "Tell Donald when he comes that no matter what he does, I'm going to have a divorce and I'm going to have Toby. No matter what it means. Disgrace, scandal, even if it means sending him to prison—no matter what."

"I'll tell him, Brenda. If he comes or telephones. But Donald doesn't listen, you know."

"I know. Well, this time he'd better. And—" She was clutching the phone so hard that a new pain climbed her arm into her shoulder pits. "And tell him that if he does anything to Toby, any more than he's already done, I'll find other ways to make him pay for all of it."

"Brenda—listen, dear, don't think that way. Don't do anything desperate or that you'll regret later."

"You just tell him. And also—that if I have to kill him to stop him, I will."

"Brenda, calm down a bit and tell me how to reach you."

"You mean you'll let me know if—"

"You have my word, dear."

So she gave him the number and then, when he asked, the area code. All of a sudden her voice was not sharp and clear. She discovered that, finally, for the first time, she was weeping.

"You hang in there," Orin said. "I don't know what I can do but you hang in there now. And Brenda—I'm sorry."

She had replaced the phone before she realized that she had not said thanks or good-bye. Then, as she gave herself over utterly to the release of tears, she stood up and walked to the front doors. Stood a moment in the spot where she had fallen after the blow. Where, later, she had wakened in pain. Had be brought Toby out the front doors—past the naked senseless body of his own mother on the floor? Or had he carried him out the back door and along the side of the house?

He was capable of anything. Anything. And—regardless of his

father, regardless of his childhood, or the stars, or his drunken mother—*he* had done this. *He* was responsible. *He* alone. . . .

Still walking in pain, every step still torture, she returned to the alcove. Her admission of hate gave her strength. Even the pain fed her sense of determination as she sat again and opened the directory to find Rex Maynard's home telephone number.

No hesitation, beyond doubt now, she dialed. Charlene and Mal should arrive any minute. She did not need their advice for this.

She could not go on waiting. Whatever had to be done—or *could* be done—she couldn't do it on her own.

"H'lo?"

"Mr. Maynard?"

"Yes. Speaking."

"Mr. Maynard, I'm sorry to bother you this time of night. This is Mrs. Forrest. Brenda Forrest—"

"Yes, Mrs. Forrest? What's happened?"

"He took my son. *Our* son."

"Mrs. Forrest—how do you know?"

"How do I *know*?" She had to be careful now. She wanted action, she wanted help but— "Donald was here. We were all three here. I put Toby to bed. Donald knocked me out—"

"He knocked you—"

"When I came to, they were both gone. Two plus two equals four."

She had, she thought, very neatly evaded any mention of sexual assault.

"Not always, Mrs. Forrest. Two plus two, in law, sometimes equals five. Or three. What I'm trying to say is, I'm sorry if he hurt you but if we assume that the boy's with his natural father and since you have no court order giving you custody, or even a divorce, it makes it a little sticky."

"Stickier and stickier," she said grimly. "What are you really trying to say, Mr. Maynard?"

"Mrs. Forrest, please understand first that I'm on your side. What you'd like is a police search, correct? Well, I could have the police come to you. But I'd want to be there. On the other hand— may I assume that you don't fear the father will do bodily harm to his own son?"

"I don't know."

"Did I hear you correctly, Mrs. Forrest?"

"After what's happened here tonight, I don't know whether it's safe to assume *anything.*"

"Mrs. Forrest, may I say something? You have every right to be angry. Hang on to that. It might help carry you through. By the way, my friends call me Rex."

A long moment. Was she going to burst into tears again?

"My name's Brenda."

"Well, Brenda—here's what I'm going to suggest. I'm going to ring up a friend of mine. Someone connected with the state attorney's office. We could come out there, but any extracurricular activity there might scare your husband off if he should change his mind. He might get the idea he's in trouble and drive by with little Toby in the car and not stop. Also, I'd like to keep this informal and off-the-record for, say, the next hour. Are you up to driving?"

"I'll drive."

"Good."

"Where?"

"Whitfield Estates. That's on the east, or right side of the Trail, just after you pass the airport driving north. Seventy-one Mango Drive. First house on the right. Spanish style with a stucco wall around it and empty lots on both sides. You got that?"

She had it. "Right away?"

"There'll be a light burning at the entrance gate, and my wife, who is now sitting up in bed and frowning, will have hot coffee for all of us."

"Thank you, Rex."

"Don't thank me yet. It's only the beginning. Oh, one more thing. Vitally important. Don't let questions throw you and . . . the total truth. Don't hold anything back. It's the only way we can help you."

She hesitated. Why would Rex and whoever *they* were need to know that she had been raped? She couldn't go into that. Wouldn't. Only Toby mattered, damn it.

"You there?"

"I'm here," she said. "And I hear my friend coming now. So

there'll be somebody in the house in case my husband comes back or phones."

"Good. See you in twenty minutes or so."

What she had heard was Mal Eggers's motorcycle. But, thoughtfully, Mal did not come in. After parking her station wagon in the driveway, Charlene slid open the door and entered and took a long look at Brenda, who had slipped into a pantsuit after hanging up the phone and now had her purse under her arm and keys in hand as she came into the room.

"My God," Charlene said. "What's he done to you?"

"The question is, what is he *doing* to Toby?" She gave Charlene a quick hug and went to the doors. "If he comes back, put Toby to bed, call me at Rex Maynard's home number. And steer clear of the sonofabitch."

"Mal will be here." Then, quickly: "Brenda—"

"Yes?"

"Did he hurt you?"

"Yes. But if the Catholics are right, the timing is perfect. If they're wrong, I've already decided. I'll abort."

"Pet, I love you! I don't think I've ever seen you like this."

"You couldn't. I've never been like this." She went out the doorway. "Thanks, Charl."

Outside, Malcolm Eggers spoke from the shadow of the shrubbery in that deep theatrical voice of his: "Good luck, kid."

"Hold the fort," she said and sank into the seat of the Lancia.

As she backed it into the night-hushed street, she wondered whether Charlene would tell Mal. It didn't matter. But she could not let the police know. Or Rex. *Something* has to be sacred, doesn't it? Even rape.

Driving, she wondered how long her hate and anger could sustain her.

————□————

"Home. That's where we're going. I've already told you about a thousand times. Home where we belong."

Toby said, very softly, staring out of the window of the car: "I heard Mama say we d-d-don't have a home."

"Your mama and daddy were having a little argument, buddy. All big people do that sometimes."

"You promised n-not to fight. Both of you."

"Sorry, buddy. All my fault."

Was it? Yes. And Christ, he *was* sorry. He was sick with being sorry. Even the Jack Daniel's wasn't helping. He had grabbed the bottle as he passed the bar on his way to Toby's room. The sliding door to the bedroom had been closed. Had Toby heard?

"Were you listening to what we were saying?" he asked.

"Only when you y-y-yelled."

Thank God the kid hadn't burst into tears. Yet. And thank God he'd been too surprised and scared to resist when he'd picked him up bodily from the bed and taken him out the rear door instead of going back through the living room.

Where she was lying sprawled naked and out cold on the floor.

Oh, God, Brenda, you'll never know how sorry I am.

"*When* is Mommy c-c-coming? You said she had to pack and bring the c-c-car. Why couldn't I go with *her?*"

"Buddy, buddy, this is Daddy. Your old man. No reason to be scared. I thought you'd like flying on a little plane. You can see everything and it's a sensation you don't often— *You're going with me because I say you're going!*"

And when Toby did not answer, he growled: "Right?"

Faintly, without turning his head, the boy said: "Right."

And then Donald regretted the quick spasm of anger. "Look, let me explain. Little boys like to know, right? This is the town of Bradenton we're going through. They didn't have any planes to charter back there in the Sarasota airport until nine o'clock. And all the regular flights are booked solid. So we're going to Tampa to hire us our own plane. Roger?"

"Roger," Toby said.

Only a half-bottle of Jack left—he took a long swig and then glanced around as they crossed a bridge with little traffic and only a few lights reflected on the water on both sides. According to the map he'd picked up from the Hertz desk in the airport building, Tampa was only about forty miles.

His body felt empty. The whiskey was not doing any good. He was still remembering what had happened. What he had done.

To Brenda.

It had been a tremendous and shattering orgasm. Like none he'd ever known before.

He'd really *had* her. She hadn't even known it but God, God, God, he'd *had* her.

But he hadn't hurt her. He was sure of that. He did not want to hurt anybody.

Especially you, Brenda.

A wave of tenderness engulfed him.

He took another swallow from the bottle.

You, Brenda, always you, only you—

A state police car passed, not going fast, cruising.

And then, after that, every time headlights appeared in the rear-view mirror he was convinced, until it passed, that it was a high-way patrol car.

What if they stopped him? What if they discovered the open bottle?

He'd been arrested twice for drunken driving. And each time his father had been able to get him off—with a fine or, he suspected, a bribe. But that was in Connecticut. Here—

Or suppose Brenda had gone to the police when she came to?

What crime had he committed? She was his wife, wasn't she?

She'd never tell anyone. Too much pride. He knew Brenda.

"You didn't get out of bed and go to the living-room door, did you, buddy?"

No answer.

"Buddy, I'm talking to you. I know you're not asleep."

"I d-d-d-d-d-didn't look," Toby said softly. Then he turned his face to stare at his father. "Why? What did you d-d-do to my mama?"

"Nothing. We talked. We made plans."

"That's a l-l-lie."

"What'd you say?"

No answer.

In the dimness he could see the boy's face but not his expression. And he felt the rage explode like a bomb detonating in his chest, his head, his blood.

"Don't call me a liar, you little brat! I'm your father!"

It was then that Toby started to cry for the first time.

"Stop sniveling. Hear me, stop blubbering!"

But now, bent double, face down between his knees, Toby was sobbing.

"You know what *my* father would've done if I'd ever called him a liar? You want to know?"

He was remembering: *I give up. Nothing else seems to work, maybe you'll understand this!*

"He'd whip me. Good. Hard. With a belt!"

The sobs continued and now the thin small figure was quivering all over and he was gasping for breath.

"Men don't cry. You're a man, aren't you? You want to be a man, don't you?"

No answer.

"You want me to stop the car?"

At last the boy spoke: "N-n-n-n-no, please, n-no."

"Then shut up or I'll show you who's in charge of this goddamn family. Just like I showed your goddamned mother."

He looked up. The wide highway was forking and he was in the left lane and the sign above read: ROUTE 19.

It came to him then: He'd stay in this lane and bear left. He remembered the map. The long skyway bridge over Tampa Bay led into St. Petersburg. Tampa and St. Petersburg were twin cities. He could circle east after the bridge and find his way to Tampa Airport. There'd be signs. And even if the police were looking, they'd be patrolling the shortest route—the Tamiami Trail, which he had just left. Once he was in Connecticut, with Toby, he'd let her know. She'd come then. She'd come home then.

Toby had stopped crying but he was not sitting up.

———□———

As one of only two female attorneys on the staff of the state attorney's office in Sarasota, Mary Rinaldi knew that certain cases were assigned to her because of her gender rather than her abilities to advise prosecution and then to conduct same. And she did not have to guess that Rex had invited her here in the wee hours of the morning because he needed her advice on some situation involving a female client. And while helping his wife, Alison, in the kitchen preparing a coffee tray, she had already confirmed her suspicion that the client was the young wife from Connecticut in whose predicament Rex had somehow become so personally involved. She remembered—at the table on the lawn at the Harmons' dinner party only last evening—chiding him for playing the knight errant on a white charger. And she remembered the odd pang of jealousy she had felt at the time. . . .

"Rex," Alison said, "usually resents even a phone call here. Says he doesn't conduct law in his home." She laughed. "Now look at us."

But she seemed pleased, even a bit excited, by the unusual circumstances tonight. Wearing a simple long green housecoat, she went about her coffee-making with a quick, simple efficiency. A plain young woman really, with a freckled country-type face and long pale red hair that hung rather than flowed down her back, Alison always seemed ageless. But her hazel eyes exuded a frank, childish innocence and naiveté that charmed one and all. Even Mary Rinaldi, who wished she could dislike this girl of whom she was admittedly quite jealous.

"Nancy didn't wake up," Alison was saying. "Lucky us. She'd expect to join right in. And ten-year-olds seem to have opinions on *everything*. But I have to admit, I'm perishing of curiosity, aren't you? Rex hardly ever discusses his business at home."

"Smart fellow."

"Listen! Someone else has come."

Mary Rinaldi stepped to the swinging door.

A heavy voice with a southern drawl said from the living room: "When a lawyer asks a police officer's advice, it usually means he wants a favor."

Lieutenant Waldo Pruitt. Surprised, Mary Rinaldi heard Rex asking the older man to sit down, thanking him for coming, and offering him a drink. She heard Waldo Pruitt's sour laughter. "Booze raises hell with my gout, goddamnit. But I do smell coffee brewin'."

"Alison's up. And Mary Rinaldi's here. Let me sort of fill you in before Mrs. Forrest gets here."

Mary Rinaldi turned from the door and took the tray from the counter. "One of my favorite characters is here," she told Alison in a whisper. "God grant me the power to bite my tongue."

"I'll bring the pot and plug it in, in there."

Detective Waldo Pruitt was wearing the same rumpled gray suit that he always wore. Ever the southern gentleman, he hoisted his 250 pounds of beef to his feet as they came in through the dining room. He nodded to Mary. "Miss Rinaldi." But he almost bowed as he greeted Alison. "Mrs. Maynard—what kind of a husband would get a lady out of bed this here time of night?"

"You go on now," Alison said. When her plain face was ignited by pleasure, she looked about fifteen years old. "And you'll all have to excuse me. Two total strangers should be enough for poor Mrs. Forrest and I don't want to be in the way." She set the coffeepot on the tile-topped coffee table set between the two long Spanish-style sofas facing each other; then she stepped, almost birdlike, to Rex and kissed him lightly on the lips. "I'll be in bed reading if you need anything. G'night, all."

And then she was gone. But, strangely, what Mary Rinaldi felt then was not jealousy, or even envy—only a kind of sad acceptance. She knew of so few good solid marriages that she had become acutely aware of one when she found herself observing it. Rex was looking after his wife as if, yes, he was sorry to see her leave the room. Christ, Rinaldi, you're getting downright sentimental—and more so as you become more cynical and detached.

"Excuse me, Mary," Rex said as he sat to pour coffee, "I was just giving Waldo what little background I have."

"I'll keep watch on the ramparts," she said, wandering to the ceiling-high arch framing the front windows and windowseat. She sat down and stared out the lead-framed, diamond-shaped panes of glass. The heavy wooden gate in the stucco wall stood open, lighted by a stained-glass lantern on a wrought-iron post. Mango Drive was a typical street of comfortable medium-sized houses, mostly of concrete-block construction and of no particular design. In contrast, Rex's house, which must have been built in the twenties, before the Florida land bust, had a sort of modest Old World grandeur, with its arches and colorful tile floors and decor. She thought of her own small apartment near the beach on Siesta Key—did Alison know how damned lucky she was?

Through the open gate now she saw a low blue car, not quite small enough to be a sports car, crawl to a stop along the curb. She stood and turned into the room. "The victim arriveth," she announced.

And Waldo Pruitt shook his square brush-cut gray head and sighed audibly as he stood up. "Victim's the word," he drawled. "The lady's on a spot, son. The lady's on a right nasty spot."

While Rex—who was wearing no glasses and an open-necked sport shirt and faded jeans, in contrast to the tan and brown suits he usually wore when she saw him—went into the foyer to open the front door, Mary Rinaldi drifted to the table to pour herself a cup of coffee. Waldo Pruitt's heavy face was wearing a scowl. He said nothing. He had never been more than grudgingly polite since that day in court when she, as a public defender then, had had to attack his testimony unmercifully. She had won the battle, and the case, but she had made an enemy. The feeling was somewhat mutual: Lieutenant Pruitt was too much the high-handed policeman of the old school for Mary Rinaldi's tastes. And she was damned if she could figure out why Rex had asked him here tonight.

What struck Mary Rinaldi first about Brenda Forrest was the look of hesitation in her brown eyes—the baffled, stunned expression of a wounded, cornered animal. She seemed so small. Mary Rinaldi was almost always self-consciously aware of her own six-foot height, but this Brenda Forrest seemed china-doll diminutive. Her body, though, had trim, even athletic lines.

Still . . . as she stepped to the chair to sit down, her step seemed uncertain, too, as if she were making an effort to move her legs.

Under Rex's gentle, almost tender questioning, she told her story: She returned to the house after dinner, he was waiting, they sent the boy to bed, they argued, he knocked her out, she awoke to discover the child gone. There was a fine thin edge of steel in her quiet tone that alerted Mary Rinaldi. And reassured her—a glint of anger, a tense sharpness, a brittle suggestion of rebellion.

"Then, although you didn't witness the act, there's no doubt in your mind that your husband left the house with the child?" Rex asked.

"None."

"And you want him apprehended—"

"Apprehended. Arrested. Whatever the word is, I want Toby back. Is that unreasonable?"

"Not at all," Rex said. "However—"

And Lieutenant Pruitt cleared his throat. Then he asked, "On what charge, Mrs. Forrest?"

"It's kidnapping, isn't it?"

Lieutenant Pruitt shook his head. "No, ma'am, no, ma'am, it ain't. Not if your conjectures are on the mark and he's with Mr. Forrest right now."

"The lieutenant's right," Rex said then. "On the other hand, you say he knocked you unconscious. How?"

"With his fist. He was a boxer in college. He knows how."

"Did your son witness this?" Lieutenant Pruitt asked, leaning forward to pour more coffee.

"Not that I know of. Do I need a witness?"

"It aids the cause, Mrs. Forrest—yessir, a eyewitness aids almost any legal cause."

"Mary?" Rex prompted.

"Mrs. Forrest," Mary Rinaldi said, "if I were your attorney, I'd advise you to forget the kidnap charge—"

"Forget it?"

"For the moment. I'd advise you to go to the state attorney's office at nine o'clock this morning and swear out a warrant for aggravated assault and battery."

Lieutenant Pruitt said, "Miss Rinaldi, you know as well's I do: We get so many of those warrants these days, we can't process them fast enough."

"Does that mean going before a judge?" Mrs. Forrest asked Mary Rinaldi.

"Yes. It'd help if we could establish his blow broke your jaw but failing that—" She leaned forward on the sofa. "What are those purple bruises on your cheeks? Did he strike you more than once?"

The bruises gave the fragile, otherwise pallid face the look of illness. The question disconcerted Brenda. She dropped her eyes. "May I have some coffee, please?"

Rex leaped to his feet, murmuring apologies and pouring coffee. But Mary Rinaldi recalled the way Brenda Forrest had walked into the room, the way she sat down.

"I should have advised you to swear out a restraining order when we first talked," Rex apologized. "But we didn't even know he was in the state then."

"Peace bond, they used to be called," Lieutenant Pruitt said. "They sometimes work. If the man has his good senses and don't drink too much. Ah, by the way, Mrs. Forrest, does your husband drink?"

"He drinks." Cautious, bitter. "Yes, he drinks."

"Is he an alcoholic?"

"I honestly don't know. I don't care. He wasn't drinking tonight! If he had been, would that excuse what he's done?"

Now Mary Rinaldi was almost certain. Thanks, Lieutenant. "Mrs. Forrest," she said, "may I call you Brenda?" And Brenda Forrest nodded, her eyes still guarded, alert. "Brenda, we ought to know the whole story." And when Brenda Forrest nodded: "Did your husband brutalize you in any other way?"

"If he did," Brenda Forrest asked, meeting her gaze with a resolute, waiting stare, "if he did, would somebody *do* something then? Instead of just sitting here. *Would* you?"

And now Mary Rinaldi knew. "We might. We'd sure as hell have more incentive to try."

So then Brenda Forrest leaned back in her chair and said, very quietly: "He knocked me out, he ripped off all my clothes, and he raped me while I was unconscious."

No tears, no catch in the throat—not the suggestion of a tear.

Mary Rinaldi broke a swift, sudden impulse to move to the chair. To reach a hand, to—

"Now," Brenda Forrest said, "now will you for God's sake *do* something?"

No one spoke. No eye met any other eye.

A low-flying plane roared overhead and the house seemed to tremble. The panes in the windows rattled.

Finally Rex spoke. "Thank you. Thanks for doing what I suggested. We do need the whole truth." And then he turned to look at Mary Rinaldi: "Thank you, too, Mary." He glanced at Lieutenant Pruitt. "Waldo?"

The big man shook his head. "A man can't rape his own wife."

"He did," Brenda said softly.

"Not legally," the policeman said.

"What he's saying," Mary Rinaldi explained, trying to control her voice, "is that legally a man *can* rape his own wife. It's his right."

"It's not against the law in the state of Florida. They been fiddling aroun' with a bill year after year—"

"Only in Nebraska and California," Mary Rinaldi said and a familiar anger sharpened her mind. "What Lieutenant Pruitt is saying," she explained, hearing the guttural, ironic bitterness in her tone, "what he's saying is that only two states have spousal rape laws—establishing that it's a crime for a man to rape his own wife. Everywhere else in this land of the free the woman's a bona-fide legalized sexual toy, and he has a license." She saw the expression of dismay on Rex's lean face and the flicker of a patronizing grin on the lieutenant's beefy lips. Furious, she stood up. "Everywhere else she's his property, his sexual slave!"

When she moved, shaking inside, to stand at the window, the silence behind her was broken only by a gurgling sound in the coffeepot.

"He knocked you out," Lieutenant Pruitt finally said mildly. "Aggravated assault is punishable by a year in the slammer."

"And rape," Rex said, "is a first-degree felony, punishable by a sentence of thirty years to life in state prison."

"Well, it ain't rape. That's all I know and all we need to know here. Get me a warrant for assault and I'll put it in the works."

"Then what?" Brenda Forrest cried, standing up. "Then what? How long? How long will it take from the time the courts open this morning to *apprehend*, to get my boy back? How long?"

"My, my," Lieutenant Pruitt said, "I'm getting it from all sides. I don't make the laws, ladies—I just try my damnedest to enforce them."

Rex stood and crossed to Brenda. "I have to warn you, Mrs. Forrest—even if the police can find your boy, they can't arrest your husband for child abduction. A smart lawyer will have him out on bail within an hour or so. And we have no grounds to get possession of your son for you. I just don't want you to get your hopes up in that regard."

"Maybe I haven't said it," Brenda said, panic in her face for the first time. "Maybe I haven't made it clear. Toby's a sensitive child. You don't know Donald. Anything can happen. Anything can be happening right now!"

"Hold on now," Lieutenant Pruitt said. "Do you think there's some possibility he might abuse your son?"

"Before tonight, I'd say no. Now—I don't know." Then her chin set and her voice rose: "He doesn't have to be harmed physically to be harmed! Don't you understand, can't any of you understand?"

Mary Rinaldi went to her then, all but shunting Rex aside. "I understand. We all do. Even Lieutenant Pruitt understands, I think. We're trying to do all we can within the limits of the law."

"The law!" Brenda's voice rose to a low shriek. "Whose side is the law on anyway?" She stepped around Mary Rinaldi and went to Lieutenant Pruitt's chair, stared down fiercely. "If he'd been kidnapped by a stranger, someone wanting *money*, you'd have your men out there looking for him now! If I'd been raped by some sex-mad pervert, you'd sound an alarm, wouldn't you? *Wouldn't you?*"

Lieutenant Pruitt was staring up into the furious face above him. He allowed a long moment to pass. Then, frowning, he asked, "What kind of a car was he driving?"

"Black. New. Wait a second—Toby asked about it. The name of some animal. Jungle animal. Cat."

"Cougar?" Rex suggested.

"Yes. Rented." Brenda said. "He uses Hertz usually."

"And where do you think he might go?"

"Home, probably. Danbury, Connecticut."

"He could be out of the state by now."

"He chartered a plane to come down." She stood away. "Why didn't I think of that? He could be—"

"Take it easy now, missie," Lieutenant Pruitt said as he heaved himself to his feet. "Take it real nice and easy and let's see where we get."

"Anything else you might have forgotten?" Rex asked.

"The boat!"

"Boat?" Mary Rinaldi said. "What boat?"

"He chartered a boat. He's to take delivery at nine o'clock."

"Good girl!" Rex said. "Do you know where?"

"Here. Sarasota. That's all I know."

"There aren't that many charter companies," Mary Rinaldi said. "Or that many marinas."

"Anything else?" Rex asked again.

"Yes," Brenda said, facing him.

"What?"

"The divorce. File whatever you have to file right away."

"Today, Brenda. This morning."

"And," Mary Rinaldi said, "I'll get an arrest warrant as soon as court opens."

"Meanwhile," Lieutenant Pruitt said, and they all turned to him, "meanwhile, there's more'n six hours. Now—we don't know for dead *certain* his old man snatched the kid, do we? Maybe he *has* been kidnapped. Lots of kooks around. Or maybe he just got tired of hearing his folks carrying on and wandered off, like. Lots of unfenced pools out Lido Shores way. And that beach, it's getting its own reputation, ain't so hot. Might get a extra car or two out in that direction. So—we got a missing person on our hands, warrant or no goddamn warrant. Won't hurt to alert the patrols on the streets, make a few phone calls. You don't happen to have a photograph of the boy, do you, Mrs. Forrest?"

"In my purse."

"Let me take it. Who knows who might get picked up for driving under the influence this time of night? And while we're at it, you don't happen to carry a picture of that lovable husband of yours, do you?"

"It just so happens I do," Brenda said. And then, rummaging through her purse, she added, "Oh, we're a close, devoted family, we are."

And then, much to Mary Rinaldi's amazement, she joined in the terribly unlikely, really incredible laughter as the four of them stood in a small circle laughing together and another plane passed low overhead.

———□———

Toby was sleepy, very sleepy, but he couldn't actually go to sleep. Maybe when they were on the plane he would. He pretended to be asleep, though—it was better that way.

Especially when Daddy acted this way. Daddy, it was funny, didn't always act the same, like Mama did. Sometimes—most of the time if he wasn't drinking a lot—he was quiet, sort of faraway, but nice. And other times he was really neat—trying to teach you something, like how you figure out the weight and stress of a new building, or how to swim. But Toby didn't want to think about that now because Daddy lost his temper about swimming. And then there were times like now when he was just sore, angry, yeah, but not really mad the way he sometimes got. And he wasn't blaming Toby but himself because he couldn't figure out on the map how to get to the airport, blaming the goddamn sonsabitches who made up the map, and the service stations for being closed.

And the only place he *could* find open was a kind of outdoor pizza parlor with sliding windows and only one man working behind the outdoor counter. The Tampa Airport—why, man, you gotta cross the causeway to get to that, not the skyway, the *causeway*, and then watch for the signs. Daddy thought the man was a dumb bastard but Toby thought he was nice and wished he had a Coke and pizza but this was no time to ask.

They were on the causeway now, practically the only car going either way, and it wasn't like the skyway, which kind of soared way up and gave you the funniest feeling because it was so high and there was only all that black water down below. Here, it was more like a road laid right down on the surface of the water itself. And the water seemed to come right up to the pavement. It was even more scary and spooky in a way.

He felt like he was lost. Lots of ways. Daddy had told him to watch for airport signs but he knew he wouldn't see any signs (except 45 LIMIT) on the causeway. Even he knew that: He wasn't as dumb as Daddy sometimes said he was.

He was cold, though, shivering, and his pajamas felt damp and clingy. Daddy should have told him to take his clothes when he got him out of bed. He should have told him they were going on an airplane. But he wasn't going to bring it up again. *Let 'em stare*, Daddy had said, even before they'd stopped way back there at the Sarasota airport a long time ago. *You're my son, aren't you? I can take you anywhere I like.*

So when they got to the airport now all he could do was pretend he was dressed and pretend he wasn't embarrassed.

Then, down the road, even before they were off the causeway and on land again, he saw the big lighted billboard with the picture of a jetliner painted on it. He was about to tell Daddy but he thought maybe he'd wait till he could try to read the printing when Daddy said: "Who's the man you and Mama had dinner with tonight?"

Man? Did he mean Barry? Who had given him the carved egret. Which he should have brought along. But he remembered other arguments and also what he'd heard from the bedroom to-night: *Donald, for God's sake, there's no other man, there never has been.* So he just shut his eyes and said nothing.

"Come on, buddy. You're not sleeping. Answer me."

"We ate d-d-dinner with Mrs. Davidson. She's an old lady, and she's g-g-got a neat house. Right on the beach."

"She writes books, right?"

"R-r-right." He wished he could stop stuttering. But he knew he never would. "Right," he said, gritting his teeth.

"That's what your mother said."

"Well, Mama wouldn't lie."

Daddy grunted. It was almost a laugh. But not a good laugh. "Like hell," he said.

So Toby didn't say anything. He waited. They were on land now and they'd passed the billboard with the picture of the plane. And to hell with it. That's what everybody said all the time. Well, if Daddy thought Mama was a liar—to hell with you, buddy.

"What," Daddy asked, "what about that guy who comes to the house all the time?"

Did he mean Mal? But Mal was Charlene's boyfriend. "On the m-motorcycle?" he asked.

"On the motorcycle. Who's *he?*"

"Mal."

"That's not a name."

"It stands for Malcolm. He's an actor."

"Where's he act?"

"In Sarasota. He took me t-t-to the theater. It's neat." Maybe if he talked about that, and not Mal—

"He took you and Mama to the theater—"

"N-n-no, just me. To rehearsal. The theater has two balconies and box seats, but it's very small, like a d-dollhouse, sort of. It was built over two hundred years ago and they brought it over from Italy, all in p-p-pieces, and built it up again. You never saw any-thing like—"

"What's his last name?"

"Eggers. Something like that. He—"

"He what?"

"I just thought. It's Friday n-n-now, isn't it?"

"It's Friday, so what?"

"The play opens tonight. Mal was g-g-going to let me watch from b-b-backstage."

"Malcolm Eggers—is he good-looking?"

"He looks okay, I guess."

"Goddamnit, I knew it!"

And Toby remembered other things he'd heard, when they were fighting, so he said, loud: "He's Charlene's boyfriend!"

"Shit."

"You t-t-told me not to say that."

"Charlene—she's behind the whole goddamn thing!" His voice rose, hard and thin and sharp like a knife. "And now you're in it, too."

"What did I do?"

"Lying. Everyone's always lying to me. She's got you fooled, too, has she, the little slut?"

He didn't know what *slut* meant but from the way Daddy spit out the word, he knew Mama wasn't one.

"She is not," he heard himself say, no stutter, but he felt something heavy turn over inside and that funny flutterylike feeling came back—like birds when they fly up from the beach together— and then he made up his mind: he was not going to cry, no matter what, he was never going to cry again.

"You'll find out," Daddy growled. "You'll grow up and you'll find out. Lying sluts—all of them!"

The car came to a stop. The brakes made a screeching sound and he was thrown forward so that he had to bring up his arms to keep from banging his forehead against the windshield.

Then the car was backing up and he was thrown back against the seat. Hard. In the headlights he saw a sign: NO U TURN. But the car shot forward again, then swung left, and it made a U-turn in the cross-over space where there was an opening in the curbing that separated the traffic.

They were going in the opposite direction.

Going fast now, speeding. The motor roared and the whole car kind of shivered. He shut his eyes again and hunched himself down in the seat. He admitted it—he was scared, oh, God he was scared!

When he figured that they must be on the causeway again, he decided to ask: "Where are we g-g-going now, Daddy?"

He could tell from the gurgling sound that Daddy was drinking from the bottle again. Did that mean he was driving with one hand?

Did that mean he was going to get really drunk?

Did that mean—

"Where the hell you *think* we're going?"

When Daddy was mad—mad like this—he sounded like some kind of wild animal caged up, trapped or wounded—

"Answer me!"

"To see Mama?"

"Not to *see* her. To *get* her!"

And then he couldn't talk again because he was scared in a different way, but at the same time he couldn't help feeling happy—it was too good to be true!

But . . .

"D-D-Daddy . . ."

No answer.

"Daddy, slow d-d-down. Please."

"We're going to get her and we're going to get on the boat and we're going home. The three of us. How'd you like that?"

A boat? The three of them?

"How'd you like that?"

"N-n-neat. Daddy. That'd be neat."

Then he heard himself screaming. But not crying. Only screaming. And he couldn't stop no matter how hard he tried.

——□——

Three quarters of an hour ago Alison had run out of coffee. And had her loving husband, Mr. Rex Maynard, LL.B., berated her, even complained, so much as groaned? Not on your legal life—cheerfully he had suggested brandy. And a fine decision it had been, too. Mary Rinaldi approved.

Alison was huddled in one corner of a sofa, her face so flushed that the freckles had all but disappeared, her pale red hair helter-skelter all over her housecoat. "Now I wish I'd stayed downstairs long enough to meet her," she said.

Her long legs dangling over one arm of her easy chair and her head resting on the other arm, Mary Rinaldi said, "You know what's going to happen? Some smart-ass courthouse lawyer's going to claim conjugal consent—or worse, enticement, enticement to husbandly lust."

Sprawled on his back on the floor, Rex said: "He'll swear he can prove she's a two-timing Lorelei with a stable of adulterous lovers and deserves whatever she got!"

"I never will understand the law," Alison said, staring at the ceiling and stretching her arms.

"What you didn't hear, Alison," Mary Rinaldi said, "was what Brenda said when she produced the ogre's picture. *Oh, we're a close, devoted family, we are.* Listen, chappies, anyone who can joke like that at a time like this, she gets my vote."

"If I were in his shoes," Rex said, "and a woman made it clear to me that she plain didn't want me, I'd say to hell with it and farewell my lovely."

"Well," Alison said, "it sounds to me as if he's sick. Maybe not psycho, but *sick* anyway."

"Here we go," Rex groaned. "There's always a psychological explanation so nobody's ever guilty. Horseshit."

"The demon lover," Mary Rinaldi said, and sat upright in the chair. "Driven by fires inside."

"More horseshit," Rex said.

"You didn't see his photograph, Alison. Handsome lad. Blond, athletic."

"Don't let that fool you. According to a classmate friend of mine who wished this mess on me, your tall Mr. All-American Boy tried to run him into some lake up there. Him *and* his wife. Because Mrs. Forrest had discussed divorce with him. Professionally."

Alison moved then. She uncurled her body and stood up, frowning.

"Relax, honey," Rex said, rolling over. "I shouldn't have mentioned it."

"No," Alison said, gravely. "I think you *should* have. And before this."

The telephone rang and as Rex leaped to his feet and started toward the arched foyer, Mary Rinaldi said, "Our good old boy Waldo."

They could hear Rex's voice in the foyer but he spoke in such a low tone that the words were only occasionally distinguishable.

"Honestly," Mary Rinaldi said, hoping to take Alison's mind from the fear she had seen take root there, "earlier tonight I couldn't understand why Rex asked Lieutenant Pruitt here. Then, just before he left, I think I glimpsed another side of his red neck."

"I hope," Alison said, "I hope the phone didn't wake Nancy."

But, Mary Rinaldi knew, it was not this that was really on Alison's mind as she strolled blindly away. "Forget it," she said. "The ogre doesn't even know Rex's name."

Alison turned. Her face, pale now, the freckles clear again. "He'll know it if he's arrested and goes to court, won't he?"

Before Mary Rinaldi, startled, could reply, Rex was back in the room.

"There's a full moon," he said. "Has anyone noticed? Or rather, there'll be a full moon tonight. And it's during a full moon that most crimes of violence are committed."

"Did Lieutenant Pruitt call to tell you that?" Mary Rinaldi asked.

"He was only reminding me. Oh, the man's been working. He has a detailed description of the Hertz car. With exact license number. And about an hour ago, a man answering our man's description unsuccessfully tried to charter a private plane at the Sarasota-Bradenton airport."

"Then, presumably," Mary Rinaldi said, "he's still in the area."

"Presumably. But if you were in a hurry to get *out* of the area and there were no vacancies in the motels—that's a safe assumption this time of year—what would *you* do?"

"I'd try to get a flight out of Tampa," Alison said.

"Give the little lady a *big* cigar. So would I. And the thought has already occurred to our policeman friend. He has the state police alerted and I get the impression that the patrol cars have informal instructions to apprehend a possible DWI offender driving a rented black Cougar on the Tamiami Trail."

"What if he's not drunk?" Alison asked.

"They'll have to release him. After they make sure. And while they're making sure, the boy has to be cared for by someone, doesn't he? How about his mother?"

"Waldo Pruitt," Mary Rinaldi said, "is a good ole boy!"

"He's working on the boat charter angle, too. But that will have to wait till they open at nine."

"Nine?" Mary Rinaldi said. "Do you both realize how soon that will be? Chappies, I am wending my way."

"One last tidbit," Rex said. "Are you ready for this? Lieutenant Waldo thinks Mrs. Brenda Forrest is a clevah li'l gal. He doesn't believe she was raped at all. He says she made that up just to shake us up and get us off our asses and *moving*. God's truth, what the big man said."

———□———

When Brenda went into the alcove to make a telephone call, closing the *shoji* screen panel behind her, Charlene asked, for the umpteenth time, "What time is it?" She was smoking one cigarette after another now.

"A few minutes after four," Mal said. "There's a line rehearsal at one and the curtain, come hell or high water, goes up at eight."

While he had waited with Charlene for Brenda to return from her lawyer's house, they had smoked two joints between them in the hope of quieting down and she had cued him from the script while he rattled off his lines of dialogue.

Brenda had finally returned in a mood of suppressed frenzy— and anger. *It seems there's been no crime committed,* she had announced. *The police feel the way Donald's mother does: Toby's his son, too, isn't he?*

The two front-door panels had been slid wide open so that it was as if part of the front wall had been removed. Pacing up and down the long room, Brenda had lapsed into a grim silence that seemed to exclude Charlene and himself. He could only guess at the furious monologue in her mind: Why hadn't she known this would happen, what sort of idiot was she not to have read her husband's character better, how had he managed to bamboozle and hoodwink and *blind* her so successfully? Mal had suggested a little grass to pull her down but she refused. A drink then? *Not on your life,* she'd said. *I'll probably never have a drink again as long as I live. I'll leave the drinking to experts!*

And through it all Charlene had been *great.* She was one hell of a girl, this Charlene, and tonight only confirmed him in his feelings: marriage or not, Charlene was the girl, or woman, for him. But he had begun to doubt, in the last few weeks, that Charlene would ever admit he was the man for her. And if that was the way she really felt—well, it was his loss. And a sad one.

She'd carefully evaded discussing what had really happened in this room earlier—to Brenda. But he'd made a guess or two without asking.

Brenda slid open the panel and returned to the room. "It seems," she said, "there are too many motels for the police to check them all. But Lieutenant Pruitt says they've checked the flights and there are none out of here till seven." She was speaking in that brittle high-pitched tone that seemed to tremble on the edge of a scream. "I'd already done that myself. Donald hasn't turned in the Hertz car. Now Lieutenant Pruitt's waiting to hear from what he calls 'Security' at Tampa Airport. They ought to be able to spot a man with a little boy wearing pajamas, shouldn't they? And if they *do*, that's *all* they can do. It's his right to take Toby home. I can't ask my parents for help. I may call Preston Brice in Connecticut."

"What you'd better do," Charlene said, "is settle down. You don't want him to pull up in front of the house and Toby to leap out, and you—"

"Lieutenant Pruitt agreed to put an extra patrol car out here." Then she began to pace up and down again. "But what the sweet hell good will *that* do?"

Charlene's eyes met Mal's. They looked bright with worry and concern.

He took his cue—and was grateful. He stood. "Well, you know where to reach me." He stepped out of the pit and went to Brenda—who did not seem to be aware of his presence as she continued to move up and down, up and down.

"When Toby comes back, Brenda"—and then he repeated the word—"*when*, let me know if he still wants to go to rehearsal." No answer. "Toby, you know, has become a sort of mascot at the theater. I think the whole company's sort of adopted him." No reply. He went on: "I'll bet he makes rehearsal." And then, feeling foolish: "If you won't smoke pot, how about Valium or something like that?" Still no reply.

He turned to Charlene, who came to him and kissed him swiftly on the lips and then placed her cheek against his and whispered: "I'll handle it, pet. But thanks, thanks for trying."

She gave him a quick hug and then turned away and returned to sit down and he was sliding open the screen panel when Brenda spoke: "Mal! I'm so sorry. I didn't mean to involve you, so many people . . ." The thin, high, brittle quality was gone from her tone. "Oh, Mal, don't think I'm not grateful." She was speaking now in a warm hoarse rush of words as she came toward him. "I'm so grateful. I had to come and disrupt— Oh, Mal, thank you, thank you, thank you!"

Close now, she took his arms in her hands and then, leaning forward, she kissed him on the cheek. And allowed her cheek to remain against his as she whispered, "I can't tell you how much I appreciate your help."

Not knowing what to say, but touched, Mal allowed her to drop her arms and to step back. Then he leaned forward and kissed her forehead.

He went outside. He slid the screen panel into place without glancing back into the room, although he was aware of Brenda's figure outlined in the light behind and of the fact that she had not moved.

While he stood in the saddle of the bike, opening the stopcock on the fuel feed, twisting the key, then kicking the motor into action and as he waited for it to warm up, strapping on his helmet, he was conscious of how much the house, with its open doors forming a proscenium, resembled a stage set. Then he adjusted the mirror on his left and revved the motor with the throttle in his right hand before kicking up the stand. As he wheeled out onto the street and shifted into second gear, he realized that, since he was helpless to *do* anything, he was relieved to be going. That feeling of utter impotence, he only now realized, was one of the most harrowing a man can experience. And he knew, too, that putting a few miles between himself and that empty, waiting, terrified house would only relieve but not obliterate his concern. Odd, very odd: he feigned emotion and drama on the stage but how little he had ever known of the real thing.

The streets were almost devoid of traffic. Sleeping dark houses. And going across the first of the two bridges on the spacious Ringling Causeway to the mainland, he allowed the vibration and the steady engine throb to lull him into a pleasant sense of detachment and escape.

Perhaps it was because of this that he did not notice the headlights in his rearview mirror until he was halfway across the second bridge. At first he was not surprised. He glanced at his tach and speedometer: he was cruising at about forty-four, not even five miles over the legal limit posted here. Still, because he couldn't make out the outline of the car behind, he turned the throttle forward with his right hand and slowed. If it was not a cop car, it would probably breeze past, especially since it was this time of morning.

But, instead, the car kept its exact distance—three, possibly four, car lengths behind.

Odd. Very damned odd. And not another moving light or vehicle anywhere in sight. On either side of the road. Anywhere.

Uneasy now, he was tempted to downshift and gun it. Hell, this little Triumph Bonneville could climb from forty to seventy in five seconds, maybe less.

But damned if he wanted another speeding ticket. Too expensive—he couldn't afford it on the bread the Asolo Theater paid its actors. And with two offenses against his record since coming here . . .

Now that he was off the bridge, he could pull off the pavement onto the shoulder. Let it pass. Probably some innocent drunk getting home from a late party on Lido Beach . . .

But the dude was making him nervous. Why didn't he go around?

And why did you always feel so vulnerable and exposed on a bike?

The headlights kept their distance.

His palms were damp and his muscles had tensed up.

Hell, he may as well downshift and get it over with. If a siren sounded and those blue and red lights started whirling, he could then pull over, take his medicine. Cops love to hassle bikes and Corvettes, especially when they have nothing else to do at night.

But what if they decided to hassle him, really to hassle him, maybe a body search just for the merry hell of it? He didn't have much but he did have some pot on him. And joint papers. Nothing heavy, because he didn't go for coke or even hash—but possession of how much was a misdemeanor, how much for a felony charge?

He was maintaining an even forty-five. And so was the car behind.

Opening night. His first really starring role in Sarasota, hell, the *title* role this time—the Asolo didn't take kindly to bad publicity. And he doubted the police gave a damn that he had no understudy. He had to go on tonight—what if they held him in jail? He had no money to post bond. He could lose his job. Worse, he could have a hell of a time finding another if—

Then, glancing quickly over his shoulder, he got a better view of the car. Dark. Cop cars here were white and blue. A black car . . .

What the hell then, he may as well lose him. He did downshift then: his right hand turned back the throttle on the handlebar, the bike zoomed forward, with a loud satisfying roar.

Too late, though, he saw the red light ahead. Suspended from above. Three red lights in a horizontal row.

He had reached the Trail.

No traffic. Should he run the light?

Why should he?

Because that damned black car was coming up fast from behind—

He had become an actor in college when most guys he knew were going in for sports. He couldn't fight. He'd never been able to fight. Or wanted to. . . .

He came to a stop at the wide white line. He was shaking.

But something in him would not allow him to plunge on, straight ahead or onto the Trail, to *run*. He'd never learned how to fight and he'd never learned how to run.

He applied the footbrake.

The car came to a screeching, shuddering stop alongside. On his right. He was supporting himself and the bike with his left foot on the pavement.

He turned his head.

Only one person in the car, the driver. . . .

He didn't have time to make out the man's features—only that he was about thirty-five or so, blond windblown hair, furious dark eyes, wild—

The door of the car exploded open.

It caught his right leg, hard, and he heard the blow as he felt it. But then everything took place so fast that, with the shock and pain together, he could not be sure what was happening.

He was on the pavement, his shoulder stabbing pain, his neck snapping, he could feel the weight of the bike, he was trapped under it, he smelled gasoline, and lights spun red and green and yellow between him and the sky, and then he saw the legs of the man coming around the front of the toppled bike, and the last thing he saw was one foot lifting and drawing back.

SHE had heard the telephone ring so often in her imagination in the last endless hour that when it did finally sound and she leaped up, she wondered even as she moved along the living room to the alcove whether the repeated ringing was, after all, only in her mind.

But the call—an efficient feminine voice—was for Charlene, who was taking a shower. Brenda, knocking on the bathroom door, wasn't sure whether she was disappointed or relieved: a ringing telephone could mean anything, *anything*!

While Charlene spoke, Brenda, for want of anything else to do, went to the wide front doors and slid them open a few feet. A damp breeze swept in and there was a suggestion of gray in the darkness now. Was the night really over? Where, where was Toby? And what was he thinking, feeling? Was he *suffering*?

The physical pain had somewhat subsided. Her whole face ached but it no longer throbbed. And she could walk with only an occasional twinge or piercing reminder.

But a sense of hopelessness had worked itself into her whole being much as her mind struggled against it; it now flowed bitterly in her blood. Like some dark and powerful drug. But she knew that she dare not give in. She had no way of knowing what was to come, or how long this might go on, or—

Behind her Charlene's voice spoke her name and then: "It was Sarasota Memorial Hospital." And then, when Brenda, stiffening as if she'd been stabbed, whirled about: "Not Toby, pet. Mal's been in an accident." And, beginning to remove the terry shower robe, Charlene disappeared into the hallway, lifting her voice. "He gave my name. They don't say much, or know much. It can't be too serious because he's not in intensive care. But he must have broken something. He's scheduled for surgery at seven thirty. That damned motorcycle, that *goddamned* motorcycle. When will the boy ever grow up?"

Then Charlene returned, wearing a dress, rummaging through her purse for her keys. When Brenda said nothing—all of this seemed to be happening to someone else, not her, someone else— Charlene looked up and stared and, appalled, said: "My God, I can't leave you alone like this."

Brenda listened to her own voice: "You can and you will. I'll be all right." Would she ever be all right again? "All I can do is wait anyway."

Was anybody doing anything? What the *hell* was anyone *doing*?

But she added: "Both Rex and Lieutenant Pruitt have promised to call." And then, realizing and abruptly ashamed, she asked: "Is there anything I can do for *you?*"

Charlene was outside the screen panel when she said, "Yes, there is. Ring Barry and ask him to meet me at the hospital. Why does everything always have to happen at the same time?"

And then she was gone, striding toward the white station wagon, and Brenda, suddenly grateful to be moving, went to the telephone in the alcove.

Her hands were not shaking as she thumbed through the directory. There was no Barry Conrad listed. She heard the sound of the station wagon receding down the street. A numbness took over. Then panic. Barry's number was not listed! Why, *why*?

But then she remembered. Of course! Barry lived on Anna Maria Island. Bradenton, not Sarasota, Bradenton. She dialed information. She thanked the operator. She dialed.

The phone at the other end of the line rang over and over and over and over. She was clutching the instrument, pressing it painfully against her ear. She was thinking of how good a thing it would be to have a brother. A brother to whom you could turn. She let the phone go on ringing. And then she remembered Toby saying: Guess what? *H-h-he has this big workshop but he sleeps on his boat. N-n-neat.*

Toby. She must not think of Toby. She must not remember, she—

"H'lo?"

She recognized his voice at once. "Mr. Conrad?" A picture flashed in her mind: the short trimmed red-brown beard, the soft shy brown eyes.

"Yes. Brenda?"

How had he known her voice?

"Barry?" she said.

"What is it, Brenda?"

"Charlene asked me to call."

"Charlene? Is she—"

"She wants you to meet her at the Sarasota Memorial Hospital. There's been an accident. Mal. Something's happened to Mal."

"I'm on my way. Brenda—"

"Yes?"

"How are *you?*"

Suddenly, wildly, she was tempted to tell him, to shout it, to burst into tears. . . .

But, instead, she said: "I'm just a bit sleepy." A lie. "This sea air."

"I don't like the way your voice sounds, Brenda."

"Well"—stalling—"it's a difficult time." To say the least, to say the *very* least! But he knew that—she had sensed his knowing in his quiet eyes over the dinner table. "Nothing I can't get through."

"I'll let you know what's up. G'bye, Brenda. Go back to bed."

And then, when she'd replaced the phone, while she sat staring at it but not seeing it, she started to cry.

Tears blinded her and covered her face and dripped off her chin, and she could hear the sound echoing through the empty house. She sat quite still and gave herself over to the deep, wracking, convulsive sobs. She lowered her head until her forehead rested on top of the telephone in its cradle.

It was then that the phone rang. Loud and jarring and harsh.

She straightened and lifted it on the second ring.

"Yes?"

"Your line's been busy." At first, but only for a second or two, she did not recognize his voice. "Who've you been talking to— your pop?"

Just like that. As casual and friendly and slightly mocking as if he'd been phoning home from the office.

She was tempted to scream: Pop's in the hospital. Because of you, *because of you!* But, stunned, she said nothing, waited.

"How are you, Brenda?"

"How am I? How *am* I?"

"Now, now, control yourself."

"Where's Toby?"

"Toby? He's here with me. We're shacked up in a flea-bitten little motel. Batch-ing it, as they say."

No rush, no urgency—sweet, sweet reason reverberated politely in his tone. She could picture his eyes now: pale and calm, without anger or rancor. The quiet, composed Donald Forrest whom everybody knew. . . .

"May I—let me speak to Toby!"

"Toby's snoozing. And playing games. He won't even talk to me."

"Please, Donald. I have to talk to Toby."

"Not till you tell me you forgive me, Brenda."

Forgive? She would never forgive him. But, suddenly cunning, she said: "I forgive you, Donald." Never, *never!* "I understand." And, with deceit to buttress the lie: "You were drinking."

"True, baby, true." A fresh confidence in his voice: "And you *know* how sorry I am, don't you?"

"Yes, yes, I know." She didn't doubt. True it might be, true it undoubtedly was—but his remorse, however genuine, meant nothing. She said: "Now wake Toby, will you?"

"Brenda—darling, you've been crying, haven't you?"

Crying? "No, Donald," she said, "I've been laughing. I've been laughing my silly head off."

"I didn't really hurt you, did I? I'm sorry I hit you but I lost my temper when you bit me."

So . . . it was *her* fault. If she had not lost *her* temper, *he* wouldn't have slugged her. "It was my fault," she lied. Because she had to talk to Toby, had to make sure . . .

"I know just how hard to hit," he said reasonably, sensibly, no problem, no problem. "I might've broken your jaw if— Oh, Brenda, I didn't really hurt you, did I? You didn't really feel a thing, did you?"

When you raped me? No, not a thing. But she asked, "When are you going to bring him home?"

"Home? Home, Brenda?"

She realized her mistake. She said quickly: "When am I going to see Toby?"

"Home. That's when you're going to see him. When we're on our way home. Together."

So . . . so that was it.

"I told you last night, Brenda. I get the boat at nine this morning."

"And if I refuse?"

"If you won't play ball, Toby and I are taking off. Mexico, Bahamas. Puerto Rico. Europe. You'll never know."

He still spoke with that detached self-composure—confident, assuming she had no choice. Assuming again that what *he* wanted, had to be.

"Well, baby?"

She wished she could afford to doubt him. She couldn't.

"It's the only way you'll ever see him again," Donald said.

Hostage. Hostage and ransom. It *was* a kidnapping after all. . . .

"You know where the Sarasota Yacht Club is, Brenda?"

"I . . . I've seen the sign."

"Not five minutes from where you are. On the right before you cross the first bridge on the Ringling Causeway."

"Yes?"

"Ten o'clock. Sharp. All packed and ready. We'll dock and pick you up."

Was this happening? Was this really happening? She couldn't do it. But she couldn't leave Toby alone with him. And on a *boat*. He'd come to hate boats since that day his father had thrown him overboard. Oh, God, she couldn't allow Toby to be alone on a boat with this madman, this lunatic, this—

"Donald, you're crazy!" She heard the shrieking in her voice. She struggled for control. "Donald, you can't do this to your own son!"

"Brenda, I'm not doing anything to Toby."

"You can't do this to me!"

Silence. She was cold but not shaking. She was very still, waiting.

"I wouldn't do anything to you, Brenda. Not ever. I love you. You know that."

"Well, *I* don't love you. I *hate* you." And she did. Now. At last! Only now, or was she only just admitting it now? "Hate, hate, hate!"

Another silence. Longer this time. She heard a mourning dove's soft cooing in the quiet. She heard a sea gull cawing. She was consumed by hate. Devoured by it. And weak all over.

"You don't mean that," the hated voice said, still quiet, still rational and low and positive, even sad. "Brenda, haven't you learned anything out of all this? Don't you realize? Can't you get it through your lovely head? You can't run away from me. I'll find you anywhere you go. Like I found you here. You're part of me, Brenda. I can't help myself. You're in my blood."

And he was in hers, too—a poison, a contamination, *pollution*! Choking, she could not speak.

"You love me, too, Brenda. I know."

How do you know? Because that's what you want—that makes it *real*. But she knew that she had no choice. He had given her no choice.

"I can't come, Donald. You come here. We'll talk—"

"We'll have days to talk. Weeks. Months. On the boat."

Hopeless, hopeless.

And then another thought slithered into her mind: What if all this self-assurance, this titanic calm, was only a symptom? What if, deep in him, he had actually cracked up? She had read somewhere that people reach a certain brink and that after going over the edge they reach a euphoric sense of well-being, a sort of self-induced high. Emotional breakdowns, she knew, took amazing turns, revealed themselves in strange and unpredictable ways.

If, if, if this had happened, then what about Toby?

"I'll be there," she said. "Ten o'clock."

"I knew you would, darling. All we need is time together, that's all."

"Now . . . let me talk to Toby."

A long sigh. "Darling, you'll see him in less than four hours. You don't want *him* to get excited, too, do you? Let him sleep. He'd only get hysterical, too. And Brenda—"

"Yes?"

"No tricks, right?"

What could she do? What tricks? She could have Lieutenant Pruitt waiting at the dock. *Even if the police find your boy, they can't arrest his own father for kidnap.* Rex Maynard had warned her: *On the assault and battery charge, the dumbest lawyer in town will have him out on bail within an hour or so.*

And then what? Why, then it would start all over again.

"No tricks," she said. Because she had none up her sleeve.

"Brenda—"

"Haven't we said enough?"

"Brenda, you lied to me."

"I always lie to you, don't I, Donald?"

"You said there was no man." His tone was soft and silken. "You did lie."

She was again tempted to scream: *Not one man, you bastard— hundreds, thousands! As many as desire me. As many as will have me!* But she said, "Good-bye, Donald."

And she was about to set down the phone when she heard him laugh. Once. Shortly. She hesitated.

"He got his," Donald said.

She listened.

"No use lying, Brenda. I saw you kiss him in the doorway. But he got his."

Click. She was holding a dead telephone.

So it had not been an accident then.

Whatever had happened to Mal—

Oh, God, had she caused that, too?

The fight had been drained out of her.

Black tidal waves of despair moved in.

She had no choices now. He had won.

She could not move.

She didn't need to move for four hours. The yacht club was only five minutes away.

———□———

"You asleep, buddy, or are you faking that, too?"

Toby was not asleep. Yes, he was faking it. But he wasn't faking the other. The other he didn't understand at all. He really couldn't talk.

"Playing games, are you, old buddy?"

He kept his eyes shut. But not too tight shut or it wouldn't look natural. Without seeing, he could picture the room; twin beds, a TV, a kind of old beat-up dresser, rugs on a cement floor that had been cold on his bare feet. Linoleum, cracked and sharp, in the tiny smelly bathroom. The whole place smelled. Mama had taken him to Holiday Inns. But he could not think of Mama now. He wished he'd been able to talk to her on the phone just now. But Daddy had told him to get in bed, cover up, and go to sleep. And he didn't want to get slapped again. Daddy slapped hard. His teeth still hurt.

Talk to me, you little brat. Stop making that damned noise and spit it out!

All he'd been trying to say, in the car, after what had happened to Mal, all he'd been trying to say was that they ought to go back, that Mal might be really hurt.

But all he could do was open his mouth and his throat would make that strange, weird sound trying to speak the words that he had formed and ready in his mind.

Then Daddy, driving with one hand, had slapped him. Hard.

Now he didn't even *want* to talk. To Mama, yes, on the phone, but he'd known Daddy'd never let him do that. And while they were talking, he thought of sitting up and screaming. He wasn't sure he could but he *thought* he could. But if Daddy had slapped him that hard for trying to talk, what would he do if he yelled? And besides, he hadn't wanted to worry Mama any more than she was. He'd heard her voice, once, almost screeching at the other end of the line but he hadn't been able to make out the words.

"Okay, buddy, you can go on playing games. I'm going to take a pee and if you try any funny business—like trying to get out of here—I'll give you what my old man used to give me. With my belt. So you remember that, you phony. Just like your mother—full of tricks, full of lies."

Then he heard the sound of the chain being hooked on the door and Daddy go into the bathroom. But he didn't hear the bathroom door close.

Was the chain too high for him to reach? He hadn't noticed. And if he could get out, where could he go? The office was probably dark but the old man who'd given Daddy the key—while Toby had been hunched down on the floor—the old man might still be awake. Watching TV maybe.

He could tell the old man he wasn't Daddy's son. Which was true. Daddy was not his father anymore. He decided that. So it wouldn't even be a lie. He'd decided that in the car when he was supposed to be looking for VACANCY signs. Daddy was not his father. Not anymore. From now on. But, because he couldn't talk, he couldn't tell him. But saying it in words didn't make it true or untrue, one or the other. Knowing it—that's what counted, that's what made it true.

Hearing Daddy using the toilet, he took the chance. He opened his eyes. The crummy room. And now, outside the closed curtains, it was beginning to get light. So it must be morning. On the dresser he saw the bottle of whiskey the old man had sold Daddy.

Which he'd been drinking ever since they got here. *Fifty bucks for a cheap five-buck bourbon and not even a full bottle at that. Florida's full of pirates, buddy—thieves.*

Then he heard the toilet flushing.

Too late now to try to run. So he turned over onto his tummy and shut his eyes again. Maybe if this man, this man who was not his father, maybe if he drank too much he'd go to sleep himself and then—

She kissed him. The little bitch kissed him, I saw her!

That was after the man got back in the car when it was parked in the driveway of the house next door to the house he'd just begun really to like, the Japanese one. He had heard voices but he hadn't been able to see because of the big shrubs between but the man had gotten out of the car and he saw. And when he was sitting there behind the wheel, kind of shaking, waiting for Mal's bike to leave, the man had said, *So that's your friend Mal, is it?*

Then that ride, following Mal, knowing something awful was

going to happen—the man had made him sit on the floor so he couldn't see, but he knew they were following the bike. He begged then, blubbering like a crybaby, till the man growled: *Shut up or I'll give you what I ought to give him.*

He must not think about that now. He must not think about that, *ever.* If only he could pretend it never happened . . .

The man was in the room again. He was pouring more whiskey into the glass. Toby could hear the clinking, and then the gurgling sound of the man drinking. He heard the curtains sliding on the rod and the click of the light switch. Then the springs squeaking on the other bed. Maybe, maybe . . .

But, while he waited, lying very very still and waiting and hoping, he remembered the scene under the stop-and-go lights. When the car had come to a jolting stop and the door had opened—like a bomb going off—and he had caught just a quick glimpse of the bike and Mal's surprised face under the helmet as the bike toppled over on him. The engine still running, the man climbing out, and after that, too scared to look, he had curled up on the floor, listening but not wanting to hear: thumps and thuds and grunts and no voices, no words, only that funny sound over and over, a flat wooden sound over and over and over . . .

That's when he'd thrown up. On the floor. On his pajamas. All over. He couldn't help himself.

He wondered whether he'd ever be able to forget. What he'd heard and then the way he felt when he saw the man's bloody knuckles on the steering wheel, and then *Christ, this car stinks* and then *Puking little coward* and then, after crying and trying to beg the man to go back but making only that hoarse funny sound till his throat ached, the man finally saying, *There's a vacancy sign, are you blind as well as dumb?*

Dumb. That meant stupid but it also meant, he knew, someone who couldn't talk. Like blind means you can't see.

He heard the man pouring another drink.

The funny thing, though, the thing that really confused him, even now, was the change in the man after they were settled and he'd had maybe half a glass of whiskey: he'd just *changed*, that's all. He became cheerful and kind of playful, like everything was a big joke, or a game, and when he'd talked to Mama on the phone, he'd been more the way he used to be, in the good times.

He'd asked Toby whether he needed any help in taking his bath and he'd said he was sorry there'd been no place open to get hamburgers and how it was too bad they had to stay here in this dump that didn't even have a snack machine or candy bars. Then, on the phone with Mama, he'd been so friendly. Like nothing at all had really happened.

Toby couldn't figure it out. He didn't *care*. He didn't even want to figure it out. Not anymore. The man was a stranger and he didn't care. He didn't hate him or love him or hate him or love him, he just didn't care.

But one thing he knew: He was not going to get on any boat.

He listened. He heard a deep, steady, heavy breathing. Not a snore, though.

He waited. Then he opened one eye.

The man was stretched out on his back and one hand hung down off the bed. With the empty glass in it.

He glanced at the door. The chain, if he stood on his tiptoes, was within reach. But he'd better wait a few minutes longer. He'd better make sure.

Ten o'clock. Sharp. All packed and ready. We'll dock and pick you up.

How long till ten o'clock? It was light outside now.

He was not going to get on any boat.

I'll bet you really can swim and don't know it. He thought of Barry. Who had taught him to ride the bicycle. *It's really a matter of confidence.* He remembered Barry driving the Jeep on their way to Barry's workshop after dinner. *Like riding the bike, same thing. But you do have to let yourself go. You have to believe your body won't go down, really believe it in your mind. Then all you have to do is keep moving your legs or your arms, or both.* Barry smoked his pipe and his lips smiled in his beard. *Main part's in your head, though. Maybe I'll have a chance to show you what I mean.*

But Barry had not had the chance. Now he probably never would.

And Toby knew, because of what had happened last summer, that he couldn't swim. So he was not going out on any boat. . . .

Was the man asleep? His mouth was open. Kind of slack. He was snoring now.

This was his chance.

Slowly he edged his body under the covers to the far side of the bed, away from the hanging arm. He paused. No change in the snoring.

He lowered himself to the small rug and then he was crawling on hands and knees, off the rug onto the bare floor in the direction of the door. The floor felt damp, smelled sour like his pajamas.

When he was beyond the bed, he could see the figure of the man on the bed, a kind of hump, and the glass held in the hand with the swollen purple knuckles.

Carefully, very slowly, he brought his body upright. The air chilled his body and the cement was cold under his bare feet.

First the chain and then, even more slowly, to turn the lock. He took a last look at the bed. Then he reached. The chain was curved above his head but his hand reached it.

He was sliding the chain, inching the round metal plug along its track, when the glass fell from the man's hand and shattered on the concrete floor with a terrible crash.

───□───

Over and beyond the call of duty: it was a phrase Waldo Pruitt's wife used to use when she was chiding him for allowing himself to become too involved in some case or other. He'd as often as not regretted that tendency himself—especially in those cases where his spleen had been stirred up. He'd done some things, some brutal things, that he didn't relish looking back on. But that was pretty much his life now: looking back. Aurora'd been dead— how many?—nine or ten years now. And since then he hadn't slept too well—she'd been a cheerful scold but just one hell of a woman—so he didn't mind spending a night like this one in a good cause. A foolish one, maybe even hopeless, but a good one.

This way he did feel connected to something. And as the reports of the night's misdemeanors and felonies drifted to his desk, as requested—he gave particular attention to the DWIs tonight—he went over them one by one, again pondering the ever-strange fact that so many human beings could waste so much of their lives doing harm to other human beings, and to themselves. Why, hell, it was hard to believe, but in Florida alone last year there'd been more than a thousand reported homicides. Disheartening. Not to mention the suicides, the maimings, the drownings, accidental and otherwise—it still gets me down, Aurora, after twenty-seven years it still gets me down.

Tonight there'd been more than the usual domestic disputes involving violence, three resulting in hospitalization, and five separate barroom altercations, two of them brawls—but you had to expect this the night before the full moon. Let 'em laugh, the smart young know-it-alls—facts are facts. The switchboard was always and invariably swamped. The kooks went really whacky this time of month, no doubt about it in his mind.

Look at this, for example: a plain case of aggravated assault and battery on a motorcyclist at Ringling and the Trail. Probably the busiest intersection in the county. Approximate time 4:30. Two hours ago. Victim a Malcolm Eggers, age twenty-five, address a rooming house on Third Street. No witnesses. No description of the perpetrator, only a general description of the car he drove leaving the scene in a southerly direction: black Mercury, late model. The report had been radioed in from car 19 by Patrolman Ned Stanley.

He threw the last batch of reports into a wire basket. Dead end. It had been this way ever since he'd left Attorney Maynard's house in Whitfield Estates around 2:30. The extra patrol car he'd put on in the St. Armand's–Lido Shores area had spotted nothing unusual and he'd had no reports from anyone else, anywhere. All he knew really, because he'd checked this out personally, was that the 1981 Cougar, black, had not been returned to the Hertz office in either Sarasota or Tampa. So the boy and his father *could* still be in the area. But that was a damned weak supposition based on a single—

Black. Mercury. Late model.

He did not reach for the wire basket. He did not need to read the report again.

Cougar.

Sign of the cat.

The Cougar was a Mercury model.

He felt a faint prickling at the back of his neck.

He heaved his big heavy body to a standing position and picked up the phone. Hell, he was stymied anyway. He had nothing better to do.

He asked to be connected to patrol car 19, Officer Ned Stanley.

Who knows? There was no law against what the papers had begun to call "childnapping." No crime if neither parent has separate custody awarded by the courts in a legal action. He'd read of cases where the parent and child had just disappeared, dropped out of existence. And he didn't have to be reminded by lawyers like Maynard and Miss Rinaldi that even the Justice Department opposed criminalizing parental kidnapping for fear it would bring the FBI into thousands of domestic disputes. Simple fact: Without an actual crime to work on, he was wasting his time here.

Unless . . .

The prickling had moved from the base of his skull out to his thick shoulders and down his beefy arms.

"Patrolman Stanley, car nineteen." The voice was young but Waldo Pruitt could not connect it with a face in his mind. "You wanted to talk to me, Lieutenant?"

"On the A and B, Ringling and forty-one couple hours ago—"

"Yes, sir?"

"Your report is incomplete."

"Yes, sir, I know. But you see, there were no witnesses, sir, only the driver of the eighteen-wheeler and all he saw was the victim on the pavement and the motorcycle on its side when he stopped at the light. And the vehicle I reported. It was leaving the scene, but south, as I stated, so the truck driver didn't get a good look."

"The victim must have seen who beat him up."

"Yes, sir. But, Lieutenant, I couldn't question him at the scene. He was almost unconscious and in a state of shock. He did shake his head when I asked if he recognized the perpetrator."

"Didn't you follow through at the hospital?"

"Oh, yes, sir. But you have to understand. The interrogation was carried out under impossible conditions. He was under medication in the emergency room and they had immobilized his jaw. He's an actor employed by the Asolo Theater and he wrote down the name and address of next of kin, who has been notified. The other data I got from his ID and driver's license."

"Theories, Officer Stanley?"

"Well . . . we found some pot on his person, but not much. I doubt he's dealing but we all know it can be bought at City

Island and/or the south end of Lido—lots of places in the area of his address, too."

"Then you think that might tie in with the motive somehow . . . ?

"No, sir. I figure he and the man in the other car had some sort of altercation over driving. Maybe he gave the other guy the finger and the driver of the car lost his temper and then caught up with Eggers at the stoplight. It's all speculation, sir. But he was beaten up pretty bad. And oh, yes, he wasn't robbed. It must have all happened very fast. That's why there were no witnesses that time of morning. The assailant really let the poor guy have it. With both fists, and at least one kick in the ribs."

"One more thing, Officer—"

"Yes, sir?"

"Did you ask the truck driver—specifically—whether the assailant was alone in the car?"

"I did, Lieutenant. He said he saw only one head in the vehicle."

The prickling sensation had gone. But of course the kid could have been asleep in the backseat. Through a fracas like that? Fat chance.

"Add those details to your report when you come in," Waldo Pruitt said; and then he added, "You did all right, kid."

"Thank you, sir."

Waldo Pruitt snapped off the radio connection. Officer Stanley had done all right but he hadn't had some of the information that Waldo had. And he hadn't had some of the questions that still nagged at Waldo's mind. So, tired of sitting on his tail anyway, Waldo decided to mosey down to the hospital, less than a mile away from the station: maybe, just to clear his own mind, he'd ask those questions himself.

On the way, no siren and driving at a normal rate of speed, Waldo told himself that he was barking up the wrong tree. This Donald Forrest, he had no quarrel with anyone but his wife. *He was a boxer in college.* Proves nothing. Implicates no one. *You don't know Donald. Anything can happen. He's capable of anything.* He was a hunter refusing to admit he was on a cold trail. Another one, Aurora. Dawn. Aurora. It was getting lighter by the minute now.

There were only two ways to the mainland off Lido Shores: the long way north up Longboat Key to Anna Maria Island, or the shorter and more likely way—across the two bridges of the Ringling Causeway to the stoplight at the corner where Ringling met the Trail.

The nurse on duty in the emergency room did not, she said, have the authority to permit him to see the patient now. The patient was, she said, scheduled for surgery at seven. But she would summon Dr. Rosser. Surgery?

Waldo went into a small waiting room. A couple was seated there: a striking-looking tall young woman with stunned eyes and a young man with a reddish beard.

The young woman stood up. "Are you going to get him?" she asked, her gray eyes on Waldo. "I heard you talking to the nurse. What are the police doing?"

"As much as we can," Waldo said, facing the two of them, hearing that familiar question for perhaps the thousandth time. "Are you a relative?"

The bearded young man stood up then. "My sister is a close friend." He had a mild, diffident manner that Waldo found refreshing. "Fact is, Mal had just left her shortly before this thing happened."

"Do you have any idea who did this to him?"

"Not yet, miss." And it was true, too. He was way out there in the cold blue yonder and only playing hunches again. "Do you?"

The young woman shook her head. "Everyone loves Mal."

"Tell me, miss—when he left you, where would that be?"

"At my house."

"And where might that be, miss?"

The brother spoke. "Eleven-sixty-eight Westway."

Waldo knew the address. The prickling returned to his neck. "Lido Shores?" And when the young woman nodded: "And Mr. Eggers considers you his next-of-kin?"

"He gave the policeman her name and address," the brother said. "His family lives in New Jersey. But now they won't let her see him because he's going to be operated on."

Scowling, Waldo asked: "Do either of you know anyone who might hold a grudge against your friend?"

The brother, his own eyes negative, regarded his sister quizzically.

But she shook her head. "I told you—everyone loves Mal. It has to be a stranger."

Waldo decided not to mention his conversation with Mrs. Forrest almost five hours ago now. Not just yet—after all, he had very little to go on. Nothing, really, except that address. So he said, "If they'll let me see Mr. Eggers, I might get some idea how to proceed."

"Lieutenant Pruitt?" It was a young voice behind him and when he turned, he discovered a chubby young doctor in white with a casual but oddly distant and yet efficient manner. "I'm Dr. Rosser. Come with me, please."

He ushered Waldo into an adjoining office, small and bare. Without further palaver Dr. Rosser said: "In a very few minutes the patient will be prepped for surgery."

"Surgery?" Waldo asked.

"Not the conventional sort," the doctor said. "There appear to be no significant internal injuries. The right knee is fractured, probably when the bike fell over on it, and there are lacerations, a dislocated shoulder, contusions, one broken rib. But the major damage seems to have been done to the face. And it is major."

"Good God," Waldo Pruitt said. He hadn't expected this, anything like this.

"They'll do the best they can this morning but there'll have to be more surgery later if the face is to be restored. And, at that, I have doubts it'll ever be the same. A lot of mutilation can be done by two fists. Our friend was lucky he was wearing that helmet."

And when Waldo—still capable of shock, still subject to revulsion and anger—did not answer, Dr. Rosser went on: "I don't know law, Lieutenant, but if you're here to determine the degree of the crime by the extent of the injuries, I'd say you have one hell of a case."

"I'd like to ask Mr. Eggers three questions. Correct that—two questions. The lady out there, Miss—"

"Miss Charlene Conrad," the doctor said. "Mr. Eggers has no relatives closer than New Jersey. I'm afraid he shouldn't be bothered with questions at this point. And he couldn't answer them even if his face were not bandaged as it is."

"Two questions," Waldo persisted. "He can nod his head yes or shake his head no."

The young doctor considered. "Is it important? Now?"

"If I'm right, we might be able to prevent something like this happening to someone else. This, or worse."

"This way, please."

They took the elevator and in an alcove off a hallway where a few patients lay on carts outside the swinging doors marked POSITIVELY NO ADMITTANCE, the two men faced Malcolm Eggers, whose bed was adjusted by a nurse in surgical green so that his head, swathed in white, was in a semi-upright position. His eyes, almost invisible, peered out. They appeared dazed and filled with dread, but there was curiosity there, too.

"Mal," Dr. Rosser said, "Lieutenant Pruitt is a police officer. He's going to ask you two questions, and only two. No matter how painful or difficult, I want you to nod yes or shake your head no. Lieutenant Pruitt thinks it's important. Lieutenant?"

Waldo stepped to the bed. "Mr. Eggers—you've already told the investigating officer that you did not recognize your assailant. Now—was there a child in the car?"

A long moment. During which Waldo thought that the young man had not heard or perhaps was considering his answer carefully. It was also possible, Waldo realized, that he himself had just suggested a possibility that had some meaning to Eggers, something that perhaps Eggers himself had not thought of until now.

At last, slowly, the head moved from side to side.

Waldo took a step. Another dead end? There was no prickling at the back of his neck now. His big body was a mass of hot sweat.

"One more," he said and reached into the inside pocket of his jacket to bring out a small photograph. The one Mrs. Forrest had produced from her purse while she made that bitter, feeble little joke about hers being a close family. Waldo took another rolling step and held the picture about a foot from the young man's eyes.

"Mr. Eggers—is this the man who attacked you?"

And then Waldo saw, or imagined he saw, a glint in the tired, pain-filled eyes. And, while he held the photograph steadily, he felt the familiar prickling return to the base of his skull and begin to spread, even before the young man, with some vigor, nodded his head.

A cold pleasant chill went down Waldo Pruitt's frame and in a moment the flesh of his enormous body was tingling all over.

———□———

When he found no one in the house but the blue Lancia Zagato parked in the driveway, Barry walked down the street a hundred yards or so, to the grove of Australian pines and through the woods toward the beach. The sky was a leaden gray and heavy clouds hovered in the west over the Gulf. It would turn breezy soon and then, later, it would probably rain in drenching showers off and on. And the tourists would complain because they expected brilliant sunshine every day, all day.

For three hours now, ever since he had joined Charlene for the vigil in the hospital waiting room shortly after six o'clock, he had been torn between his loyalty to Charlene, her need for him, and—once Charlene had told him that Toby was missing—his feeling that he, somebody at least, should be with Brenda. *Nightmare,* Charlene had whispered as she came into his arms when he arrived, *the whole night's been a nightmare, Barry. First, Toby— and now this. It makes no sense. I can't believe it's happening.*

Trying to comfort and reassure her, his words sounding like tired truisms in his mind, he could only hope that his presence would be more meaningful than the trite and feeble phrases. All the while, though, he had been thinking of Toby, too. All Charlene knew really was that the police were not doing much because Brenda was convinced his father had taken him and although she insisted this was all she knew, he suspected otherwise: there was something more. What? Did it have to do with Brenda?

Then, while Mal was in surgery, he had phoned Brenda and had then reported to Charlene: It was definite that Toby *was* with his father and Brenda was leaving with them both on a boat at ten o'clock. Brenda had sounded faraway, lifeless, resigned—but determined. And she had inquired over and over about Malcolm Eggers—almost as if she had transferred her concern for her son to Charlene's friend, whom she could not know very well. As he, Barry, did not know Brenda; and now never would.

On the long stretch of white beach there were only a few figures:

a pot-bellied man jogging, two elderly women shelling, two or three strollers. And Brenda. She was walking slowly, head down. She wore slacks and a pale soft sweater and she was carrying her shoes. She didn't see him until he had crunched across the surf-crushed shell and fine sand and stopped in her path a few yards away.

Then she brought one hand up as if to shade her eyes, although there was no sun, and at this distance he could not be sure but it appeared that her lips trembled very briefly. She lowered her arm and stood waiting for him to join her. She looked frail and lost and alone—abandoned. But then her chin lifted, her shoulders asserted themselves, and she spoke in a clear controlled tone: "How's Mal?"

"He's out of surgery."

"And?"

He hesitated. Could he tell her what the surgeon had told him and Charlene? That even with extensive plastic surgery, over a period of time, the boy's face would never be quite the same. Would she burst into tears as Charlene had done?

"Barry," Brenda said, "I'm a big girl. Tell me, please."

Still, he evaded. "His jaws will have to be wired together for eight to ten weeks. He'll have to exist on a liquid diet."

"It's worse than that," Brenda said. "Tell me."

Puzzled by her quiet intense interest concentrated on Mal instead of on herself at a time like this, he said: "He'll never look the same, Brenda. If that's what you're asking."

She nodded. "It is." And she began to walk along the edge of the surf line where wet sand met dry. "Poor Charlene, poor kind Charlene. I knew, I *knew*."

He was walking alongside, quiveringly aware, as he had been all through last evening, of her physical presence—not so much of her body in itself or of her appearance, but of her *presence*, her being. It was a new and strange feeling for him and suddenly he knew that, in years to come, he would never forget this moment.

"You said you're going north," he heard himself say, wondering if it sounded like a question. "Around ten?"

"At ten. *Ten* sharp, per instructions." The sharp bitterness of her tone surprised him. "My jailer calls," she said. "Life sentence, no parole."

And she changed direction, turning toward the shadowy cave of woods leading to the street and house beyond.

"Charlene's not here," he said. And when she missed a step, then stopped and turned: "Some of Mal's friends from the theater are making breakfast for her."

Brenda's dark brown eyes, meeting his, took on a knowing, accepting look. "She blames me, doesn't she?"

Baffled, he asked, "For what, Brenda? Why should she blame you for anything?"

"I should never have come," Brenda said and turned to walk again.

And he remembered. *You go, pet. I don't know what sort of spell she placed on you but you give yourself away every time her name is mentioned. I really don't know how I feel yet but you tell Brenda good-bye for me.* It had mystified him then, a half hour ago, and now the mystery was deepening. Again he had the disconcerting sensation that he was trying to put a puzzle together but that a key piece was missing. What? What did Mal's mishap, or whatever it was, have to do with Brenda? And what could Charlene possibly blame Brenda for?

Abruptly he felt the impulse to step into Brenda's path, to take her into his arms, just once, to say good-bye, to kiss her lips, just once before she disappeared forever, just once . . .

But it was Brenda who spoke: "Barry, you've been kind. You and Charl and Lavinia—you've all been so kind. I'll never forget you. Will you tell Charl? No matter how she feels now—will you tell her? Promise?"

"I promise," he said bleakly, even more bewildered. Then they were on the narrow paved street, walking side by side, strangers.

On the large platformlike porch he heard the telephone ringing inside the house.

Brenda halted. He glanced at her. Her face looked stricken—again unprotected, defenseless. A frightened child.

"Shall I get it?" he asked.

All the fixed determination had drained from her face. She only nodded. Once. And as he went inside and crossed to the alcove, he had the impression that she was a woman—a girl, a *child!*—who had coped with as much as she risked coping with at this particular moment.

"H'lo?"

"Who's this?" The voice of a stranger: deep, startled, on the verge of hostility.

"This is Barry. Whom did you want?"

Behind him, Barry heard the screen panel slide open and shut. Brenda had come inside.

"Did you want to speak to Charlene? She's not here."

"I want," the voice said, "I want to speak to my wife. *Please.*"

"Brenda?"

"Mrs. Forrest. My wife. Yes. Now."

"Mrs. Forrest is not here, either. May I take a message?"

"Yes, you *may*. *If* you'll be so fucking kind. Tell her I'm calling from the boat. I've got the boat and I'll see her in twenty minutes exactly at the yacht club. Who the hell are you?"

But before he could answer, Brenda took the phone from his hand. Very close, he caught a quick startling view of her face: pale, tight, scowling, her brown eyes black with anger. He relinquished the phone and moved into the living room. He did not close the panel that separated the alcove from the main room. Damned if he would!

He went to stare out the front doors, which were open wide.

He heard her voice: "It's none of your business but he's Charlene's brother. . . . It's not ten yet. I said I'd be there and I will. . . . I don't have to answer any more questions. Let me talk to Toby. . . . If you don't I'm not coming."

If he had not known who was speaking, Barry would not have recognized Brenda's voice: flat, cold, decisive—tinged, Barry thought, with contempt, or worse.

"Toby? Toby, are you there?"

Now her voice had changed again. She spoke with a hot rush of feeling.

"Toby, it's Mama. Talk to me . . . Toby?"

And then she waited. A delivery truck passed along the street. Brenda said nothing. Barry heard Charlene's mockingbird from atop the electric wires in the rear.

Otherwise, nothing.

Until Brenda's voice erupted in a heartrending plea: "Toby, Toby, please stop making that sound, don't try, don't try to say anything now, just *listen*: I'll be with you in a few minutes now, darling. Soon, soon. You don't have to say anything, don't try. Mama understands. Now, give the phone to Daddy—"

And while she waited, Barry heard her whisper: "My God, oh, my God, what has he done to you?"

Then, in a scream that filled the house: "What have you done to him? What have you done to Toby? . . . Liar, liar, he is *not* playing games, he is not asking for sympathy, he can't talk, oh, you bastard, you bastard, you put Mal Eggers in the hospital, you smashed in his face and now this, now this!"

But she did not hang up.

Now he knew. Now he, blind stupid Barry Conrad, knew what had really happened to Malcolm Eggers—who had done it, why Charlene felt as she did, why Brenda felt responsible.

"I'm coming," Brenda said at last—and in still another tone that Barry had never heard before—a bitter, contained wildness, harshness grating in every word. "Oh, I'll be there, Donald, you can count on that. I'll be there and we'll all three go sailing north together, ride, forever ride!"

She threw down the phone with such violence that Barry could hear the clatter from where he stood.

He walked toward Brenda, who in a low hopeless tone said: "You heard, so now you know."

"I still don't understand, Brenda." It took an effort of will not to go to her. "Why Mal?"

Her eyes were almost mocking but her tone remained the same, low and flat and ugly. "I kissed him on the cheek. To thank him."

"Jesus."

"And now Toby doesn't stutter anymore. He stammers so bad he can hardly say a single word."

"You think Toby saw what happened?"

"I know he did."

He moved then, but only a few steps. "Brenda—you can't go back to a man like that."

"Oh? Do I have a choice?"

"I'll take you to Holmes Beach. You can stay with Lavinia. He'll never find you."

Brenda snorted a laugh. "And Toby?"

"Let the police handle it."

But she was shaking her head slowly from side to side. "No

crime, no help, sorry. Possession is nine tenths of something or other."

"Brenda—"

She exploded. "Barry, stay out of this! Get out! I can't bring any more trouble to anybody, you or Lavinia or anybody! Get out now and good-bye! It's not your life. You have nothing to do with this! You're not *in* it!"

He went to her then. "I'm in it, Brenda. I don't know how it happened, or why, but I'm damned well in it."

And then he did reach. He did take her into his arms.

And, as if the hard coldness had gone out of her, her body came against him and he held her.

He reached with one hand and took her face in it and tilted her head back and kissed her, very lightly at first, on the lips.

Then, as if her whole being had quickened to vibrant, pulsing life, she responded. She placed her hand behind his head and held his mouth against hers and he could feel her whole body quivering against his.

But then the quick desperation died. She drew her head back and then her body began to move protestingly in his arms so that he released her.

They stood facing each other a long moment and then she moved away, almost strolling.

"Why," she asked—and she had changed again—"why do men always imagine everything can be solved by sex?"

It was like a blow. For a split second he thought he might double over from its impact.

"Thanks, Barry, but no thanks. I've had enough of that for one lifetime. I'm not in the market. Comfort me with apples."

He had no idea what to say. But another part of the puzzle fell into place—that piece that Charlene had withheld. Probably out of loyalty to Brenda. He knew now what had happened between the moment her husband had knocked her out and the time he had taken her son. He was sick, and furious. And now he began to hate a man he had never met, a man he had never even seen. He began to hate him murderously.

He heard himself say, "Let me get on the boat when you do."

She was frowning. "I told you, Barry. I refuse to bring any more . . . any more destruction. Any more *pain!*"

"But *you* haven't, Brenda. Keep it straight for God's sake! You haven't done anything. *He* has."

"Through me. Because of me!"

"Damn it, you can't blame yourself!"

She turned away—changed again. When she spoke, her tone was as rigid and severe as her back. "I know what I can do. The *only* thing I can do. Now, if you'll get the hell out of here, I'll get on with it. I said good-bye. I meant good-bye."

But he couldn't leave. He had to know: "What are you thinking of, Brenda? What are you planning?"

She whirled about to face him again, her eyes wild and terrible. "That's my business. None of this has anything to do with you. Can't you get that straight? Whatever happens now, it'll be my doing."

"But what, Brenda, what? You can't let him drive you to do something even more terrible."

"Please, Barry." And now she was meek, pleading, desperate. "The car's packed. If you have any feeling for me at all, you'll go home and let me do what I damned well know has to be done."

He hesitated only half a minute. If she did not appear at the Sarasota Yacht Club, what might the bastard do to Toby? If she did go—what did *she* plan to do to Donald Forrest?

He turned and slid back the screen and went out. As he climbed into the Jeep, he knew that he was not going home, or back to the hospital. He knew that he was going to stay with Brenda.

But he had no idea what he could do.

————□————

Lieutenant Waldo Pruitt was traveling south on the Tamiami Trail and he had become more than a bit edgy. He was tracking down what might or not be a workable, valuable lead.

The sheriff's office of Lee County had phoned in response to the missing child alert that Waldo had put out at three o'clock after questioning the child's mother at Attorney Maynard's house. A man and a child, male, had checked in at one of those small mom-and-pop motels about ten miles north of Fort Myers and had left at around seven this morning under what appeared to the owner to be suspicious circumstances. All the sheriff's office had ascertained was that he'd registered in the name of D. Woods and the car license was that of a rented car. The license number corresponded to the one that Waldo had been searching for during the last six hours. The name D. Woods was close enough to Donald Forrest to convince him completely. Then what the hell did he hope to learn by questioning the motel owner?

You never know. Police work's a combination of reason and guesswork, logic and hunches. And hard evidence was something that you often came by *after* you'd used your experience and your goddamn cop's intuition born of that experience. Asking that poor actor fellow in the hospital bed to identify the picture of the handsome young Donald Forrest—that had been based on a hunch that had paid off. Now they had a prosecutable crime, didn't they? Waldo had put out an arrest order even before young Miss Rinaldi had obtained an official warrant when the court opened less than an hour ago. He'd like to explain to that poor Mrs. Forrest that he could do this only after an actual crime had been committed, and he had probable cause to think her husband had committed it—in this case, an eyewitness, the victim himself! Frustrating and infuriating as they often were, those were the rules of the game. And, if nothing else, if this Donald Forrest was arrested, at least she'd get her kid back, wouldn't she?

But what really bugged the bejesus out of him was that he couldn't come up with, couldn't even *imagine*, a motive for the bloody attack on Malcolm Eggers. Without asking that Charlene Conrad any questions, he had ascertained through his own methods that she and Malcolm Eggers were more or less shacked up together in her house and that Eggers and Mrs. Forrest had only a casual acquaintanceship *through* Miss Conrad. Then why a vicious attack like that? Waldo never expected to see an open-and-shut case but there had to be, there just had to be a motive.

He'd tried to reach Rex Maynard earlier but he hadn't been in. Driving, he decided to try again. He radioed headquarters. When the operator said, "I have Mr. Maynard, sir, go ahead," Waldo brought Rex Maynard up to date in a sketchy but very precise way, not giving the lawyer any time for expressions of surprise, and then he drawled: "Now you tell me, son. You tell me. Why?"

"All I can do is take a stab in the dark," Rex Maynard said.

"Well, you go ahead, son, take your stab. Playing around in the dark's all I been doing all night. Shoot."

"You ever hear of compulsive sexual jealousy, Lieutenant?"

"Maybe not in them words but I heard of almost everything. Proceed."

So then he listened while Rex Maynard told him of what had happened to a friend of his in Connecticut who'd taken on Mrs. Forrest's divorce case—how the husband had first accused him of being paid by sexual favors and had then tried to drive the attorney and his wife off the road and into the lake. "What we're up against is a twisted mind, Lieutenant."

"What we're up against," Waldo growled, "is a criminal who shouldn't be running around loose and free and able to mutilate and cripple his fellow citizens."

"True enough. But if he's still in the area and hasn't taken the boy home up North, what the hell's the point?"

Waldo's mind was operating now the way he liked it to operate. It was beginning to get a clear picture. "I'd say he's holding the boy for ransom."

"Ransom?"

"*She's* the ransom. The wife."

"If that's true, why hasn't she called me? Or you?"

"Same reason the families of most kidnap victims don't—for fear of what he might do to the kid if she brings in the police."

"Then . . . then she could be on her way to meet him right now. What can we do about that?"

"We can try to get the bastard first. That's what I'm doing now."

"And if we don't?"

"We got the other charge. Assault with intent to kill. Attempted homicide's an extraditable offense—maybe we can put him away and she can have a few years' peace. I got to sign off now. Keep in touch."

Click. He flipped the switch and then made a U-turn on the highway and brought the car to a halt in the parking area of the Buckeye Motel.

There he met a Mr. Oscar Robb, originally from Lima, Ohio— a small wizened man with whiskey-streaked eyes and an obsequious manner. Oscar Robb showed him the registration card. "D. Woods" had given his address as New Milford, Connecticut, and had paid for the room in advance and in cash. "He had a slew of fifties in his billfold and when I couldn't break one—catch me showin' cash to a stranger that time o' night—he asked if I had any booze and I sold him my own bottle for the difference. Nice-dressed sorta man—blue blazer, white buck shoes, but I notice things."

"Like what, Mr. Robb?"

"Well, he don't take no suitcases in. And he don't carry in the little fella, let him walk in his bare feet. *First* thing made me suspicious, though—the boy had on pajamas. I couldn't get back to sleep for wonderin'. Comes to me maybe he had no proper intentions to that boy, if you know what I mean. Lotsa screwballs runnin' around and majority of 'em get to Florida, y'ever notice?"

"Did you happen to notice which direction he went when he left here?"

"He went back the same direction he come. North. Toward Sarasota."

Another dead end. He could have saved himself the drive. But he'd been itching for action anyway and there was nothing more he could do at headquarters.

"Mr. Robb?"

"Yessir?"

"You must've had *some* reason to notify the sheriff."

"I told the young deputy. He acted like it didn't mean nothin'. I don't think he even believed me."

"Try *me*, Mr. Robb. If I'd been in your place, I'd have made damn sure this Mr. Woods wasn't up to what you thought he was up to. I'd have figured it was my duty."

"I figured that. Yeah. So I looked in."

"Good for you."

"Them curtains don't come together so good. It was just gettin' light and there was a lamp on inside, too."

"We can arrest him, you know, if what you suspected was true."

"I was wrong."

"They were both asleep, were they?"

"No, sir. The boy was stretched out on the bed on his belly. He didn't have no shirt on then. And this man, said he was his father, he was standing over him and what he was doing is, he was beating the mattress. With a belt. He never hit the boy once, just the bed, first on one side of the boy, then on the other, over and over and over. You could hear that belt smackin' the mattress like a gun going off each time. And every time he hit it, the boy went stifflike and then his whole body jumped till he almost doubled up. But he never cried, didn't utter a sound, and had his eyes squinched together. But he was crying all right. His face was all shiny wet and he was shaking so hard you could see the spring wobbling under him."

It took effort for Waldo to ask, "What did you do, Mr. Robb?"

"Me? I was scared. You shoulda seen that man's face. It wasn't even humanlike. It looked mad, angry-mad but mad some other way, too. Because even if he was drunk, you never saw eyes so bright. Like maybe, some way, he was enjoying what he was doing. I almost threw up. It couldn't have been worse if he'd been doin' what I thought he might be doin'. You know—what them fruits do. This was worse."

Waldo, himself sick all through his huge body, asked again: "What did you do, Mr. Robb?"

"I'm an old man, that young fella's six feet—"

"What did you *do*?"

"I come back to the office and I slammed the door and then I sung out, 'Emma, I think I heard someone prowlin' around here.' My Emma's been dead three years but *he* didn't know that. And sure enough the light went off in number seven."

"How"—he was having some difficulty in his throat, which was very dry—"how long was that before they left?"

"Less'n an hour."

"Is that when you called the sheriff?"

"I didn't know *what* to do. First, I figured he *was* what I suspected, then I thought he probably *was* the boy's old man and he probably had a right to chastise his own son any way suited him. I went through hell till they left and that's when I made up my mind to get it off *my* conscience by telling somebody. So I called the sheriff's office. But that was a mistake, wasn't it? Nothin' you can do, is there?"

"You . . . you did the right thing, Mr. Robb."

"What *can* you do?"

It was a good question. A damned good question. Waldo said, "The man took the kid from his mother. We're trying to get him back."

Relief welled up into Oscar Robb's wrinkled face. "And I helped some then, did I?"

"You helped," Waldo said. But had he? In what way? "Thanks."

"I feel better myself anyway. In my gut."

"We'll get him," Waldo said, opening the door. "One way or the other we'll get him."

But how?

He strode to the car. A thin rain had begun to fall. He climbed in. He felt strong and determined and helpless. Anger flowed hot in every vein. Hate.

Disgust.

Driving north again, he radioed and asked for his office.

Dutch answered. "That you, Lieutenant?"

"Anything new?"

"We been trying to get you."

"Anything new, goddamnit?"

"Plenty. Pay dirt maybe. Donald E. Forrest took possession of a charter boat at nine. Almost an hour ago. The kid's with him. We've got a description of the boat, ID numbers, the works. He took it out into the bay after getting operating instructions. Well, my friend, you said to cover every angle. You're still the best hound dog in these parts, Lieutenant."

"Save the bullshit, Dutch. Didn't he have to give the leasing people his destination?"

"Only that he has permission to tie up at the Sarasota Yacht Club. But he changed the charter so the boat will be delivered to some company in Westport, Connecticut."

"Then get on it. Get some cars out to St. Armand's. Fast. They're to go aboard at the yacht club and arrest! Assault and battery with attempt to murder."

"Got you, sir."

"Get the Harbor Police over there and alert the Coast Guard in case we need them."

"Hey, Lieutenant, simmer down."

"Don't tell me what to do. I'm sixty miles away. I want this sonofabitch in handcuffs within the half hour. I want him behind bars before I get up there. And, Dutch—"

"Yes, sir?"

"Don't forget. There's a kid on board."

"I'll pass the word."

A kid on board. A kid who's been through enough. More than enough.

He reached and switched on the dome light and siren. He eased into the left lane and pressed down on the accelerator.

Aurora and he had always wanted a child. No such luck.

And then a bastard like this has one and—

His big shoulders hunched over the wheel, Waldo realized that another element had entered the case. An element inside Waldo Pruitt.

Revenge.

Yes, damn it, revenge. They could say all they wanted, write all they wanted about prisons and capital punishment—what none of the fancy talkers, none of the fancy writers, could get around was the simple fact that justice and revenge are not too far apart, not so very damn different in the showdown.

Right now he wished it was the old days. He wished he could have about ten minutes alone in a cell with this Donald E. Forrest!

———□———

Barry had parked the Jeep in the deserted parking lot of the Sarasota Yacht Club so that he could get at least a partial view of the bay. The clubhouse was a handsome low building set in a shaded curve of land on the bay, accessible to the Gulf by two passes but protected from it by the length of Lido Key. Because of the rain and clouds, no boats had come into or departed from the club's marina, so he had had no occasion yet to use the binoculars he always carried in the Jeep and which were now strung around his neck. He was sitting behind the wheel waiting for either the boat or Brenda to arrive and wondering when it had been that he had actually realized what Brenda really intended to do. Brenda, Brenda, how could you let him drive you to this? Despite his incredulity, he knew. He was certain.

He was certain that, on the boat, somewhere en route north, at some point when they were far offshore, probably at night so that the fact or the body would not be discovered till morning, Donald Forrest was going to be lost overboard.

To drown at sea.

An accident. They happen on boats all the time. And if the victim were known to be a heavy drinker, with alcohol discovered in his blood—

To Brenda it had to seem her only way out. And Toby's only hope for a life—

Perhaps it was.

What he could not understand was not Brenda's decision to act but his own ready comprehension of it.

But not approval.

No, he could not let it happen that way.

When he saw the little blue car turn between the stone entrance posts and stop, and while he watched her get out and take the suitcases out of the trunk—no wasted motion, all graceful and determined and lovely, lovely—he tried to decide what he could possibly do, or say, even as he climbed out into the thin windswept rain and went to where she stood picking up two of the three pieces of baggage.

She saw him. Her lips opened, slightly, then closed into a firm thin line and her eyes, as he reached her, looked lustrous but like hard, brown opaque marbles in a face that had lost its softness in the clenching of her jaws.

But he knew now and time was running out. "I won't let you do it, Brenda."

Her chin was set and the muscles in her cheeks flared. "How do you expect to stop me, Barry? I'm going back to my husband."

"To kill him."

Her face, wet in the rain, went awry then, trembling. She blinked, fast, and her lids continued to flutter as her shoulders went slack. "How . . . what makes you think a crazy thing like that?"

"Even if you don't get caught, even if he deserves it—you'd have to live with it the rest of your life."

The quivering reached her body and she stooped to fumble blindly for the handles of one of the suitcases. "You're as crazy as he is."

"I don't think so."

She straightened, suitcase in hand. "What . . . what kind of a man are you?" she demanded, but piteously, shaking her head which glistened black in the falling rain. "How could you even . . . guess? Do you have some kind of magic powers? How, how, how did you know?"

"I care," Barry heard himself say.

"No," she cried. "No, please not now, don't say that, please." And she picked up another suitcase in her other hand and turned toward the clubhouse. "Not now, not now, damn it!"

He swooped up the third suitcase and followed. She did not go to the portico entrance of the clubhouse but turned alongside the building and, hurrying, went to the marina, which extended behind the building. All sorts and kinds of craft were moored in the complex of docks and the area, in the rain, was deserted. She walked out to the farthermost point over the water and set down the luggage. And stood, shoulders fixed, waiting.

He joined her. "Brenda, after what happened to Eggers, the police must be looking for your husband. Let them handle it."

She whirled about. "I told you, I told you! They won't, they can't. They can't stop him. He's done enough. Especially to Toby. I won't allow him, ever, to do any more. Don't you understand, can't you understand, don't go on torturing me!"

Over her shoulder he saw only two boats on the water: a small rowboat with an outboard motor idle, drifting, with a single figure aboard, a man in a yellow raincoat fishing in spite of the rain, and a yacht approaching in the distance, its prow on a direct line, pointed to the docks.

And then something happened to her. She let go of the suitcases, one fell over onto its side, her shoulders heaved and he saw her arms and hands shaking, not trembling, *shaking*, and she clenched her arms close to her body as if to stop the compulsive agitation in them, and her body bent forward slightly, her head moving from side to side as she seemed to struggle for breath.

He dropped the suitcase and stepped to her and reached for her face.

At his touch she straightened and came against him, head down, gasping, her whole body a quivering mass of anxiety and desperation.

He held her and whispered, "You're all right, Brenda. You're going to be all right. Toby's coming. We'll take Toby and—"

But it was at that moment that he heard the siren.

———□———

"Who's that with her?" the man yelled, one hand on the wheel, the other holding the field glasses. "Toby, take these and tell me who that red-haired sonofabitch is!"

Toby was too stiff with fear to move. He was sitting on the floor of the cockpit, trying not to see the water. He hated the water. He was a scaredy-cat, he was a crybaby, he couldn't help it, he hated the deep terrible water on all sides. The man had promised him he'd see Mama, they were going to pick up Mama now, but even that didn't help. He wasn't crying, he'd been crying, inside and out, for a long time now, ever since the man had done what he did in the motel, but now it was like he'd run out of tears and all he could do was sit hunched down here in the rain and keep his head down and wait and hope and—

"You heard me," the man yelled over the sound of the motor, "you heard me, you little faker, come over here and tell me who your goddamn Mama brought with her!"

But he didn't move. He couldn't. All he could do was sit like this and—

"Toby!"

His hate was a tight, hard, hot ball in his stomach but otherwise his body was freezing cold and wet. He didn't turn his head to look at the man behind the wheel. He wished he could never see the man again, ever again. . . .

Then he heard another sound. At first he couldn't make out what it was—a kind of wailing over and over and over. Far away but getting closer.

He heard the man cursing and growling behind him and he heard the sound getting closer, not one sound now but a lot of sounds; he had to know, so he lifted his head a little and felt the rain beat against his face and he forced his eyes open. Directly ahead he saw a building with boats tied up and the outlines of two people on the dock, but he couldn't make out who—was it Mama? So then he looked up and off to the right of the building, where there was a kind of flashing, and he saw two police cars on the causeway bridge moving fast, and then he knew what the wailing sound was.

"She tricked me, she tricked me!" the man's voice was yelling, and then something happened to the motor, it stopped roaring, it made a funny gulping sound and he felt a kind of bumping as the boat slowed, and then he felt it turning. He saw a little boat with a man in it wearing a yellow raincoat and he thought first of standing up and waving his arms and yelling *help, help, help,* but he knew the fishing man couldn't hear him, and then he almost toppled backward when the motor started to roar again.

The man was still yelling but he couldn't hear the words now and the boat was going faster and all he could see now was water, more water—

"Little bitch, little bitch, she'll pay for this!"

He heard that. It was a howl. But all he could think of was, we're turning around, we're going away!

"I'll be back, I'll be back, little slut, I'll be back!"

He stood up. His knees wobbled. He caught sight of the small boat again, a flash of wet yellow, and he saw that he was going to go past the little boat, close, not close enough but close, maybe he could make it, if he could swim he could make it, he could swim a little, not much, if he could just remember what Barry had told him, let yourself go, *believe* you won't go down, if he didn't try he would go back out on the water, maybe out in the Gulf even, he had to try, he had to believe, you won't sink, just keep moving your arms and legs and—

——□——

Brenda screamed. She lowered the binoculars and, bent almost double, staggered to the edge of the pier.

Barry grabbed her and held her body with one arm as his other hand took the binoculars and lifted them.

He brought the boat's stern into view. He had seen it make the turn and he had watched its wide silver wake reverse direction. He had wondered, seeing the juxtaposition of the two craft, whether that wake might swamp the smaller one. Now he saw the larger boat slowing almost to a stop. He focused in more closely and could make out the figure of Donald Forrest behind the wheel, looking out over the water. She shifted the glasses slowly to the surface of the water and then he realized why Brenda had screamed.

He saw Toby in the water, thrashing, but his head above the

surface, his head remaining above the surface and his forward movement slow, almost indiscernible, in the direction of the rowboat. The man in the yellow slicker was no longer fishing: He was pulling the rope to start the outboard motor and then he was sitting down to drive it. A steady gust of dark smoke appeared behind.

"He's all right!" he heard himself shout. "He's going to be all right, Brenda!" And he felt her body regain life in the grasp of his arm. He released her.

"Look," he said, and extended the glasses.

Brenda took them.

Without the binoculars he could see, even in the falling rain, the small boat swerve in a small semicircle as the fisherman cut the motor and the boat drifted close to the swimming body in the water. The fisherman was reaching and the boy was hanging on to the gunwale.

Brenda spoke. "He swam," she said. "Barry—Toby swam!"

The large ketch, which had been unmoving during this, drifting some twenty or thirty yards away by now, spurted to life and started off, leaving an angry wake behind.

Well, at least the bastard had waited to make sure his son was safe.

Behind, Barry heard the sound of the sirens, closer now, in the parking area behind the clubhouse, as they subsided into silence.

The outboard boat was heading toward the dock.

Brenda, when he finally looked at her face, appeared dazed and very still. She was no longer shaking.

"Imagine that" was all she said as she handed him the binoculars. Then their eyes met. And she said, "Thank God."

By then several uniformed policemen had joined them. But only Barry knew that while she was thankful for her son's salvation, she was also grateful for her own. Now she would not have to do the terrible thing she had come here to do.

AFTER looking over the black Cougar in the parking area at the charter boat company, Lieutenant Pruitt obtained from the manager a photograph of the yacht itself. The manager was obliging; he had already supplied the police with the boat's ID numbers and now he was worried: Why were the police involved, had he made a mistake in turning his valuable property over to a man who was wanted by the authorities? Waldo Pruitt did not attempt to reassure the man because Waldo himself was not reassured in the slightest. His own frustration had deepened ever since he had left the docks of the Sarasota Yacht Club. The damned boat had apparently disappeared. By now it could already be on its way to Connecticut, but Waldo couldn't help hoping that the sonofabitch was still within reach.

Driving, he pictured the entire area in his mind: a complex of bays and inlets with hundreds, maybe thousands, of private docks and marinas on the mainland and along the bay side of each key and the whole damned Gulf of Mexico on the west. How could a single craft be spotted by the two Harbor Police boats and the Sheriff's Department helicopter now searching?

He'd asked assistance from the Coast Guard, but the single cutter assigned to the Sarasota area as well as the various planes and copters were involved in an important drug bust somewhere fifty miles north in Tampa Bay. Since Florida had become the gateway for illicit drugs from the Caribbean islands and from Central and South America, the Coast Guard, always shorthanded, was forever waging its war against smuggling, by air and by sea. Cooperative when possible, they, like all law-enforcement agencies, had to set their own priorities. And the search for a single fugitive wanted for a minor felony such as aggravated battery, even with intent to commit murder—a charge that Waldo had gratuitously added in order to get as much police action as possible—had to be the responsibility of the local authorities involved. Waldo understood, cursing the fact even as he acknowledged its necessity. There was simply too damned much serious crime everywhere for all of it to be handled adequately. Well, somehow he had set his own priorities, too—and he was not yet sure exactly why.

The boy was safe now. In the hands of his mother and, as Waldo understood it, under the care of a doctor in Sarasota Palms Hospital. Which probably meant that he was under the care of a psychiatrist. Which probably meant that he had suffered some sort of emotional shock or damage. Maybe from witnessing that vicious violence on the street or from the way his father had treated him. Waldo's mind shied away from the scene that the shocked little motel owner had described. But he began to understand why he himself had set his own priority.

He radioed Dutch. Anything new? Nothing. They were alerting all the boatyards and marinas where Forrest might put in to refuel but this was only more wasted motion. At nine o'clock, not yet two hours ago, the boat had two full tanks of fuel. Enough to carry it to Texas or Mexico. "And he knows we're looking for him," Dutch said. "He's either holed up somewhere or sitting out there in the Gulf thumbing his nose at us."

"Let's just pretend he's holed up. And let's just pretend we're going to find him."

"Okay, Lieutenant. But if he's gone, maybe we could get on with some of the important work that's been stacking up on your desk."

"I'll be in, in ten minutes, Dutch."

Little Miss Coleen Lyons was waiting in his office. Damn! Pert and tiny and playful as always, she did not stand up when she greeted him with her usual: "What's world-shaking, Lieuten-ant?"

And as usual, lowering his bulk into the swivel chair behind his cluttered desk, he said, "Nothing for publication, Miss Lyons. Sorry."

"Like hell you are."

Waldo remembered when the *Herald-Tribune* had assigned only hard-bitten but always respectful young men to the courthouse beat. Now he had to deal daily with this fresh Irish kid who de-manded every detail even before you could put the details together yourself. He was not in the mood for Miss Coleen Lyons just now, thank you.

"Busy night," she said. "World-shaking enough to interrupt *your* sleep anyway, wasn't it?"

He was sorting the reports into individual stacks without looking up. What irked him about the girl was that she sometimes did her job too damn well—and you had to guess *how* she'd done it. Cau-tiously he waited.

"Do you have any leads in the manhunt for the motorist who beat the hell out of a Malcolm Eggers at approximately four thirty this morning?"

"Not yet."

"There was a missing-child alert in effect from two thirty until about an hour ago. Any connection?"

"I don't see why there should be, do you?"

"Now that's the kind of evasive answer a working gal appreci-ates." She flipped the pages of her notebook. "When my editor's in a good mood, he sometimes lets me review plays at the Asolo. How serious are the injuries to Malcolm Eggers, Lieutenant?"

"Check with the hospital."

"I have. The man you're looking for is named Donald Forrest. The father of the so-called missing child and the suspected assail-ant of Malcolm Eggers. *That's* the connection, Lieutenant. I fol-lowed the patrol cars to the Sarasota Yacht Club an hour ago. I saw the boy come ashore after jumping into the drink."

"You're a busy little girl," Waldo said, but slowly, sparring for time now because an idea had occurred to him. "There *is* a con-nection as you say and I'll fill in the gaps for you, if you'll do me a favor in return."

"Giving me the facts isn't exactly doing me a favor, Lieutenant."

He was tempted, sorely tempted, to say something else, something profane or scatological, but he shoved the paper work aside, having made up his mind, and said: "Tit-for-tat or no deal, Miss Lyons."

"What do you want me to do?" she asked.

He reached into his pocket and handed her the photograph of the boat. "I want this picture reproduced in the afternoon paper and, if you can manage it, on the local TV news at noon."

"Twelve thirty," she said, glancing at the photograph. "You can arrange that yourself, Lieutenant. Why ask me?"

"A forty-one-foot Morgan Out Island ketch. Named the *Wanderer*. Make sure they include the ID number. If some alert citizen spots it, he's to call headquarters."

Miss Coleen Lyons was peering at him across the desk with a new, puzzled expression in her blue eyes. "In other words," she said, "if you do it yourself, it becomes official. And you may be making more of this than the actual crime really warrants." It was not quite a question, not quite an accusation. "And if I do this little favor, you'll tell me why you're so eager to nab this character. Tit-for-tat?"

"I'll tell you," Waldo said and he stood up, glaring down on her. "Not for publication, off the record. I'm convinced this sonofabitch is a dangerous man and maybe capable of a hell of a lot more than he's already done."

In the silence that followed, Waldo realized that his gut was quivering. He heard a siren approaching outside, its wail dying as it arrived. He saw Coleen Lyons stand up and he saw a small but offensive smile flicker on her lips.

"Lieutenant, you surprise me."

He made an angry slashing gesture with one hand. "Will you do it?"

"I've had several dates with the manager of the TV station. And if my city editor objects, I'll use my feminine guile. Now . . . how about filling me in on the whole story? Off the record."

"Sit down and listen," Waldo Pruitt growled.

———□———

He tried to avoid looking into her face. He couldn't bear it. Her brown eyes, staring straight ahead but not seeing the activity in the hospital waiting room, had a stunned blank expression. Despair? More. Much more. Barry had no way of projecting himself into her mind. After all, he had known her for only two days. Did not really know her at all. But it was odd: he did not question why he was here with her waiting for the doctor who was examining Toby. Less than two hours ago he had declared himself in. *I care,* he had said when he picked up the suitcase and followed her down to the dock at the yacht club. . . .

In those bleak months after Jenny had died, killed by a drunk on the highway, *he* must have looked the way Brenda looked now—withdrawn into a depression that, even this many years later, often threatened to return, to overwhelm him. He'd found his way to live with it, to survive, but how could he help this strange, lovely young woman face the wreckage of her life? His mind rebelled angrily at his own inadequacy.

"Mrs. Forrest." It was Dr. Seymour, who had returned. A heavyset short man with gold-rimmed glasses and a graying beard whom Brenda's lawyer had brought into the case, Dr. Seymour spoke in a gentle voice again, repeating her name. "Would you like to come with me, please?"

Brenda's eyes did not blink. She moved her head slightly but she did not seem to see the doctor. "I want to see Toby." Her tone was flat.

"I want you to see him," Dr. Seymour said, "and I'm sure he wants to see you. But I think you and I should talk first. Would you mind?"

Brenda stood up. "Can Toby talk?"

Dr. Seymour glanced at Barry for the first time. "That's what you and I should discuss, Mrs. Forrest." The doctor had dark eyes, almost black, and in that moment Barry saw in them an expression of naked pain—a compassion so strong that, seeing it, Barry recognized a reflection of his own misery and sense of helplessness. And realized that he could like this man; realized that, in that second, he did like him. And trusted him. "Excuse us, Mr. Conrad," Dr. Seymour said. "We may be a while."

"Brenda," Barry said, careful to break the impulse to touch her arm, "Brenda, I'll wait."

Her eyes met his then—and flinched away. But a tremor passed along her pale lips.

And when they had gone, Barry walked to the glass doors that led out onto the quiet neighborhood street. The building was small and low and on the lawn a modest sign read SARASOTA PALMS HOSPITAL. It did not identify it as a facility for neuropsychiatric care. Only a few blocks away Mal Eggers lay in a bed on the third floor of the much larger Sarasota Memorial Hospital. Two casualties. And Brenda? Was she a casualty too?

The rain had stopped. The pavement and the few passing cars glittered wet but the sun had come out. Strong and bright. White clouds had replaced the gray ones already and soon the beaches would be crowded. Florida weather.

He spotted a phone booth on the street and wondered whether he had any change. He probably should have reported to Charlene before now. What would he tell her? Well, only some of what happened in the last two hours. He would not reveal that Toby was in the hospital or what he knew Dr. Seymour was telling Brenda: that Toby no longer stuttered, that he did not stammer, that ever since he had been pulled out of the water he could not speak at all. He'd spare Charlene that—as he could not spare Brenda.

———□———

The sun was shining on the Gulf now but Donald knew that it had been the rain that had saved him. Because of the rain there'd been only a few stray boats on the bay. Lucky for him, though, there'd been that one outboard; otherwise he'd have had to go back for Toby. Crazy stupid kid, jumping in like that! Once he'd seen the fisherman pull Toby aboard, he'd been free to continue south on the bay, full throttle, and then west, out into the Gulf.

Would you have gone back?

Hell yes!

With those cop cars and people running down onto the docks?

Yes, goddamnit, *yes!*

But there remained a troublesome lurking doubt, even now. He'd gone haywire just for a while. Wild! He hadn't known what he was doing. Only that he had to get away. What the hell did the police want with *him?* Toby was his own son, wasn't he? And, no matter what he'd done, Brenda was still his wife. And they don't send three or four squad cars after you just because you beat the shit out of a man who's playing around with your wife.

Panic. He'd never known such panic before. It was a frame-up! They were all against him. As usual. He'd had to grip the wheel to keep control of the boat. Shaking, sweating, weak all over— Christ, he'd lost his mind there for a while—he'd headed straight out into the Gulf in the rain. Where was he going? Texas? Mexico? He had enough fuel. Maybe he should turn east into the next pass between the keys, try to lose himself in the backwaters, the channels and inlets. Maybe find an empty house with a dock somewhere. You can't *hide* a boat this size! And what if the police had a description, the ID numbers, what about Harbor Police, did they have any here, the Coast Guard, a cutter or a chopper?

By the time he'd recovered his senses, he was heading south about five hundred yards offshore. Siesta Key, according to the map.

If only he had a drink . . .

Below Siesta was Casey Kay. If he turned in through Midnight Pass, there'd be channel markers. He could hit the Intracoastal Waterway—and then what? On to Miami, the East Coast? Where the hell was he *going*?

He couldn't leave Brenda. Brenda was back there in Sarasota. With that man. Whoever he was. Red hair, red beard. *Another* man! Whoever he was, he was in on it, too.

And Brenda—she'd tricked him. She'd set up a trap to have him arrested. The bitch. The conniving little bitch. Christ, if he had one drink, just *one*, he'd be able to *think*!

If he could get the police off his back, just that, he'd be free to make up his mind what to do about Brenda.

God, how he hated her. She'd send him to jail. If she could. To prison. And then what? Then she'd be free to ball every man she met. While he sat in a cell somewhere going bananas. He'd lose his mind, he'd—

And then it came to him: there was a radiophone on board. He could call his father. The old man'd know what to tell him to do. It meant calling the marine operator. It meant giving the ID number of the boat. Well, he'd fox them there, too. He'd give the number with one digit wrong. And he'd reverse the charges and give a false name. He'd give his mother's last name, her *maiden* name, and her father's first name, which was the same as Toby's. . . .

———□———

"It's long distance, Mr. Forrest," his secretary said over the intercom. "Person-to-person, charges collect. A Mr. Tobias Carpenter."

Orin sat there for a second or two without picking up the phone. Tobias Carpenter? Rosamond's father. But the man had been dead for more than twenty years. . . .

"Shall I accept the charges, Mr. Forrest?"

"Where's the call coming from?" he asked.

"Sarasota, Florida."

I'm going to go get her myself, Donald had said. *She's in Florida, not Phoenix, and I'm flying down now.*

"Put him through," Orin said, and snapped off the intercom. His tall lean body had tensed and he took a deep breath, knowing, not accepting but knowing: It had happened, the inevitable had happened even if he couldn't imagine what it might be.

"Dad?"

"I'm here, son." It was not a snarl or growl—it was, he realized, the voice of a very tired old man. "What have you done?"

"I'm in trouble."

"I know that. What sort of trouble?" He didn't want to know. He had to know. "Spit it out."

"I got into a fight."

"Is that all?" He knew it wasn't. "How bad?"

"I lost my temper."

"How bad?"

"I don't really know. That's the truth. All I know is the police are looking for me."

Rosamond must not know. Even this. He'd see she didn't find out. Somehow.

"And Brenda?"

"Are you going to do something, Dad? Tell me what to do."

"How's Brenda?" He was slightly relieved that Donald's voice did not sound as if he was drunk. Now, anyway. "Have you talked with Brenda? Have you seen her?"

"Brenda's being stubborn but she'll come round."

Tell Donald when he calls that no matter what, I'm going to have a divorce and I'm going to have Toby.

"Where's Toby now?"

"Dad, are you listening? I'm in a boat out on the Gulf of Mexico and I don't know what to do."

The low desperation in his son's tone, painfully familiar, stirred that part of Orin that he had come to hate in himself, but a terrible anger had begun to seethe in him too. "I'm coming down."

"You don't need to, Dad."

"I'll be on the next plane."

"Don't you *understand?* I can't wait. I'm out here by myself and Brenda's turned against me, too, and I'm going to be arrested."

No matter what it means, Brenda had said. *Disgrace, scandal, even if it means sending him to prison—no matter what.* And Orin had promised to tell Donald this if he phoned.

But Orin decided to ignore that promise. Donald, after all, was his son.

"Where can you be reached?" he asked.

"I can't. I don't want to risk it. Christ, Dad, I'm going nuts out here by myself. If they throw me in jail—"

"Shut up and listen. Call me back here in one hour."

"What are you going to do?"

"I'm going to get you a lawyer down there who'll know how to handle this. When you call back, I'll have the information." And then he asked, because he had to: "Are you all right otherwise, son?"

"I will be," Donald said. "I will be now, right?"

"I hope so," Orin said. It was what he hoped but not something he could be sure of, ever. "You keep your nose clean now." How many times over the years had he used those foolish words?

He replaced the telephone slowly. Was he being had again? Donald had not answered his question about Toby. He had also evaded talking about Brenda. He had revealed nothing, really. As usual. But Donald was getting what *he* wanted, needed, had to have. And Orin was helping him get it. As usual. He reached for the phone and dialed.

———□———

"And," Dr. Seymour said, from behind the desk, "and, Mr. Conrad, I don't want you to feel that you've betrayed any confidence by filling in these details for me. We're both trying to help, and considering the circumstances, I'll need all the assistance I can get."

"I warned you," Barry told him, "I've only known them both since the day before yesterday."

"A hell of a lot's happened in that time, though, hasn't it? Well, Mr. Maynard gave me a brief rundown when he asked if I'd take this on." Dr. Seymour took off his gold-rimmed glasses and peered at Barry owlishly. "So I knew what Forrest did to the young actor. And that the boy must have witnessed it. But Rex also told me that Forrest assaulted his wife. Sexually. If you don't know that, I think you should."

"I know it," Barry said, hearing the flat dullness of his tone and conscious of the hot sharp blade twisting in his stomach. "I've known it for some time, I think."

"Well, I'm sorry but it's too late to conceal anything now." And then he added: "Even from ourselves. Agreed?"

"Agreed." He swallowed the poison that came spewing up and into his mouth. The doctor was right in that, too: he had been refusing to accept what he really knew. "Agreed," he said again.

"The one who should really be getting psychiatric care is the man himself. But by now I guess he's several hundred miles from here, don't you?"

"Does Brenda think so?" Barry asked.

"No. Do you?"

"No."

Dr. Seymour was still studying Barry with his black bright eyes. "He's a victim, too, you know—"

"Knowing that doesn't change what's happened. It doesn't make Toby talk and it doesn't—" But he stopped himself. "Now *you* tell me. What about Brenda?"

"She's traumatized, too. Shock. A series of shocks. Frankly, Mr. Conrad, I'm as concerned about her condition as about Toby's. Hate's a corrosive, destructive emotion and frankly I think she's consumed by it."

"Do you blame her?"

"My job's not to blame anyone." He put on his glasses and adjusted them. "Ironic, though, isn't it? It was only a brief and superficial examination—of both of them—but I get the gut feeling that if the boy could ever admit that he really hates his father, he'd have a fair chance at regaining his power of speech. And if his mother could get *her* hate under control, at a very deep level, she'd recover, too."

"It *is* ironic," Barry said, liking the doctor even more for admitting his educated conjectures. "Are you advising me of something, Doctor?"

"Take it that way. She's agreed to let Toby be admitted to the hospital but she absolutely refuses to admit herself." He stood up. The two men were about the same height. "Whoever she's going to be with now may as well have the advantage of my very limited guesswork. Agree?"

"Thank you."

"She also consented to take the medication I've given her—simple tranquilizers, really—but frankly I wish she felt more . . . well, fear."

"Maybe she's felt enough fear."

Dr. Seymour came around the desk. "It's a protective emotion. And quite valid in these circumstances, I'd say. Mr. Conrad, do you realize what a man with his mind and in his present state is capable of?"

"I've some idea."

"Well, impress this on Mrs. Forrest. Whatever else is going on inside her—and it's almost more than she can handle right now—she seems to have run out of terror."

"He won't get to her," Barry said.

The short gray beard twisted into a grin. "Well, Barry, let's just hope you can handle him if he does."

It was Barry's turn to grin. But there was no mirth in it. "Well, Ezra," he said, recalling the other man's swift expression of compassion an hour ago in the waiting room, "let's both rely on each other." It was the closest he could come to expressing his confidence and gratitude.

"I doubt she should be with Toby much longer—although God knows what's best really. I'll give them another few minutes. By the way, she refuses to contact her parents up North, says her father's not well—"

"That leaves a few of us, though." He handed the doctor a slip of paper with his own name printed at the top—one of Lavinia's gifts last Christmas. "I've jotted down the two phone numbers where she can be reached. One's mine. The other's Mrs. Davidson's. Neither one is in Sarasota."

"Good. Anything else?"

"Yes. What kind of security do you have here?"

"Well, normally we're concerned about patients leaving. But, as you may have noticed, the exterior doors are always locked. Both sides."

"If I can handle it, would you object to a private guard if he wasn't in uniform and kept himself inconspicuous?"

"I don't think so. Under those conditions. The only access to Toby's room is through the lobby and I've already given instructions he's to have no visitors. Anything else?"

"Yes. Good luck."

"You too, Barry. We'll both need it."

They shook hands.

And then Barry went across the street and into the phone booth to call Rex Maynard. A lawyer would know how to hire a private bodyguard—damned if a man like Barry Conrad did. He was already in waters that were way beyond his depth. How long could he go on swimming in them?

Swimming. Toby had jumped off the boat and had actually *swum* to safety. Remarkable. Well, if it indicated nothing else, it revealed how much he hated his father. Whether he could express it in words or not.

Waiting for Rex Maynard to answer his phone, Barry felt a great wave of tenderness flood through him and he remembered the carving of the egret and the book of Florida birds that he had given Toby. Did he have time now to drive to Lido Shores and get them and return before Brenda came down from Toby's room?

———□———

Donald could wait no longer. It had been only forty-five minutes since he had called his father but he doubted he could make it through another fifteen minutes of this hell. It was like being in prison. He'd moved the boat three times. He had never needed a drink more. His arm ached from holding the binoculars. His eyes were stinging because the sun was burning down now. He was starving. And his whole body and mind were quiveringly alert as he continually scanned the sky (no planes or copters), the glittering water's surface, and the entrance to the pass (no Coast Guard boats). He didn't know when he might have to start the engine and take off again. Or where he could go if he had to. The Gulf was calm as a lake now as he allowed the boat to drift.

He couldn't go on like this.

His body was drenched in sweat. His hands were shaking again. He didn't have a drink to settle that churning hungry shotaway emptiness. . . .

He went down the companionway into the cabin and put the call through. In the same manner as before.

"The attorney's name is Hollis Sanford," his father said. "He's an old-timer there, knows everyone. My old friend Kyle Glendinning contacted him and he's waiting for your call now. His number is 555-2933. You got that?"

"I can remember."

"And Donald—"

"Yes, Dad?"

"Do whatever he tells you. Let *him* decide."

"He doesn't think I'll have to go to jail, does he?"

"His job's to keep you *out* of jail, son."

"Thanks again, Dad."

"The way you can thank me is— Oh, for God's sake, stop *saying* thanks and start *acting* thankful. Call the man now."

The conversation had calmed his nerves. He was accustomed to his father's anger; it was oddly reassuring in its own way. At least he had one person on his side. Not Mother, though. . . .

He put the call in through the marine operator. And waited.

No, not Mother: she blamed him for everything. Always had. Bitch. She might have fooled Dad. She didn't fool him. He'd had her number since he was thirteen years old. And she knew it. Bitch. Women are all alike.

"Hullo, Mr. Forrest. How are you?" Hollis Sanford spoke with a hearty, throaty drawl that was full of friendliness and good cheer. "Still out on that boat, are you?"

"Yes, sir."

"Turned into a right fine day, didn't it? There is a warrant out for your arrest, you know that, do you?"

"I was pretty sure, yes."

"Well, I've had the charges read off to me over the phone. Ag-

gravated assault, bodily injury, battery with intent to commit homicide, leaving the scene of a vehicular accident, unlawful flight to
evade prosecution. Sound grave enough to you?"

Christ! All he could manage to say was "Yes, sir."

"Someone's throwing the book at you, boy." He heard the older
man chuckle. "Somebody's being a mite too overzealous in his
use of words. Could be some law-enforcement officer's got his
back up, got some beef against you personally. Never know. Policemen are people, too. Now—you been involved in any other
illegal activities that I'm not cognizant with? You're not implicated
in any drug business, are you—buying, selling, transporting?"

"No, sir."

"Then here's what. You're going to turn yourself in. You *just*
learned the police want to question you. Had no idea until now.
I'll be right alongside and I'll do the talking. Let 'em arraign you,
plead not guilty, put up the bail—that's all arranged for—and I'll
have you in and out of the courthouse in less'n an hour's time.
How's that sound, son?"

"Then what?"

"Then you're a free man till the trial comes up, months from
now more'n likely. Now here's what: You tie up at the Field Club.
That's on the mainland south of town. I'm a charter member, use
my name. Better'n that, I'll be waiting for you, drive you to the
courthouse myself, we can get acquainted. You got a map aboard,
I take it?"

"I'm looking at it now. I'm only about twenty minutes from the
Field Club, I think."

"Make it thirty. I'll be there draped over a martini. By the way,
Mr. Forrest—"

"Yes, sir?"

"You came to Florida like any other tourist, understand? When
we get before the judge, I won't let any state attorney muddy up
the waters with any kidnapping tomfoolery, irrelevancies like what
they call spousal rape, wife assault, anything like that. You don't
say a word in court, hear?"

"I hear." Christ, the man knew everything! "Half an hour, Mr.
Sanford." How the hell did he know? "I'll be there. And thank
you, sir."

"Before you hang up—"

"Yes?"

"*I'm* going to have the martini—not you. Not a drop until you're a free man again, hear?"

Donald returned to the cockpit to start the engine.

A free man. In only an hour or so now.

Then he was *not* going to jail after all.

Which meant that soon now, very soon, he could go to get Brenda and they could leave for Connecticut together. Once they were back in their own home, they could put this whole miserable mess behind. . . .

————□————

"My car." It was the first time she'd spoken since they left the hospital. They were passing the Sarasota Yacht Club, where she had left her car when she got into the police cruiser with Toby to go to the hospital. "Barry?"

Pleased—relieved, actually—that she was speaking at all, he said: "I don't think you're in any condition to drive."

She sat stiffly beside him in the Jeep and said no more. From the Ringling Causeway he could not see the various boats moored behind the building of the yacht club and he wondered whether the police had stationed an officer there in case the bastard should risk coming in that way. But the police probably had plenty of other and more important work to keep them busy.

The sun was high, the sky bright and almost cloudless now. And tonight the moon would be full. But it was only a little after two in the afternoon and he was in no mood to contemplate what might happen by nightfall. His mind was having some difficulty with time anyway: so much had happened in such a short space of it—and there'd been so many mysterious and amazing changes inside him—that he couldn't yet assimilate it all.

Then he heard Brenda speak again. Listlessly. As if she were speaking to herself.

"What difference does it make whether they arrest him or not?"

And what could he answer? Knowing what she meant, what could he say? Except: "It might give Toby time to get out of the hospital."

She didn't reply. He knew, he knew. She would never be free; she would never be able to feel free. Always running, always hiding—how could Toby grow up like that, how could she live? And if the bastard were sent to jail, it wouldn't be for long. It could not be forever. He'd found her here; he'd find her anywhere. Sooner or later. And waiting, wondering, she'd be more a prisoner, wherever she was, than she'd been in that house in Connecticut.

After he'd turned north around St. Armand's Circle and had crossed the short bridge and was approaching Morningside Drive, which led off to Westway, she moved in her seat. And as he passed the turn, he glanced: She was frowning, questions in her eyes.

"The first place he'll look," he explained, "would be Charlene's house."

"But," she said, "that's what I want. I *want* to see him."

Astonished, he asked sharply: "What will that accomplish?"

"Why did the police have to come when they did?" she said, that same bleak flatness in her tone. "If they hadn't come when they did . . ."

But she allowed the sentence to die away vaguely.

If they had not come, would she have gone through with her plan—an accident during the night at sea, drunk man overboard, his absence not discovered for hours?

"Listen," he heard himself saying, "listen, Brenda. Stop thinking that way. I don't blame you, I wish I did, but that's wild, dangerous thinking. You couldn't live all your life knowing you'd killed a man. Even if he deserved it. Even if you could really do it in the first place. Which I doubt."

She didn't answer. Had his feeble words reached her? Then she made a sound, without moving. It was a terrible sound, deep in her throat—part laugh, part sneer, so low and bitter and scornful that he turned to look at her again. Her eyes were open and narrowed and in them, although they did not meet his, he saw such cold rage that he recalled what Ezra Seymour had said about the corrosiveness of hate. She did not even seem conscious of his presence. And her delicate face, jaw clenched and muscles flaring, was ugly for the first time. He realized that no matter how much he cared, his mind could not plumb the depths of fury and despair behind that quiet facade of composure and cold control.

So he drove up Longboat Key in silence.

Finally she spoke again—in that distant lifeless way that she had spoken at the hospital and while he had all but led her sleepwalking figure out to the Jeep: "He should have his books."

"I took the Florida bird book and Lavinia's *Bluebird* to the hospital while you were in his room."

"And the egret?"

"The carving, too. I have a key to Charlene's house."

"Thank you, Barry."

"I had to have something to do."

"Poor Barry. I bet you wonder how you ever got involved in all this, don't you? I'm sorry."

"I'm not."

Several miles went by. Had she heard him? Had he meant it? Yes, he had meant it.

His mind went to Jenny. As it had done several times before. He had never really loved any other woman but Jenny. And he had come to accept the fact that he never would. That he never could. But today, in the midst of all this, he had felt a mysterious and puzzling sense of renewal. He had become a part of something again, however cruel and tragic that something might be. Whatever its outcome.

"Stop the car!" Brenda screamed. "Stop the car, turn around!"

He pulled off onto the shoulder of the road and eased the Jeep to a halt. Brenda was staring at him, wide-eyed.

"I can't leave him." She was no longer screaming. Her words came in a breathless rush. "There'll be nobody with him after Dr. Seymour leaves. Take me back, Barry, please, I can't let Donald have him again, don't you see?"

"It's taken care of, Brenda," he said. "I spoke to your lawyer and he put me in touch with a Lieutenant Waldo Pruitt. He's sending an off-duty sheriff's deputy to stay at the hospital all night."

She blinked, frowning.

"The guard should be there by now. If you want, we can stop at the next phone booth and make sure."

She continued to stare at him. Her eyes, withdrawn and vacant before, became dark and lustrous and moist.

She started to speak but did not. She sat back in the seat instead and looked ahead. "No need," she said.

So he threw the Jeep into gear and eased it out onto the road and into the line of midday traffic.

"No need," she said again. "If Lieutenant Pruitt said he'll do it, he'll do it."

"I," Barry said, breathing again, "I had the same impression when I talked to him."

He hoped she would not thank him again. She didn't.

Instead she said, "When I was driving along here last night after dinner, Toby asked me why everyone was so nice. . . ."

"And what did you say?"

"I told him that maybe that's the way people really are."

It was all she said then. A few miles beyond, as they approached the bridge to Anna Maria Island, she reached out and placed her hand over his on the wheel.

Neither spoke.

Then, off the bridge with Coquina Beach on the left, the glittering Gulf beyond its Australian pines and picnic tables, she said, "I'm sorry I ever came. I'm so sorry."

"You can't blame yourself, Brenda."

"That's what my mother always says. But how can you help it if that's the way you are? We can't help being what we are."

And with her hand over his as he drove in a line of even slower traffic through Bradenton Beach, he felt hatred seep through him. Poisonous and acrid through every fiber and nerve of his body. To bring this woman to this—this girl, this child, this human being! As he drove along the sunny street filled with swimsuited merrymakers going and coming from the beach, he gave himself over to an emotion that he had never really known before—savage primitive hate.

It was then that Barry Conrad came fully to life for the first time in many, many years.

———□———

"Free? What do you mean, free?"

"He's on the street, Rex," Mary Rinaldi's voice said on the phone. "Turned himself in, arraigned, bond posted, smooth as ice. No longer a fugitive from what we laughingly call justice."

From his office window Rex could see the rooftops of the town with the bay beyond, peaceful and quiet in the sunshine. "Free to do whatever occurs to that sick mind now," he said. And then: "I detect the fine Italian hand of Hollis Sanford in this."

"Careful what you say about us Italians, chappie. But you're on target. How'd you know?"

"That fine southern gentleman of the old school called me during my mythical lunch hour. Said he understood I was representing a Mrs. Brenda Forrest in a divorce action and slyly inquired about the character of *Mr.* Forrest. I got the drift so I laid it on the line. The works, a complete rundown. Divorce, wife-battering, kidnap, even rape. Hell, Mary, I did everything but suggest to the old boy that he not take the case."

"Damned unethical of you. Well, I shot my bolt in the courtroom just now, too. Over our cracker friend's objections I argued against any bail whatever and then demanded a half-million-dollar bond at least. Danger to society and all that. Well, Bonnie Bielinski herself was sitting so when everything else failed I asked to examine the defendant's knuckles. The old gal can't stand violence and she breathed fire but set bail at fifty thousand. While Sanford snorted indignation. Trial's been set for May so meanwhile Mr. Donald Forrest is at liberty and at leisure, a respectable citizen even as you and I."

"Shit."

"I heard that," Mary Rinaldi's voice said. "My sentiments exactly."

"Well thanks, Mary. But I don't know what I can do about it except let his wife know."

"Don't tell me your troubles. Do you realize that I don't have a single third-person witness to the Forrest-Eggers assault? Only the victim himself. That's how people get away with murder. Give Alison my best. And Rex—"

"Yeah?"

"Don't despair. This character—and I didn't expect him to be so all-fired, all-American handsome in the flesh—the ogre won't be able to stay out of trouble."

"That," Rex said, "is what scares the hell out of me."

"Get on it, friend."

He looked up Brenda's phone number in his wallet notebook and punched it out himself. And waited. Picturing the houses on

Lido Shores. No answer. She might still be at the hospital. Should he dump this on her there? The girl had enough on her mind, didn't she? Maybe he could call Ezra—

Before he could decide, a button lit up on the base of the phone and he reached to touch it.

"It's Nancy, Mr. Maynard."

"Put her on."

Forcing his mind to shift gears, he waited for her voice. "Hi, Daddy, are you busy?"

"How are you feeling, punkin?"

"Oh, that." He could see her face squinching up, dismissing it. "It's only a cold, you know." Ladylike now—the lofty sophisticated woman of the world. Then in a rush, the ten-year-old hoyden he liked most: "One question, Daddy, and I'll let you go. On the twelve thirty Channel Seven news there was a picture of a boat that the police are looking for. Did you know that?"

"I had no idea."

"Well, this morning at breakfast when you and Mommy were talking about that woman who came to the house in the middle of the night—"

"And," he said, relaxing, enjoying the sound of her voice, "and while you were conning us into staying home from school because you caught a cold from those snowbirds from the North—"

"You're not listening, Daddy. You both talked about someone leasing a boat to take up to Connecticut—remember? Well, my question is, is that the same boat? They didn't give any names on TV. Only the numbers and all that stuff. It's called the *Wanderer*."

"I suspect it's the same boat, yes." Lieutenant Waldo Pruitt was leaving no stone unturned. The thought brought him back to the problem at hand. "Don't worry your pretty head about it, punkin."

"I'll let you go now. And, Daddy, I hope you get him."

"Where's your mother?"

"She's gone to Sears to get that part for the dishwasher that you promised to put in tonight. We're both kind of sick of washing dishes the old-fashioned way. Well, g'bye."

Walking along Main Street the three blocks to the courthouse— he could imagine what Hollis Sanford's argument would be: A man's innocent until *proved* guilty. Every citizen is entitled to his day in court. He'd been indoctrinated by the idea, the whole philosophy, and he accepted it. In most instances. But every once in a while things came to his attention that made him doubt the system—a convicted felon receiving a five-*hundred*-year sentence in Chicago becoming eligible for parole in *nine*; and an Iowa parole board releasing a criminal after he'd served two years of a *seventy-five*-year sentence.

And now Donald Forrest climbing aboard his fancy chartered yacht—and then what?

In the old marble lobby of the courthouse he used a public phone to call Ezra Seymour's office. Only to be told that the doctor was at Palms Hospital and was not expected back in the office all day. So he had to reach him at the hospital. Ezra provided him with two phone numbers for Mrs. Forrest, both beginning with the numbers 555. He dialed one and asked for her. The cautious, slightly husky voice of an older woman told him politely he had the wrong number. He was about to hang up when he decided to identify himself as Mrs. Forrest's attorney. The woman, who then introduced herself as a Mrs. Davidson, informed him apologetically that Mrs. Forrest was not in. He left his office number and repeated his name and thanked her, adding that his message was urgent. Then he dialed the second number and there was no answer.

Passing through the courthouse, he turned into the new city police station and went directly to Lieutenant Pruitt's office. Waldo was not alone. Seated in a chair as if she felt right at home was a small young woman with short dark hair whom he recognized as one of the reporters he'd seen many times but whose name he could not recall.

Without his usual courtly preliminaries Waldo said: "I know what you want. Well, we're fresh out."

"What are you doing now?" Rex asked.

Waldo's big beefy face scowled. "Not a damn thing," he said. "Look at that desk. Do you have any idea how many crimes have been committed in this jurisdiction in the last twenty-four hours?"

The girl smiled at Rex and then she winked.

"I know what's eating you, Waldo," Rex said. "Well, me too. Where do we go from here?"

"I'll tell you what's eating me," Waldo said. "Lawyers like your colleague Mr. Hollis Sanford buttonholing me outside the court-room and warning me that his client is not to be followed or harassed. Harassed, got that? The man's got it all worked out in that legal brain of his that I'm the one behind everything that's happened to his poor *harassed* client!" He stood up behind the desk. "Well, I'll tell you what I'm doing since you asked. We're trying to find a way to keep the sonofabitch under arm's-length surveillance. With so far no luck at all. His Hertz Cougar is still parked in the boat-charter lot and the boat has dropped out of existence. Again. There's a lot of water around here. All we know for sure is that the boat's not at the Sarasota Yacht Club. He's too smart to tie up there again, but the dockmaster will report here if he should. The Coast Guard's busy chasing drug runners in the Tampa–St. Pete area and the Harbor Police are alerted. Again. If that's harassment, it's the best I can do." He took a long, heavy stride toward Rex. "And what are *you* doing, Mr. Maynard?"

"Trying to get in touch with Mrs. Forrest."

Waldo nodded. He looked tired. Yet somehow younger and more vigorous than he had seemed last night. "Well, you'd better do that little thing, Rex. And the sooner the better."

The reporter stood up. She looked first at Waldo and then at Rex before she said: "Gentlemen, I'm impressed." And when Waldo made a gesture of annoyance: "No, I mean it. I had no idea that this much effort ever went into trying to *prevent* a crime. I mean it—I'm impressed."

"Listen, missie," Waldo said, and his tone had softened, his face had become thoughtful, perhaps even cunning.

"The name's Coleen," the girl said. "Not missie. You want to see my ERA card?"

Waldo ran an impatient hand over his face. "Remember that deal we made?"

"I did my part. The picture of the boat was on the twelve thirty news."

"Well, the deal's off. Print the whole story. It's no longer off the record. Print it any way you can."

Rex was tempted to ask what good that might do—Forrest would probably never see it and if he did, it wouldn't scare him off. Not a mind like that. But he said nothing.

"I saw him in court a while ago," the girl said. "I'll describe him—blue blazer, all-American–hero type—"

"Here," Waldo said, and reached into his pocket. "Get this back to me but see if they'll print it." He handed the photograph to the girl and then shambled away to stare out the window. "Maybe someone'll see him and tip off his whereabouts."

"It's a long shot," Rex said.

"Well, I don't have any short ones in sight, do you?"

The girl stepped toward Waldo. She touched him on the shoulder, very lightly. "I'll do what I can, Lieutenant." And then she added, "Don't worry so."

She turned and flashed Rex a quick fleeting smile as she left the office.

Rex said, "I'll be in touch, Waldo. Thanks."

When Waldo only nodded and sat down to face the chaos on his desk, Rex followed the girl and joined her on the stairs.

"You know what bugs me," Coleen Lyons asked. "This Forrest dude, he's off the wall. He's a kind of love freak. A lunatic lover. I know a lot of women, mister, who'd give one hell of a lot to be loved like that today."

Rex halted. When she paused, too, and turned to look up at him, he said, "Miss Lyons, you're an idiot."

"Maybe." She smiled. "But the man's a lover anyway, isn't he? There aren't too many around."

Rex passed her then, going down the stairs fast. Idiot, idiot, idiot! He had to hurry back to his office so as not to miss Brenda's call when she returned his. So that he could tell her to hide from her lunatic lover. To hide so that her romantic lunatic lover couldn't find her and beat her and rape her.

Or worse. . . .

———□———

After the phone call from Brenda's lawyer in Sarasota, Lavinia had found it impossible to go back to work. She had returned to the screened-in room facing the beach where, if the day was cool enough, she preferred to write. Today the sun was high and bright and there was no surf whatever. She missed its pleasant lapping rhythm.

Tense and expectant, she found herself listening for the familiar sound of the Jeep's motor. She really had only the vaguest sort of idea of what had been going on. Barry had phoned about an hour ago from some hospital in Sarasota. His words had conveyed little but his tone had suggested much. And then, knowing he did not have to ask, he said: *I'm bringing Brenda up there.*

So be it, but where were they? Then Brenda's lawyer, a man named Rex Maynard, had phoned. He had obtained the number from a Dr. Seymour and said he had an urgent message for Brenda. Urgency: it was a quality that had been missing from Lavinia's life for many years. And now, as she had last evening at dinner, she realized just how self-satisfied and complacent and eventless her life had become. She was, she admitted to herself, in an odd mood—with a dark tinge of dread in it.

Giving up on the work, she stood up and went outside—and there were the peacocks come to call. Flamboyant yet dignified and sedate, nine or ten of them together as usual, they were approaching the wooden barrier that separated the dead end of the street from the sea grapes and beach grasses and the sloping white sand. They roamed the neighborhood at will and she had no idea where they slept. They'd been around as long as she could remember and each time they appeared, she was pleasantly, almost childishly amused.

She heard the motor of the Jeep then and looked to see it approaching and turning into the shell driveway that circled the banyan tree. She went to greet Brenda, intending to ask no questions but simply to lead her to the bedroom that she had prepared.

But when she saw the girl's face, she stopped. Still seated in the Jeep, Brenda was staring—not at her but at the peacocks. And she was weeping.

Barry climbed down and came around and offered the girl his hand. Barry cast Lavinia a quick glance revealing nothing and then, unable to help herself, Lavinia took Brenda into her arms and felt her slim body quivering against her as it erupted into sobs.

Together then, the two women went inside and Barry followed.

Urgent, Mr. Maynard had said. But should she tell her now?

"I'm sorry," Brenda said at last, staring around the room, as if she were wondering how she had come to be here, and why. "I'm so sorry."

"It's my pleasure," Lavinia said and heard the gruff sincerity behind the conventional words. It *was* her pleasure—and more. But the man had said urgent. "Your attorney called, Brenda." She caught that expression of bewilderment and quick alarm again, sharper now than it had been last night. "Do you have his number, dear?"

Nodding dumbly, Brenda glanced around the room.

"I moved one of the phones into the guest bedroom," Lavinia said, leading the way into the short book-lined hallway. "Take your time, dear."

And after she'd closed the bedroom door, she returned to the living room. Barry had disappeared but in a moment he came in from outside, carrying three suitcases.

"Has she been crying like that all the way up here?" Lavinia asked.

Barry set the luggage on the floor. "Not a tear, not a whimper. Till she saw the peacocks."

"The peacocks?"

Barry smiled in that slightly abashed way of his. "After dinner last night, remember? You told Toby about your family of peacocks and he got so excited that he made Brenda promise to bring him back to see them. Remember?"

Now she did remember. But Barry had known at once.

"Tell me about Toby," she said.

Barry shook his head and sat down on the couch and took out his pipe. "He can't talk," he said. And then quickly: "Or won't. Dr. Seymour's puzzled, too, but he tried to explain. The kid either can't talk, or refuses to talk because he knows he'll stammer for minutes on end before he can say a word—or it's all beyond his will or even any conscious desire or refusal on his part." He was packing his pipe. "It's beyond me, Lavinia. The human mind. His. His father's." He struck a wooden match on his boot. "I'm way out of my depth."

Lavinia sat down into her wicker rocking chair. "No one knows his depth till he tests it, does he?"

She waited. Barry lit the pipe and the harsh and pleasant smell of his familiar tobacco filled the room. His eyes found hers.

"Dr. Seymour is as concerned about Brenda as he is about Toby." And then, in a hushed voice, he told her what had happened during the night, not leaving out the fact that, before taking his son, the man—whom Barry called "the bastard"—had knocked out his wife and had then raped her while she was unconscious. "She'd like to kill him," Barry concluded, "and so would I."

Trying not to reveal her shock, Lavinia said mildly: "You don't mean that, of course."

But, blowing smoke, Barry only stared at her, clenching the pipe between his teeth; his eyes were narrowed, and instead of looking troubled or contemplative they answered her question. Their feral intensity caused her to shiver.

To throw off the feeling she asked: "And the young man, Charlene's friend?"

"He's been out of surgery for hours. Charlene's with him." But that did not really answer her question. And the shiver turned into a shudder that passed through her entire body.

Then she heard the door of the guest room open, she saw Barry's gaze move to the hallway, and then Brenda appeared.

No tears now. Her face was fixed and cold. Her brown eyes were sharp and furious.

"Lavinia," she said, "do you have a gun?"

For a stunned instant Lavinia could not speak. Far out across the quiet water a boat's horn sounded. At last she managed to say, "I hate guns."

"So do I," Brenda said. "Do you have one?"

"No, I don't, Brenda."

"He's been arrested and he's out on bail."

It was all she said. She crossed the room and went out the door.

"But," Lavinia said, watching Brenda out the window as she moved toward the beach, "but he'll never come here. How would he know?"

Barry did not rise. His pipe had gone out. "He came to Florida, didn't he?"

Lavinia stood up. "Do *you* have a gun?" she asked.

"My father's old deer rifle. A keepsake. It hasn't been fired in years."

"Well?"

Barry knocked out his pipe and shrugged as he got to his feet. "I'll get it if it'll make you feel any better." He faced her. "And if you're prepared to use it."

She thought this over. Good God, was she actually standing

here pondering whether she was capable of shooting a man? Killing a man?

But instead of answering, she said, "I have a feeling *you* wouldn't hesitate," she said.

"I have a feeling you're right," Barry said.

When he'd gone out, she realized that she'd gone weak and slightly faint. She returned to the chair. She sank into it.

Nightmare. The sun was streaming into the pleasant room, everything was in its familiar place, her work was spread over the table in the next room—all comfortable and fixed and secure. But she had somehow stumbled into—or been drawn into—a nightmare. And from now on, what?

Her mind flinched from the violent grotesque images that began to crowd into it. She had written about killing—murder as a polite puzzle. But now her dear, dear friend had gone to get a real gun; he was going to bring it into *her* house.

Was the nightmare only beginning?

——□——

On her way to Lido Shores after leaving Mal asleep in the hospital room, Charlene kept reminding herself that she could not blame Brenda. It wasn't fair. But if only she had not invited her, if only Brenda had not come . . .

It had been several long hours now since Mal had regained consciousness after surgery, but in that time she had sensed that after the trauma he had begun to realize how really serious his injuries were. She attributed at least some of his mood to the medicines and the shock, but there was more: She had seen a kind of bleak despair gather in his eyes, which were encased in an ugly, heavy white mask that hid his face, and no words of hers had been able to reach or dispel it. Which she understood because she shared it, too. His jaws would be wired together for eight to ten weeks while he existed on a liquid diet. And afterward—more plastic surgery with no assurance that his face would ever look the same. She had not dared to think what this might mean to his career, his life. Whenever that question flickered through·her tired and confused mind, she felt a terrible anger take over. How unfair, how accidental, how idiotically unnecessary!

She parked the station wagon and let herself into the house. Which was empty. Where had Brenda gone? On the phone when he'd reached her at the hospital, Barry had told her only that Toby was with Brenda and that they were both all right now. *I'll handle it,* he had said. *You stay with Mal.* And Charlene had felt both relieved and let down at the same time. She had missed Barry's company, his quiet strength. But she was damned if she was going to resent Brenda for that. Or for anything! God knows Brenda had enough to bear. Still . . . if only she'd never come—

Should she stretch out and try to sleep? Hopeless. Her body was almost weak with weariness but her mind was in a turmoil. Probably the shock had not quite caught up with her yet. She decided to go over to the beach. Maybe a good swim would renew her strength, calm her mind. Or at least temporarily numb it. . . .

Only tourists swam in the Gulf this time of year. Well, if it was too cold, she could wade and walk the beach.

In the bathroom she changed into her bikini and then studied her face in the mirror. Well, pet, you show it. You look about ten years older. And, God, she felt it, too.

She put on her short terry robe and returned to the living room.

And there he was. She hadn't seen him for nine or ten years but he hadn't changed. He was sitting on the low built-in couch along one side of the sunken conversation pit, legs crossed, a smile on his lean, handsome face. The face she had seen on the photograph that the police had shown Mal in the hospital hours and hours ago.

Her impulse was to run but she stood there frozen.

"What the hell are you doing here?" she heard a strange voice, her own, demand. "Get out of here or I'll scream."

"You do, Charlene, and I'll put that lovely ming tree through that lovely plate-glass wall."

And he would, too. She knew. She remembered what Brenda had told her. She did not move.

"Aren't you going to offer me a drink? It's after four o'clock."

His tone and his manner were relaxed and friendly and his blue eyes seemed pale and pleasantly distant but, like his voice, coldly mocking, or amused. She remembered what Brenda had said: *He doesn't so much change when he drinks as to get more so.*

"I have some Jack in the car," Donald said. "Plenty of Jack. But I don't feel like going out now that I'm here."

She was still considering the possibility of making a run for it, but it was not her house really and Jason Drake and family in New York didn't deserve to have anything happen to it because of her.

"I could call the police," she said, still not moving. "They're looking for you, you know."

Donald smiled. "Not anymore, Charlene."

Mal's face flashed into her mind. The way it had once looked. "Shall I phone them then?"

Donald shrugged but did not stand up. "I don't think I would, no."

She took a deep breath. "Haven't you done enough? What do you want now?"

"My wife. And my son."

"I don't know where they are, either one of them."

"It won't do any good to lie."

"I'm not lying. I came in just now—"

"I saw you."

"—I came in and they weren't here. That's all I know."

"I hate lies, Charlene."

"Maybe . . . maybe they've gone north. Maybe—"

"Cut the crap, right? Her car's still parked at the Sarasota Yacht Club. I just came by there. I just saw it."

"Perhaps they caught a flight."

"I checked. There's no space out of here this time of year."

So she decided on another tack. "I'll cut the crap, pet, if you will." She stepped down into the pit, careful to keep the huge lacquer table between them. "She's had it. The girl's had it. Now why the hell don't you be a good little boy and leave her, all of us, alone?"

"I haven't done anything to anyone. Yet."

Hearing the word yet, she measured the distance to the open door out of the corner of her eye. But even as she did so, the anger burst in her chest, exploded. "How can you say that? Do you really believe that? Don't you even *know*? Mal is in a hospital bed with his face caved in—who did that?"

"Malcolm Eggers, right?"

"You don't even *know* him!"

"I know enough."

"What did you have against Mal, what?"

"Same thing I have against you. You're in it together, all three of you."

She was staring at him. His eyes had darkened. "In what? What are you talking about?"

"She came down here to meet him, right? You helped her."

Stricken, incredulous, Charlene could not speak for a second. "Right?"

"My God," she said in a whisper, knowing. "My God."

"Right, *right*?"

"No. How did you ever—" But she stopped herself. "Donald, Mal Eggers is *my* friend. Not Brenda's—mine. He hardly knows Brenda."

"You'd lie for her."

"I'm not lying."

"He had it coming." Donald stood up. He was much taller than Barry, even taller than Mal. He was beginning to glare. "I saw him kiss her. I saw *her* kiss *him*."

"Mal and I have been lovers for four months. He just met Brenda two—no, three—days ago. I doubt he even knows her last name."

Silence.

Donald's eyes looked stunned but he did not blink. Then they darkened and he took a step around the table. "Then who's the guy who brought her to the dock? The one with the red beard?"

Barry. Stiff all through now, poised for action, she said, "I don't know."

"More lies. I'm suffocating in lies." He seemed to break an impulse to step closer. "She came down here to meet a man. That's all I know."

She would have to warn Barry. God knows what this flake would do if—

"You're off your rocker," she breathed. "You need help."

Donald made a slashing downward gesture with one arm. "Don't you start that. That's what she's sold you on, right?" And then his manner changed again. He even turned away. And this time he seemed to be mocking himself. "Easy, Donald. Cool it, Donald." He uttered a low, mirthless, scoffing laugh. "What they all tell me, *pet*. My old man, my lawyer, that ugly bitch of a female judge. Keep your nose clean, Donald."

"It's damned good advice," Charlene said. "Considering that you've already ruined at least one life. Mal's the wrong man, goddamn you. Mal's the wrong man. You did it for nothing!"

"Then who is he, who's the right man?" He moved so quickly that he had grasped the lapels of the robe in two hands and had her pinioned in his grip before she even realized what was happening. His face was close, eyes black, intense and demanding, inches from her own, and his breath smelled of whiskey. "No more lies. Who is he? Where is she?"

Helpless, she choked down her terror. And asked: "What are you going to do—rape me the way you raped her?"

His scowl turned into a frown. He released his hold and stepped back.

"I didn't rape Brenda," he said in a tone of astonishment and chagrin—genuine disbelief. Now he *was* blinking. "I didn't *rape* her, I made love to her."

Amazed, bewildered, Charlene moved backward. But she couldn't resist saying, "When she was unconscious?"

For the first time Donald raised his voice. "I wouldn't hurt Brenda!" It was a bellow. "I love her!" In that instant she was convinced that the man actually *believed* that. And, realizing this, she managed a furtive movement to the step leading up from the pit in the direction of the door. He was sick, crazy, sick—

Donald, moving away, did not notice when Charlene stepped up to floor level. "As for you—" And now he was staring at her, his eyes dropping from her face to take in her body where the robe had fallen away. "As for you"—he spoke in a harsh scornful whisper now, his face contorting with disgust—"you could walk in here stark naked and give yourself to me like the slut you are. I wouldn't touch you." His gaze rose to her face again. "You're not Brenda."

As if that explained it. Explained everything. And perhaps, in some weird inscrutable way, it did.

The man had said he was not going to rape her and instead of being relieved or reassured, she was more terrified than ever.

"Now," Donald said at last, again reasonable, again the polite

guest, even smiling, "now, if you don't tell me where she is—"
He stooped and picked up the ming tree in its ceramic base. He
hefted it and lifted his blond brows and waited.

She could guess where Brenda was. She was almost certain.
Brenda was with either Barry or Lavinia, or both. But she was
damned if he could make her say it.

"I don't know," she said. "I don't know where she is."

Donald shrugged his wide shoulders and, without glancing at
the huge window, tossed the ming tree through it. The wall of
glass shattered and the plant crashed into the Japanese garden beyond. The sound was like an explosion and the glass caved in,
collapsing in huge shards and panels, shattering.

But Charlene realized that she had already moved. She was
clawing at the sliding screen panel and then she was out on the
platform, across it, running on the brown pebbles, wildly, toward
the street, shouting. She did not know what she was shouting as
she tore down the street between the rows of houses, screaming
and weeping and giving in utterly to the hysteria that had been
threatening her all day.

IT was a radiant afternoon with twilight still two hours away and sunset another hour after that. The Gulf was smooth as any lake. Lavinia was standing inside, watching Barry swim out toward the rowboat. The water, holding the sun's warmth, had to be cold regardless. Brenda saw him at last and then pulled on one oar and held the other steady until she had straightened the small boat into a position to row toward him.

When Barry's arms were holding on to the gunwale—he did not attempt to clamber aboard—Lavinia wondered how Brenda would react to this intrusion on the privacy and isolation she probably needed. At this distance Lavinia could not discern facial expressions without using the telescope that sat on its tripod within arm's reach, but she did see Brenda's hand go out to touch, very briefly and impulsively, Barry's wet arm.

Before he had decided to swim out, Barry had said, *She's taking tranquilizers but damn it, I wish she'd scream, go into hysterics, curse God, anything but this.* But then, after Dr. Seymour had called to speak to Brenda and, failing that, had asked for Barry and after they'd talked in the way of old friends for a minute or so, Barry had faced her, his short-bearded face smiling vividly: *Toby's swimming. Apparently there's a pool in the hospital. Toby saw it and he must have asked with his eyes or somehow. Ezra thought it might be a good idea in view of what happened earlier. Anyway, he and Ezra have been swimming and the boy's having a hell of a time!* And then he had gone into the other room to change into his swim trunks without telling her what he planned to do.

Now she saw Barry floating on his back, pushing away from the boat, and she watched as Brenda again took the oars into her hands. Barry struck out for the shore and Brenda was rowing again in the opposite direction when the phone rang.

In the next room Bobo set up a raucous racket, screeching protest as he always did and, going to the phone, Lavinia recalled Toby's delight when he'd been introduced to the parrot. It didn't seem possible that that had been only last evening.

At first Lavinia could not recognize the voice that said, "Let me speak to Barry, please."

When she finally did identify it in her mind, she said, "He'll be here in a few minutes, Charlene. What's happened?"

"Is Brenda there?

"Yes, Charlene, dear, what is it?"

The bitterness in Charlene's tone was harsh and guttural and ugly. "Tell her he's looking for her, that's all. I didn't tell him a thing but he's looking for her. And he's looking for Barry, too. He saw Barry on some dock this morning. He doesn't know who Barry is or even that he's my brother but he saw his red beard— Oh, Lavinia, that man's insane. He'll do anything!"

"Charlene, please. What's happened? What has he done?"

"He wouldn't have done anything if Barry'd been with *me* instead of with *her!*"

"Charlene, you're not yourself at all. Why don't you come up here, dear? You know you're welcome."

"Don't invite strangers into your house, Lavinia, don't. I'm making that a cardinal rule from now on."

"But Charl, we're not strangers." Although Charlene *was* a stranger to her now. "You can stay with Barry on his boat if you're afraid."

It was as if the young woman had not heard her. "*She* wasn't a stranger, either. But look at me, look at this house! You should see what he's done to this house!"

"Please, let Barry come get you."

"Barry's too busy taking care of *her*, isn't he? Besides, I can't be twenty miles away from Mal. And I do still have a job, Lavinia. I only called to warn her. I had to do that much."

"I'll have Barry ring you."

"No, don't. I won't be here. You think I can stay *here*? I don't really want to talk to either one of them. I hope I never *see* her again."

"Charlene, whatever's happened, it's not Brenda's fault. Try to be fair."

"Fair? Nothing's fair. Do you think I'll ever believe again anything in this world is ever fair? What did *I* do? Why should this happen to *me*?"

"Please, dear, be reasonable."

"I'm *being* reasonable. I'm going to do just what *she's* doing now. I'm going to *hide*. Tell them both what I— Oh, by the way, how's Toby?"

"He's better, I think. He's still in the hospital but—"

"Hospital?"

"Didn't you know?"

"No. No, and I don't want to know. Not anymore. I don't want to know any more about any of it! Tell Barry not to call me!"

Click. The line went dead.

Lowering the phone, Lavinia glanced around the pleasant, familiar room. Would the nightmare never end? She'd never been involved in anything like this. But now she was a part of it, for better or for worse, and she would have to decide what, and how much of what she'd just been told, she would reveal to Barry. Through the window she saw him now, standing up and beginning to wade to the beach, his slight limp obscured by the water. The relationship between Barry and Charlene had always been one of the truly admirable ones that Lavinia had observed—and had, in a sense, shared. When Charlene had come here after her divorce, brother and sister had both discovered how much they cared for each other—even needed each other. Until now, this minute, it would have been unthinkable that anything, anything, could shake or even cloud that relationship, that devotion. The tentacles of destruction that a strange young man could put out and the poison they could spew into the innocent lives of strangers. . . .

Saddened, tense, she waited for Barry to appear. She heard him using the outdoor shower to get the sand off and then he came in, still toweling his brown, finely muscled body.

She told him that Charlene had called. She repeated Charlene's warnings. Carefully—and with doubts as to her right not to do so—she did not mention Charlene's acrimony or her resentment toward both Brenda and himself.

"But what happened?" Barry demanded, stepping to the telephone.

"She was too overwrought to say very clearly." She watched Barry as he dialed. "But I don't think anything to her personally beyond a good deal of terror." And while Barry listened to the buzzing on the phone: "But the house—he must have wrecked the house."

At last Barry replaced the phone. His eyes met hers. Both, she knew, were recalling what they knew about that other house in Connecticut. She saw the conflicting impulses in his mind: to go to find his sister, wherever she had gone, or to stay with Brenda. She waited. She did not mention even now Charlene's hurt, her painful and bitter sense of abandonment, betrayal. Should she, in all fairness?

"My father's deer rifle is in the Jeep," he said. "I'll show you how to use it before Brenda gets back." He moved to the door. "If I can remember how to use the damned thing myself."

After he went out again, she remembered that he'd told her once: *If my father was ever disappointed in me, I think it was because I could never develop a taste for hunting.*

As that sense of being trapped in a nightmare again settled through her, Lavinia choked down her own abhorrence of anything and everything violent. But in a nightmare there had to be violence. Violence and terror are the stuff of nightmares.

———□———

The trick was to keep control. Hang on.

The phone was not in a booth but in a stand-up plastic hood outside a busy shopping center. The maroon T-bird was parked between a camper and a pickup truck—sandwiched in, just in case.

Hot. Jesus, the sweat was sticking to his clothes and dripping off his forehead. Almost five o'clock—wasn't it supposed to cool off this time of day, even in Florida?

The man's name in Tampa was Grimsby. Up North, it had been Collins. Grimsby was ready to close his office for the day, he said, but he wanted to be obliging. "You got to understand, Mr. Forrest—we need something to go on. Even Forsythe Investigations don't work miracles." He chuckled. "We only walk on water." He giggled. "Maybe what I ought to do is come down there to Sarasota in the morning."

"Morning?" At the rate he was going, the way his heart was pounding and his mind was threatening to explode, he'd never last till morning. "I won't need you in the morning."

Grimsby chortled. Grimsby thought that was *funny*. "Waal, we're always available. Now why don't you see what you can do? Rack your brain. Try to get us some sorta lead. Even a phone number would help. I think you said that's what our Danbury office had luck with, didn't you?"

He gave up. Forsythe would be no help. He was on his own. "If I can get something like that, how'll I reach you?"

"Just use this here number you got. It's connected to my home phone during the night. And before I leave the office, I'll call Danbury and get all the backup data. Oh, we'll locate the little lady for you, sir. Sooner or later."

It was almost exactly what Mr. Collins had said. And *he'd* come through, hadn't he?

Panic threatened again as he stepped back from the phone.

On the way back to the mainland from Lido Shores, he'd made sure again: The blue Lancia Zagato was still parked at the Sarasota Yacht Club. Maybe she'd taken Toby and rented a car—

No cars for rent this time of year. He had the maroon T-bird only because Hollis Sanford—not even questioning why he didn't want to return to the black Cougar now that he was legally free to do what he wanted—had made some sort of arrangement with the local Ford dealer. Hollis Sanford, he had to admit, sure as hell knew how to get things done. For a price, of course.

He was about to get back into the car when the idea came to him. If the little bitch had filed for divorce—and Hollis Sanford had confirmed this—then she'd have a lawyer here in town. But who was he? He should have asked that bitch Charlene. He had to control himself, goddamnit. He'd lost his temper again back there. Maybe enough to put the police on his tail again. That's what scared him most: the way his mind could go blank, the way he could go wild before he even knew what he was doing, or going to do.

Hollis Sanford would know who Brenda's lawyer was. And the lawyer'd know where she'd gone. . . .

He climbed in and slouched down in the seat and took a long swig from the bottle of Jack that he'd planted on the floor under his legs. It braced him. And he'd have to pick up another bottle soon. Couldn't run the danger of being without it again, the way he'd been on the boat with Toby. . . .

Used to be called the Plaza Restaurant, Hollis Sanford had said on their way to the Ford showroom from the courthouse. *Used to be the gathering place for the whole town a few years back. Including the town's literati, such as they were. Now it's changed hands three or four times. Folks go to their private clubs now. But I still go every evening after work. Old dog, new tricks.*

Fat feisty old tub of lard. Donald had to admire the old boy. And he was grateful, too. If he was going to get any help in this town, it'd be from Hollis Sanford. Thanks, Dad—you always come through.

With the air conditioner on he didn't feel so hot and feverish now as he parked in a public lot across First Street from the restaurant-bar, now called Merlin's. Wasn't Merlin the name of the court magician in the legends of King Arthur? Well, Mr. Merlin Hollis Sanford, work your magic.

As he crossed the street in long confident strides, he realized that the panic was gone. He was even feeling a little high. He went into a dim lounge. He'd make it. Nobody gets the better of Donald Forrest. Nobody.

Hollis Sanford—bow tie, rumpled seersucker suit, cigar, and all—was seated at the bar, flanked by several younger people, all dressed as if they belonged over in the beach area instead of in a downtown cocktail lounge. "Buy you a martini?" he said into the older man's ear.

Hollis Sanford studied Donald in the mirror behind the bar before turning his huge soft body. "Here now, let's find us a booth where I can spread my wings." And when they were seated across from each other and had ordered, he took a puff on his cigar and asked, "How's the car? Meet with your approval, son?"

Donald had his number. He knew what his father must have told the old crock: *Money's no object.* Donald nodded, already aching for the drink to arrive. So he decided not to waste time. "What's the name of my wife's lawyer?"

Hollis Sanford peered at him from between the soft gray puffs that all but obliterated his small shrewd eyes. "Time, son, time. We'll get to all that in due and proper time."

"What's the man's name?"

"Here, here, not so fast, not so precipitous, as they say. Divorce now, that is far into the future. Where you been this afternoon? Been behaving yourself, have you?"

The waitress arrived and went away. The Jack was short and cold. Hollis Sanford's pate, bald beneath a few stray strands of white hair, was discolored by the same liver spots that covered his bulbous hands. Braced by the whiskey, Donald ignored the older man's question and said, "What's the guy's name? It's an innocent and logical question, right?"

"Depends on what you want the name for."

"A man has a right to know where his wife is."

The shaggy white brows lifted. "Does he now? Well, that sort of depends on *why* he wants to know, doesn't it?"

"Whose side are you on, Mr. Sanford?"

"Yours, son, yours. Reason I have to remind you—you were indicted and arraigned this afternoon for the commission of one felony. And there're folks I could name who are not overfond of you, one reason or another."

"Who? I don't give a shit what people think. Who?"

"A certain lieutenant of detectives who's taking a certain unhealthy interest in your comings and goings and doings, God knows why."

Donald realized that he was leaning across the table and that he had already finished his drink. "All I want to do is talk to my wife." It seemed so clear-cut and simple—why did he have to spell it out? "That's all."

"Talk? *Is* that all?"

How much did this fat old guy know? And how had he learned it?

"Could be, son, that after what happened last time you 'talked,' could be she's in no mood to hold another palaver with you."

So that was it. Hollis Sanford was in on it with them. He knew everything, so someone had told him. He'd *changed* sides. Or had that Charlene bitch gotten to him in this short a time? Was he saying that what Donald had done to that goddamn house was another crime?

"You're *with* me," Donald said, "or you're against me."

Hollis Sanford hesitated only a second before he lifted his glass to signal for another drink. "Oh, I'm with you, son. That's the reason I'm trying to suggest: go easy now, relax." Then he added: "Considering where your boy is—and I don't presume to know why—your wife isn't going to be willing to sit down and have a friendly chat with you right now, is she?"

Toby? What the hell was he saying? "Where *is* my son?" Donald asked.

"I didn't mention it earlier today because I was hoping you'd be smart enough not to carry this on—"

"Where?"

"He's in a small psychiatric hospital."

Donald stood up. "What's the name of it?"

"The Palms, on South Osprey. But they won't let you see him, so I don't advise your trying."

"If he's there, she'll be there."

"Sit down, sit down. Your wife left the hospital around two and is not expected back today. Doctor's orders. See how I do my job?"

Donald slid into the booth. So . . . so Toby was still playing games. Getting attention and scaring people. What a phony that kid was. But now he knew. She had not gone! Now he was positive.

The drinks came and he polished his off in one long satisfying gulp. He set down the glass.

He was all right now. Great, in fact. Brenda was still in town. And since she was, he'd locate her.

"I'm sorry about Toby," he said. "He's a sensitive boy. Oversensitive. He could *use* a little professional help." But Hollis Sanford didn't reply; he only sat squinting at him as if he were judging him. Damned if he wanted someone on his side who was *judging* him! "Mr. Sanford," he said, "sir, if you want to go on representing me, you'll tell me the name of my wife's lawyer. Now."

The old man seemed to consider that carefully before he grinned and lifted his glass to his thick soft lips. "His name's Maynard. Rex Maynard. Ellis Bank Building. His number's in the book."

Donald stood up again. And went out without glancing back.

——□——

If Toby could swim, it was because of Barry.

Brenda had taken the light Fiberglas rowboat out in some vague hope that, alone, she'd be able to sort out her thoughts, to deal with the chaos of her emotions. To arrive at some sort of perspective so that she could somehow assert herself again and take some sort of action. She couldn't go on running like some scared little rabbit!

Instead of reaching a decision, though, she had worn out her body. Her arms and back and legs were aching and her hands were so raw that she knew they were going to blister.

Then Barry had swum out to her—in that freezing water—to tell her that Toby, too, was swimming. *Ezra thinks it's a very hopeful sign and so do I.* What had that news done to her?

Something certainly. Quite a lot, because now, with the golden light beginning to fade over the water, she was returning to the cottage. Rowing in a straight determined line. Now she knew exactly what she was going to do. And why.

She was going to thank Barry. Not just for what he'd done for Toby—for what he'd done for her, too. What he was continuing to do.

She was going to make love to him. She was going to allow him to make love to her.

Now.

Now, before anything else happened.

It was what Donald had always suspected her of, wasn't it? It was what he'd *accused* her of.

After her marriage there'd never been any man but Donald. Not once. Well, that marriage was over now—maybe it had been over for a long time. She had played her role out with simple honesty and devotion—and look where *that* had brought her.

She had no doubts. No qualms. Barry was the most gentle and appealing and attractive man she'd ever met. And he was alone, and lonely, as she was now. . . .

Her body had fallen into a rhythm of determination, excitement, and, now, desire.

————□————

The bar and lounge waggishly named The Five O'Clock Shadow was one place where a woman alone could go after working hours without fretting about being propositioned—unless she made the first move. Frequented by the younger executive and professional types, with a sprinkling of tourists in Hawaiian shirts and Bermuda shorts, the Five O'Clock offered a conviviality that Mary Rinaldi really enjoyed—because the rest of her evenings were usually spent alone. Tonight's opening at the Asolo had been canceled because of the "illness" of the leading man, so she'd probably make do with a TV dinner and TV. Unless, by some unlikely chance, a likely male should suggest a one-night stand.

After she'd been served her first gin-and-tonic at the bar, she lit a cigarette and then glanced around the smoke-clouded room.

Rex and Alison were at a corner table and waving an invitation so, balancing her glass and cigarette, she shouldered her way through the bibulous geniality to join them.

She asked, first, whether Alison had been able to get up on time this morning after last night's brandy-soaked pow-wow and then whether there was any late-breaking news on the ogre.

"There is," Rex said. "Less than half an hour ago I had a personal phone call from the man himself. He identified himself quite openly."

"Why not?" Mary Rinaldi said. "He's as free as a bird, why not?"

Alison straightened. "You didn't tell me. What'd he want?"

"He wanted me to tell him where his wife had gone."

"You lied, I hope?"

"I stalled. Said I had no idea. Said she'd probably gone north. But he wouldn't buy that. Her car's still here and he'd just learned their son was in the hospital so she had to be around. All he wanted to do was talk to her about Toby."

"I hope," Mary Rinaldi said, "you told him to go to hell."

"Not at first. I tried to reason with him. All the time feeling like an idiot. And then he said she *had* to be staying with somebody: did I have a name?"

"Do you?" Alison asked.

"Only vaguely. A Mrs. Davison or Davidson, with or without a *d*, who gave Brenda a message when I called one of the two phone numbers I have. But I wasn't going to hand over even that much to this nut. No, I'm afraid I just blew. He crowded me too far, I just let him have it—hadn't he caused enough trouble, didn't he even know *why* his kid was in the hospital? And Malcolm Eggers was in another one and he was out on bail himself, did he want to go to prison?" Rex took a swallow of his manhattan. "I was trying to throw a scare into him, I guess. I told him *you'd* see he went up for ten years, Mary—because of the permanent damage to the actor's face, if nothing else."

"Oh, thanks, friend. I hope you mentioned me by name."

"He didn't even raise his voice. I'd have been less appalled if he had. He was cold as ice. Very calmly he warned me: He had every right to talk to his wife and if I wouldn't give him her number, he'd find another way. He knew my time was expensive, so good-bye. He was so cool it was eerie."

"You mentioned two numbers—" Mary Rinaldi felt that angry feeling coming back. "So you *do* know where she is."

"Ezra Seymour gave me two phone numbers. But no addresses. No, I don't know where the girl is and I don't *want* to know. All I want is to pick up three barbecue-rib dinners and go home and try to fix the goddamn dishwasher. I've had enough of Donald E. Forrest for one day."

"You also didn't tell me the little boy was in the hospital," Alison said, and took a wipe at her uncombed reddish hair as she pushed back her chair.

"There's a hell of a lot I haven't had time to tell you, honey," Rex said; and then to Mary Rinaldi: "Want me to make it four rib dinners?"

"Sure," Alison said. "Are you handy with dishwashers?"

But, tempted, Mary shook her head. "Thanks but no thanks. It's been quite a day."

"Let's hope it's over," Alison said. "Rex, I think Nancy'd prefer the pork dinner, not ribs. Her braces, remember? So long, Mary."

And then they were gone. And Mary Rinaldi felt more alone than ever. She debated returning to the bar. She was really sick of her life. Up to here with it. Fed, fed. She paid for her drink and went outside. She had times like these; she lived through them. She was too tall and too heavy and too dreary. And here she was, not tired in the slightest, with no place to go.

The sun was lower and it was a few degrees cooler, but still not dark on the street. There was a gray car parked at the curb and, as she started away, its driver stepped out on the far side of it.

"Could I have a word with you, missie?"

Lieutenant Waldo Pruitt. In person. His tall hulk did not come round to the sidewalk.

"If you don't call me missie," she said, "I'll be happy to chat with you." She strode to the car. "Your place or mine?"

The lieutenant didn't bat an eye. He came round then and opened the door for her, and held it. Somehow the act delighted her. "You may call me missie," she said, and stepped in.

While Waldo Pruitt drove, she waited. Your move, Lieutenant. But she didn't have long to wait.

"Miss Rinaldi, I'm in a picklement."

"Shoot."

"You know that Japanese house out on Westway? Well, it's a shambles. Inside, anyway. Like a hurricane went through it."

"And," she prompted, "you think you know the name of the hurricane?"

"The young woman who occupies the residence insists it was done by vandals. No names, no descriptions, perpetrators unknown."

"But you and I know better."

"I know better because the woman in question was found running down the street in hysterics till some neighbor took her in and notified headquarters. By the time I got there, her story was that she walked in, took a look at the place, and started screaming."

"Why, Lieutenant, wouldn't she want the vandals, or vandal, identified and apprehended?"

"You tell me."

"We both know, don't we? Worse than that, we both understand, don't we? She's terrified."

"She refuses to even sign a complaint. How the hell can I do my job if the *victims* of a crime don't cooperate?"

"And is that your question for me?"

"No, that's not my question. My question for you, missie— sorry."

"Proceed, Lieutenant."

"My question is: Without any evidence to link the sonofabitch to the crime, can I bring him in for questioning without Hollis Sanford yelling harassment and false arrest and my trampling on the legal rights of a law-abiding, upright citizen?"

Mary Rinaldi considered this. If such interrogation should produce enough evidence to warrant a charge, would it prejudice the prosecution's case that there had been no tangible reason to justify the apprehension and interrogation in the first place?

"Any substantiating or outside evidence at all, Lieutenant?"

"A neighbor across the street, a doctor's wife, saw a late-model maroon-colored T-bird parked in front of the house and a Negro maid on her way to the bus saw a similar vehicle speeding out of Lido Shores at about the same time. License number not known and no description of the occupant."

"Well, a crime's been committed; a certain car was observed. What's to prevent your issuing an alert for a maroon T-bird, driver wanted for questioning only?"

"I don't want to jeopardize the Eggers prosecution for you. At least in that one we got a victim who's a witness, we got a signed complaint and an indictment."

"On the other hand, if the ogre's in a cell being held for questioning on a completely different charge—then for that length of time anyway he wouldn't be free to continue his hunt for the quarry he really wants, would he?"

Waldo Pruitt turned his big square head to face her. "Lady, you got a head on those shoulders."

"Thanks, chappie."

"I'd started feeling hog-tied again. Now you said just what I guess I wanted to hear only I couldn't put it together. Excuse me."

And then he took a hand mike from the dashboard panel and

began to give orders to a sergeant named Dutch at headquarters.

Mary Rinaldi sat back in the seat. Well, it could be an exciting evening, after all. And it was, she suspected now, far from over. She wondered whether Waldo would object to her going back to headquarters with him.

But it was Waldo Pruitt himself who, replacing the hand mike and without turning his head, asked: "You hungry?"

———□———

The moment Brenda came in and Lavinia saw her face, Lavinia knew that something inside Brenda had changed. Her brown eyes had lost that stunned vague look; they were bright and alive with an odd soft expression in them, somewhat satisfied, slyly secret. Even her body, the way she held it, suggested that she had come back from rowing with some sort of decision made. But what?

" 'Home is the sailor,' " Brenda quoted.

In that instant Lavinia experienced an unreasonable upsurge of hope and she felt her lips smiling. Then, perhaps catching the smile, Brenda stepped to where she stood and, very briefly, hugged her.

And as swiftly turned away to regard Barry, who stood quietly observing, his eyes assessing, his stance shy. He was again wearing the denims and plaid work shirt.

"Thanks, Barry," Brenda said, remaining two or three feet away from him, but her body straining forward, chin lifted almost challengingly. "Thanks, Barry, for teaching Toby how to swim."

Barry did grin then, in a puzzled way. "I've never even been in the water with him," he said.

But Lavinia then remembered Toby's grave report when he had come back from Barry's workshop last night: *Barry says all I really have to do is let myself go and believe I can do it and I will.*

Had Brenda remembered while she was out in the boat?

Brenda's gaze had never left Barry's face. But his drifted down to her hands.

"How do they feel?"

"What?"

"Your hands. They'll blister, you know."

Then Brenda did look down, lifting her hands and turning them palms up. They were both an ugly red color.

"Brenda, child," Lavinia cried. "Don't they hurt?"

"A little."

"Well, let's *do* something. First, you soak them in cold water and I'll get the ointment." She started toward the hall, pleasantly aware that she was giving in to the maternal instincts that some accident of nature had cheated her out of indulging. "I know I must have something here . . ."

But when she was in the bathroom at the cabinet, she heard Brenda's voice from the other room: "Do you have cold water on your boat?"

"I even have ice," Barry replied.

"Then let's take the ointment along and I'll use it on your boat."

Half-empty tube in hand, Lavinia returned. They had not moved. Barry was no longer staring at Brenda's raw red hands. Their eyes were locked. Brenda's were luminous now, vivid and direct and, Lavinia realized, kindled.

Barry's face appeared slightly bewildered. "The old man in Hemingway's book soaked his in salt water," he said.

"Then," Brenda said, a breathless quality in her voice now, "then let's go out in the Gulf and I'll dangle them overboard. Do you have an anchor?"

"Sure."

Lavinia, it was clear, was not invited. Nor, suddenly, did she wish to be. For now she comprehended, and instead of feeling excluded, she gave herself over to a sense of utter satisfaction— almost as if she, instead of chance and fortuitous circumstances, had arranged it so.

Brenda went outside. Barry stared after her a moment, then turned to Lavinia and took the tube of ointment from her hand.

"Don't cook," he said, going to the door. "I'll bring back hamburgers."

He was gone. Want to bet, Barry, my dear? Want to bet that if you bring back anything, it'll be bacon-and-egg sandwiches for breakfast?

———□———

Damn them, goddamn them all! *Ten years*, that bastard lawyer had said. *You could get ten years for assault with homicidal intent, Forrest, and I'm not alone in hoping that's what they give you! I'll help any way I can.*

Dad always said someday you'd go too far.

Well, if he had—by accident, by *accident!*—it didn't matter what else he did now, right? It didn't matter whether he used the blue steel revolver, did it?

He had thought it'd be a big deal getting a gun. What a cinch, what a joke. Let your fingers travel over your Yellow Pages. First two sports and gunsmith stores had insisted he fill out papers, state law. To hell with that. So he'd told the pockmarked owner at the third shop—guns everywhere, a regular *arsenal!*—that he was a tourist passing through, with two of his ex-wife's brothers on his tail, and this got to the red-neck's sense of drama, this and six fifty-dollar bills extra, over and above the cost of the gun, cash under the counter. *Y'all have a good day, come back and see us, heah?*

He stopped and bought another quart of Jack at a liquor store. Had to clear his head.

He opened the bottle and took a long drink while he drove. He couldn't get smashed; that'd foul up everything. He just had to *think*.

If Toby was still in town, Brenda was still in town. Period. He knew Brenda.

Yeah, he knew her. And if he went to prison, he knew what she'd be doing. Ergo and therefore, he could not let them put him in prison, right? He'd go raving mad in there, nothing to drink and knowing, knowing—the bitch, the little bitch!

But none of that would happen, it wouldn't happen that way if he could just *find* her.

He took another swig. The Jack was doing its job—his mind was working again. *Clickety-click.*

Mango Drive. He'd passed the Whitfield Estates sign, seeing it but not seeing it so that it only registered on his mind when he saw the street name a few blocks farther north. He didn't have to look again at the street map he'd bought at a place called Charlie's News. He had the map in his mind. Proving he was not smashed, right? He made the right turn off the Trail. He had Rex Maynard's home address—it was printed just below his office address in the phone book. Hell, he knew how to do things. Even his father had to admit he had a good business head. Pleasant street, lawns, cement-block houses, middle-class comfortable, mostly retirees probably. . . .

He drove very slowly, looking for house numbers. He had to be careful not to draw attention to the car—who knows, who knows what those cops are up to, how much they know? Even Hollis Sanford had admitted at least one of them was out to get him. . . .

Seventy-one Mango Drive. Rex Maynard's house was older than the others along the street. And larger. One of those stucco Spanish-looking things left over from the twenties or thirties. The only one with a wall around it! And with no other house close to it on either side! Who could ask for anything more?

All he had to do now, what he had to do, was lay off the booze, drive around the neighborhood, find some inconspicuous place to park the car, and then walk back concentrating, really *concentrating*, on the plan he already had worked out in his mind.

——□——

"What is it?" Barry asked.

"The smell," Brenda said. "Toby told me your workshop smelled nice. Or did he say neat? Well, it does. It's a lovely smell."

From the small balcony that served as an entryway from the outside, he looked down on the high and very large but very cluttered room, aware now that he himself had become so accustomed to the scent of freshly sawed and carved and sanded wood that he was no longer conscious of it. Brenda, as if preoccupied yet intensely alert at the same time, had gone down the steps and was wandering about, drifting in a curious way, between the benches and drawing tables, her eyes taking in everything, her hands touching the lathe, the various electric saws, the hand tools—knives and mallets and chisels—stroking the sculptures, lingering almost tenderly, almost sensuously, on their as-yet-unpolished surfaces. Her mood baffled and challenged him. It had been different since she had returned from rowing and he was relieved that she had somehow thrown off that unreachable, frightening despair. In the Jeep coming up the island she had been even more quiet than before, but in a different way. Although she hadn't spoken more than ten words or so, she had seemed less remote.

"Do you want to bathe your hands?" he asked.

"In the salt water," she said, softly, still moving. "On the boat."

"I brought the ointment, but if you want the best results, I have several aloe plants growing along the dock. It's a magical jungle weed really. Called the century plant in this country but originally from Africa, or maybe South America." He was talking too much, and too fast, and he realized it but damned if he knew why. "Shall I get you some?"

"We'll take some out on the boat as we go."

The light had begun to change, to dim toward evening, but the sun was still high enough so that, as it fell through the slanting skylight that he had installed when he first came here, she appeared almost dark against it, shadowy, indistinct. Almost unreal.

"I'll tell you what I want, Barry," her voice said, firm but slightly fearful at the same time. "I want to go out on your boat with you. Very far out. But first I want you to come down here and kiss me."

———□———

He drove through the open gateway into the walled yard and, passing Alison's VW, directly into the arched doorway of the single-car garage that was a part of the house's Spanish design. To save himself juggling the front-door keys and the three plastic plates, which were covered and stacked, and because the barbecue was still hot (he hoped), he went in through the kitchen without pulling down the garage door. No rain predicted, full moon tonight. Because of the delicious aroma in the car, he had been getting more and more hungry on the way from the Old Hickory Restaurant. Now he was starving.

There was no one in the kitchen, which always looked festive because of the colorful tilework, and the breakfast nook was empty. There was no one in the dining room, either; nor was the table set.

"Anybody home?" he called out, as he did nine evenings out of ten. He placed the plates on the long refectory table and stepped to the arch leading into the living room.

Alison was sitting in one of the big chairs by the fireplace. She was smoking a cigarette; she hadn't smoked in two years. Her narrow country-girl face was so pale that the freckles stood out vividly. And her eyes were furious.

"We have company," she said in a mocking drawl.

Then Rex saw him. For the first time. And recognized him at once. *Oh, we're a close devoted family, we are.* He wore a blue blazer and gray slacks and a composed, pleasant expression.

"Come into my parlor," Donald Forrest said. He was seated on one of the couches, motionless, one leg thrown casually over the other. His blue eyes were blank, unreadable—but friendly. "Your wife won't offer me a drink. Will you?"

A tremor of anger passed down Rex's tall frame. "You've had enough, haven't you?" He came down the flat-stone step into the room. *Had* Forrest been drinking? And if so—

"I haven't had too much," Donald Forrest said. "If that's what you mean." And then he grinned—a guest come for cocktails, frivolous chitchat.

"How'd you get in here?"

Before Donald Forrest could answer, Alison said: "Nancy's not here. And you know *her*: she never locks the door."

"So I made myself at home."

"He won't tell me what he wants," Alison said.

Very quietly Donald Forrest said, "Your husband knows what I want."

Rigid now, trying to assess the situation reasonably and realistically, cautious, Rex made no move to sit down. "I don't practice law in my living room, Mr. Forrest. Sorry."

"If you take that tack, *Mr.* Maynard, you could be a lot sorrier."

"If you'd like to make an appointment for Monday—"

"Shit."

Rex sized up the other man: about his own height, but heavier by fifteen or twenty pounds, and probably fitter. A boxing champion in college, his wife had said. And face it: you haven't been in a fight since grade school. Where you learned that logic and words were more effective weapons. And keep in mind what he did to that actor kid . . .

"Let me remind you," Rex said. "You're out on bond. That's a kind of parole, you know. It can be revoked."

"For what? What am I doing?"

"Trespassing. Breaking and entering if the door was not unlocked."

"Which is what you'd claim, right?"

"Right."

Alison had not said a word during this. Now she stubbed out the cigarette and her thin body seemed to relax slightly as she leaned back in the chair. But, remembering all that he knew about Donald Forrest, Rex himself wondered how long he could stall and how much if anything that he could say in words would penetrate the mind he was up against.

"I'm parked in the lot at the golf club at the end of the street," Donald Forrest said, and stood up. "All you have to do is tell me what I want to know and I'll be on my way. No big deal."

How could he convince that mind that he really did not know? "The only address I have is one-one-six-eight Westway."

Very slowly, his tone almost silken, Donald Forrest said: "If there's anything I can't take, Maynard, it's a lie. That's a friendly warning. You get that clear and straight and we'll get along, right?"

"Tell the creep what he wants to know," Alison said. "Before Nancy comes home."

Rex stepped toward her. "I can't tell him what I don't know!"

Alison's eyes met his. There was a shadow of mistrust in them. "I believe you, Rex." But did she?

Now Donald Forrest began to move around the room in long strides. "She believes you, Rex. Hell, she even called *me* a liar, got really sore, when I told her how my wife pays her legal fees."

At once Rex remembered: *Ask your friend Preston Brice what Donald accused me of!* Well, he *had* asked him. It had given him one of the first insights into the disordered, irrational mind of this man. And he remembered, too: *He tried to kill us both, I swear he did.* Rex let the realization seep into his mind. You'd better play this out with great care. You've never really dealt with anyone like this before.

"Well," Donald Forrest asked, stopping to study them both, "well, aren't you going to deny what I just said?"

"He doesn't have to," Alison told him, her anger sharp in her eyes and body. Her scornful disgust. "He doesn't need to." Then, as if to remind Rex, perhaps to warn him, she said: "The man's teched."

"I'll try to have the information you want on Monday morning.

I'll give it to your attorney." But even as he spoke, he knew the maneuver wouldn't work.

"By Monday morning she'll be somewhere else. By Monday morning she could be in Europe, and Toby, too. By Monday morning you could have me arrested again. Breaking and entering. Don't play games with me, Maynard."

The flat monotone of the man's voice, his composure, could be deceptive. No telling what was happening inside. But Rex had to risk the bluff anyway.

"Then I'll have to call the police," Rex said and moved toward the foyer, knowing the danger, chancing it, but damned if he could give the sonofabitch information he didn't have. He stepped up to the tile-floored entry hall and picked up the phone from the wrought-iron table.

"He pulled out the wires," Alison said.

And then Rex glanced back into the room. Too late.

·What he saw caused him to freeze, phone in hand.

Alison was still in the chair. Donald Forrest was standing beside her. And his arm was outstretched. In his hand was a gun. Its muzzle was an inch from Alison's ear.

He could not see Alison's face.

He did not have to.

"You love her?" Donald Forrest asked. "You love her the way she loves you?"

Rex set down the phone and stepped down into the room on hollow legs. Weak, incredulous, he stared at the scene. It wasn't really happening, was it?

Then he heard Alison's voice: "He won't do it, Rex."

But Rex did not know. How could he be sure?

"If you kill us," he heard himself say, "one or both, you'll go to prison for life, Forrest. Is that what you want?" And then, wary but cunning, he added: "Then you'll *never* see her."

Would it work? Would anything work?

The arm did not come down, even an inch, but a new tone—uncertainty? fear?—came into the voice: "Ten years, you said on the phone. Might as well be life, right?"

"In Florida," Rex said, "they've reinstituted the death penalty."

"I don't care. I don't want to live without her, anyway."

And there it was—a plaintive cry, an almost pathetic plea. But against it, what weapon did he have, what chance?

Alison, not turning her head, said: "Rex—the phone numbers."

Bewildered at first, Rex did not comprehend. "Phone numbers?"

"You told Mary and me that you had two phone numbers."

God, how could he have forgotten? In the shock, certain that his mind was functioning perfectly, he had completely forgotten the two telephone numbers that Ezra had given him. A jetliner, climbing, passed overhead. The house shuddered. He reached into the inside pocket of his jacket and took out the gold-rimmed leather memo book that Alison had given him on his fortieth birthday. His fingers were trembling. "Take the gun down!" he shouted. He heard the sound fill the room. He tore out the small page. He heard his hoarse cry echoing through the house. "Here. This is all I have." Quickly he memorized the two numbers as he extended the paper. He would warn Brenda. Fast. It was the best he could do.

He saw the arm with the gun come down. He saw Donald Forrest's other hand reach out and take the slip of paper. He felt himself moving around the man with the gun and he felt Alison's body as, standing up, she came into his arms. She was not crying, but her body was taut and shuddering.

At that moment he heard another sound. He heard the front door open and close.

The three figures in the living room whirled about at the same time.

Nancy was standing in the foyer. Frowning. Her face—part child, part woman—looked surprised at first, her eyes squinting. She wore shorts and a bandana shirt tied by the tails at her middle. Then her eyes widened and her mouth opened.

"It's all right, Nancy," he heard her mother say, in a breathless rush of sound; then he saw Nancy's eyes drift down to the steel-blue glitter of the gun in Donald Forrest's hand. With all the gunplay and violence on TV and in the movies, he knew she had never seen a real gun before.

Out of the corner of his eye then he saw the gun move. It lifted till it was pointed at the child.

Sensing her impulse, Rex called her name before she moved.

But she had already turned in panic and was tugging at the door, clawing at its thick heavy wood.

He reached her before she could open it and, close, he caught a quick glimpse of the profound and terrible terror filling her face before her mouth opened to scream. Kneeling, he pulled her against him, oblivious of everything but the wild shrill wails all through the house and her clinging, kicking, hysterical body, small and convulsive and quivering, against his.

Which was why he did not see the blow. It came from behind and he heard a crunching thud even before he felt the pain. His head seemed to explode and as he rolled to one side, he caught a brief inflamed glimpse of Nancy's face again, a white mask with its mouth open; there was a furious eruption of sound, deafening, and then there was a vast hollow silence that no sound could penetrate as the pain blotted out everything. . . .

But only momentarily. He had no idea how long. He emerged from the dark depths. He could not breathe, he could not move, there was a smell of blood, and suspended over his eyes as they cleared was a face, a face he could not recognize—mouth contorted, jaw twisting, eyes black with fury—and above the blond head the gun, discolored with blood, lifted again, poised to crash down on his head again, and he was too weak even to twist his head.

And he thought he could hear words. A long low snarl. Words. Something about lies . . . everyone always lying . . . drowning in lies. . . .

Then through the unreal pain-clogged swirling miasma a voice cut like a clean knife of sound. He heard every word distinctly. "Stop, stop, stop. I know the address!"

Alison's voice. He could not see her. The face above him turned to look into the room.

Then, even though the gun did not come down on his skull again, he felt his mind sinking once more, slowly this time, into those deep soundless depths.

7

WHEN she awakened, she did not open her eyes. Only momentarily and pleasantly startled at finding herself naked under a light soft flannel blanket, she did not move. Or wish to move. She gave herself over to such a sensuous sense of well-being, physical and emotional—almost spiritual—that she longed to extend the time, to hold it, to prolong it without end.

The engine was silent. Far off a whistle of another boat sounded. There was a gentle swaying motion and she could hear the water riffling against the hull, so without opening her eyes she knew that the tide had changed and that the lakelike surface was no longer so calm and smooth.

How long had she been here? She had had no idea that making love could be so tender and yet so profoundly consuming. She had never known that the exquisite paroxysm of a physical orgasm could be more, so much more—as if the bodies were not bodies at all.

And now her whole being was in a state of total repose. Not spent but sated—tranquil. How long, oh, God, how very long since she had known such utter peace?

Lying here on the wide bunk built into the prow of an old

trawler, over a thousand miles from any place that she had ever known as home, with the unfamiliar smell of salt air all through her head, she had never felt more herself. Or in less doubt as to who that self really was.

She opened her eyes at last. She did not have to lift her body to look out the small portholes on either side. There was a sail in the distance and the surface of the water was fringed with narrow white lines now and the low sun cast a glow over it—red and gold and orange, an impossible luster.

She sat up then and looked out through the opening in the bulkhead. She could see past the galley and the cabin. He was nowhere in sight but she could picture him as clearly as if he were in plain view.

And a slow astonishment engulfed her. He was not like any other man she'd ever known—the boys in school and college clutching and reaching for her body with selfish lust, her first lover who had never bothered to know anything about her but her body, and Donald, who had to possess for possession's own sake, Donald whose own swift satisfaction was timed to Donald's own urgency—

No, she must not think of Donald now.

But of Barry. Barry Conrad, who had been tender and caring. For her—her, not himself, *her*. Was he a new, different breed of man altogether? No swagger, no mocking macho grin of male self-confidence, mastery . . .

And then, out of nowhere, a black cloud descended, closed over her. Everything came flooding back, all the cruel uncertainties, the dismal realities, the hopelessness—

And guilt.

But why? Guilt over what?

That she had flagrantly and adulterously made love to a man she had met only two days ago? That she had done so with abandon and defiance and exaltation?

No. She was no longer married. She had betrayed nothing, no one!

No one but Barry.

But how, in what way?

She couldn't get up, dress, go out there. She couldn't face him. Why, Brenda, why?

Because she had used him. Taken advantage of that gentleness, that compassion, that manliness. After all he had done for her, she had used him, coldbloodedly, to escape. An hour's oblivion. An hour's crazy desperate passion—no more, nothing more. Don't confuse it, don't romanticize it. Certainly not love. Love is a delusion anyway. Haven't you learned that? If nothing else, *that*. Not love. Don't fall into that trap again. Ever, ever. Oh, God, how could she have taken such advantage of the understanding sweetness of the man?

And could she face him now when—knowing, accepting—she hated herself so much?

——□——

The bitch had lied. 3800 South Tamiami Trail. It was an office building. The bitch had tricked him. The windows were dark. The front door was locked for the night.

He'd lost his head when the little girl came in the front door and the lawyer had run to stop her from going out again. The lawyer had just given him the slip of paper with the two phone numbers on it and he'd realized the bastard had had them all along and had lied—that's when his mind had gone blank, that's when he'd lost control. He'd had enough lies, nobody could get away with lying anymore to Donald Forrest!

But you could have killed him with the barrel of that gun. You might have fractured his goddamn skull.

Now, getting back into the car, he wished he had.

He'd warned the wife, after she'd shouted the address two or three times, blubbering, what he'd do if she were trying to trick him.

But he couldn't go back there now. The house'd be swarming with cops. Maybe an ambulance for the lawyer.

The parking lot behind the building was deserted. He couldn't sit here—the woman would sure as hell give the cops this address.

He took a long swallow from the bottle and drove west a block, then made a right turn. North. Now what?

You have the phone numbers. Find a booth.

The gun was in the pocket of his blazer. He'd have to get rid of the gun. It had blood on it now.

Oh, Christ, Brenda, how can you put me through all this? Why do you force me to do these things?

He sneaked another drink. There were only a few cars on the streets.

What'd happen once the lawyer told his story?

Hell, let him talk. They didn't even know what kind of car he was driving. They were looking for the black Cougar that was still parked at the marina where he'd leased the boat. And if they were looking for the ketch itself, it was still tied up at Hollis Sanford's club south of town.

Maybe . . . maybe he ought to take the boat, make the calls from there. But maybe those cops, especially the one Hollis Sanford had warned him about, maybe they'd be monitoring calls placed through the marine operator.

So many goddamn things to think of, to worry about!

Why two numbers? Two different guys?

He spotted it a block ahead—an old-fashioned aluminum-framed booth with glass panel walls. And on his side of the street. Luck was running with him again. He parked along the curb and then stepped across a strip of crisp grass and a cracked sidewalk and pulled open the folding door.

Dialing the first number—555-2726—he saw his hand trembling slightly and he saw the brown stain of blood on his fingers. Lawyer deserved what he got—how many times had he balled Brenda on his office couch?

He heard the distant ringing. Over and over. He waited. Oh, Christ, had he been tricked again?

No one answered. Not Brenda. No one.

The booth held the day's heat. He was sweating. Face, arms, back, armpits, crotch—he could feel the sweat all down his legs.

He replaced the phone. He slumped against the glass. If he'd done all that, if they'd put him through all that for nothing—

He placed the coin again and dialed the second number: 555-2466. The phone rang three times only before there was a sound of the receiver being lifted.

He stiffened.

"Yes?" a woman's voice answered. But not Brenda's voice. "Yes?"

He managed to say: "May I speak with Mrs. Brenda Forrest, please?"

A brief silence. Then the woman's voice—pleasant, self-assured, almost bluff: "I'm terribly sorry. You must have the wrong number."

"Mrs. Brenda Forrest," he repeated. Was the woman lying, stalling?

Her tone was still polite, low-pitched, almost husky: "I'm afraid there's no one here by that name."

"Who . . . who is this speaking?"

"My dear man," the voice said, "since I am *not* Mrs. Forrest and since there is no one here of that name, I fail to see what interest you could have in my identity. Good-bye."

She had rung off.

She was in on it. She was one of them. He knew, he knew. . . .

He slammed a quarter into the slot and dialed again, shaking all over, his mind clogging with anger. She knew who he was, she knew who Brenda was, the old bitch.

"Yes?"

But even as he spoke, he recognized the same voice. Even as he asked for Mrs. Brenda Forrest again, he knew she'd lie again.

"Look here," the woman said, her annoyance crisp and authoritative, "look here, you've dialed the same number. Now kindly don't disturb me again. I'm an elderly lady and a busy one and I won't stand for this harassment, do you understand?"

"You're a lying old whore!" he bellowed, his lips against the mouthpiece. "You tell Brenda her husband's on the phone. I have a right to talk to my wife!"

Click. Again he was holding a dead telephone. The bitch, the old bitch. They were all alike—her, the lawyer's smart-ass wife, Brenda, his mother, all of them, *all women were the same!* For a second he thought that he was going to rip the whole phone box out and pitch it through the glass.

But then, breathing hard, his ears deafened by his own shout, he asserted control.

If he did that, he wouldn't be able to call Tampa and give the numbers to Mr. Grimsby—Mr. Grimsby who did not work miracles, Mr. Grimsby whose company had a 90 percent record of success in such cases. . . .

Mr. Grimsby, who, when he answered, indicated by his tone that he was annoyed to be reached at home but who listened patiently, and then asked him to repeat the numbers. "Offhand, 555 doesn't sound like a Sarasota exchange, but I'll get right on the matter on Monday morning."

"Tonight," Donald said.

"Mr. Forrest, you must realize that our sources of information are within the phone company. The weekend has begun."

"Two thousand dollars," Donald said.

"Would you repeat that?"

"Two thousand dollars over and above the regular fee."

A brief silence.

And then: "Where can you be reached, Mr. Forrest?"

"I'll call you."

"Give me two hours."

"I'll call you in one hour," Donald said and hung up.

He was done for. He didn't know whether he could go on. He didn't know where he could go.

It was then that he turned from the phone and saw the police car. It was parked along the curb behind the T-bird and the blue lights on its roof were flashing.

He thought of the bloodstained gun in the pocket of his blazer.

———□———

Barry did not know what to expect when he became conscious of Brenda's moving about in the cabin. He had been hoping that she would sleep for hours. She had to be exhausted. Then when he turned to face her as she emerged from the companionway, an electric jolt of joy went through him, followed by a throat-stopping diffusion of tenderness that left him shy and wordless.

She was, in that moment, the most beautiful human being he had ever seen. As beautiful as Jenny had been.

But he did not step toward her because something in her eyes, in her stance, would not permit it. What?

"Are you ready to go back?" she asked.

Shocked, he said, "Sure. I didn't want to wake you." But he did not speak her name. Nor she, his. Why?

"Then let's go," she said.

He turned, numb, and stooped and began to hoist the anchor, unable to look at her any longer. Her face was lifeless. And devoid of any hint of happiness or excitement. If anything, a shadow of bitterness in her eyes. Or regret.

When he had the anchor aboard, he went, almost blindly, to the wheel.

"How long?" she asked.

He flipped on the engine. "How long?"

"Will it take? To get back."

He spotted the tip end of Anna Maria Island and said, "Half an hour." His voice did not sound like his own.

She was behind him now, having moved aft, her back turned to him. He eased the throttle forward as he put the boat on course.

He realized that he was not quite breathing. Whatever he had expected—a kiss, an embrace, a few moments of smiling uncertainty and even embarrassment perhaps—he had not anticipated this. Whatever the hell it was. Whatever the hell it portended.

Behind him, she spoke. "Thank you."

A prickling irritation caused his body to stiffen slightly and his tone to take on an unfamiliar edge of irony. "Thank *you*," he said, wondering if he was going to be angry.

"I mean it," she said. She still did not use his name. "I do mean it. I'm grateful."

He could not find the words so he did not reply. A cabin cruiser was bearing in from the north, cutting arrogantly across his bow. He ignored it but slackened speed.

"And I'm *sorry*, too," she said.

"Sorry? Well I'm *not*."

Her voice came closer. "Not for what happened—I don't mean that."

"Then what?" he asked.

At last she spoke his name. "Barry—do you know the Bible? I think it's in the Old Testament. 'Comfort me with apples.' "

" 'For I am sick of love,' " he quoted. And now he knew what she was saying. "How do you know?" he asked.

"Know?"

"That you are sick of love?" His mouth and throat were dry. His voice was hard. "How can you know when you've never been loved?"

What a cruel, hateful thing to say. How could *he* say a thing like that? What the hell right did he have to tell this lovely, suffering girl that she had never been loved?

"Until now," he heard his voice say, grimly and loudly, over the steady thrum of the engine. "Until now."

———□———

Rex Maynard was a shattered man. This is what kept going through Mary Rinaldi's mind while she listened. A shattered and terrified man.

She had been with Waldo in his office, after having had a spaghetti-with-Chianti dinner with him at his favorite restaurant named Gigi's, when Rex phoned. He had to talk to Waldo at once, he'd said, but not at police headquarters. When Waldo had told him that Mary was with him, Rex had asked whether they could meet in her office. So she and Waldo had walked the single block to the offices of the state attorney and now the three were seated in the waiting room in the otherwise deserted building.

And while she was listening to Rex's words, she was concentrating on his condition. And longing to be able to do something for the pain that she knew was throbbing and swelling in his head which, he had said, Alison had bandaged the best she could. He refused to go to the emergency room of the hospital, or to see a doctor, and he was trying to explain why: He did not want to answer any questions. And as he spoke, she began to understand.

When he had told his story—quietly, economically—he concluded by saying: "It was Alison who got rid of him, not me. My mind wouldn't work, that's all. All I could do was stare at that damned gun."

Eyes wretched, even ashamed, he took off his shell-rimmed glasses and passed a hand through his thinning brown hair. It came to her clearly then: Poor Rex, he felt guilty. As if he had reacted inadequately, or even ignominiously, in the clutch.

But before she could put her reassurances into words, Waldo jumped up. There was an expression of relief and satisfaction on his square raw-boned face and a low rumble of triumph in his voice. "We got him. Mary, you do the paper work—breaking and entering, assault with a deadly weapon, fleeing to elude, possession of a concealed weapon, everything you can think of. I'll get back there and see he's detained."

"Detained?" Rex asked, frowning, getting to his feet.

"I didn't tell you," Waldo said, "but our friend was picked up a while ago on a driving-under-the-influence charge at Osprey and Laurel. It must have been just after he left your house. He's being processed now. Breathalyzer test showed he was legally intoxicated. That's all we had then. I had a squint at him in the holding cell. His lawyer's on the way. But *now* we've got charges, *real* charges. So you take it easy and let old Uncle Waldo do his job."

But by now Mary knew why Rex had not wanted to meet in Waldo's office. She sensed what Rex was going to say.

"Hold on, Lieutenant. Listen. You don't understand. I'm not bringing any charges."

Waldo's face hardened but his eyes opened wider. "You don't have to. I will."

"I mean, Waldo—I mean I won't press them."

"Are you saying you won't sign a complaint?"

Rex's chin set. "I mean everything I've told you—legally it didn't happen."

Waldo visibly overcame his shock. He glanced at Mary, frowning: Was this possible? Then, almost in a whisper, he asked: "And your wife?"

"Alison and Nancy are on their way to her brother's. In Asheville, North Carolina. In her VW. I'm on my way, too." Rex took a step. "Do you think I'd leave them in that house? You didn't face that weirdo. You don't know."

"But we've got him," Waldo said. "He's in custody right this goddamn minute."

Rex replaced his glasses. "Sorry, Waldo. I've been through all that in my mind, believe me. But it's my family. He warned Alison before he left that if she was lying to him, he'd be back. You don't *know* that guy, Waldo. You didn't see him put a gun to your wife's head. You didn't see his face *after* he opened up my skull. He could have killed me because he thought I'd lied to him. He could have killed any one of us."

Almost softly, Waldo said, "You or somebody else. You think he's going to stop here?"

"I don't care about that now. God help me, I can't. For all I know he's come back and burned the house down by now. I'm sorry but I know what I have to do and I'm going to do it."

Waldo's head nodded. "I wish I knew what *I* was going to do," he said very quietly. Then suddenly, his pawlike hands reached out and he grabbed the lapels of Rex's jacket and brought Rex's body to him and growled: "I *know* him. I know what he did to that kid of his. I know things you don't know. Not prosecutable offenses maybe but *crimes*. You saw the wife's face—what do you think he'll do to her if he gets near her again?"

Mary stood up then. She saw the stubborn anguish in Rex's face as he remained motionless in the other man's clutch and she saw the fury in Waldo's eyes. "Waldo," she said. And only that.

The older man released his grasp. Almost gently. As if he wanted to apologize. Rex stepped away.

"Waldo," she said then, "Waldo, did Forrest have a gun on him when he was arrested?"

"Not to my knowledge." He seemed to be having trouble with his voice. "Half-empty bottle of booze on the seat. Routine search." He moved toward the next room. "Which one is your office in here?"

"Third on the right, Waldo. Light switch on your left."

She heard him shamble to her office and pick up the phone.

"I guess you think I'm a bastard, too," Rex said.

"I think you must love your family very much." And as she said it—something she'd been painfully aware of all along, of course—she realized how really foolish and hopeless her attraction to Rex had always been. Her forlorn girlish yearning, her lubricious desire . . .

"It was Alison who really *did* something," Rex said. "Not me. I was too goddamn petrified."

Mary smiled. "Well, chappie, you were petrified for *them*, weren't you. That hardly makes you a coward."

His eyes narrowed behind the glasses. "Alison said something like that just before she took off in the car."

"Smart girl."

"Both of you."

"We try, chappie. We try. Now, before *you* take off—you mentioned giving the ogre two phone numbers."

Rex nodded. "I did have enough sense to memorize them, as we used to say in school, before I handed him the slip of paper. 555-2726. The other one's a 555 number, too: 2466. Those are Manatee County prefixes, aren't they?"

"Anna Maria Island, I think. Bradenton Beach, Holmes Beach,

and the village of Anna Maria. I'll ask Waldo to check it out."

"I don't suppose she has to be told that he's on the prowl for her but I was going to try to reach her by phone on my way north."

"I'll do it," Mary said.

"Thanks. I should wait a minute and try to make Waldo understand."

"Waldo understands."

"Like hell."

"That's what really bugs him. The man's quite a human being, Rex. It's kind of exciting watching him discover the fact."

"You're all right, too, Mary."

"Thanks. I could say the same for you. How's Nancy taking all this?"

He shook his head and stepped to the street door. "I don't think the kid ever witnessed actual violence before. She'll get over it but maybe now when she sees it on television she'll know what the real thing is." He turned. "Well, Mary—"

"Well, Rex?"

"I'll be back once he's really behind bars."

After he's actually killed somebody? But she didn't say this. What she said was, "Have a doctor look at your head when you get there."

Rex stepped to her then and kissed her on the forehead.

Then he turned and went out onto the street. She heard his car start and pull away. In some odd way she knew that she was saying good-bye to Rex Maynard. As if she had ever said more than hello.

She lit a cigarette. The light outside was changing. The sun was probably about to set over the Gulf.

In the empty building she heard the sound of Waldo replacing her phone. In a moment he appeared and went directly to the door.

"They've done another body search. No concealed weapon. But bloodstains on one hand—and not a damned thing we can do about it. They're going over the T-bird again." He held the door— dear old Waldo. "His trusty attorney is on the scene and the usual DWI bond has been posted. For a lousy two hundred dollars he's ready to walk out. Again. Twice in one day."

"Maybe he panicked and threw the gun into some empty lot," Mary said, matching her stride to Waldo's on the pavement.

"Or maybe he threw it out the window onto the street somewhere—for some innocent kid to stumble on."

Possible. Quite possible. The proliferation of evil possibilities— where would it end? To the more immediate point: Where would he zero in next?

"Waldo," she asked, "are you ready for some more bad news?"

"What other kind is there?"

"I thought of telling you at dinner but the spaghetti was so good. And I was enjoying the company."

"Cut the bullshit."

"Why, Lieutenant Pruitt!"

"You've heard the word."

"Well, I sent young Dan Gregory of our office to try to get more details from Malcolm Eggers this afternoon. Strictly routine."

"And?"

"Well, Mr. Eggers has somehow become uncertain as to his identification of his assailant."

"Uncertain? He identified him to me personally."

"Yes, but only with a nod of his head if I recall. And when he was en route to surgery only hours after the assault. He gave Dan a note he'd written. He claims *now* he was full of medication and still in a state of shock at the time."

They walked in silence.

Then Waldo said flatly: "Charlene Conrad."

"Married name Scherwin. His sleep-in friend—yes, what about her?"

"One-one-six-eight Westway," Waldo growled. "Lido Shores."

And then Mary understood. She recalled Waldo's description of the vandalized house. She remembered that Charlene Conrad had also refused to press charges.

"My God," she said, "he has the whole damn world terrorized."

"So terrorized," Waldo snarled, "that the sonofabitch's going to get away with anything he wants to do."

They had reached police headquarters. Lights in the jail windows above. Shadows behind bars. And Donald Forrest in a holding cell. Or was he?

But Waldo was not giving up. In his office he flipped on the intercom and spoke with someone named Dutch. No gun had been found in the car; they had taken the Thunderbird apart. And Donald Forrest was leaving the building with his lawyer.

Waldo snapped the lever and slumped down into his swivel chair. "Our old friend Hollis Sanford," he said.

Mary reached and helped herself to a sheet of paper, wrote down the two numbers that Rex had given her, shoved it across the desk and said, "May I use your phone?"

Waldo glanced at the numbers. "Bradenton exchange. Anna Maria Island." And while Mary was dialing: "When you get the address, I'll alert the three town police departments up there. Not that they can do anything but keep an eye out." He looked tired again—and older than he had at dinner. "I just wonder why we're going to so much damn trouble on one case."

But she didn't have to answer that and they both knew it.

The phone was ringing at the other end.

"Tell her," Waldo said, "that we're doing all we can. Don't tell her it probably won't be enough. Or in time."

——□——

Until now. He had shouted it over the throbbing of the boat's motor. She had said she was sick of love and he had asked her how she could know since she'd never been loved—

Until now.

Then, startled, more confused than ever, her mind in total turmoil, she had retreated to sit in the stern, trailing first one hand in the water, then the other.

Too much, too much. She couldn't deal with it. Everything was happening too fast. And was continuing to happen. Too much, too much . . .

She had tried to think of Toby. He was safe. Wounded in his own way, but safe, alive. And possibly recovering.

She had tried *not* to think of Donald—where he might be, what he might be doing. All she could hope was that she'd never see him again, hear his voice.

She would no longer hope for his death. But, God forgive her, she would not mourn it.

She heard the sound of the engine change. They were in a long inlet, moving between a line of palmetto islands on one side and, on the west now, the long strip of the key with a public park, cottages, docks, and not far ahead she could see the roof of Barry's workshop. Panic stirred her to action. She could not go ashore, return to Lavinia's without . . . without what? There was so much she had to tell him, explain, ask him . . . but what?

She stood up, rubbing her blistered palms against her slacks, and moved to stand behind him at the wheel, close enough so that he could hear her voice.

"You said that I have never been loved."

"If I hurt you"—his voice was gentle again—"if I hurt you, Brenda, I'm sorry."

"It's true," she said. "Maybe I've really known for some time. Maybe it took your saying it."

His pipe, unlit, was clenched between his teeh. "If that's what it took, I'm *not* sorry I said it."

She accepted it fully then, but with no sense of loss, only a faint sadness, hurtful as the light dying, the sun disappearing over the roofs and the trees. She had never really been loved—she surrendered to the hard ugly fact and, again, she was grateful to him.

So she said, "Thanks, Barry."

"It's not your gratitude I want," he said.

"What is it you want?"

"I want you to get it through your head that I know one thing for sure now and so should you: It was no fault of yours, so shuck off the lousy guilt once and for all. You can't blame yourself for *his* failings. Put the goddamn blame where it belongs once and for all."

So . . . he had known that, too. But he sounded almost angry again. At her?

"It's taken me a while," he went on, manipulating the wheel, eyes narrowed, "to get it straight myself. I've been standing here feeling hurt and resenting the way you came out on deck a while ago. Well, no more. I've figured out what's eating you."

Had he? Could she tell him, in words, how sorry she was that she had taken advantage of the very qualities she most admired in him? Oh, God, what kind of a human being was she to have done that?

"I know what's eating me, too," she said, staring away.

"You're giving yourself hell again, aren't you?" He did not even sound like himself. "You imagine you've victimized me in some way and you're bleeding over it." He reached and one hand took hold of her shoulder and swung her body around. "You think I care that I could help you get your revenge on the sonofabitch?"

She stared into his eyes. Revenge? What was he saying?

"We both know the one thing he fears most. Well, you gave it to him. *We* gave it to him. I only hope one of us has the chance to tell him."

But . . . but she'd had no thought of revenge. She felt his strong fingers digging into her shoulder. She began to shake her head.

"Don't deny it, Brenda."

She wrenched herself away.

"Admit it, Brenda, savor it, revel in it. He had it coming. Revenge is sweet as hell!"

Was it possible? Now she was even more confused. If making love to Barry had really been only—

The stern was swinging out into the channel and she could hear the water thumping against the hull.

"That's terrible," she said. "That's *worse*."

"Like hell. Look, what's so terrible about revenge? Or pity?"

"Pity?"

"Sure. You felt sorry for me, didn't you? Well, I felt sorry for you, too. Damned sorry and I still do. So what? Who said pity can't be a part of love? And gratitude—you're grateful that I came along and could help and I'm grateful I finally have someone *to* help. It's all part of it, so what! Who the hell cares where love comes from, Brenda?"

The gray wooden hull touched the gray wooden pier, with a soundless precision and delicacy, and there was not so much as a tremor through the boat.

Until now.

"Make yourself useful," he said, turning from the wheel and picking up a coil of rope. "Jump up there and tie off the line."

She did as she was told, every nerve on fire, her body flushed, her fingers clumsy and trembling. Then she straightened. He was poised to leap off the gunwale.

"Love?" she said.

"You heard me."

———□———

"Where're you taking me?"

"Hyatt House," Hollis Sanford said.

"No vacancy," his client said.

"There's always room for one more if you know the right people."

Young Forrest was in a sullen gloomy mood. Well, all that photographing and fingerprinting and treating a man like a criminal just because he'd hoisted a few too many drinks, it was not exactly what you'd call an uplifting experience, and hard on the old ego. Too, probably the young man was panting for another drink.

"Be there in less'n five minutes," Hollis Sanford said, lighting a cigar. "Could've waited to make that important call you had to make back there." He was curious about that: Forrest'd been downright stubborn—while Hollis had cooled his heels waiting on the police station steps. "What was so all-fired vital? Anything your legal counsel can help you with?"

"Maybe." Caution in the thick voice now, a note of shrewd wariness in the foggy mind. "I have two phone numbers. I need the addresses. The bastard I spoke to in Tampa promised he'd have them in an hour but he's let me down."

Hollis Sanford considered this. Time for *him* to be a little cautious himself. No telling what this screwball might do next time he saw his wife. "Maybe on Monday. There're ways."

"Fuck Monday."

"Short, but not to the point. Irrelevant, young sir, irrelevant. Give me the numbers anyway."

"555-2726 and 555-2466," Donald Forrest said dully.

Hollis Sanford committed them to memory. Mind still perky at sixty-seven. Wits still in fine fettle. "Sounds like Bradenton," he said. "Not Sarasota. I'll get the addresses."

No answer. Young Forrest stared morosely ahead. Well, he was up against an odd one here. But there was mazuma in them thar hills: The weirdos got into the deepest thickets, and extricating them, if they were also rich, provided the funds to make a man's declining years as painless as possible. Sometimes sort of challenging to boot.

"Why don't you take me to the car?"

"The one you were driving while intoxicated? Well, son, there are regulations about things like that. One thing, your driver's license has been revoked for three months. Another, the vehicle's been taken to a service station. Normally, you could recover it by paying the towing fee. But the Thunderbird's been impounded for reasons I'll delve into on Monday."

"Then take me to the boat."

"The Field Club? Young man, you are in no condition to pilot a yacht. And in addition, we are going to indulge in a voluptuous dinner together, replete with as many alcoholic beverages as you desire, while we await the arrival of your daddy."

He'd hoped this might jolt the hungover young scalawag out of his lethargy. But if anything, the news seemed to drive him deeper into the doldrums.

All he said was "Christ" and he mumbled that and slumped deeper into the seat.

Ungrateful pup. Orin Forrest had phoned to say he'd be in on the 7:15 flight from Hartford and he'd sounded like a damned concerned parent. The kind that's willing to pick up the tab for a fiasco like this without questioning the amount.

So Hollis decided then that maybe he did have a duty here, for the father's sake—if he could bore through to whatever sanity this spoiled mixed-up brat had left.

So he said: "Hear me now, and *listen.* Advice is what your daddy's paying me for, so listen. I got my finger on the pulse of this town, that's my business. Certain shenanigans I don't have the straight of yet—like why you haven't been charged for what you did to that house on Lido Shores. But I do know they're out to nail you on the assault-battery charge, that actor fellow. And I have been told by your wife's attorney what you did to your wife. Son, you got certain quarters in this town mighty damned upset and that's unhealthy in the extreme. Especially if you pull off anything else. *Anything.* When Waldo Pruitt calls me personally, that's bad, bad medicine. What sticks in his craw, reading between the lines, has something to do with whatever you did to your son. That ring any bells?"

"I never did anything to Toby. I love my son."

"Well, he's in a psychiatric hospital all the same. And Lieutenant Pruitt blames you."

"You said they won't let me see him." Donald Forrest was sitting up straight for the first time. "What's the name of his doctor?"

"Now that particular little fragment of information I failed to obtain. *Mea culpa, mea culpa.*"

He made the turn onto West Sixth Street, now called the Boulevard of the Arts. A block away the Hyatt House rose up on the left, overlooking the bay. The sun was out of view, beyond the keys. Well, if you've seen one sunset, you've seen them all.

"Palms Hospital, you said—they'd have to give me the name of his doctor, wouldn't they?"

Hollis Sanford gave up. There was only a certain amount a man could do. This fool was living in a world of his own.

He drove to the end of the street to turn around and return on the other side of the planted median to the sloping circular driveway in front of the hotel. He pointed out the new library and the strange-looking theater building on the edge of the bay. "Designed by the Frank Lloyd Wright people, locally dubbed The Purple Cow. It seems that lavender is the favorite color of the great man's widow. Old ladies love the place."

But he knew Donald Forrest was not listening. It didn't matter. Some good victuals, a few martinis—let his daddy take over from there.

When he stopped and let the young uniformed attendant open his door, he maneuvered his weight out of the car, saying cheerfully, "All ashore."

But Donald Forrest made no effort to get out. Instead, before the attendant could climb in, he slid over on the seat, fast, slamming the door and taking the wheel and throwing the car into gear, all in one smooth movement.

Hollis stood there and watched his handsome white Cadillac Seville move in a curve down the ramp and onto the Boulevard of the Arts toward the stoplight at the Tamiami Trail.

Now what? Well, one thing he *couldn't* do was report that his own client had stolen his car. He tipped the attendant, shaking his head, and went into the elegant high-ceilinged lobby. The kid was a freak. Beyond reason—a real freak.

Well, if he got in any deeper, it was not his lawyer's responsibility. His job was to defend the accused, not to try to forestall a crime that might or might not be committed.

He went to the desk and left word that when a Mr. Orin Forrest checked in, he—"Hollis Sanford's the name"—would be dining in the Peppercorn Room.

Well, if the young bullhead wouldn't listen and if he continued on his merry way—who knows? In all his years at the bar Hollis Sanford had never had the opportunity to argue a capital case. Wouldn't be a bad way to end a career—a sensational murder trial. Go out in a blaze of glory.

——□——

Sunset. While she stood watching the great orange-red disc touch the horizon of water and then, always swiftly at that point, descend out of view, Lavinia heard the motor of the Jeep and realized that she had been expecting it even though her hopes were set against its return. They should have stayed till morning. Not only because they both deserved it but because Brenda would be safer out on the Gulf in Barry's old fishing boat.

During the eternity since the angry and frustrating phone call from Brenda's husband, whether she was chattering idiotically with Bobo or tidying up the rooms that were already tidy, she had been waiting—would he come to the door, would he knock, would he burst in? Or would the phone ring again? When it had, the caller had not been Donald Forrest but a woman named Mary Rinaldi, who had left a number.

As soon as Brenda came in, before Lavinia could get any impression of her mood or condition, she said: "The police! We saw three cars in five miles. Have they been here?"

"Not exactly," Lavinia said, seeing Barry's face behind Brenda's, both alert, inquisitive, not quite alarmed. "Not exactly, but two cars have come down the street and turned around at the barrier. One Holmes Beach police, one sheriff's. But no one came to the door." Then she said what she had known for more than an hour that she would have to say: "Brenda, he called. He asked to speak to you."

"And—?"

"I told him I'd never heard of you." She did not mention what she had wanted to tell him. Or that she had been called a whore for the first time in her life. "Whether I was convincing or not, I don't know."

Brenda did not answer. Barry placed a hand on her shoulder.

"Anything else?" Brenda's tone, like her face, was expressionless. "Dr. Seymour?"

Lavinia shook her head. "Sorry. But a Miss Mary Rinaldi. I tried to be cautious. She said she was calling for Mr. Maynard so I said you'd be back." Then she added: "But probably not till morning."

"Did she leave a number?"

"It's on a pad by the other telephone. Brenda, she asked for this address. Was I wrong to give it to her?"

Her pale delicate face still inscrutable, Brenda shook her head. "No," she said. "Thanks, Lavinia." And she went into the hall and then into the guest room.

Barry looked after her a moment, then sighed. He went to sit on the rattan couch and then as if to answer Lavinia's unworded question, he asked, "Can a man fall in love in less than a week?"

"If he's got any sense."

Barry grinned. "Or if he hasn't." And then his grin disappeared. "Anything from Charlene?"

Lavinia sat down beside him. They could look out through the screened-in room where they'd had such a pleasant dinner only last evening, and out across the water. The afterglow was really the best part of the sunset—gentle, soothing, refreshing. "Not a word," she said, knowing what was on his mind. "She'll come to see it in perspective." She only hoped that he was not tormenting himself; she only hoped the rift between brother and sister would not become another piece of the wreckage. She placed her hand over his. They rarely touched each other, or had occasion to. "There *are* times when one has to choose, aren't there?" It was the best she could do. Barry had chosen to be with Brenda. Lavinia was glad. "You didn't bring hamburgers."

"I forgot."

"Well"—and she stood up again—"more gourmet leftovers. I wish I kept cans on my shelves like most people. Do you know, I haven't opened a can in twenty years."

Brenda had returned. But she did not speak. She did not seem to see them.

"Brenda?" Barry prompted, as he stood. "Who's Mary Rinaldi?"

"Assistant prosecuting attorney," Brenda said. Her face looked dazed now. "Something like that. Very nice."

"And . . . ?"

Brenda blinked. "Donald went to see my lawyer a while ago. In his home. With a gun."

They waited. Lavinia thought of the hunting rifle standing hidden behind the door in her bedroom. Barry reached to touch Brenda's arm.

"I no longer have a lawyer. Whatever Donald did, it was enough to chase Rex Maynard off the case. And out of town."

"Wasn't he arrested?" Lavinia asked.

"Not for that. I don't know why. He was arrested for drunk driving." She meandered into the screened room and her hands wandered across the glass surface of the table.

Barry followed. "Then he's in jail?"

Brenda only shook her head. "No one knows where he is." Then she turned to Barry and her eyes were curious but slightly accusing. "What did Donald do to that lovely house?"

Quietly, meeting her gaze, Barry said: "He trashed it."

"Another one," Brenda said. "And you didn't tell me." It was a soft flat statement of accepted fact, only faintly tinged with reproach. "Someone else had to tell me."

"I knew," Barry said, "that you'd take it on yourself."

She seemed to ignore that. She glanced at Lavinia. "And is Charlene coming here?"

"No, dear."

Brenda nodded. "She doesn't want to see me." She turned to Barry. "Or you. Does she? First Mal, now this."

Barry did not lie. "She'll get over it."

Brenda nodded again. Lifelessly. "She shouldn't have to."

Barry reached again but this time she evaded his touch, drifting away to stare out at the sail sculpture on the beach.

"I said it on the boat and I'll say it again." Barry's tone had taken on a different timbre. "No more guilt, damn it. You can't go on blaming yourself for everything *he* does!"

"Everywhere I go, everything I touch, everyone I meet—" Her voice, forlorn and miserable, asked, "Is there anything else I should know?"

But before Barry could answer, the ringing of the phone cut harshly through the two rooms.

Brenda turned. Barry glanced at Lavinia, who stood up and stepped toward the table as it shrilled again.

But Brenda, on the third ring, said: "I'll take it."

Startled, Lavinia asked, "Are you sure?"

Brenda was in the room now and she picked up the phone just before it could sound again.

"Hello?" And then: "Yes, Doctor, this is Mrs. Forrest." And then, not knowing whether to go outside or to stay, Lavinia simply stood without any pretense of not hearing. She was conscious of Barry's stiff tense silence and of the fact that Brenda's face revealed neither anxiety nor relief. She could hear the other voice speaking without pause but she could not make out the words.

Finally Brenda spoke again. Her face was still composed, almost blank, as if the shocks she had been experiencing in the last few minutes had driven her into a state of apathy—or possibly a kind of stoic despair. Her voice, however, and her words, contradicted this impression. "Thank you, Doctor. You can't *know* how much I thank you." And then, after a long pause: "You are a kind man and I love you."

Astonished, dumbfounded, Lavinia could not take her eyes off Brenda, who, very slowly, lowered the phone. In that long moment Lavinia saw—or perhaps imagined she saw—her own amazement and incredulity reflected on Brenda's face. Had the girl ever said anything like that before? And to a person who was almost a stranger . . . ?

Brenda let her gaze move from one to the other before she spoke. "Toby is not talking but Dr. Seymour has found a way to communicate. He asks questions and Toby types out a word or two. Types." A small smile trembled along her lips. "Dr. Seymour called to say he is more hopeful than ever."

Lavinia remembered what Barry had told her: that the doctor wished Toby could acknowledge his hate and that Brenda would not be consumed by hers.

When Barry, not speaking, only smiled his shy smile, Lavinia said, "Then I say it's time for wine and sustenance. I'll bet not one of us even thought of lunch and now it's time for—"

"Wait," Brenda said. And when Lavinia paused on her way to the kitchen: "From now on I'll be here and I'll take all phone calls if you don't mind, Lavinia."

"Do you really think—"

"*Do* you mind?"

Lavinia's eye caught Barry's. He was frowning. "Whatever you say, Brenda."

"And from now on," Brenda said, "I would appreciate it very much if you would not go on protecting me. Both of you. I'm a big girl now. I do not want to be spared."

"What are you going to do?" Barry asked.

"I don't know," she said in a rushed whisper. "Don't ask me that, I don't know, I don't know. *Yet.*"

Then, as if the pressures had been gathered and seething in the crater, the volcano erupted.

"What I am *not* going to do," Brenda cried, "is go on running! Hiding. Skulking like some terrified animal in a cave! I have *had* it." Her eyes flashed brown fire and her face contorted and she was moving, junglelike, around the room. "I won't *take* any more!" It was a shriek. "I won't let anything else happen—to anyone, to you, to Toby, to me, to *anyone!* I . . . refuse . . . to . . . take . . . any . . . more!" Then, moving in a gust of fury to the phone table, she snarled: "*You heard me!* If he calls again, I'll talk to him." Hatred, naked and savage, howled in her voice: "And if he doesn't call, I'll find out where he is and go to him! I am not going to sit here shivering and weeping, not anymore. He's done enough. I won't take any more if I have to kill the cruel, vicious sonofabitch myself!"

—— □ ——

Thank you, Doctor. You can't know how much I thank you. Some days were good days. Gratifying.

Ezra Seymour removed his jacket and tie and adjusted the shade of the lamp over the desk and went to stretch out on his own couch in his own office. It had been a long day but a good one. Nevertheless, he was relieved to be away from it, even though the small brick building that housed his office and only three others, each with a private entrance from outside, was less than a mile from the Palms. It was dusk now and the building was deserted, so he had a few minutes at least, perhaps even half an hour, before

Dolores would come. Then they would spend another hour, or less, making love before going on to dinner, probably at the Café L'Europe on St. Armand's. Afterward, he would drop her off at the hospital where he had spent the whole day. She was on the night shift this week. Then on to his bachelor's pad on Longboat Key and some well-needed rest. God, he was tired. He'd canceled all his appointments and he'd been on the one case, with some interruptions, since Rex Maynard had called him shortly after ten this morning. But it had been worth it. That was the feeling that he depended on to sustain him. For there were other times, dealing with those sick and miserable and often baffling minds, that he had to wonder whether all the work and devotion were worth it.

You're a kind man and I love you. The woman didn't strike him as the kind who expressed herself that way. In the short time he'd spent with her before noon, he'd even been slightly skeptical of her muted hysteria. Her intense concern for the child—might it be too much for the boy's own good? But there was no denying the depth of her gratitude on the telephone.

Love. Why are we all so reluctant to put it into words? Although he had to deal with it every day in its myriad forms and contradictions and complexities, he had long ago acknowledged and surrendered to the fact that he himself was incapable of it. Possibly this deprived him of certain insights and sympathies that would be helpful in his professional dealings with souls in crisis, in turmoil, on the verge of chaos. On the other hand, his own failing, if that's what it was, might be the factor that provided the objectivity that in *some* instances, at least, led to success. And those successes were the reason for his living. They made each day a challenge and few men, he knew, at age thirty-nine were fortunate enough to have that feeling about their work.

Yes, today had been one of the good ones. He didn't know now how he'd hit upon the idea of the typewriter—possibly only because he'd seen the boy fingering it curiously. Mocking himself silently—after all, the word-association method was so elementary that its use was outmoded—he'd set it up with Toby at the keyboard and himself pacing idly around the office as if they were playing a game. Each time he spoke a word, he gave the boy plenty of time to locate the keys and type out a word or two. If the kid couldn't talk, or refused to, well, possibly, just possibly—

Then, when he stood at Toby's shoulder and read off the capitalized words typed on the paper, he had to recall the sequence in which he had suggested each subject.

MISS HER . . . that would be Mama.

SEXY . . . that would be in response to nurses. Very good, Toby!

And *NEAT* . . . thank you, Toby. Dr. Ezra thought he was pretty "neat" himself.

THANKS . . . who was he thanking? Oh, yes, Barry Conrad. For what?

And then *STINKS* . . . that would be his estimate of the hospital.

HATE.

The word that Ezra had saved for last had been the key word: *Daddy.*

He had felt a distinct stab of triumph as he stared at the typed response. It was almost always hard, sometimes impossible, for a patient to admit hatred for a parent. Hard enough for adult patients. But a child, unless in a fit of anger and rebellion—

Breakthrough. Now, if that complex dam inside had really been penetrated, no telling how soon the flood waters behind might be released. So that the debris in them could be explored and dealt with. . . .

But now, full length on the couch, Ezra knew that, however satisfying the thoughts, he had to shut the day away from his mind. A half hour, preferably an hour, and he would be renewed, eager for the always-surprising delights of Dolores and her games.

But after he'd removed his glasses and thrown an arm over his closed eyes and before he had really begun to feel his mind drifting away, he heard footsteps on the brick walkway outside. Damn. Then he heard the door to the waiting room, which he had left ajar by arrangement, open fully. It did not close. And she did not playfully call his name, as she usually did.

He got to his feet and went to the office door, which was wide open.

It was not Dolores.

The man who stood there was tall and broad-shouldered with blond hair, wearing a blue blazer jacket and an expression of hesitation and apology.

"Dr. Seymour?"

There had been a series of robberies in the hospital area lately but this man did not strike him as a thief.

"Dr. Seymour, I need your help."

And the tone of voice, the slumped stance, the beseeching blue eyes—he did look pathetic, almost desperate.

"I'm sorry," Ezra said. "You'll have to make an appointment through my secretary, who won't be in till—"

But then he stopped. The intruder had stepped into the office. He was glancing around the dimness.

And a suspicion leaped into Ezra's mind. Along with incredulity.

"Mr. Forrest?"

"Yes. The hospital gave me your name. There was no answer at your home, so I took a chance and came here. I saw the light. Luck." The man's tone was bleak. "I have to know about my son."

Ezra recalled quickly what he had learned about Donald Forrest. Not too much. Only that he had raped his wife and abducted his son. And that his wife feared and hated him intensely. . . .

"Toby is showing signs of improvement," Ezra said cautiously. "He'll need therapy, though, and I'll need a lot more time with him before I can say much more."

"Everybody blames me," Donald Forrest said. "Well, I accept that." He sat down without being asked, in the patient's chair facing the desk. "I'd never do anything to harm my son, Doctor."

"Mr. Forrest, I'm really not prepared to have a conference. I can see you're distraught—"

"I'm not drinking," Donald Forrest said. "Right?"

Possibly not at the moment. But Ezra had some of his history now and he recognized alcoholic depression when he observed it.

If he could query the man, probe more deeply into that mind itself when it was completely sober, it might better prepare him to cope with Toby tomorrow. He moved to sit behind the desk.

Donald Forrest lifted his head. His face was filled with abject despondency. "I take all the blame," he said. There was a plea in his eyes, in his voice. But something else, too—unless Ezra was imagining it. He had had vast experience with the cunning of a sick mind. And of the alcoholic's mind, too. It fools itself as slyly and cleverly as it fools others. "You can help me, Doctor."

"If," Ezra said, "you're suggesting becoming a patient, putting yourself in my care—"

"Anything you say, Doctor."

It was a situation that Ezra had never encountered before. If Donald Forrest was acknowledging his need for counseling . . .

"I don't want to go on the way I am," Donald Forrest said. "I'm scared."

Ezra sat down in his chair behind the desk. "Of what, Mr. Forrest?"

"I don't seem to be able to . . . to . . . to . . ."

There was no doubt in Ezra's mind that the man was being sincere: at this moment Donald Forrest undoubtedly believed his own words and felt that fear.

"Able to do what?" he prompted, because there was also little doubt that certain minds were capable of sincerity even while feigning it for their own ends and to themselves as well. There was no limit in the spectrum of self-deceit, ambivalence, and duplicity—and the more disturbed the mind, the more obscure the distinctions. Wary now, but intrigued, he said, "Are you saying you're finding it harder and harder to discipline and contain your emotions?"

Donald Forrest nodded his head. "I do things before I know I'm going to. But—"

"Yes?"

"I don't want to hurt anybody. I really don't."

Ezra considered his predicament. He decided to carry this on one more delicate step before suggesting that the man turn himself over for further professional and possibly, just possibly, effective treatment. "You haven't asked about your wife," he said.

"Brenda?"

"She's going through an ordeal, too—you realize that."

"Because of me, right?"

"In a complex human situation such as this, Mr. Forrest, it's not my function to fix who's at fault, but, with luck and hard work, to reach solutions. For everyone. Including yourself."

"I'll do anything."

This was his opportunity. He asked, "Are you prepared to enter a hospital where we might be able to explore all the possibilities?"

"Hospital?"

"It would be the better way. The first step, ideally, would be a program of detoxification."

"You're saying I'm drunk, right?" The streaked eyes stared across the desk. "Right?"

"I'm saying, Mr. Forrest, that the first step would be to clear your mind."

This time he actually saw the cunning enter the blue eyes, and recognized it. "The same hospital where you've got Toby? The Palms?"

Cautious, remembering the private guard that Barry Conrad had arranged, Ezra said: "I'd recommend Sarasota Memorial or Doctors Hospital."

Donald Forrest leaned forward in the chair. "Brenda's always saying I need a shrink." His tone had hardened and his eyes had darkened. "Like hell, like hell, like hell!"

There was no point in reminding him that he had all but begged for help. "Perhaps not. You do need medical attention."

"All I need," Donald Forrest said, "is to see Brenda."

Ezra had dealt with obsessions—of various kinds, with various objects, fixations of every sort and kind. And he was aware of the dangers. But, helpless, all he could say was: "I don't think that is advisable. At least not tonight and in your present condition."

"Who are you to decide?" Donald Forrest demanded. "Where is she?"

"I honestly don't know." It was the truth.

"She's behind this, isn't she? *She's* the one who wants to get me in a mental ward."

Hopeless, hopeless. But he spoke very gently: "How could she know you would come here, Mr. Forrest?"

In a tone of despair rather than anger, Donald Forrest said, "You're all in it together."

The last straw, the final admission, the classic symptom—the line was always a thin one, and often deceptive, but Donald Forrest was further along than Ezra had recognized. He knew, though, the futility of reason, even of words, now.

"If I'm in the hospital, she can get away, can't she? Is that what you want?" Donald Forrest was leaning forward now, his streaked eyes peering, demanding. "Is that what you're all trying to do?"

Before Ezra could speak—aware that any denial was futile anyway—he saw the man's hand reach into the side pocket of his jacket. Momentarily too dazed to do anything but stare, he saw the hand emerge holding a blue-steel revolver.

It was, some distant part of his mind realized, the moment all doctors in his field always secretly dreaded, always anticipated, even sometimes joked about socially, but always tried to evade facing in their minds. There was an awesome sense of unreality about it. Nothing in his training or experience could have prepared him for facing a deranged mind and a loaded gun.

Donald Forrest did not lift the weapon. Or point it. "It was still in the phone booth," he said somewhat dreamily, but reasonably, as if for some vague reason he had to explain. And then he said, "I don't want anyone to get hurt." The simple pathetic sincerity in his tone was more terrible than a shouted threat. "All I want is Brenda."

Ezra's mind went to the only address he had: 1168 Westway. And then to the memo that Barry Conrad had given him in the hospital office. He made up his mind. He was not going to get killed. He was thirty-nine years old and he was not going to die. He'd do whatever he could to get rid of this sick man and afterward he'd do what he could to protect the man's wife.

But Ezra had one other alternative. "Your wife is staying with friends."

"Where?"

"On Longboat Key."

But Donald Forrest shook his head. "More lies," he said. "I've already been lied to enough."

Ezra tried to keep his eyes off the gun. "One-two-oh Sands Point Road. Apartment three-oh-three."

He saw the doubt in the reddened eyes. A flicker of hope, too—Donald Forrest wanted to believe him, longed to believe him.

But then the gun came up to rest flat in Donald Forrest's bruised hand on the desk.

"Clever, aren't you?" He sounded almost sad.

"She gave it to me in the hospital this morning. When your son was admitted."

Donald Forrest shook his head and turned over his hand so that the barrel of the gun was pointed directly at Ezra's chest. "That's *your* address," Donald Forrest said.

Ezra gave up. He had not been clever at all. Only foolish. He cursed himself silently and stared at the pointed gun. If Donald Forrest had looked him up in the phone book—

"Is she staying with you?" Donald Forrest asked. "Is that how she's paying you?"

God, he'd been stupid. He remembered what Barry Conrad had told him about a young actor named Malcolm Eggers. . . .

He could not take his eyes off the gun.

"I was lying," he said. But the gun did not move. "I don't really know where your wife is." The gun, clutched in that hand, was pointed directly, firmly, at his chest.

He had really known fear only a few times in his life. The woman patient who'd come at him with a knife in the ward when he was a resident in Bellevue, the first bombardment in the hospital in Saigon . . .

He was not shaking. He was glacially cold, and motionless.

He managed to say, "I have two telephone numbers."

"Where?"

"In my shirt pocket."

But since he did not lift his arm, Donald Forrest stood up and leaned across the desk, bringing the gun even closer until it touched his shirt. He felt a hand take the paper from his pocket.

"More tricks," Donald Forrest said almost wearily. He must have read the numbers. "I already have these."

Ezra simply could not open his jaw to speak. He could not explain that these were all he had, the best he could do. . . .

"Who's Barry Conrad?" the voice above his head asked—and now there was a new grating strain of wildness in it. "Who's Barry Conrad?"

The man who had given him the slip of memo paper. The man whose name was printed on it together with the image of a sea gull in flight.

"He's the one she's with, isn't he? He's the bastard with the red beard, isn't he?"

Ezra wondered how Donald Forrest could know this. Had he seen Barry Conrad? The muzzle of the gun was pressing against his breastbone now. Harder. If he had been able to speak, he would not have been able to say anything. Words had failed him.

There was nothing more he could say. Everything had failed him. He closed his eyes.

Then, in the silence, smelling the whiskey breath of the man above him but unable to see his face, he heard a sound outside. A step on the brick sidewalk. And then he felt the point of the gun shoving more deeply into his chest and heard a voice in the next room calling playfully, and then Donald Forrest's whisper: *"He's the one she came here to see."*

There was a metallic click, which he did hear, but it was the last sound he ever heard.

Mary Rinaldi returned to Waldo's office from the beverage
machine with two *more* cups of hot weak coffee. Waldo had fallen
into a gloomy mood and damned if Mary could blame him. A
man like Waldo Pruitt was not the sort to reconcile himself easily
to being "hog-tied"—his word.

Standing in front of Waldo's desk now was the reporter named
Coleen Lyons whose diminutive size always made Mary feel like
the Jolly Green Giant. Waldo was reading from a long rolled sheet
of paper—and scowling.

"What are you doing here?" the reporter asked without preliminaries.

Mary placed one cup on the desk and said, "Oh, Lieutenant
Pruitt's adopted me. I might ask you the same."

"I thought he'd adopted me," the girl said, and went to sit in
the corner chair.

A siren wailed, a car leaving the building in the rear. Footsteps
and voices in the corridor. No commotion. It was a quiet time of
evening.

Back in her chair, Mary thought of a story she'd read once—
The Pattern That Gulls Weave. A woman was sitting near the
seashore and watching the gulls dipping and wheeling and criss-

crossing each other's paths and she began to ruminate: If each gull had in its beak a thread of a different color, the design woven would be like the pattern of life. What, indeed, was she, Mary Rinaldi, doing here tonight? And why was little Coleen Lyons in the office of a lieutenant of detectives when, in the editorial rooms of the building a few blocks south of here they were hustling to put the morning edition to bed?

Waldo rolled up the sheet of paper and picked up his coffee cup. "Your editor won't print it?"

Coleen Lyons shook her helmet of flat dark hair. "Says it's too speculative. Fiction, he called it. Not enough hard facts. I told the asshole it was a human interest piece, not a news story, obviously, since I didn't use names."

"I agree with your editor." And when Coleen Lyons all but leaped out of her chair: "Who may be exactly what you called him, missie, but young ladies don't use language like that in my office."

Coleen Lyons stood there with her pretty mouth only slightly wider than her pretty eyes. "*He* doesn't want me to believe things like rape and child abduction and brutality at a main intersection can happen in this idyllic community. Might scare the tourists away. And the tourists' money. Have *you* joined the Chamber of Commerce?"

But Waldo was not amused. "Those aren't my objections."

"What then? I got in everything you wanted." She stepped to the desk, furious. "Description of the Cougar, the license, the yacht, the ID numbers, the photograph."

Waldo sipped his coffee. His big face did look miserable, as if his helplessness had penetrated every part of him.

"What I object to," Waldo said, handing over the roll of typing, "is the way you make some kind of romantic lover out of the sonofabitch."

"I didn't intend to do that exactly." Coleen Lyons glanced at Mary. "Maybe I did get kind of carried away. Rex Maynard called me an idiot when I said there were a lot of females who'd like to be loved that much."

Waldo did not speak. So Mary Rinaldi, to bridge the gap, said: "His mind has to be sick. Probably a borderline psychopath."

Waldo stood up. He continued to glower. His tone was flat: "He may be a demon lover to you, Coleen. And a poor sick soul to you, Mary. But to me he's a criminal and to me criminals should not be on the streets."

Before either of them could reply, a buzzer sounded and Waldo took one step and flipped a switch on the intercom.

"Yeh, Dutch?"

A filtered voice said, "Dutch went off-duty a long time ago, Lieutenant." The same businesslike boyish voice: "This is Sergeant Vendig, sir."

"What?"

"Homicide. One-eight-five-nine Hibiscus. Officers are on the scene."

"Victim?"

"Doctor by the name of Ezra Seymour. A psychiatrist."

"Witnesses?"

"A nurse. She's being interrogated by criminalistics officers now. Everything under control."

"Thanks, Sergeant. I'm on my way." He snapped the switch.

Coleen Lyons had already disappeared.

At the door Waldo turned. "You coming?"

"Lay on, Macduff."

And in Waldo's car, light flashing and siren urgently *wow-wow-wow*ing, she lifted her voice to shout: "You can't tie in every crime in town with Donald Forrest."

Waldo had come to life. "Any bets? My *gut* tells me, missie. Any bets Dr. Ezra Seymour, psychiatrist, has—had—an eight-year-old patient named Tobias Forrest in Palms Hospital? Any bets, missie?"

———□———

Murder.

He had to stop the car. He had to stop the car because if he didn't stop the car, he'd crash into something sure as hell, the oncoming headlights, a palm tree, one of those houses . . .

He managed to turn the Caddy into a dark side street and to come to a stop at the curb. His long lean body exploded into wild convulsive jerks and he tried to grip the wheel. His hands were wet and cold, and his fingers and arms were too weak to hold on.

Oh, God, what was happening, this was worse than the shakes, he'd had the shakes two or three times, scary, but nothing like this.

He'd left the lights on. Someone will see the headlights, some cop, but body twisting and wriggling, mind giddy, threatening to go blank, every nerve twitching—he couldn't find a way even to reach and punch the headlight knob. He felt vaguely that there was something he had to do. Something. But what?

And then, instead of getting it clear, his mind veered in the *other* direction. His mind veered to what he *had* done.

You're in trouble now. Real trouble.

But it hadn't really happened, had it?

You killed him.

He hadn't intended to kill anyone. Only to scare—

Oh, Jesus, it all came back in a vivid shattering unreal burst that threatened to blow his skull apart: the sound of a girl's voice from the other room, the click of the trigger being cocked, followed by that deafening, world-shattering blast, the look in the man's eyes, no surprise, no change whatever, and the blood spreading almost instantly on the white shirt, and then the shrieking behind him.

Even now he could hear the girl screaming, one long terrible sound over and over and over, as he brushed past her, their stunned eyes meeting only once, an instant, before he was out and running, stumbling, toward the—

The bitch. Why had she come in just then? What was she doing there, who was she, little whore, like all the others, he knew what she was doing there this time of night, offices closed, she was like all the others, same as his mother, same as Brenda.

Brenda. He almost had it now—something he had to do. If he didn't push it, if he just let it come, he'd remember.

His right hand, limp, no longer shaking, was resting on something smooth. Glass. The bottle of Jack. Of course, he'd left it on the seat.

Holding the bottle in two hands, he managed to tilt back his head and take a long swallow, hearing the glass chattering against his teeth.

The whiskey was cold and wet in his mouth, then scalding in his chest, then shocking and hot as it reached his stomach. How could he have forgotten the booze, right here in the car all the time. . . .

Almost at once he felt steadier. Able to move. He took another drink and straightened. His mind would clear soon. He reached to turn on the headlights—but they were already burning. He started the engine. Now what? He drove, slowly.

Don't panic. Take it easy now. If you panic, you know what will happen, don't you? You know what they'll accuse you of—

Murder. First-degree murder.

But not if he didn't *intend* to murder.

See, your mind's working now. All it needed was a blast or two of booze.

But . . . but you did go there with a gun, didn't you? You went back to that phone booth where you'd dropped the gun earlier, when you saw the cop examining the T-bird, remember? And—some kind of miracle, your luck still working for you—there was the gun still on the floor of the booth.

But he'd only wanted it to scare the doc. To find out where—

Then why'd you pull the goddamn trigger?

Barry Conrad. Now he had it. *That's* what he'd been trying to remember. The name *Barry Conrad* printed along with a picture of a bird at the top of the slip of paper he'd taken from the shrink's pocket. . . .

Seeing that, knowing for sure then—Brenda *had* come to Florida to be with a man!—*that's* when he'd squeezed the trigger too hard.

That's when he'd known that he was going to kill Barry Conrad. *Not* the goddamn doctor.

He had it all clear and straight again now.

He pressed the gas pedal and began to look for another booth. Now he not only had the phone number, he had the name.

But could he risk stopping?

He had to get rid of the gun, too.

No. If you throw the gun away, how can you do what you have to do?

A sickening certainty came over him. What he had to do before he was arrested, what he had to do while he could still do it—he had to kill Barry Conrad. Because . . . because as long as Barry Conrad lived, he'd have the memory in his mind of having screwed Brenda. The only way to blot out that memory was to blot out that mind. And then . . . why then, it hadn't really happened at all, had it? If there was no memory of it, no consciousness of the act, then there really hadn't been an act. It . . . had . . . not . . . happened.

There—nothing the matter with his reasoning. His thinking was sharp and lucid and logical again.

All he needed now was a little help. He could call Tampa again. But to do that he had to be able to use a phone. In private.

. . . *We are going to indulge in a voluptuous dinner together, replete with as many alcoholic beverages as you desire, while we wait the arrival of your daddy.*

The Hyatt House. Now, remembering, he knew where he could use a phone privately. It meant facing his father but, hell, he'd handled the old man before. And his father had always taken care of him, hadn't he?

But the Hyatt House was north—he couldn't risk driving through the center of town. That bitch back there had seen the car. . . .

The boat! The goddamn *Wanderer*. He'd seen boats moored at the Hyatt House. They might be looking for a white Caddy but they couldn't even reach him on the boat.

The Field Club was south of town. Hollis Sanford's Caddy would be right at home at the Field Club.

His mind was really working again. *Clickety-click.* He started the motor.

——□——

The phone rang for the first time since Brenda had returned with Barry from his boat. Tensing and at once remembering Brenda's demands—or commands—Lavinia did not answer it. But she heard Brenda pick up the extension in the guest room after the second ring. Then she heard Brenda's voice but could not distinguish the words. Outside, the last light was fading over the Gulf. It would soon be dark. The sound of the surf was more distinct now and there was a breeze off the water that threatened to grow stronger.

If that was Donald Forrest on the phone, then what?

Brenda had retreated to the bedroom after her outburst—for which, thank God, she had not made any attempt to apologize.

To pass the time Barry was tinkering with something under the hood of his Jeep in the shell driveway that circled the big banyan tree. Had he heard the ring?

She brought the huge wooden salad bowl from the kitchen and set it on the table in the screened room. Oh, damn it, she was not hungry and neither were they, what was she doing and what was being said on that telephone?

What did Brenda have in mind? Did she propose to see the maniac? Confront him, try to reason with him? To threaten him? How could she threaten him? With what?

I won't take any more if I have to kill the cruel vicious sonofa-bitch myself.

Lavinia was opening the Chablis when Brenda spoke from the living room: "It wasn't Donald."

Thank God, thank God! Lavinia turned.

And was shocked. Brenda's delicate face was paler, ivory white now, and fixed. Her eyes were brilliant points of brown color, small and hard. She came into the room and reached and took the wine bottle. "I let you do it all, don't I?" But she spoke as if the words were not a part of her. She moved and spoke now like a person who had made up her mind and knew exactly what she was going to do and how to do it. "Donald's father," Brenda said, working the cork between her two thumbs. "He's in Sarasota. He wanted to know whether there was anything he could do. For me." The cork came out with a long sighing sound. "Odd. I think I've been unfair to Orin." Even the meditative tone, though, did not seem to alter the concentrated resolve that lay darkly behind and under everything she said and did. "I even blamed him. And Donald's poor mother. Who blames *every*thing on the stars." She was pouring the clear pale wine. "In the end, though, if there's anyone to blame it has to be the person himself, doesn't it?"

Lavinia, for some puzzling reason, felt a slow shudder of apprehension. Why?

Less than an hour ago Brenda had been wild with emotion, a character out of Greek tragedy. Medea herself. Antigone. Intense and livid. *I won't let anything else happen!* Now, quiet and composed, she was resolute and committed.

But committed to what?

To avoid asking the questions that she dared not ask, Lavinia placed the bamboo-handled flatware by the pewter plates, and asked instead: "How'd Mr. Forrest know how to reach you?"

"He's with Donald's lawyer at the Hyatt House. Donald must have given his lawyer this number. How Donald got it, I don't know." Her voice missed only a beat. "I told Orin to have Donald call me here."

And then, and then? But Lavinia again could not ask.

"I'll get Barry," she said abruptly, and went through the living room to the door without glancing back.

Because she had to force herself to stop conjecturing. That cataclysmic eruption a while ago—had it been a purging catharsis, as she had hoped, or had it been only a bridge to some further horror? Dread pulled at her muscles as she walked between the sea grapes.

Oh, God. Oh, God, had the man driven the poor child over some invisible emotional brink—toward what, toward what?

——□——

It had been Mary Rinaldi's first on-the-scene homicide investigation and she was relieved when it was over. And shaken. The sight of the dead man—short chubby body still upright, bearded head lolling to one side, eyes flat, not bulging, flat black glass, his white shirt bright with blood. Real death, actual murder—it was not like words printed in a newspaper, or in a lawbook, or spoken in a courtroom. While the police photographer moved around clicking his camera over and over and over. Then the interrogation of the witness in the waiting room, the constant chatter of voices and the wail and squawk of approaching and departing sirens—all of it had been unnerving. Now, waiting in the passenger seat of Waldo's car, she felt spent and drained. Almost desperate to put it all behind her—the flashing and revolving lights, the commotion, the growing throng of curious and awestruck neighbors and sightseers on the sidewalk. She saw Coleen Lyons, pert and businesslike, accost Waldo as he emerged from the small brick building. As they came closer, all she could hear was Waldo asking, with bitterness: "What do you think of your romantic demon lover now, missie?"

"Is that official?" Coleen Lyons asked. "He did this?"

"There's an APB out," Waldo said and climbed in. "Suspicion

of homicide. Suspicion, hell! Eyewitness, missie, positive identification, eyewitness!"

Coleen Lyons hurried off, probably hoping to make the morning edition.

Driving, Waldo was a changed man. When she'd showed him the card from the doctor's files with the words *Tobias Forrest* typed on it, there had been no surprise whatever on his face. And when he'd stared at the dead man, no incredulity. Only, she thought, a wondering sense of inevitability. Which she shared. He had spent the long day hoping to prevent just what had now fatally occurred.

"Poor guy," he said at last, "just doing his job, just happened to get in the way, didn't he? Well, it's a whole new ball game now." He was no longer the tired old man he had appeared to be in his office. He picked up the hand mike, barked, "Dutch?"

"Dutch is gone for the night, sir. This is Sergeant Vendig."

Waldo's voice crackled with vigor: "Well, Sergeant Vendig, what I need to know is the make and color car Mr. Hollis Sanford drives. Full description, and license number."

"Mr. Hollis Sanford, the attorney, sir?"

"Everybody knows good ole Hollis Sanford, don't they? The one and the same, Sergeant. I'm not coming in. Get on it!"

"Right away, sir."

"Another hunch, Waldo?" Mary Rinaldi asked.

"What kind of vehicle would you guess a well-heeled upstanding pillar of society like Mr. Hollis Sanford would own?"

"White Caddy, maybe. This year's model . . . ?"

"Well, that's the color and make vehicle our one and only witness, Miss Dolores Sanchez, saw parked back there before she went in, isn't it? That's the kind every patrol car in the area is looking for by now, isn't it?"

"Waldo, Waldo, oh, how you'd like to pin an aiding-and-abetting charge on our mutual friend—well, I'm with you. But Sarasota's crawling with late-model white Cadillacs."

Waldo considered this, shaking his head. "Whole world's crawling with Hollis Sanfords."

"My turn for a hunch?"

"Fire away."

"You've had the address traced from a number I used, haven't you?"

"Holmes Beach, one-four-one West Forty-sixth Street."

"And you've already alerted the police up there?"

"Ten minutes ago. Not alert this time—*arrest* on sight."

"And now you're trying to decide whether to tell Mrs. Forrest about Dr. Seymour."

"Not whether—*how.*"

"And we'd be friends for life if I volunteered to do it—"

"For life, missie. For life."

"Waldo, I'm going to hate doing it, but you got yourself a friend."

At dinner, devouring the salad ravenously, Brenda had said, *So you'll both stop wondering—I'm going back to him.*

It had been then, in that instant, that Barry had known. It was not a suspicion but a realization. She was lying. After that volcanic eruption a while ago, she had to know that they wouldn't believe this.

So after Lavinia had gone out to walk the beach, he followed Brenda when she again retreated to the bedroom to wait for the phone to ring.

"I'm not going to let you do it," he said.

"Do I have a choice?" She sank down on the bed. "He's won. I can't allow anyone else to get hurt. And it's best for Toby."

But he shook his head. "You may as well tell the truth, Brenda."

Her chin lifted, set with defiance, and her voice, not angry, only unyielding, said, "It's my life, isn't it?"

He made an impatient gesture and closed the door so that Lavinia, if she came back from the beach, would not hear. "I know what you're thinking," he said.

"Do you?"

"We're back to ten o'clock this morning, aren't we?"

Her gaze faltered and she looked away.

How many hours ago had it been since they had stood staring at each other in the rain waiting for the boat to come in at the yacht club? Suitcases packed, mind made up. And now that same mind had returned to the same idea: the only way out—an accident at sea, man overboard, a man too drunk to swim. He had understood her impulse then; now, after all that had happened since, he understood it even more.

But he said: "I won't let you."

The defiance returned but her tone was flat, empty: "I can't let anything more happen. To anyone else."

But she had not denied what he knew. Nor had she changed her mind.

"Let the police handle it. You can arrange to meet him, inform the police where—"

"And then what? He'll be arrested. Maybe, in time, they'll put him in jail. And Toby and I will live with our eyes on the calendar. Waiting. Wondering when they'll release him, whether he'll break out. Knowing that sooner or later—"

"The police can arrange protection."

She turned her head to face him. "All my life? Can they arrange protection for the rest of my life?"

She had thought it through. Her logic was unassailable. But . . . "If you go through with what you're planning, what then?"

She shook her head. "No one will know."

He took two steps. Somehow, with words, he had to get through to her. "I'll know."

Her eyes met his. But they remained unconvinced. Relentless. "You said you loved me."

"And *you'll* know. It'd destroy you, Brenda. Just knowing. Bit by bit, year by year. You're you. And then you'll become something else. Someone else. The guilt would always be there and in time it'd destroy you. I can't let that happen."

A long moment passed. In the other room Bobo stirred in his cage and made chattering sounds.

Had his words reached her?

No. She stood up. The fixed resolution remained in her gaze and she spoke as she had before. "It's the only way. For Toby. For me. For everyone."

He was tempted then to use the word that had been fluttering, sinister and cruel in his mind: *murder*. But he said instead: "Back to the jungle—is that it? Now he *has* won. You're just like him."

"Survival," she said. "Self-preservation. I didn't make the rules. God did." Her eyes were colder than he had ever seen them. She moved past him to the door.

His voice stopped her—one last desperate try: "If you go through with this, Brenda—" And while she waited, face fixed and expressionless, doorknob in hand: "We're finished. Even if, God help me, I do understand—we're finished. Not because I give a damn what happens to him. He deserves it. Or worse. Only because I do give a damn what happens to you."

Her hand dropped from the knob. Her stiff back went slack and her shoulders slumped, and she turned to place her forehead against the closed door.

"Damn you," she whispered. "Oh, damn you, damn you, Barry."

He waited.

"I could have done it," she breathed. "I *would* have done it." Then she raised her hands and beat with her fists on the door, over and over. "I can't lose you, too. I can't lose you, too, I can't lose you, damn you, not now, not now—"

And her fists continued to hammer the door and Bobo began to squawk in the other room and then he had her in his arms and the parrot went into a wild and jumbled series of sounds, giggles and cackles and shrill laughter and shrieks and squalls and hoots until the whole house was filled with an insane and strident cacophony. . . .

———□———

Before she went downstairs to have a sandwich and coffee in the hospital cafeteria, Charlene wrote a note and placed it between Mal's fingers while he slept.

The cafeteria was abuzz. One of Mal's nurses joined her and, when she asked, explained across the table: "It's awful. A doctor was murdered a while ago. Dolores Sanchez—she's a nurse at Palms—saw it happen. And she identified the killer. From a photograph. Rumor has it he's the same kook who put your boyfriend in here. There's a manhunt on. Didn't you know?"

"No."

She left the table. She had to find a phone. To call Brenda. She tried Barry's number. No answer.

Had Brenda heard, did she know? Well, Charlene decided, she couldn't be the one to tell her. Brenda had had enough. Too much, too damned much!

Barry was with her. Probably at Lavinia's. Well, Brenda needed him more than she did. How the hell could she have resented that? Maybe Barry had discovered how much he needed someone, too. Isn't that what she'd always hoped? She was glad that he was with Brenda. Glad.

She went up on the elevator.

Mal was awake. The note was in his hand. She stepped to the bed.

And saw his eyes in the white mask. They were no longer bleak with misery. No longer dull with despair. They were bright and excited—the way they would have been at about this time if he were in his dressing room at the Asolo waiting to make an entrance.

"Well?" she asked.

The head, encased in the white helmet, nodded.

The answer was yes.

She took the note from his hand and, sitting on the edge of the bed, read what she had written: *Will you marry me? You'll always be handsome to me. Love.*

Her ploy had worked. He was alive again. Nice work, pet. And now her whole life would change.

Again.

Because of Brenda.

She really ought to thank the girl instead of blaming her. What if she'd never come here . . .

———□———

"Dead?"

Because she had not known what the relationship was between Brenda Forrest and Mrs. Lavinia Davidson, who had opened the door to her, Mary Rinaldi, intent on what had to be done, had asked to speak to Brenda Forrest in private; and Mrs. Davidson had led her into the bedroom. Where now Brenda Forrest repeated the word she had just uttered, but this time it was not a question: "Dead."

"I'm sorry." The words rang hollow and feeble in her own ears. "Lieutenant Pruitt thought you had to be told."

Brenda nodded. Numbly. Her face, which had been alive and angry, even fierce, in Rex Maynard's living room last night, now looked haggard, defeated.

Brenda Forrest shook her head of disheveled black hair. "How

. . . how'd he ever get to—" But she did not finish the question. "I might have known . . ." In her tone was the same flat sense of inevitability that Mary had glimpsed on Waldo's face less than an hour ago as they stood staring at the lifeless figure in the office chair. "*Should* I have known?"

The tears came then, at last, not in a gush, only a slow brimming in her hollow, saddened eyes. They did not run down her bone-white delicate cheeks.

"Your son's all right," Mary Rinaldi said. "He's safe."

"He'll never be safe," Brenda said. "No one's safe." And then: "Except *him. He's* safe, isn't he?"

"We're doing all we can. There are police outside here now. He'll be arrested in time."

Brenda Forrest shook her head, once. "He's going to get away. He's going to get away with all of it."

The wan face, the weak knowing voice, the exhausted body that now fell back on the bed, the empty eyes staring blindly at the ceiling—Mary felt the woman's despair invade her own being. She glanced around the small room. How unfamiliar and impermanent it must seem to Brenda Forrest. How like a homeless refugee *she* must feel.

To restrain the upsurge of her own feelings, Mary turned and stepped to the hallway door. "Do you want Mrs. Davidson with you?"

But Brenda Forrest only moved her head from side to side. "No thank you. You . . . you're very kind. Everyone has been so very kind." And then, as if the words had stirred a memory too cruel to bear, she rolled over on the bed and wept.

"Hang in there, Brenda," Mary said helplessly, and went into the hallway, closing the door.

In the living room Mrs. Davidson was seated in a rocker with a book open on her lap, but she was not reading. A rather short man with rust-colored hair and beard came in from the Florida room, smoking a pipe. His manner was refreshingly diffident and he walked with a limp.

"Hello," he said, "I'm Barry Conrad."

Mary took a deep reluctant breath. She had no choice. "There's something I have to tell you both. I'm afraid there's been another crime committed. . . .

———☐———

"Where are you?" Orin asked.

"In the lobby."

"Come on up, son," Orin said, replacing the phone and fighting anger, still struggling with the fear that had tormented him on the plane and that had only been exacerbated in the time he'd been with Hollis Sanborn.

The lawyer's hearty reassurances had worked on Orin's nerves and made him suspicious that he *still* did not have the whole story.

Youth, Mr. Forrest—wild oats.

You said the motorcyclist was in the hospital. No question my son put him there, is there?

That don't count. Not in law. Don't matter whether he did it or did not do it—he's not guilty till he's had his day in court.

Orin had been relieved when the garrulous old shyster had finally decided: *Well, it appears he's not going to return my car tonight. I'll get me a taxi downstairs. And you—you relax now, hear? You leave it all up to Hollis Sanford.*

There was a hell of a lot more that Orin didn't know. Yet. But he was damn well going to get to the bottom of it.

The door buzzer sounded.

But when he went to the door and saw Donald standing there, he was stunned. The anger went out of him in a gush of compassion and love. "God, son, what's happened to you?"

Without a word, without a handshake or a hug, Donald came into the room. His eyes had a blurred look but he seemed set on what he was doing even though he looked like a sleepwalker.

Orin shut the door. "I'll order some coffee. Why don't you go in there and take a shower?"

As if he had not heard, Donald went to the table between the two beds and took up the telephone book and, still standing, began to flip through the pages. Orin, bewildered, felt a bellow of rage building inside, but a greater force smothered it down—dread took over. He stood staring, helpless, weak, while all the fears of a lifetime broke through him in a black, overwhelming tidal wave.

"What have you done with Mr. Sanford's car?"

"Fuck Sanford, he's in it, too."

"In what?" Orin heard himself ask.

"They're all in it."

"Who are *they*," Orin demanded, "and what are they *in?*"

Donald looked up, frowning, blinking. "There's no Barry Conrad in Sarasota," he said—in a tone of wonder, of utter disbelief. As if this were impossible, could not be.

"Who the hell's Barry Conrad?" Orin asked. But behind the familiar annoyance and exasperation, there was an unfamiliar current of terror. "Donald, answer me!"

Abstracted, as if Orin were not even in the room, Donald paged the book again, desperately, ran his finger down a column, stared—and then he threw the book to the bed.

"The bastard doesn't live in Sarasota," he said—as if he still could not believe it.

The fear in Orin hardened. He had never seen Donald like this. He had never seen *anyone* behave like this. Now he *hoped* that Donald was drunk. And only drunk. He could deal with that.

"Son, I've come all this way to—" But he broke off. "Goddamnit, you're going to talk to me!"

"Dad," Donald said in a tone of great reasonableness and even sadness, "Dad, don't *you* join them, too."

"Join *whom?*"

"Everyone," his son said. "Everyone."

Orin felt a chill pass down his spine and his scrotum tightened. He'd heard this before, but in a whine, a complaint, never in this accepting, knowing way.

"I'll get some hot coffee from room service, you take a shower—"

But when Donald finally collapsed into a chair, Orin accepted the fact: Whatever was happening to the boy—or had already happened—it could not be remedied by hot coffee, a cold shower, or even a good night's sleep.

By what, then?

"Donald," he said, "I don't know whether this is the time to tell you, or even whether I should tell you this at all." He took a shallow breath and plunged on: "I talked with Brenda over an hour ago."

Donald's flat pale eyes were on him, but they did not seem to be seeing him.

Tell him, Brenda had said on the phone, *tell him it's over. I'm going back to him.*

"She wants you to call her, Donald. 555-2466."

Donald frowned then. "That . . . that's the number I have." He took a slip of paper from the pocket of his shirt and stared at it. In a wondering tone he said, "I have this number. I had it all the time. Even before—"

But he didn't finish. He glanced blindly around the room and then drifted toward the telephone.

"Dial nine first," Orin said, "and then the number."

He was giving instructions again, as if Donald were a little boy again.

Tell him I'll be waiting for his call. I'm ready to go home.

But Orin, moving to sit weakly in the chair that Donald had vacated, knew—knew in his marrow, in his blood—that it was not over. Too much had happened now, more than he even knew.

He closed his eyes. Was he now ready to accept the fact that his son had cracked up? Or was cracking up now, minute by minute?

He heard Donald's voice: "Brenda?"

Listening, Orin wondered what he always wondered: Had he done the right thing?

"Brenda, where are you, darling?"

—— □ ——

Barry put down the telephone in the living room. To hell with whether she heard the click or not—to hell with any niceties now. He was in or he was not in. He strode to the door of the bedroom and threw it open.

Brenda had heard the click. She was standing straight, still alongside the extension phone, waiting for him, her eyes expectant but unflinching. "You shouldn't listen to other people's conversations on the telephone," she said.

No evasions, damn it, no stalling. "Back to the jungle, after all?" he demanded. "I meant what I said, Brenda—you go through with this and you and I are finished."

"And I told you I couldn't lose you and that I wouldn't let *him* force me into killing him. I meant it, Barry."

"What then?"

"You heard me try to get him to come here."

"I also heard you offer to go to the Hyatt House."

"I thought I could hold him there long enough for the police to get to him—"

"What then, Brenda? You intend to get on that boat, and then what?"

"I'll call Lieutenant Pruitt and tell him where Donald is now." She picked up the telephone and dialed. "If they don't arrest him, I'll have to handle this myself."

"But how, goddamnit, how?"

"I'll tell you, Barry. But you can't stop me." Then into the telephone: "Lieutenant Pruitt, please. Hurry."

——□——

Orin was facing his son in a way he'd never faced him before. "I'm not going to let you go, Donald, I can't."

"But I just told you. She's waiting for me. Brenda's waiting."

"Son, you're sick. Look at you—you're coming apart at the seams."

"Dad, get out of my way. Please. Brenda's got it all worked out. She's going with me."

"Where? Home?"

"Dad, please. I can't go home."

"Why not? You just told Brenda you couldn't stay here because the police are looking for you."

"Get away from the door, please, please, please. . . ."

"Hollis Sanford says you're free. Unless—"

Donald took a step.

Orin refused to step away from the door. "What have you done, Donald? What else have you done? Tell me."

"Goddamnit, you heard me. Brenda's waiting. She loves me. Me. She said it. She's going to help me get away!"

"What have you done?"

"Get out of my way!"

Orin saw the movement; his body tensed, his guard came up by reflex, and he went into a crouch—but not quickly enough.

The fist exploded in his face, he tasted blood, and then he felt himself staggering sideways, trying to regain his balance, and then he heard the door opening and slamming as he sprawled across the bed, head down, the pain beginning . . .

DAMN you, Barry.

She was standing on the beach side of the cottage, staring at the sail sculpture. And at the area around it. All illuminated by the spotlight, which she had just turned on from inside.

The rowboat was no longer there on the sand.

Now, when Donald arrived—he had said it would take more than an hour—he would see the light and the wooden sails and he would know where to stop and wait for her two or three hundred yards offshore, as she had instructed, but now . . . now there was no way to get out to him.

Damn you, Barry.

He did not have the right. Even if he loved her, he did not have the right—

She knew. When he had left, he had hauled the rowboat off in the back of the Jeep.

I can't let you do it, he had said after he'd listened to her conversation with Donald on the telephone. *We know now—he's a killer.*

All the more reason he has to be arrested—

Brenda, he killed Ezra with a gun. He must still have it.

That's why he has to be stopped, damn it, he has to be stopped somehow!

Not by you, Brenda, not this way. It's a damnfool scheme and I won't let you be on that boat with him even for a few minutes!

Just long enough to get the key. You said all boats with engines have to have keys to the ignition. Well, there's no wind tonight so he can't put up the sails! With no engine, all he can do is sit out there and wait to be arrested.

If you can swim back to shore, he can.

Barry, I've thought it through. I got the idea while I was talking to him on the phone. If the police don't arrest him at the Hyatt House now, I'll tell Lieutenant Pruitt what I'm doing and he can put men all along the beach in case Donald's sober enough to swim—

But Barry had shaken his head. *No, Brenda, no. Use the light, use the sculpture, let him come—but from then on it's up to the police.*

She had agreed. Verbally. But she could not take the chance that Donald would realize he'd been tricked and cruise away. So she'd lied to Barry—*Whatever you say, darling*—and had continued with her own plan.

And Barry had accepted her agreement, verbally, and had quietly gone on with a plan of his own.

Now . . . when Donald came, he would blink the lights on the boat to signal his position and he'd search the surface of the water in the moonlight and, not spotting the rowboat, would decide he'd been tricked. Then what?

He'd curse her and the world and he'd get away again.

And there was no way for her to prevent that unless, when she saw the boat, she swam out to it.

She went back into the cottage to wait for Lieutenant Pruitt to call and let her know whether Donald was under arrest.

While she waited, she would put on her swimsuit under her slacks. In case . . .

—— □ ——

"No, there's no doubt about it, Mr. Forrest," Waldo said. "There's a witness. I'm sorry." It was the best he could do—and not enough. The steel-hard shaft of frustration and helplessness had been driven even deeper in him now as he stared at the ravaged face. "There's no doubt he did it and we *are* looking for him, yes."

No answer. Orin Forrest lowered his head and Waldo was staring at the bald pate and hunched strong shoulders, which had gone slack.

"His wife said he might still be here at the hotel with you."

No answer. He had to ignore the grief. He had to do his job.

"How long ago did he leave, Mr. Forrest?"

No answer. No movement.

"I'm sorry, sir. We have to know."

Without lifting his head—sparing Waldo the necessity to look into those stricken eyes—Orin Forrest said: "I won't tell you."

Waldo nodded. Accepting. "What kind of car was he driving?"

"I don't know."

"Where was he going?"

The head lifted then. Waldo was forced to look into that miserable face. Orin Forrest said: "I know you'll get him. I know he won't get away. But I'm goddamned if I'll help you."

Waldo wished *he* could be so sure the sonofabitch wouldn't get away. He said: "We'll try, Mr. Forrest. We'll go on trying." He went to the door. "And I'm sorry, sir, whether you believe it or not."

He went out into the corridor, passing the elevators to hurry down the stairs. Brenda Forrest had said on the phone that she'd spoken to her husband, who was then with his father at the Hyatt House. *Whether you arrest him or not, let me know, please.* Well, he'd let her know but not by phone.

He was on his way up there now. And so, he suspected, was her husband.

———□———

The speed of the boat should not be greater than would enable her to change from headway to sternway when danger presents itself. How's that for remembering? Word for word! Rules of the sea, pilot's regulations. Word for word.

And the shrink had wanted to put him in the hospital. But he couldn't think about that now. The shrink—he wouldn't be in this mess if it weren't for the shrink.

Only a few other craft visible from time to time. Moon bright. He didn't turn off the running lights. Against the law.

Son, you're sick. Look at you. You're coming apart at the seams.

Like hell, Dad, like hell. Never better. On top of it, on top of everything now, never better!

Quarter mile offshore, maybe closer. Plowing NNW. Full throttle. He could set the automatic pilot but he needed to have the wheel in his hands. He had to hold on to the wheel to keep from floating away. It was all too much, too much. . . .

Brenda—darling, where are you?

Did your father give you my message?

I'm with him now.

Donald, I've only just now learned what trouble you're in. I want to help.

Because you love me. Say it, Brenda.

I've just realized how much. Yes.

Say it, Brenda. Say the words.

I love you.

I knew it, I knew it! Where are you?

Stay there at the Hyatt House. I'll come to you.

I can't stay here. They're liable to bash in the door any minute.

Then come here. I'll tell you exactly where. Listen . . . do you still have the boat?

That's how I got here, but—

Then come here by boat. Stay out in the Gulf.

Can you get hold of a small boat?

Yes. It doesn't have a motor but I could row out. The Gulf's calm enough tonight.

Brenda, do you love me! You—

Don't shout. Shut up and listen. We'll get away, Donald. Listen now.

Remembering, he also remembered what had happened this morning when he'd tried to dock at the yacht club with Toby. . . .

What if this was another trick?

He couldn't believe that. Not now.

You always believe what you want to believe, son.

Poor old Dad. He hadn't understood. He hadn't understood that Brenda was waiting, that the police might come, that he had to get on the boat, that Brenda was going to take care of him—

He remembered the look of surprise on his father's face when he had swung. And the blood on his lips as he fell across the bed. He hadn't swung hard, really, only hard enough to get him away from the door. He didn't want to hurt the old man. He didn't want to hurt anybody, ever—

With one hand on the wheel, he reached for the Jack Daniel's on top of his blazer on the seat of the cockpit. He wouldn't drink much more now. Just enough to keep this good feeling coursing through his blood. Not so much that he'd hear that little click in his brain. He didn't want his mind to go over that line and into that dead gray world—not tonight, not now that he had her again. Only a swig or two to get him through the next few miles.

—— □ ——

When the pain in his jaw became intense, Mal bore it for as long as he could—Charlene knew this—before lifting his arm in the signal they had worked out between them. Then she summoned the nurse and explained. "He should really be sleeping anyway," the nurse said and then went away and returned in a few minutes to administer an injection.

Charlene waited until he was snoring softly, then touched his hand with hers—sleep, my pet, sleep—and went down to her station wagon.

She was about to turn north toward Mal's rooming house to spend the night when she changed her mind. If Brenda was at Lavinia's, who was with Toby? At the corner of Osprey, she turned south, fully anticipating that they would not let her see him.

"Are you a relative, miss?"

"Almost," she said lamely. "He's been staying at my house."

After the elderly woman in the pink uniform had unlocked the door to allow her inside, she continued to frown. "Well, Dr. Seymour left orders that he was to have no visitors till tomorrow. Even his mother. But—" She moved off. "Excuse me."

While she was gone, Charlene realized that she knew so very little of what had been going on since ten this morning. She didn't really know why Toby was here or even what the symptoms of his illness might be. Or in what condition she might expect to find him.

She glanced around the reception room. It was unoccupied except for a uniformed sheriff's deputy seated on a couch. He smiled cordially and went back to his magazine.

The woman returned, sitting down behind the counter to riffle through a file as she spoke: "Dr. Hunter has countermanded Dr. Seymour's order. In view of the circumstances . . ." She looked up.

"I know what's happened to Dr. Seymour," Charlene said.

"Isn't it dreadful? We're all stunned. Well, Dr. Hunter thinks it might do the little fellow good to see a familiar face. In case he may have learned somehow." She handed Charlene a visitor's pass. "But Dr. Hunter insists that you *not* mention or discuss Dr. Seymour." She smiled. "Sweet boy, that Toby. We all love him."

Toby was in a room by himself. He was wearing pajamas that were too big for him and appeared to be hospital issue. And he was staring out the window, his back to the room.

"Toby?"

He turned. And his eyes frowned, then brightened. And then he came flying across the room and into her arms.

Kneeling, she held his small body until he drew back and looked gravely into her face.

"Charl—d-did Dr. Ezra have an accident?"

Carefully she asked, "Do I know Dr. Ezra?"

"He's my doctor."

"What makes you think anything's happened to Dr. Seymour?"

He leaned back. "You *do* know. That's his l-l-last name. Seymour. So you know."

"Nothing's happened to him that I know of, Toby."

He climbed up onto the bed. "You're l-l-like everybody else. But I can tell. Every t-time I come up to two nurses talking in the hall, they stop." He was sitting now, legs dangling. "I have something very important to t-tell him. I wanted him to be the first to know." He shook his head and stared over her head at the wall.

How had she stumbled into this? And just what the sweet hell could she say?

"I wish people'd start g-getting wise," Toby said, disgust and even anger in his tone. "I can take it."

"Can you, Toby?"

His blue eyes met hers. "Try me."

But she couldn't. She had her orders. Still—could she leave him here all night, wondering?

"Well, Charl?"

"Dr. Ezra did have an accident, Toby." She said it very softly, very gently. And waited.

"He's dead, isn't he?"

Startled again, she considered a moment. Then she nodded her head. It was the best she could do. She'd already said too much. What would happen when he learned the whole truth?

There were tears in his eyes now, and on his cheeks. But he was not sobbing. He sat very straight.

Her heart twisted but she realized that it was not her place to reveal the whole truth. But there was no doubt in her mind that when he learned, the kid really could take it.

Then—a diversionary tactic—she asked: "What was it you wanted Dr. Ezra to be the first to know? Can you tell *me*?"

"You already know."

"Know what, pet?"

"I really knew I could do it all day, the way I can swim. . . ."

"Could do what, darling?"

"T-t-talk," he said. "Don't you hear me?"

———□———

The traffic on the single narrow thoroughfare running north and south on Longboat Key was thin this time of night. Mary Rinaldi, again in the passenger seat next to Waldo in his car, had already spotted three police vehicles parked inconspicuously off the road between buildings at different locations since they'd crossed the short bridge over New Pass. And she knew there were others. Waldo was driving fast, light flashing overhead, siren wailing urgently.

He'd been leaving the Hyatt House when she caught up with him—after traveling this same road south and then learning at headquarters where he'd gone—and she'd reported that she had informed Brenda Forrest of the murder of Dr. Seymour. Waldo had said, *Leave your car and come along. If you want to be in on the arrest. But don't count on it. I just struck out again.*

Since getting into the car, he'd occupied himself barking orders on the radio: setting up roadblocks on the three bridges giving access to Anna Maria Island, trying to position cars out of sight in the immediate vicinity of the house at the Gulf end of Forty-sixth Street in Holmes Beach, and asking whether there was anything new on the car the subject was presumably still driving—1981 white Cadillac Seville, registered in the name of Hollis Sanford.

"Nothing yet, sir."

Waldo didn't so much as glance at her but she knew: His hunch had paid off. "Fugitive is armed and should be considered extremely dangerous. Get on it. Out."

He replaced the mike and growled: "That damned gun. Why didn't one of us think of it two hours ago?"

"Think of what, Waldo?"

"The sonofabitch stashed the thirty-eight in the phone booth when he was apprehended on the DWI. And *we* wasted time taking the T-bird apart. All he had to do was go back and get it and drive to Seymour's office and *use* it."

"Proving what?" she asked. "That even Waldo the Great can't think of everything?"

"Proving," he snarled, "that if we *had* thought of it, the doctor might be alive! There's no room for that kind of mistake in police work."

Then, crouched heavily over the wheel, he lapsed into silence.

The road curved slightly between a mobile-home park on the right and the Gulf on the left. Out on the water she could see the lights of a few boats and their shadowy outlines. The moon, brilliant and still low over the pines and roofs to their right, was huge and full. And there were few clouds—a fine night for a manhunt, wasn't it?

Full moon. She remembered Waldo's theory: On the nights of the full moon the loonies went loonier. Well, who was she to scoff? Evil spirits, devils, dybbuks—how explain the unexplainable? She thought again of the gulls wheeling against the sky with invisible threads in their beaks, weaving a mysterious pattern.

By the time they reached the long narrow bridge between Longboat Key and the south end of Anna Maria Island, roadblocks were already being set up: revolving and flashing lights, red and blue, several different kinds of uniforms and police cars, an atmosphere of grim efficiency.

After they'd been waved through, she heard a crackling sound and then the boyish polite voice of Sergeant Vendig again. "Lieutenant?"

"Yeah, what've you got?"

"The stolen vehicle, Mr. Sanford's Cadillac—it's been located, sir. Parked at the Field Club, south of town. Unoccupied."

"And Mr. Sanford?"

"Shall I have him informed?"

"Informed, *hell*—bring him in for questioning. Suspicion of accessory to murder but don't book him. Let him cool his fat ass. I'll interrogate him when I get back. And, Sergeant—"

"Yes, sir?"

"Do you happen to know whether there's a marina at the Field Club?"

"Yes, sir, there is."

"Question the dockmaster—use the phone, we can't spare any men—find out whether the goddamn *Wanderer* has been tied up there all day."

"Right, Lieutenant."

But, hanging up the mike, Waldo knew—and so did she.

"Roadblocks," he said, "road surveillance, law-enforcement agencies of two counties out in force chasing their tails—and all the time Mr. Donald Forrest is cruising north in his fancy yacht and giving us all the finger."

"Now what, Waldo?"

"Now," he said wearily, "now we can contact the Coast Guard, again, and let *them* give us the finger."

——□——

Only twenty-four hours had passed since she had met Brenda—right here, last evening—but Lavinia had come to feel that she had known the girl for years. Probably because so much had occurred in that time. Not only violence and terror but a reaffirmation within her of the faith she'd always had in the decency and compassion and selflessness of which human beings were capable. The composed pattern of her own life had been shattered. But at the same time, astonishingly, her whole being had been revitalized.

Giving herself over to thoughts such as these did nothing to quell the uncertainties and apprehensions quivering through her tired body. Nor did Haydn's lovely *Farewell Symphony* on the hifi.

Brenda was alone in her room, waiting for another phone call—*Maybe Lieutenant Pruitt will arrest him and it'll all be over—* but when the phone finally rang, it was not Lieutenant Pruitt calling.

Brenda came out of the bedroom and her eyes looked stunned. She was shaking her head from side to side.

"Charlene," she said in a disbelieving whisper. "She's with Toby. She has permission to stay with him all night. And, Lavinia, he's talking!"

Then, as if she could say no more, as if the relief were too much to bear, she whirled about to return to the bedroom, then stopped. Now she spoke again but this time in a low, harsh groan: "All the more reason, all the more reason—" And she was gone.

All the more reason his father must never see him again— Lavinia knew. And agreed. All the more reason the man must be arrested and put away.

She changed the record blindly, her hands trembling, afraid to give in to her own relief, her own hope—nothing, nothing could reach the fears beating like the wings of wild birds in her breast.

Where was Barry? What had he meant when he said: *The bastard's on his way here by boat but he can't get ashore unless he has a dinghy on board, or swims. The police are parked out there now so you two are safe if he's crazy enough to try it.* And then he'd driven off in the Jeep with the small Fiberglas rowboat in the back. But by now he'd had all the time in the world to get to his place and back. It wasn't like Barry not to take her into his confidence.

The bedroom door opened and Brenda came in. Her expression was unreadable but there was a bitterness in her voice: "Lieutenant Pruitt promised to call me. So I called him. He's not in. But no one by the name of Donald Forrest has been arrested." She moved into the dimness of the screened room. "Do you have binoculars, Lavinia?"

"No, but I have a telescope in the closet. And a tripod. Shall I get them?"

"Please."

So Lavinia, relieved to be moving, stood up and went into her own bedroom. And then she thought of the old hunting rifle that Barry had shown her how to use before placing it upright behind the bedroom door. It was fitted with a telescopic sight.

But when she looked behind the door, it was not there.

Barry must have taken it.

Where?

Her heart had begun to hammer, fast and hard.

It was then that she realized where Barry had gone. Onto his boat. With a gun.

———□———

Mary Rinaldi was still learning, minute by minute.

"Reporting on the Coast Guard situation, Lieutenant," the filtered voice was saying as Waldo turned the car west off Gulf Drive onto Forty-sixth Street.

"Let's have it."

"Coast Guard's trying to get a cutter free, but on top of the drug operation up Tampa way, there's an oil tanker aground down south, off Key West. No available aircraft."

"Priorities," Waldo said, nodding.

"What's that, sir?"

"Never mind."

But Mary Rinaldi understood. What's more important overall— a million-dollar narcotics bust, an oil spill, or a murderer with a loaded gun who's sure as the devil going to get away again?

"Did you check on the Sheriff's Department helicopter?"

"In repair. It crashed last week on that bank robbery capture in Myakka, remember?"

"Why wasn't I told that this morning?"

"I can't say, sir."

"Jesus. What about our Harbor Police?"

"Already dispatched. But it'll be two hours even with the Gulf smooth as the bay. And they already told me—they're not equipped to overtake a forty-foot Morgan with diesel power, especially in the Gulf."

"Then how about police boats here, Manatee, Bradenton area?"

"Negative. One boat. Nineteen-footer. Limited to inland waters and only one marine officer—who's in Tallahassee for three weeks at some training school."

Yes, Mary Rinaldi was learning. Apparently there was such a plethora of crime—at any given time, anywhere, everywhere—and such limited police facilities that it was a sheer miracle that any criminal case ever reached her office for prosecution; yet that office was always overburdened and behind schedule.

Instead of parking the car at the striped wooden barrier that separated the end of the street from the beach, Waldo turned into the driveway that circled the banyan tree on the east side of the cottage. Then he got out and shambled over to the Holmes Beach Police car parked at the barrier and told the officer: "Stash your vehicle out of view of the Gulf and radio instructions to all cars— approach this area with care, no lights, no sirens." Then he rejoined her on the walk to the side door and allowed himself a deep sigh. "Now let's see what the little lady has up her sleeve."

The "little lady" was waiting, and Mary saw Mrs. Davidson behind Brenda in the next room, seated at a telescope set up on a tripod, its aim directed through the screen over the beach and the water. "You promised to call me," Brenda Forrest said. It was an accusation, flat and questioning at the same time.

"I decided to tell you face-to-face, Mrs. Forrest."

"He got away, didn't he?"

"He left the hotel within minutes after talking to you on the phone." It was Waldo's turn to accuse. "Mrs. Forrest, I made the mistake of assuming he was traveling by car—if you knew he was coming by boat, you should have told me."

"And what would you have done, Lieutenant?"

"Just what I've done now, only sooner. We've got an officer at the marina behind Pete Reynard's restaurant. That's the only public dock within walking distance. And we've alerted all the other facilities on the bay side of the island. The whole neighborhood's crawling with squad cars. Is it your idea he'll anchor out there and come in? Does he have a dinghy on board?"

"*My* mistake, Lieutenant. I didn't think to ask him. We all make them, don't we?"

"But there's no doubt in your mind that he's heading this way?"

She only shook her head, but with an air of cool certainty.

"Then what?" Waldo asked.

"Then it's up to you. Arrest him."

Waldo heaved another sigh and shook his head. "We've summoned the Coast Guard. It'll be some time."

"He won't wait."

"Mrs. Forrest—I'm trying. Honest to God I am. I know his mind's all snarled up, and more so now that he's killed a man, but what does he hope to do by coming here on a boat?" Then his eyes narrowed; he ran a thick hand through his short gray hair and took a step toward her. "Or was that *your* idea?"

At once—and not because of any change of expression on Brenda Forrest's face, because there was none—Mary knew that Waldo's suspicion was on target. Again.

But whatever the woman was thinking now, she was not going to reveal it. "Ever since I've been in Florida, every time I pick up a paper, there's a story about the illegal drug traffic from South America." She turned her head to one side. "Would the Coast Guard be in more of a hurry to arrest my husband if he had hundreds of pounds of narcotics on that boat?"

Mary Rinaldi glanced at Waldo's face. And on it she saw the same shock that she felt, like a jolt of electric current through her veins.

Then something that was not quite a grin came into Waldo's big beefy face. "Missie," he said, and it was not a growl, "you're not only a right pretty lady, you got a head screwed onto those shoulders. Excuse me."

And he left the three women in the house to go out to the radio in his car.

———□———

As he rounded the northern tip of Anna Maria Island at the wheel of the clumsy old trawler that he had come to love, as he pointed her prow south to hug the shoreline, Barry Conrad was still trying to decide what the hell he was going to do.

The Gulf looked like a pale enormous lagoon, smooth and placid. Only a few small pleasure craft and, miles to the west, he could see the lights of freighters and tankers in the shipping lanes to the port of Tampa. The moon was higher and its radiance turned the night into twilight.

Should he kill his running lights? Not yet. Whatever kind of boat the bastard had chartered, it could probably do eight or ten knots. The trawler was shuddering at full throttle but he doubted he was doing five knots—just possibly four.

Had the bastard already arrived down there?

What the hell did he hope to do even if he got there in time?

Any boat capable of going north in the Atlantic to Connecticut had to have too deep a draw to get very close to the beach. Of course the bastard could drop anchor a safe distance offshore and, if he had a dinghy, row in. Or swim if he had the guts. And if he didn't drown of shock when he hit the cold water, if he did reach land, the police were with Brenda. And sooner or later—surely, *surely*—the Coast Guard would have to arrive.

Was he trapped then? Hell no. At any point he could turn out to sea. Then . . . Brenda would never be safe, never.

Well, at least she wouldn't be with him on that boat for even a few minutes. If he'd done nothing else, Barry himself had scotched that wild idea.

But she'd been willing to risk it—to get on board and get that key. Even knowing the bastard had a gun—

Even knowing what he'd done to Ezra Seymour.

A flash of fury went through him.

The rifle.

He did not even know how to use it. He didn't know its power, its range. Or even whether it would be possible to aim and fire from one boat to another. Whether they were moving or not. And in this light . . .

But the impulse was in him, fierce and urgent—to rid the world of this bastard once and for all! Then Brenda would be safe, not only now but forever.

But he thrust the savage primitive craving aside in his mind. And in that instant understood Brenda's.

The bastard had brought them both to it.

What then, what the hell can you do?

Another picture took shape in his mind: a boat with a huge jagged hole in its hull. Water gushing in—

Accident at sea.

Two boats colliding. It happened often.

He reached and pushed the throttle. But the old trawler was already giving all she had.

He gave in—with relief, with ferocious anticipation—to a cold feral determination. As if he were a jungle animal stalking his prey.

——□——

"Hello."

"Mr. Forrest, thank God you're still in your room. This is Hollis Sanford speaking."

Orin's jaw, aching steadily, sent stabs of pain into his skull and down his neck when he talked. "What is it, Mr. Sanford?" As if anything the lawyer had to say would surprise him, or could reach the cold knot of despair in his gut.

"I'm afraid the authorities are claiming your son committed homicide. First degree."

But he already knew that. He'd already accepted that fact. Had he always known that someday it would come to this? He hadn't really been surprised when that detective had told him.

"Mr. Forrest, are you still there?"

"I'm here." But he seemed to be detached . . . distant . . . as if he were living through something now that he had always known he would have to endure.

"There's an APB out on him and they're holding me in the police station for questioning."

"Rough."

"Just remember what I said: He's not guilty till he's been proven guilty in court."

"He's guilty. He's guilty as hell."

"Mr. Forrest, the boy's your son—"

"I don't care."

"You got to care. Your own flesh and blood."

Was it possible? When had he *stopped* caring? Had it happened when the detective had told him? Or had it happened even before that—when that fist had smashed his jaw and he had tasted blood, sprawled on the bed while he heard the door slamming?

Whenever—he'd let go. At last. And forever.

"Mr. Sanford, listen carefully." He spoke very, very slowly: "I don't give a shit."

———□———

His goddamned mind was playing tricks on him. It wasn't the booze. He'd had only three or four snorts the whole day. All those miles and miles—

Longboat's about ten or twelve miles long—her voice had sounded so calm and positive and reassuring on the phone, how long ago, hours ago, years ago now, why couldn't he concentrate, what the hell was happening to his mind?

. . . long bridge between Longboat Key and Anna Maria Island and then a public beach—

He lifted the binoculars from his chest. Too dark to see much at this distance—tall shaggy trees behind a stretch of sand, picnic tables, a few parked cars . . .

. . . *four or five miles north, you'll see another public beach, with a small bathhouse—*

Four miles? Five? At eight knots, one statute mile equals one nautical mile, not by much, eight knots—

He had to be smashed. Drinking off and on all day. Only explanation. Unless . . . unless—oh, God, had he freaked out?

He was so tired. He sat down behind the wheel, holding it with one hand as he leaned down to set the automatic pilot. Then he released the wheel altogether. Risky business. But he'd keep watch. No other craft in sight. Except way out: lights, freighters, tankers, Tampa shipping lanes . . .

He reached for the Jack on top of his blazer on the seat. But with the familiar square-shaped bottle in hand, he decided against it. Couldn't risk passing out. Couldn't risk hearing that *click* sound in his mind. *Click*, then everything going gray and black and then dead.

If that happened, how could he pilot the ketch to Mexico?

Brenda's idea: *We'll be safe there—*

Mexico. Once she was aboard, he'd set their course WSW, full throttle. Brenda, Brenda darling, you do still love me, we'll escape together, just the two of us, to hell with the world, to hell with everything and everyone but us!

What about Toby?

To hell with Toby, too. He'd never really wanted Toby. *She's* the one who wanted Toby. He'd never wanted to share her. With anyone. Damn Toby—he'd always been there between them. Well, now she was choosing. She was choosing him, not Toby, him, not anyone else, him!

But first, once they were really out to sea—first, he'd set the autopilot and they'd go down to the cabin together, beautiful, and he'd watch her strip, beautiful, and then . . .

He fell into a reverie and let his mind drift. Memory mingled with desire. And the steady thrum of the engine and the cold salt spray and the high dome of sky and the bright moon and the sharp stars—all came together to lull his mind into a strange pleasant passive harmony.

Time passed.

He became conscious of a sound underneath the boat. He leaped up, grabbed the wheel with one hand, and stooped to switch off the automatic pilot with the other. The engine stuttered, the boat lost speed, the sound was more distinct now—a rubbing, scraping against the hull. Christ, he'd gone aground! He pulled the throttle back, swung the wheel hard to port, then slammed the throttle forward again. And the boat swung free, engine thundering, and charged out to sea.

Sandbars. She hadn't mentioned sandbars. All she'd said was to drop anchor two or three hundred yards offshore.

He looked back over his shoulder. There was the second public beach. Lights on the bathhouse roof. No swimmers. A few parked cars. He was almost there!

He eased the wheel to starboard. Pointed north again, he cut speed.

You'll see a row of cottages—

He was awake now, alive. In control. He saw the cottages.

In front of one of them you'll see a light—

He saw it.

. . . a wooden sculpture, maybe fifteen feet high, in the form of sails . . .

He saw it, he was here, there it was!

He killed all the lights, bow and stern.

When you're on a line straight out from the cottage, flash your lights on and off and then wait—

He lifted the binoculars from his chest and focused in on the sculpture, the light, the darkened house behind.

When I see your lights flickering, I'll signal with the spotlight.

He eased back on the throttle all the way and twisted the key to turn off the ignition. The boat continued forward, but drifting.

Cautiously then he moved the glasses to the right: a painted barrier at the end of the street, no cars. Then to the left: a wide tangle of trees and shrubbery between cottages. He brought his view back to the lighted sculpture. And the beach. In the spill of light around the sails, he could not see a rowboat. Not anywhere.

Christ, what if it was a trick? What if—

He went weak again.

Should he flash his lights?

Brenda, Brenda—

He lowered the glasses and reached for the switch. Brenda loved him. Brenda had realized how much she loved him. He flicked the bowlight. On and off and on and off. Then once again.

And waited.

How could he live through the minutes before he saw her again? Before he touched her . . . ?

——□——

"Brenda, what are you doing?"

But it was perfectly clear what the child was doing: She was turning the spotlight on and off, not once but several times.

Lavinia stood in the open French doors between the two rooms. Brenda had stood up from the telescope where she had been sitting for the last hour and she gave the wall switch a final flip before leaving the light on outside. "Brenda, shall I inform Lieutenant Pruitt?"

"They're watching, they saw." Going into the living room, she was taking off the blouse of her pantsuit. "They've had their chance. They've had him in custody twice." She stopped to step out of the slacks. "Don't interfere now, Lavinia. Please." Brenda was wearing a black one-piece bathing suit.

The invisible hand that had been gripping Lavinia's heart for hours tightened. "Brenda, you can't. That water's freezing."

Brenda was tucking strands of black hair under a tight white swim cap. "I know—only tourists swim this time of year. Well, I'm a tourist, aren't I?"

"You've never doubted he'd come, did you?"

Brenda came toward her. "Donald always believes what he wants to believe," she said, and placed her cheek against Lavinia's. "Don't look so frightened, Lavinia. I'm a *very* good swimmer."

"But . . . but what are you going to do?"

"Tell Lieutenant Pruitt he might try to swim in. But if I get there before the boat moves, he won't get away this time."

Then Brenda was running, quick and graceful, through the living room to the outside door. "Thanks for everything, Lavinia—"

And then she was out the screen door and dashing, head low, toward the beach.

Lavinia heard her own voice. Shouting. Not screaming, bawling—not words, sounds.

She was stumbling toward the screened room, then she was fumbling for the switch. She turned off the spotlight.

Then she pressed her forehead against the screen and saw Brenda's white and black body in the dimness: wading out into the icy water in high running steps until she was in waist-high and then plunging headfirst, arms flashing.

She sank weakly into the chair in which Brenda had been sitting.

Without the light, had he been able to see Brenda go into the water? If not, would he go away?

She heard heavy footsteps running outside.

What could the girl have in mind? What could she hope to do?

Behind her the screen door opened and closed.

Brenda, Brenda, what will happen to you now?

Steps behind her in the living room. She turned.

Two uniformed officers were standing there. Their eyes were darting in all directions. Both had guns in their hands.

10

AFTER questioning Mrs. Davidson, per Waldo's instructions, and after failing to convince her to take a sedative, Mary Rinaldi left the elderly lady seated stiffly at the telescope and went to rejoin the lieutenant. Several feet back from the edge of sand in the wooded area north of the cottage, he'd positioned himself in a clump of underbrush behind the trunk of a scrub pine where he could observe the Gulf but could not be seen from it.

"Well?" he asked, field glasses fixed on the boat. "Well, is it true?"

Still not quite able to believe it herself, Mary Rinaldi said: "What Mrs. Davidson told the officers is true."

Waldo swore under his breath and, without lowering the glasses, spoke into the walkie-talkie that he held in his other hand: "Get men spread out up and down the beach. But out of sight. Mrs. Forrest is trying to swim out there. She may change her mind in that water and turn back. Get some experienced lifeguards if you can and get a medical unit here. *Move.*"

Mary Rinaldi, without binoculars, could make out only the dim shadow of the boat—a long low hull and two masts without sails. Without lights. If there'd been no moon, she would not have been able to see it at all. And if she hadn't known it was out there, she would never have noticed it.

"Did Mrs. Davidson say what the girl's up to?" Waldo demanded.

"Mrs. Davidson blew her cool, that's all. She's old and—"

"What's in Mrs. Forrest's mind?" Waldo growled.

"She gave Mrs. Davidson a message for you. Something about the police having had their chance and that he won't get away this time."

"What the hell can she do?"

"How do I know, how do I know?"

"Easy now, easy."

"*You* take a stab in the dark," she snapped.

"She can't sink the boat!"

"How could she put it out of commission?" And then Mary Rinaldi had it. Just like that. "She could throw the ignition key overboard—"

Waldo lowered his glasses. Slowly. "Jesus," he said.

"First, though, she has to get hold of it. . . ."

"Maybe if he's sauced up enough—"

"If he's sauced up enough, he's capable of anything," Mary Rinaldi said. She did not need to add that he also had a gun.

Waldo heaved a drawn-out audible breath. "It's a very, very long shot."

"Long swim, too. And a cold one."

"It's a harebrained idea. She's an idiot."

"She's one gutsy gal and you know it."

"This is police work!"

"And look at us!"

"Hold it—"

"What do you see?"

"These damned cheap glasses. I'm not sure. Something white. Moving. Only a kind of white blob . . ."

"She's wearing a white swim cap."

"Here, you look, damn it. Maybe your young eyes—"

She took the binoculars and, bracing her shoulder against the tree trunk, peered out over the water. She located the boat almost at once—clearer now, the silhouette sharper. It was still motionless. Adjusting the lens, she could not force the glasses to zoom in closer. So she lowered her view to the quiet surface. My God, what an expanse of water between the shore and that boat!

"Can *you* see her?"

She moved her gaze over the surface in a straight line from boat to shore. "No," she said, and felt a shiver pass down her body.

"Holmes Beach boys have commandeered a private motor launch," Waldo said. "They're bringing it by trailer from Pete Reynard's marina."

"I can't see her, Waldo. I can't see anything but that god-damned, goddamned—" She broke off.

"The Coast Guard's promised a copter," Waldo said.

"I don't care," Mary Rinaldi snarled. "I don't care what happens to *him*. If she gets stomach cramps in that cold water, or leg cramps—"

"Steady," Waldo said. "Steady now, missie."

"And stop calling me missie!" she cried.

Then, quivering all over, she felt a pair of arms around her, a huge hard body close, and a gruff voice at her ear whispering "Ssshhh, ssshhh, ssshhh—"

———□———

When Barry had first seen the spotlight, he had been too far away to make out the shape of the sculpture itself, even through his binoculars. But by moving his view out to sea on a line from the light, he had been able to see the yacht, but only its profile. The bastard was out there waiting. But he wouldn't wait long. When he realized she was not coming, he'd head out into the Gulf.

Or would he? Barry had been tempted then to change course. To move in a more southwesterly direction; to maneuver the trawl-er so that if the bastard turned west, he'd be between the yacht and the open sea.

But he decided against that. He couldn't afford to lose time.

Instead he had pointed the prow on a direct line with the shadow of the other boat.

And now he was closer—close enough so that, through the bin-oculars, he could see with some clarity even though the other boat showed no lights. She was a sleek white beauty—ketch-rigged, sails furled. He tried to bring the cockpit into focus but the distance was still too great.

He lowered the binoculars to his chest, wondering whether the telescopic sight on the rifle would reveal more.

He searched the sky—no planes. He ran his eyes over the surface on all sides—no other boats of any sort now. What were the police doing? Where was the Coast Guard? The bastard wouldn't stay out there waiting forever.

And when he realized that Brenda was not coming, or if he spotted the trawler and became suspicious—

There was no way that the trawler could give chase and overtake the ketch, no way.

Barry killed his running lights.

He kept both hands on the wheel. No use to push the control any further—the trawler had no more speed to give.

But if she could get in close enough before the bastard heard her engine—

His eyes were peering over the cabin top.

The ketch was lying east-west, with her stern toward land, her bow pointed out to sea. If she stayed so, he could come in amidships.

At the last instant before impact, he'd leap overboard and let the prow plow into the hull.

If the crash didn't knock the bastard out, he'd have to swim for it. If he made it to shore, they'd have him. If he was injured and drowned—

I won't take any more, if I have to kill the cruel vicious sonofabitch myself!

He had understood Brenda then and he understood her now.

If the bastard drowned, it would be no more than he deserved. And Barry would have no regret.

All he had to do was get there before the other boat moved.

He glanced shoreward. For some unaccountable reason the spotlight had been turned off.

———□———

Brenda's coming.

She's not coming.

She must.

Then where was the rowboat? It was too dark to see clearly, even with the moon. She was coming, she had to come—

He couldn't go on waiting. He had to go! The boat was drifting. Go where?

He couldn't go now. He was this close, he'd come this far, all this long long long way, oh, Christ, it was a trick after all, there was no rowboat, he'd searched and searched, all sides, no rowboat, she'd seen his light, she'd flashed the spotlight, but she was not coming, she'd tricked him!

And now the spotlight was off. She was sitting in there, in the cottage, in the dark, looking out, laughing, laughing at him—

The little bitch. It was a trap. Brenda, you little bitch, you set me up!

If it *was* a trap, if they sent him to prison . . .

He knew why she'd set him up. His mind was working again now. She'd set him up so that they'd put him in a cell again and then while he sat there, knowing, locked up, knowing that she was out there somewhere doing what she'd been doing here, what she'd always done, fucking, fucking, fucking—

I'll kill you first, Brenda!

The gun was still in the pocket of the blazer.

His mind was about to explode.

There was only one way then: Run the boat up on the beach, take the gun, keep it out of the water—

No one else is ever going to have her, ever, ever. . . .

He dropped the glasses to his chest and stepped to the wheel. His mind reeling, he twisted the key. The engine coughed angrily to life.

He was about to thrust the throttle forward when a flash of white caught his eye.

On the surface of the water. Several yards off the port side.

At first it looked like a white ball floating.

And then he saw her arms break the surface and he caught a quick glimpse of her face as she turned her head to take in air—

He twisted the key to kill the motor. And he reached to switch on all the lights. So that he could see her. So that when she climbed into the cockpit he could really see her at last, at last, at last—

———□———

Lavinia had been concentrating for so long on the dark surface of the water—her left eye closed tight, her right eye clamped painfully to the end of the long telescope—that when she heard the boat's engine growl and then heard it die at once, she had been too startled to realize what was happening. By now the helplessness in her had turned to hopelessness. Then, through the telescope, she had seen the sudden illumination on the water's surface.

She withdrew her eye from the instrument now and sat back. All she could see were the shape of the boat and its lights glittering on the water.

Had he decided to go? Then why had he turned off the engine?

She found the strength to lean forward again and to swing and tilt the telescope as she placed her eye against it once more.

She adjusted the focus. It blurred momentarily and then—

She could see the boat close up. Motionless. At an angle, its stern toward her.

There was a figure standing on the deck. No, not the deck, it was called the cockpit. His back was to her. She had never seen Donald Forrest. Not even a photograph. And now, even if he turned, the lens was not powerful enough so that she could hope to make out his features. Wide shoulders. Blond hair. He was not moving. The lower part of his tall body was framed in the circle of the boat's wheel.

Why had he turned on the lights?

And why was he just standing there?

Then she saw the other figure in the cockpit.

Bare flesh. White cap. Black swimsuit.

A warm wave of relief broke over her. Brenda had made it.

Then, instantly, like a blast of wind off a glacier: What would happen to her now? Oh, God, hadn't she really been safer in the water?

Brenda disappeared. Where? Had she gone into the cabin? For warmth, for blankets. The child must be freezing.

Or was she seated low in the cockpit? Head down, struggling for breath—

The man made no move, none whatever. Didn't he realize

what she'd done? That she had to be chilled to the bone, exhausted? Didn't he care?

What a silly stupid question—the man was a murderer.

—— □ ——

Brenda.

She had come.

As she had promised.

He still could not believe it.

She had climbed aboard herself. And now there she sat. Only a few feet away across the cockpit.

Her head was down between her knees . . . her bare shoulders heaving.

And his panic was gone. Why had he started the engine? Where had he intended to go? Oh, God, what if he had not waited?

He continued to stand behind the wheel—drained, slack, unable to move. Or to speak. A vast sense of peace had closed over him. It was like being softly, pleasantly drunk just before that click came in his head and everything went dim and gray and then black. Never, never in his life had he felt so high and cool, so *calm*. Like the silence all around—the pale sky, the huge moon, the dark water stretching away.

"Brenda—" He heard his voice as if it were not his. A whisper. It seemed to drift from far away, like an echo. "Brenda, you came—"

"I said I would." It was almost a question. But not angry. She was no longer angry at him.

"Brenda . . . I want to see your face."

He waited. Slowly she lifted her head. Very slowly. She reached with one hand and took off the wet white cap. Her hair tumbled dark and soft around her face.

Then she stood up. Her mouth was open as if she still could not get her breath. Her eyes seemed to be frowning—as if she were surprised, or puzzled. Her jaw was quivering. And her flesh, glistening wet—

Her flesh. White. Soft. She was almost naked.

Her beauty drifted through his consciousness. Took possession of every part of him.

But she was still frowning, her dark eyes studying him.

He longed to tell her that he was not really sloshed. To reassure her. He ached to tell her that nothing mattered now but himself and Brenda, who had really, really come. She had swum all that way—

To reach him—

Because she loved him—

As he loved her.

Why didn't she smile? He longed to see her smile. He had to find a way to make her smile again.

But later. He'd find a way.

All he could do now was to stand with both hands on the wheel and gaze at her with tenderness and wonder. . . .

————□————

Through the telescope it appeared to Lavinia that the two figures on the boat stood frozen there—like two images on a tapestry, or carved on a frieze.

Brenda was standing now. Hugging her body with her arms. Her husband had not budged from behind the wheel. What were they saying?

The car radios outside were still chattering and crackling. The police were probably as bewildered as she was—and probably felt as helpless.

Now, uncertain at first, Lavinia became conscious of another sound. In the distance. Over the water. Off to her right. A low, continuous chuddering, barely audible.

Unmistakably another boat.

No light.

A Coast Guard cutter? A police craft of some sort?

No boats ran without lights at night.

She knew.

She should have known at once.

Dear God, oh, dear God—Barry, what are you going to do?

Her heart, fluttering before, began to hammer now, and as she swung the spyglass to the right, it began to thump so hard and fast that she lost her breath entirely.

She scanned the water. Slowly. Back and forth. She could not see the trawler.

But it was there. And Barry had taken the hunting rifle.

Barry, in God's name, what do you imagine you can do?

Brenda's on board now—you can't fire the rifle.

Should she shout for the police? What could they do?

Controlling the impulse, she moved the telescope very, very slowly—

And saw it. Only a movement at first, and then, as she worked the lens, the shadowy contours of its ponderous bulk—

Moving south. How far away?

Then she eased the telescope to the left until it was on the other boat.

And realized: The trawler was bearing down on a straight line toward the yacht.

Barry did not intend to use the rifle.

If Donald Forrest did not hear or see the trawler approaching, if he did not move the boat out of its path, Barry was going to ram it.

And at once she understood: It was the only way that Barry could hope to make sure that Donald Forrest did not get away.

But—her heart seemed to stop altogether—Brenda was on board now.

And Barry did not know this.

No, Barry, no, for God's sake no!

She knocked the tripod over as she stood up. Her mind filling with cruel images of more violence, more disaster, she stepped to the switch on the wall and turned on the spotlight.

Then, as Brenda had done earlier, she flipped it off and then on, off and on, over and over, hoping, hoping, wondering what Donald Forrest would do if he saw it, wondering what Barry would think when he saw it, *if* he saw it—

Would he understand? How could he?

Barry, you can't, you can't, you'll be killed, too!

If anything should happen to Barry—

She continued to flick the switch, seeing the spotlight flashing off and on outside the screen, flooding the sail sculpture that Barry had carved for her.

If anything should happen to Barry, she would not want to live.

Brenda, Brenda, you're a dear child and I love you, but if only you had never come here—

—— □ ——

Out of the corner of his eye Barry saw the flashing light on-shore.

Sorry, Brenda, sorry—you can't stop me now.

She had seen his boat, or heard it, and she had guessed what he was going to do. Now she was inside working the switch—the spotlight continued to go on and off.

Sorry, darling, it's the only way—

The ketch lay dead ahead. Its angle had changed slightly—but its bow still pointed out to sea. Its starboard hull lay directly in the path of the fishing boat's prow.

When the lights of the ketch had come on a few minutes ago, he'd taken a look. Was convinced, then, that the bastard was preparing to leave. In which case he'd get away. No way for the trawler to overtake the ketch in pursuit. No way. But the ketch had not moved.

At full throttle, if the bastard did not hear the engine, it was only a matter of minutes, a very few damned minutes.

Clutching the wheel with one hand, he lifted the binoculars from his chest. Was Brenda begging him not to ram the bastard or was she trying to tell him something else altogether?

Closer now, he adjusted the lens. The bastard was still at the wheel.

But he was not alone.

Brenda was standing in the cockpit facing him.

This couldn't be.

He adjusted the glasses again.

All he could see were the two figures.

She was wearing a black swimsuit.

He went hollow inside.

Dropping the binoculars, he swung the wheel hard right rudder and pulled the control back all the way.

Brenda, Brenda, you fool. Damn you—

He killed the engine.

He thought of the rifle.

Then he lifted the glasses.

Brenda stood only three or four feet from the bastard.

Now he could not use the rifle.

There was not a damned thing he could do.

Brenda, you idiot, you bullheaded, sweet, brave, unpredictable, crazy little idiot—it's up to you now.

———□———

"Donald, can you hear me? I said I'm standing here freezing."

He only continued to stare. Or was he staring, was he seeing at all? Minutes had gone by. He had not said a word since demanding—almost begging—to see her face. And in this endless time her shock had deepened.

Now, behind him in the distance, the spotlight in front of the cottage was flashing on and off. If he turned and saw it—

She was at a total loss. She could not think of anything to say, or do, to rouse him from his weird stupor. At first she had thought he was blind drunk. And then she had begun to hope so. She had pleaded with him—were there blankets on board, would he please go below and turn on the heat in the cabin, couldn't he see that she was so cold that she was sick, she could die! Anything, anything to get him to move from the wheel, to go below so she could get hold of that damned key. And then what? Back into that terrible icy water? Yes. Did she have the strength to swim that distance again? She didn't know.

But when he only continued to stand there—motionless, his face a pale haggard mask, eyes glazed—a new terror had invaded her mind. Had he flipped out? Was he really catatonic? If so, did she have a better chance?

Or was he likely to emerge from this staring silence to realize his own danger? To suspect—

Why did that light keep going on and off? Barry? Lavinia? What did it mean?

"Donald, can you hear me?" she shouted. "Donald!"

A sudden fury sent a flash of heat through her shivering body, through her bewildered mind. Why should she have to stand here, wet, in this brutal night air, *pleading*? He didn't give a damn, he had never really cared, hadn't she learned that?

The anger sharpened her mind. Even as she heard herself speak, she recognized the devious cunning: "At least get me a drink." *His* language now, something he could understand. "I'm cold, Donald, I want a *drink*, goddamnit!"

At last he moved. His face even twisted into a smile, or knowing grin. But instead of going toward the companionway and down into the cabin, he sat down behind the wheel and reached to his jacket that lay in a heap beside him. Slowly, dreamlike, he lifted and extended a bottle. She had not seen it lying there. She recognized the hated shape of it and its black label.

She had to step toward him to take it. She had the strange impression that everything was happening in slow motion.

With the bottle heavy in her hand, she felt the abrupt impulse to act. Now, at once, now! To take advantage of his mood, bash the bottle against the side of his head with one hand and try to locate the key with the other.

But if she took that chance, if she shocked him into full consciousness, into action—

"Donald—" And then she forced herself to say the word again. "Darling, you know I never could drink from a bottle."

He spoke then, and stood up. "Glasses in the galley." His voice sounded distant, hollow—frightening. He stepped past her to the open hatch. And turned. "Go below and mix us both a drink and take off the bathing suit." Then, eyes clearing, eyes dropping from her face, he spoke the word, the hated word that she heard even before it left his lips: "Strip." It was like an obscene caress.

Retching, she broke the impulse to lift the bottle over his head and whirled to step to the wheel, reaching, fingers and eyes searching the controls, and then she heard the bellow behind her.

Before she could turn, she felt his hand in her hair, lifting her to her toes, pain blinding, his hand twisting, her skull exploding, her mind blanking an instant, but hearing the low savage snarl close against her ear: "Liar, lying little bitch, *look*, tricks, look over there, what's that light mean, look, I said, *look at that goddamn light!*"

And then: "You did it, you did this to me!"

She felt herself being lifted—off the floor, suspended, body dangling, being carried, she saw the open hatchway, a cave of darkness, and then her hair was free, head wobbling, and she was falling down the steep steps into the dark. . . .

———□———

Barry had seen it all.

He acted in cold fury, fast.

He dropped the binoculars to his chest and grabbed the rifle. It felt heavy and unfamiliar in his hands.

Without bracing his body he lifted it, flicked off the safety, found the lighted boat quickly, located the bastard in the cross hairs of the scope—he was at the helm again—and squeezed off a shot without hesitation.

The sound exploded in his ear and echoed across the water.

Smelling burnt powder, he slammed back the bolt, then jammed it forward, lost the image through the scope, heard the big diesel cough angrily to life; he took a step, braced the rifle over the deckhouse roof, his finger tight and wet on the trigger, located his target—

The bastard had turned his head, he was peering out over the water toward the trawler, lifting his binoculars.

Barry fired again. And tried to hold the image in view against the impact of the jolt against his shoulder.

When he found focus again, the cockpit was empty.

Had he killed him?

The lightning bolt of murderous rage that had shot through him when he'd seen the bastard pick her up by the hair and fling her down the hatch was nothing to the sick shaking fury that was in him now.

After a fall like that, she could be dead—

And now, this bastard who did it could be dead, too.

He hoped he was.

Do you have the right? To kill. To try to kill—

Barry waited. The ketch had drifted farther, had changed angle.

Yes, he had the right. If not the legal right, the moral right—

If the bastard hasn't already killed her, he will if he gets the chance.

He might be on the floor of the cockpit now, wounded or not, crawling toward the companionway—

Or he might already be in the cabin.

With Brenda.

But he wasn't. He was standing up, scrambling very fast, to the wheel, reaching for the control lever.

Barry steadied the rifle. Not even sure the other boat was in range—

He saw the bastard ease the lever forward, the ketch moved, his view vibrated, he pulled the trigger, this time knowing he'd missed.

The sound of the shot drowned out the sound of the ketch's engine.

By the time he had the cockpit in focus again, the bastard was not at the wheel.

He shifted the scope toward the hatchway in time to see only a quick shadowy movement—

Barry stepped back from the rifle, staring at the other boat across the water.

It was not only moving, it was swinging about, it was veering slowly, its prow changing position, pointing west, out to sea—

But there was no one at the wheel.

He could hear the big diesel thundering, the boat gaining speed and straightening out—

Christ.

He started his own engine.

Why the hell hadn't he thought of it?

He turned on the lights and shoved the throttle and swung the wheel hard.

Why hadn't he realized that a yacht like that would have an automatic pilot? Standard equipment.

While the bastard had been down on the floor of the cockpit, he'd been setting the direction.

The ketch had reached full speed.

With a sinking sensation of utter hopelessness he fixed his own course on a line with its silver-edged wake, careful to stay outside its fanlike pattern so as not to lose speed, and jammed the throttle full forward.

What could he hope to do now? What was there to do?

One bullet left. But he'd never be able to get within range. He wasn't even sure he'd been in range when he fired—

And Brenda was in the cabin with the bastard—

I'm here, Brenda. For whatever that's worth, I'm here.

Already the yacht was pulling away, widening the distance—

He could only grip the wheel and try to urge the boat to greater speed by some superhuman effort of will. Pain climbed up his arms into his shoulders and he gave in to the angry despair as it settled bleakly through him.

Brenda had swum out to trap the bastard and now she was the one who was trapped.

If she was alive—

In the distance, beyond the ketch, he could see other lights. Moving north and south.

Freighters. Tankers. Cruise ships.

Oh, Christ, the ketch was plowing straight toward them. The Tampa shipping lanes.

And there was no one at the controls.

No one even on watch.

———□———

To Mary Rinaldi, everything seemed to be happening all at once.

The three shots reverbating over the water—

The lights coming on revealing a second boat out there—

And now the lights on both boats moving out into the Gulf—

On the way out of the woods, Mary Rinaldi explained to Waldo: "The old lady's holding up. Feels pretty proud of herself. She prevented Barry Conrad from ramming the other boat with Brenda aboard."

"Too bad the girl got in the way," Waldo growled. "What about the shooting?"

"Hunting rifle. Barry Conrad's."

"Jesus. All we need—some trigger-happy screwball. It's not open season on fugitives from justice. Let's hope he got the sonofabitch."

They arrived at the dead-end barrier and could see the water again. Two stern lights receding—they could not make out the shapes of the boats at all.

Coleen Lyons was there, beside a young man bristling with photography gear. "Cop cars behind every bush," she said. "Officers deployed up and down the beach—what's happening?"

"Nothing, missie," Waldo said. "Absolutely nothing at all."

Whrow-whrow-whrow—a police car was charging down the street, fast and loud, tires screeching, roof lights flashing blue and red. Waldo cursed and, waving his arms, brought it to a stuttering halt. Furiously Waldo shouted: "Didn't you have orders, no sirens, no lights, didn't—" But he gave up, his shoulders sagging, and returned. "Happens every time. Every goddamn time. What the hell does it matter now?"

A uniformed officer appeared on the run. "Motor launch you

commandeered, Lieutenant—we're going to try to get it into the water at the end of Forty-fifth Street."

"Do that," Waldo said. "I hope it has enough fuel to get to Texas."

"Better late than never," the officer said and went away, not running.

Then the walkie-talkie crackled: "Coast Guard's dispatched a chopper from St. Petersburg. Estimated arrival: fifteen minutes."

"Thanks" was all Waldo said, hopelessly. Then he joined her at the barrier looking out at the two receding lights. "God help her now," he said. And then without bothering to use the glasses and without turning his head: "I've forgotten how to pray. I hope you haven't."

——□——

She was a prisoner. And the boat was moving, the engine rumbling through the cabin. If it was moving away from land, she'd never be able to swim back. Even now it may have gone too far.

He was sitting on the steps. Staring again. But not at her now. At nothing.

He hadn't said a word, made a move since he'd come down after the shooting up there.

When she had regained consciousness, pain had held her on the floor at first. Head, body, every bone—she was a solid mass of pain. And then she'd heard the shots and as she forced herself to stand, she had heard the engine and had felt the shuddering beneath her. She'd made her way to the steps, head throbbing and so bursting with agony that she lost her balance, and then, her foot on the bottom step, he had loomed in the companionway above her. She'd had to slither aside quickly or he would have trampled her.

Since then—she had lost all track of time now—he had been sitting on the steps. The bottle of whiskey dangling in his hand between his knees. He must have picked it up from where she'd dropped it when he'd grabbed her hair.

Nothing she'd said had reached him.

Who's at the helm, Donald?

No answer.

Get out of the way, I'll take the wheel.

No movement.

Donald, you'll wreck us!

She had found the light switch on the bulkhead. Two low bunk-couches. A narrow table. The cabin was so small that she was only a few feet away from him.

Donald, get me a blanket. Please, I'm cold. An echo of an earlier plea—anything to get him away from those steps.

But he remained seated. And in the light now his eyes had that same glazed emptiness that she'd seen before. Had he really gone off the deep end?

Where did he imagine he was taking her? Did he know? Or care?

The thrumming of the engine filled the small cabin.

He might have *killed* her! But she could not give in to anger now. Or hysteria. She had to choke down the hate that could drive her to make the wrong move, say the wrong word—

She had to be careful. Shrewdness. Guile. Her knowledge of him. But if his mind had already moved beyond reason—

"Donald," she said now, softly, "where are we going?" And then she forced herself to add: "Darling."

But he did not look at her. "They were *shooting* at me—" His tone was wondering, almost a whisper, disbelieving. "They were trying to kill me."

She did not hesitate. "Who, Donald?"

Then he frowned and his eyes seemed to try to focus. "You . . . you heard the shots."

She had. But what if she could make him doubt . . .

"What shots?" she asked.

"Three shots—"

"I didn't hear any shots."

"They're out there. They're trying to get me—"

"I'll look—" She took a single careful step. Then, not an accusation, a gentle teasing: "Oh, darling, you always think people are against you. Let me by—"

But instead he stood up. His head almost touched the ceiling. He reached to set the bottle on the table and turned to climb the steps.

He stopped in the hatchway. His body filled the opening.

She glanced at the bottle. Then she picked it up. Heavy enough? The ceiling was low. She'd have to swing it from the side. *Hard.* Did she have the strength left? Even if the blow didn't knock him unconscious, would it cause him to fall to one side long enough for her to get up the ladder and get to the controls?

She was still holding it when he turned and came down again. His eyes held the same shimmering glassiness, but they were darker now. Brighter. He was holding binoculars in one hand and the other swept through his blond hair.

"He's there," he said, and did not sit down.

"Who?" she asked—although in that instant she knew. She should have known when she heard the shots.

"Same guy." His voice was no longer wondering. It was hard and sharp: "Same goddamn red beard."

Her hand tightened on the bottle. But he did not sit down again. He was more alert now, looking at her.

She couldn't risk it.

"It's all true, isn't it?" Donald asked. "He's the reason you came to Florida."

Now what? If he stepped toward her, she'd have to—

"No more lies, Brenda."

She was tempted to shout: *Yes, yes, yes!* But she said, "He imagines he's in love with me, Donald. I scarcely know the man."

"Did you let him screw you?"

She managed a light laugh and moved toward the galley. "We both need a drink, darling."

If Barry's boat was still in sight, she might have a chance. Without botching it, without triggering Donald's anger—

She was opening cabinets.

Had she convinced him?

She found the glassware.

He had not erupted. Was this, too, part of the strange change taking place in him?

Bottle and two tumblers in hand, she came around the edge of the bulkhead and stopped.

He was naked.

Standing exactly where he had been before. Long legs planted. Arms akimbo. Waiting.

His clothes lay in a heap at his feet.

His penis had begun to stiffen. As his eyes drifted from her face and down her body.

She swallowed the acid that rose bitterly in her throat.

She took two steps and set the glasses on her end of the table. Which was between them.

"I have to have a drink first," she said, opening the bottle, trying not to let her hand shake, trying not to scream. Or vomit.

His penis was rigid now.

She poured an inch of whiskey into one glass.

His eyes were brilliant with pleasure.

She poured the other glass to the brim. "I need it," she said. "I've never been so cold."

Carefully, she left the full glass where it was. His gaze rose to her face, a glint of mockery in his eyes—triumph.

His tall body leaned forward, he stretched a long sinewy arm and picked up the glass. He had not moved out of position.

She took the other one and lifted it to her lips. And quaffed the whiskey. The glass clattered against her teeth. The whiskey went scalding down in a spurt of flame through her chest and exploded hot in her stomach. The warmth spread through her frigid body. And reached her mind: What did she hope to do now, stupefy him further?

Eyes fixed on her face, lips twisting almost derisively, he drank down half the glass.

She felt a stab of satisfaction. His two obsessions—her body and booze.

If only she could use them, one or both, to get hold of that key, turn off the steadily rumbling engine—

"Take off that goddamn bathing suit," he said, and then he made a slight mocking bow as he took a breath.

Tipping his head back, he drained the glass.

Now his eyes reddened and moistened and returned to devour her body.

She poured more whiskey into her own glass. But did not drink.

She stepped away from the table so that it would not obstruct his view.

Without looking into her face, he tossed the empty glass to the bunk. "You," he said, "you are going to be fucked like you never been fucked before." And then he brought his eyes up to her face. Hatred was naked in his eyes. "You're going to be fucked over and over and over—for every bastard you ever let do it."

Legs apart, planted, he still stood between her and the companionway.

His eyes glittered—with a cruel, wild anticipation.

"Strip," he said.

The hated word, spoken quietly, was like a shattering concussion in her brain.

She grabbed the bottle from the table with one hand and with the other, as she took three quick strides, she hurled the whiskey from her glass into his face.

She heard his gasp, saw his hands clawing at his eyes, realized he still stood as before, legs planted apart, so instead of lifting the bottle, she dropped her glass, hearing it shatter, and shifted the bottle to grasp it by the neck in both hands and lowered it as she stepped closer. She spread her own legs wide and swung the bottle back and low between them and brought it up from the floor between his.

There was a sickening crunching sound.

His hands came away from his face, his mouth gaped wide, his eyes bulged blindly, and then he doubled up, struggling convulsively for breath, face gone chalk white. He staggered, lurching toward her—

She stepped aside and he dropped to his knees, hands clutching his groin as she moved around his body just as it toppled forward to lie in a writhing knot on the cabin floor.

Clambering up the steps, she heard the howling begin behind her—inhuman, beastlike, furious.

She emerged into the chill dimness and, without hesitating, plunged across the cold floor of the cockpit to the wheel.

———□———

As the distance lengthened yard by inexorable yard between the two boats, Barry had found it more and more difficult to keep the empty cockpit of the ketch in view through his binoculars. The large white wheel was all he could really make out over the stern and then even that began to blur. But, holding his course steady and fighting the dread that was threatening to turn to despair, he could not banish from his mind the projections of what might be, or could be, taking place in the cabin of that boat—which was plowing, pilotless, toward the paths of those enormous ships whose lights were becoming more and more visible.

When it happened, he was not certain at first that he saw anything at all.

A flash of black and white behind the wheel—

Then a ghostly figure rising up on the port side of the cockpit, pausing full-length on the narrow deck—

One white arm lifting, moving in an arc, a split-second's action—

And then the body diving, a clean diagonal black and white line into the water—

As he dropped the binoculars—easing the wheel left rudder, reflexively ramming the throttle that refused to budge farther—he saw the ketch slow down. Its masts bobbed crazily, its prow dipped, the stern lifted, and as this action repeated itself, the boat continued forward, but on momentum only. He saw the churning beneath the stern die away and then the wake behind narrowed and began to close together.

Brenda.

He lifted the glasses again. And searched the water. Beyond the reach of his bow light's narrow beam, the surface was dark.

Oh, God, that water must be cold!

Brenda, Brenda. I'm here, I'm coming, where are you?

I know what you did, Brenda. I saw you throw the key. You did it, you did it on your own!

Oh, Christ, what a woman.

Blankets on board, Brenda. Keep swimming.

Can you see the light?

He reached to the foghorn and jerked the cord. The harsh sound blasted, then echoed. He yanked it again and kept pulling it over and over, in long, loud, slow pleas—

Blankets and my old wool jacket—I'll make you warm, Brenda. Let me make you warm again—

He could see nothing on the surface. Nothing. Could she see the light, hear the horn?

Oh, God, where are you, where are you?

Estimating that he was now approaching the area where she had dived, he lowered the glasses and reduced speed, the engine chuttering.

Closer now, but still more than fifty yards away, the ketch was drifting sideways. Like a huge white fish that had floated to the surface, quite dead.

He drew the throttle back even farther, until the trawler was crawling, almost at a standstill. He eased the wheel now to allow the beam of the bow light to sweep slowly over the water.

He moved his eyes with the light, squinting. No movement. He searched the dark surface on both sides of the beam, then beyond it.

Nothing.

He became conscious of another sound. In the distance. Off to the north. A thrumming motor and the *plut-plut-plut* of revolving blades chopping the air. Too late? No—the bastard was just where Brenda had made certain he'd stay.

He gave the horn a long final blast and released the pull to reach for the rifle on the flat cabin roof. One shell left—

Keep swimming, Brenda. I'm here. I'm here. I'm doing all I can do.

Without taking his eyes from the water and without taking aim, he pointed the rifle straight up over his head and fired into the air.

The report was deafening and its echo reverberated out over the vast expanse of the Gulf.

Can you hear *that*, Brenda?

He dropped the gun to one side and resumed sounding the foghorn.

Can you hear this, Brenda? You've got to hear this, or see the light.

If you're still alive—

———□———

He thought he heard a rifle shot but he couldn't be sure. Maybe someone was hunting somewhere. He had the peculiar feeling of being in a dream. He couldn't focus his mind, it was playing tricks on him again, he couldn't really be sure he heard the shot, he couldn't be sure of anything—

Except the pain. The grinding in his groin and that sick, hollow, shotaway emptiness in his gut, his chest.

But the vomiting had stopped, his ribs ached, his mouth tasted of rot, but the awful heaving had finally stopped, giving some relief. Enough so that he could breathe again, every gasp agony.

But something else had happened, too, something weird, something scary, something inside his mind—he seemed to be floating about, underwater, in hushed green depths.

Only he wasn't floating, he was inching his way up steep steps, like a ladder on a boat—how did he come to be on a boat, whose, where? He couldn't lift his legs so he was climbing, hand over hand, like an animal, naked, puke all over him, stinking, like some dirty wounded animal.

Balls crushed. Could he ever be a man again? How the hell had that happened?

Another sound. Long drawn-out blasts, over and over. Like a ship in a fog. So he had to be on a boat but there was no fog, he was in the open hatchway, night, cold, dim, but no fog. Then who was sounding that horn out there? Why?

He had to stand up now. He couldn't. So he crawled on his hands and knees over the damp cockpit floor. Toward the wheel. Which wavered and blurred.

All he had to do was to start the engine; if he could start the engine again he could get away. Where? How could he know where he was going to go when he didn't even know where he *was*?

If he could pull his body up now, using his arms, maybe then somehow his mind would clear and he could remember what he had to do.

Crouched, not really standing, clutching the wheel for support, he couldn't find the key. Very strange, as strange as everything else—he couldn't go wherever he had to go without the key, what could have happened to it?

Now there was another sound. No mistaking that one, that clattering, a chopper, maybe the Coast Guard, he could see it coming low, lights blinking, he'd been in some sort of wreck and they were sending help—

Oh, Christ, was the boat sinking, was he going down?

So that was it then—there'd been a collision and he'd struck his head so he couldn't think but that didn't explain the pain in his balls, it was all too goddamn confusing, too much, too much, the foghorn, the racket, the chopper, the boat going down, too much—

He sank back onto the seat. Let it happen, it would happen

anyway, let whatever was happening go on happening, he didn't care now, he was too weak, too sick, too faint, fuck it all—

Why did they always do this to him? All his life—

He saw the other boat. The one that must have run into his. Looked like a fishing boat. Foghorn sounding distress, long blasts one after the other—

In the light on the water something was moving. Fish? Shark?

If he had the binoculars—what was he doing on a boat without glasses?

But he didn't need them.

A flash of white arms, black hair trailing—

Brenda.

But what was Brenda doing out there?

She must have gone overboard in the collision. She'd been thrown over by the impact or she'd panicked and jumped.

Well, Brenda was a good swimmer.

But she was swimming away. Toward the other boat. She must be confused—

Brenda, not there—*here*. This way, here! But she couldn't hear. Had he shouted? She was going away, she was leaving him again—

Again. If only you hadn't left me, Brenda.

And then he remembered. But not clearly—

Only enough to know who was on that other boat—

Only enough to know she was going to *him*.

Again.

It wasn't happening. He couldn't let it happen like this—

Brenda, you can't leave me. Ever, ever, ever—

He was behind that light on the other boat.

Where was the gun?

What gun?

He had a gun somewhere. A revolver.

If only he could *think*, if only he could remember where he'd put it, he could kill the sonofabitch before she got to him.

And when he was dead, he wouldn't be able to remember, so then it hadn't really happened.

Whatever it was—

He'd known once and it had been important, vital—

And it had hurt, too—that knowing. Whatever it was.

He turned and lifted his knees to the seat, first one, then the other, fuck the pain—

He knew now what he had to do.

He was kneeling, seeing her out there, going away from him.

He stood up on the seat. He had to get to her, he had to stop her, she couldn't leave him, not again—

And when he reached her, she'd know. She'd realize how much he loved her.

He stepped up onto the narrow deck, no pain at all now, strange, very odd, all he had to do was swim out to her and bring her back—

Easy, easy, all very clear and easy now, nothing to it—

He bent his knees and stooped low, then leaped—

He felt his body flying, up and out, buoyant, weightless, then stiffening to brace for the shock of cold below—

And then, before he reached the water he heard a familiar sound inside his head.

Click.

——□——

She was swimming with renewed vigor.

With each breath, head twisting, she could hear the horn, more distinct and louder every time her face broke the surface. The pattern of sound had changed—instead of the long drawn-out blares that had caught her attention and carried her into the triangular path of light, now the horn was blasting in quick short spurts of urgency.

He had seen her. He was telling her that he had seen her.

She was aware, too, of the helicopter—hovering, lights blinking. So it was over now, really over. She would have time—years and years at least. In which she could live. Years in which Toby could grow up. Possibly even a lifetime—

And there was no room in her for sadness, or regret. No guilt—was it possible that she was free of that, too? At last—

The chuddering of the boat's engine had changed into a low throbbing that seemed to reach her under the water. And when she opened her eyes on the next few strokes, she could see the source of the light moving closer. And then, beneath it, over the glittering plate of water, she could make out the prow of the boat itself.

Barry's boat. Where they had made love. Where she had learned what making love really means.

The rhythm within her changed. She was no longer swimming in order not to drown. She was swimming freely, buoyantly, as she had swum when she was a girl. When the future had been a mystery bright with wonder and promise.

The raw raucous blasting of that old foghorn became the most joyful sound she had ever heard.

——□——

The official coroner's report defining the cause of death of the nude male body washed up on the sands of the Manatee County Public Beach two days later read simply: *Asphyxiation by drowning, accidental.*